Household Papers and Stories

Harriet Beecher Stowe

THE WRITINGS
OF
HARRIET BEECHER STOWE

Riverside Edition

*WITH BIOGRAPHICAL INTRODUCTIONS
PORTRAITS, AND OTHER
ILLUSTRATIONS*

IN SIXTEEN VOLUMES

VOLUME VIII

HOUSEHOLD PAPERS
AND STORIES

BY
HARRIET BEECHER STOWE

1896

CONTENTS

The frontispiece is from a photograph of Mrs. Stowe taken in 1884. The vignette of Mrs. Stowe's later Hartford home is from a drawing by Charles Copeland.

INTRODUCTORY NOTE

Mrs. Stowe had early and very practical acquaintance with the art of housekeeping. It strikes one at first as a little incongruous that an author who devoted her great powers to stirring the conscience of a nation should from time to time, and at one period especially, give her mind to the ordering of family life, but a moment's consideration will show that the same woman was earnestly at the bottom of each effort. In a letter to the late Lord Denman, written in 1853, Mrs. Stowe, speaking of *Uncle Tom's Cabin*, said: "I wrote what I did because, as a woman, as a mother, I was oppressed and heartbroken with the sorrows and injustice which I saw, and because, as a Christian, I felt the dishonor to Christianity." Not under the stress of passionate emotion, yet largely from a sense of real responsibility as a woman, a mother, and a Christian, she occupied herself with those concerns of every-day life which so distinctly appeal to a woman's mind. How to order a household, how to administer that little kingdom over which a woman rules, and, above all, how to make family life stable, pure, and conservative of the highest happiness, these were the questions which she asked herself constantly, and which she tried to solve, not only incidentally in her fiction, but directly in her essays, and in that field of one tenth fiction and nine tenths didacticism, which constitutes most of the present volume.

A Scholar's Adventures in the Country and *Trials of a Housekeeper* appeared in the miscellany to which she gave the name of *The Mayflower*, and reflect humorously the viii Cincinnati experiences which again are playfully recounted in letters published in her son's *Life*. The former, contributed in 1850 to *The National Era*, was drawn pretty closely from the experiments of Professor Stowe. It is noticeable that in this paper and in *Our Second Girl*, which was contributed to *The Atlantic Monthly* for January, 1868, the author poses as the masculine member of the household, as if this assumption gave her some advantage in the point of view. At any rate, she adopted the same rôle when she came more deliberately to survey a wide field in a series of articles.

The House and *Home Papers* were contributed first to *The Atlantic Monthly*, and afterward published in book form as the production of one Christopher Crowfield, though there was not the slightest attempt otherwise at disguising the authorship. The immediate occasion of the papers was no doubt the removal of the Stowes from Andover and their establishment in Hartford, an event which took place shortly before the papers began to appear in *The Atlantic*. The years which followed during the first Hartford residence saw also a marriage in the family and new problems of daily life constantly presenting themselves, so that a similar series appeared in the same magazine, purporting to be from the same householder, entitled *The Chimney Corner*. This series, indeed, entered rather more seriously into questions of social morality, and deepened in feeling as it proceeded. The eleventh section is a warm appreciation of the woman who figured so largely in Mrs. Stowe's early life, and the last two papers rose, as the reader will see, to the height of national memories. Mrs. Fields has preserved for us, in her *Days with Mrs. Stowe*, a striking record of the mingling of the great and the near in this writer's mind. The period of which she writes is that in which *The Chimney Corner* series was drawing to a close:—

"In the autumn of 1864 she wrote: 'I feel I need to write in these days, to keep me from thinking of things that make me dizzy and blind, and fill my eyes with tears, so that I cannot see the paper. I mean such things as are being done where our heroes are dying as Shaw died. It is not wise that all our literature should run in a rut cut through our hearts and red with our blood. I feel the need of a little gentle household merriment and talk of common things, to indulge which I have devised the following.'

"Notwithstanding her view of the need, and her skillfully devised plans to meet it, she soon sent another epistle, showing how impossible it was to stem the current of her thought:—

"'*November 29, 1864.*

"'MY DEAR FRIEND,—

"'I have sent my New Year's article, the result of one of those peculiar experiences which sometimes occur to us writers. I had planned an article, gay, sprightly, wholly domestic; but as I began and sketched the pleasant home and quiet fireside, an irresistible impulse *wrote for me* what followed,—an offering of sympathy to the suffering and agonized, whose homes have forever been darkened. Many causes united at once to force on me this vision, from which generally I shrink, but which sometimes will not be denied,—will make itself felt.

"'Just before I went to New York two of my earliest and most intimate friends lost their oldest sons, captains and majors,— splendid fellows physically and morally, beautiful, brave, religious, uniting the courage of soldiers to the faith of martyrs,—and when I went to Brooklyn it seemed as if I were hearing some such thing almost every day; and Henry, in his profession as minister, has so many letters full of imploring anguish, the cry of hearts breaking that ask help of him.'"...

HOUSE AND HOME PAPERS

I

THE RAVAGES OF A CARPET

"My dear, it's so cheap!"

These words were spoken by my wife, as she sat gracefully on a roll of Brussels carpet which was spread out in flowery lengths on the floor of Messrs. Ketchem & Co.

"It's *so* cheap!"

Milton says that the love of fame is the last infirmity of noble minds. I think he had not rightly considered the subject. I believe that last infirmity is the love of getting things cheap! Understand me, now. I don't mean the love of getting cheap things, by which one understands showy, trashy, ill-made, spurious articles, bearing certain apparent resemblances to better things. All really sensible people are quite superior to that sort of cheapness. But those fortunate accidents, which put within the power of a man things really good and valuable for half or a third of their value, what mortal virtue and resolution can withstand? My friend Brown has a genuine Murillo, the joy of his heart and the light of his eyes, but he never fails to tell you, as its crowning merit, how he bought it in South America for just nothing,—how it hung smoky and deserted in the back of a counting-room, and was thrown in as a makeweight to bind a bargain, and, upon being cleaned turned out a genuine Murillo; and then he takes out his cigar, and calls your attention to the points in it; he adjusts the curtain to let the sunlight fall just in the right spot; he takes you to this and the other point of view; and all this time you must confess that, in your mind as well as his, the consideration that he got all this beauty for ten dollars adds lustre to the painting. Brown has paintings there for which he paid his thousands, and, being well advised, they are worth the thousands he paid; but this ewe lamb that he got for nothing always gives him a secret exaltation in his own eyes. He seems to have credited to himself personally merit to the amount of what he should have paid for the picture. Then there is Mrs. Crœsus, at the party yesterday evening, expatiating to my wife on the surprising cheapness of her point-lace set. "Got for just nothing at all, my dear!" and a circle of admiring listeners echoes the sound. "Did you ever hear anything like it? I never heard of such a thing in my life;" and away sails Mrs. Crœsus as if she had a collar composed of all the cardinal virtues. In fact, she is buoyed up with a secret sense of merit, so that her satin slippers scarcely touch the carpet. Even I myself am fond of showing a first edition of "Paradise Lost" for which I gave a shilling in a London bookstall, and stating that I would not take a hundred dollars for it. Even I must confess there are points on which I am mortal.

But all this while my wife sits on her roll of carpet, looking into my face for approbation, and Marianne and Jenny are pouring into my ear a running fire of "How sweet! How lovely! Just like that one of Mrs. Tweedleum's!"

"And she gave two dollars and seventy-five cents a yard for hers, and this is" —

My wife here put her hand to her mouth and pronounced the incredible sum in a whisper, with a species of sacred awe, common, as I have observed, to females in such interesting crises. In fact Mr. Ketchem, standing smiling and amiable by, remarked to me that really he hoped Mrs. Crowfield would not name generally what she gave for the article, for positively it was so far below the usual rate of prices that he might give offense to other customers; but this was the very last of the pattern, and they were anxious to close off the old stock, and we had always traded with them, and he had a great respect for my wife's father, who had always traded with their firm, and so, when there were any little bargains to be thrown in any one's way, why, he naturally, of course — And here Mr. Ketchem bowed gracefully over the yardstick to my wife, and I consented.

Yes, I consented; but whenever I think of myself at that moment, I always am reminded, in a small way, of Adam taking the apple; and my wife, seated on that roll of carpet, has more than once suggested to my mind the classic image of Pandora opening her unlucky box. In fact, from the moment I had blandly assented to Mr. Ketchem's remarks, and said to my wife, with a gentle air of dignity, "Well, my dear, since it suits you, I think you had better take it," there came a load on my prophetic soul which not all the fluttering and chattering of my delighted girls and the more placid complacency of my wife could entirely dissipate. I presaged I know not what of coming woe, and all I presaged came to pass.

In order to know just what came to pass, I must give you a view of the house and home into which this carpet was introduced.

2

My wife and I were somewhat advanced housekeepers, and our dwelling was first furnished by her father, in the old-fashioned jog-trot days when furniture was made with a view to its lasting from generation to generation. Everything was strong and comfortable,— heavy mahogany, guiltless of the modern device of veneering, and hewed out with a square solidity which had not an idea of change. It was, so to speak, a sort of granite foundation of the household structure. Then we commenced housekeeping with the full idea that our house was a thing to be lived in, and that furniture was made to be used. That most sensible of women, Mrs. Crowfield, agreed fully with me that in our house there was to be nothing too good for ourselves,—no room shut up in holiday attire to be enjoyed by strangers for three or four days in the year, while we lived in holes and corners; no best parlor from which we were to be excluded; no silver plate to be kept in the safe in the bank, and brought home only in case of a grand festival, while our daily meals were served with dingy Britannia. "Strike a broad, plain average," I said to my wife; "have everything abundant, serviceable, and give all our friends exactly what we have ourselves, no better and no worse;" and my wife smiled approval on my sentiment.

Smile? she did more than smile. My wife resembles one of those convex mirrors I have sometimes seen. Every idea I threw out, plain and simple, she reflected back upon me in a thousand little glitters and twinkles of her own; she made my crude conceptions come back to me in such perfectly dazzling performances that I hardly recognized them. My mind warms up when I think what a home that woman made of our house from the very first day she moved into it. The great, large, airy parlor, with its ample bow-window, when she had arranged it, seemed a perfect trap to catch sunbeams. There was none of that discouraging trimness and newness that often repel a man's bachelor friends after the first call, and make them feel, "Oh, well, one cannot go in at Crowfield's now, unless one is dressed; one might put them out." The first thing our parlor said to any one was, that we were not people to be put out, that we were widespread, easy-going, and jolly folk. Even if Tom Brown brought in Ponto and his shooting-bag, there was nothing in that parlor to strike terror into man and dog; for it was written on the face of things that everybody there was to do just as he or she pleased. There were my books and my writing-table spread out with all its miscellaneous confusion of papers on one side of the fireplace, and there were my wife's great, ample sofa and work-table on the other; there I wrote my articles for the "North American;" and there she turned and ripped and altered her dresses; and there lay crochet and knitting and embroidery side by side with a weekly basket of family mending, and in neighborly contiguity with the last book of the season, which my wife turned over as she took her after-dinner lounge on the sofa. And in the bow-window were canaries always singing, and a great stand of plants always fresh and blooming, and ivy which grew and clambered and twined about the pictures. Best of all, there was in our parlor that household altar, the blazing wood fire, whose wholesome, hearty crackle is the truest household inspiration. I quite agree with one celebrated American author who holds that an open fireplace is an altar of patriotism. Would our Revolutionary fathers have gone barefooted and bleeding over snows to defend air-tight stoves and cooking-ranges? I trow not. It was the memory of the great open kitchen-fire, with its back log and fore stick of cord-wood, its roaring, hilarious voice of invitation, its dancing tongues of flame, that called to them through the snows of that dreadful winter to keep up their courage, that made their hearts warm and bright with a thousand reflected memories. Our neighbors said that it was delightful to sit by our fire, —but then, for their part, they could not afford it, wood was so ruinously dear, and all that. Most of these people could not, for the simple reason that they felt compelled, in order to maintain the family dignity, to keep up a parlor with great pomp and circumstance of upholstery, where they sat only on dress occasions, and of course the wood fire was out of the question.

When children began to make their appearance in our establishment, my wife, like a well-conducted housekeeper, had the best of nursery arrangements,—a room all warmed, lighted, and ventilated, and abounding in every proper resource of amusement to the rising race; but it was astonishing to see how, notwithstanding this, the centripetal attraction drew every pair of little pattering feet to our parlor.

"My dear, why don't you take your blocks upstairs?"

"I want to be where oo are," said with a piteous under lip, was generally a most convincing answer.

Then, the small people could not be disabused of the idea that certain chief treasures of their own would be safer under papa's writing-table or mamma's sofa than in the safest closet of their domains. My writing-table was dockyard for Arthur's new ship, and stable for little Tom's pepper-and-salt-colored pony, and carriage-house for Charley's new wagon, while whole armies of paper dolls kept house in the recess behind mamma's sofa.

And then, in due time, came the tribe of pets who followed the little ones and rejoiced in the blaze of the firelight. The boys had a splendid Newfoundland, which, knowing our weakness, we warned them with awful gravity was never to be a parlor dog; but somehow, what with little beggings and pleadings on the part of Arthur and Tom, and the piteous melancholy with which Rover would look through the window-panes when shut out from the blazing warmth into the dark, cold veranda, it at last came to pass that Rover gained a regular corner at the hearth, a regular status in every family convocation. And then came a little black-and-tan English terrier for the girls; and then a fleecy poodle, who established himself on the corner of my wife's sofa; and for each of these some little voice pleaded, and some little heart would be so near broken at any slight that my wife and I resigned ourselves to live in a menagerie, the more so as we were obliged to confess a lurking weakness towards these four-footed children ourselves.

So we grew and flourished together,—children, dogs, birds, flowers, and all; and although my wife often, in paroxysms of housewifeliness to which the best of women are subject, would declare that we never were fit to be seen, yet I comforted her with the reflection that there were few people whose friends seemed to consider them better worth seeing, judging by the stream of visitors and loungers which was always setting towards our parlor. People seemed to find it good to be there; they said it was somehow home-like and pleasant, and that there was a kind of charm about it that made it easy to talk and easy to live; and as my girls and boys grew up, there seemed always to be some merry doing or other going on there. Arty and Tom brought home their college friends, who straightway took root there and seemed to fancy themselves a part of us. We had no reception-rooms apart, where the girls were to receive young gentlemen; all the courting and flirting that were to be done had for their arena the ample variety of surface presented by our parlor, which, with sofas and screens and lounges and recesses, and writing and work tables, disposed here and there, and the genuine *laisser aller* of the whole mènage, seemed, on the whole, to have offered ample advantages enough; for at the time I write of, two daughters were already established in marriage, while my youngest was busy, as yet, in performing that little domestic ballet of the cat with the mouse, in the case of a most submissive youth of the neighborhood.

All this time our parlor furniture, though of that granitic formation I have indicated, began to show marks of that decay to which things sublunary are liable. I cannot say that I dislike this look in a room. Take a fine, ample, hospitable apartment, where all things, freely and generously used, softly and indefinably grow old together, there is a sort of mellow tone and keeping which pleases my eye. What if the seams of the great inviting armchair, where so many friends have sat and lounged, do grow white? What, in fact, if some easy couch has an undeniable hole worn in its friendly cover? I regard with tenderness even these mortal weaknesses of these servants and witnesses of our good times and social fellowship. No vulgar touch wore them; they may be called, rather, the marks and indentations which the glittering in and out of the tide of social happiness has worn in the rocks of our strand. I would no more disturb the gradual toning-down and aging of a well-used set of furniture by smart improvements than I would have a modern dauber paint in emendations in a fine old picture.

So we men reason, but women do not always think as we do. There is a virulent demon of housekeeping not wholly cast out in the best of them, and which often breaks out in unguarded moments. In fact Miss Marianne, being on the lookout for furniture wherewith to begin a new establishment, and Jenny, who had accompanied her in her peregrinations, had more than once thrown out little disparaging remarks on the time-worn appearance of our establishment, suggesting comparison with those of more modern furnished rooms.

"It is positively scandalous, the way our furniture looks," I one day heard one of them declaring to her mother; "and this old rag of a carpet!"

My feelings were hurt, not the less so that I knew that the large cloth which covered the middle of the floor, and which the women call a bocking, had been bought and nailed down there, after a solemn family council, as the best means of concealing the too evident darns which years of good cheer had made needful in our stanch old household friend, the three-ply carpet, made in those days when to be a three-ply was a pledge of continuance and service.

Well, it was a joyous and bustling day when, after one of those domestic whirlwinds which the women are fond of denominating house-cleaning, the new Brussels carpet was at length brought in and nailed down, and its beauty praised from mouth to mouth. Our old friends called in and admired, and all seemed to be well, except that I had that light and delicate presage of changes to come which indefinitely brooded over me.

The first premonitory symptom was the look of apprehensive suspicion with which the female senate regarded the genial sunbeams that had always glorified our bow-window.

"This house ought to have inside blinds," said Marianne, with all the confident decision of youth; "this carpet will be ruined if that sun is allowed to come in like that."

"And that dirty little canary must really be hung in the kitchen," said Jenny; "he always did make such a litter, scattering his seed chippings about; and he never takes his bath without flirting out some water. And, mamma, it appears to me it will never do to have the plants here. Plants are always either leaking through the pots upon the carpet, or scattering bits of blossoms and dead leaves, or some accident upsets or breaks a pot. It was no matter, you know, when we had the old carpet; but this we really want to have kept nice."

Mamma stood her ground for the plants,—darlings of her heart for many a year,—but temporized, and showed that disposition towards compromise which is most inviting to aggression.

I confess I trembled; for, of all radicals on earth, none are to be compared to females that have once in hand a course of domestic innovation and reform. The sacred fire, the divine furor, burns in their bosoms; they become perfect Pythonesses, and every chair they sit on assumes the magic properties of the tripod. Hence the dismay that lodges in the bosoms of us males at the fateful spring and autumn seasons denominated house-cleaning. Who can say whither the awful gods, the prophetic fates, may drive our fair household divinities; what sins of ours may be brought to light; what indulgences and compliances, which uninspired woman has granted in her ordinary mortal hours, may be torn from us? He who has been allowed to keep a pair of pet slippers in a concealed corner, and by the fireside indulged with a chair which he might *ad libitum* fill with all sorts of pamphlets and miscellaneous literature, suddenly finds himself reformed out of knowledge, his pamphlets tucked away into pigeonholes and corners, and his slippers put in their place in the hall, with, perhaps, a brisk insinuation about the shocking dust and disorder that men will tolerate.

The fact was, that the very first night after the advent of the new carpet I had a prophetic dream. Among our treasures of art was a little etching, by an English artist friend, the subject of which was the gambols of the household fairies in a baronial library after the household were in bed. The little people are represented in every

7

attitude of frolic enjoyment. Some escalade the great armchair, and look down from its top as from a domestic Mont Blanc; some climb about the bellows; some scale the shaft of the shovel; while some, forming in magic ring, dance festively on the yet glowing hearth. Tiny troops promenade the writing-table. One perches himself quaintly on the top of the inkstand, and holds colloquy with another who sits cross-legged on a paper weight, while a companion looks down on them from the top of the sandbox. It was an ingenious little device, and gave me the idea, which I often expressed to my wife, that much of the peculiar feeling of security, composure, and enjoyment which seems to be the atmosphere of some rooms and houses came from the unsuspected presence of these little people, the household fairies, so that the belief in their existence became a solemn article of faith with me.

Accordingly, that evening, after the installation of the carpet, when my wife and daughters had gone to bed, as I sat with my slippered feet before the last coals of the fire, I fell asleep in my chair, and, lo! my own parlor presented to my eye a scene of busy life. The little people in green were tripping to and fro, but in great confusion. Evidently something was wrong among them; for they were fussing and chattering with each other, as if preparatory to a general movement. In the region of the bow-window I observed a tribe of them standing with tiny valises and carpetbags in their hands, as though about to depart on a journey. On my writing-table another set stood around my inkstand and pen-rack, who, pointing to those on the floor, seemed to debate some question among themselves; while others of them appeared to be collecting and packing away in tiny trunks certain fairy treasures, preparatory to a general departure. When I looked at the social hearth, at my wife's sofa and work-basket, I saw similar appearances of dissatisfaction and confusion. It was evident that the household fairies were discussing the question of a general and simultaneous removal. I groaned in spirit, and, stretching out my hand, began a conciliatory address, when whisk went the whole scene from before my eyes, and I awaked to behold the form of my wife asking me if I were ill, or had had the nightmare, that I groaned so. I told her my dream, and we laughed at it together.

"We must give way to the girls a little," she said. "It is natural, you know, that they should wish us to appear a little as other people do. The fact is, our parlor is somewhat dilapidated; think how many years we have lived in it without an article of new furniture."

"I hate new furniture," I remarked, in the bitterness of my soul. "I hate anything new."

My wife answered me discreetly, according to approved principles of diplomacy. I was right. She sympathized with me. At the same time, it was not necessary, she remarked, that we should keep a hole in our sofa-cover and armchair, — there would certainly be no harm in sending them to the upholsterer's to be new-covered; she didn't much mind, for her part, moving her plants to the south back room; and the bird would do well enough in the kitchen: I had often complained of him for singing vociferously when I was reading aloud.

So our sofa went to the upholsterer's; but the upholsterer was struck with such horror at its clumsy, antiquated, unfashionable appearance that he felt bound to make representations to my wife and daughters: positively, it would be better for them to get a new one, of a tempting pattern which he showed them, than to try to do anything with that. With a stitch or so here and there it might do for a basement dining-room; but, for a parlor, he gave it as his disinterested opinion, — he must say, if the case were his own, he should get, etc., etc. In short, we had a new sofa and new chairs, and the plants and the birds were banished, and some dark-green blinds were put up to exclude the sun from the parlor, and the blessed luminary was allowed there only at rare intervals, when my wife and daughters were out shopping, and I acted out my uncivilized male instincts by pulling up every shade and vivifying the apartment as in days of old.

But this was not the worst of it. The new furniture and new carpet formed an opposition party in the room. I believe in my heart that for every little household fairy that went out with the dear old things there came in a tribe of discontented brownies with the new ones. These little wretches were always twitching at the gowns of my wife and daughters, jogging their elbows, and suggesting odious comparisons between the smart new articles and what remained of the old ones. They disparaged my writing-table in the corner; they disparaged the old-fashioned lounge in the other corner, which had been the maternal throne for years; they disparaged the work-table, the work-basket, with constant suggestions of how such things as these would look in certain well-kept parlors where new-fashioned furniture of the same sort as ours existed.

"We don't have any parlor," said Jenny one day. "Our parlor has always been a sort of log cabin, —library, study, nursery, greenhouse, all combined. We never have had things like other people."

"Yes, and this open fire makes such a dust; and this carpet is one that shows every speck of dust; it keeps one always on the watch."

"I wonder why papa never had a study to himself; I'm sure I should think he would like it better than sitting here among us all. Now there's the great south room off the dining-room; if he would only move his things there and have his open fire, we could then close up the fireplace and put lounges in the recesses, and mamma could have her things in the nursery, —and then we should have a parlor fit to be seen."

I overheard all this, though I pretended not to, —the little busy chits supposing me entirely buried in the recesses of a German book over which I was poring.

There are certain crises in a man's life when the female element in his household asserts itself in dominant forms that seem to threaten to overwhelm him. The fair creatures, who in most matters have depended on his judgment, evidently look upon him at these seasons as only a forlorn, incapable male creature, to be cajoled and flattered and persuaded out of his native blindness and absurdity into the fairyland of their wishes.

"Of course, mamma," said the busy voices, "men can't understand such things. What can men know of housekeeping, and how things ought to look? Papa never goes into company; he don't know and don't care how the world is doing, and don't see that nobody now is living as we do."

"Aha, my little mistresses, are you there?" I thought; and I mentally resolved on opposing a great force of what our politicians call backbone to this pretty domestic conspiracy.

"When you get my writing-table out of this corner, my pretty dears, I'd thank you to let me know it."

Thus spake I in my blindness, fool that I was. Jupiter might as soon keep awake when Juno came in best bib and tucker, and with the cestus of Venus, to get him to sleep. Poor Slender might as well hope to get the better of pretty Mistress Anne Page as one of us clumsy-footed men might endeavor to escape from the tangled labyrinth of female wiles.

In short, in less than a year it was all done, without any quarrel, any noise, any violence,—done, I scarce knew when or how, but with the utmost deference to my wishes, the most amiable hopes that I would not put myself out, the most sincere protestations that, if I liked it better as it was, my goddesses would give up and acquiesce. In fact I seemed to do it of myself, constrained thereto by what the Emperor Napoleon has so happily called the logic of events,—that old, well-known logic by which the man who has once said A must say B, and he who has said B must say the whole alphabet. In a year we had a parlor with two lounges in decorous recesses, a fashionable sofa, and six chairs and a looking-glass, and a grate always shut up, and a hole in the floor which kept the parlor warm, and great, heavy curtains that kept out all the light that was not already excluded by the green shades.

It was as proper and orderly a parlor as those of our most fashionable neighbors; and when our friends called, we took them stumbling into its darkened solitude, and opened a faint crack in one of the window-shades, and came down in our best clothes and talked with them there. Our old friends rebelled at this, and asked what they had done to be treated so, and complained so bitterly that gradually we let them into the secret that there was a great south room, which I had taken for my study, where we all sat; where the old carpet was down; where the sun shone in at the great window; where my wife's plants flourished, and the canary-bird sang, and my wife had her sofa in the corner, and the old brass andirons glistened, and the wood fire crackled,—in short, a room to which all the household fairies had emigrated.

When they once had found that out, it was difficult to get any of them to sit in our parlor. I had purposely christened the new room my study, that I might stand on my rights as master of ceremonies there, though I opened wide arms of welcome to any who chose to come. So, then, it would often come to pass that, when we were sitting round the fire in my study of an evening, the girls would say,—

"Come, what do we always stay here for? Why don't we ever sit in the parlor?"

And then there would be manifested among guests and family friends a general unwillingness to move.

"Oh, hang it, girls!" would Arthur say; "the parlor is well enough, all right; let it stay as it is, and let a fellow stay where he can do as he pleases and feels at home;" and to this view of the matter would respond divers of the nice young bachelors who were Arthur's and Tom's sworn friends.

In fact nobody wanted to stay in our parlor now. It was a cold, correct, accomplished fact; the household fairies had left it,—and when the fairies leave a room, nobody ever feels at home in it. No pictures, curtains, no wealth of mirrors, no elegance of lounges, can in the least make up for their absence. They are a capricious little set; there are rooms where they will not stay, and rooms where they will; but no one can ever have a good time without them.

II

HOMEKEEPING VERSUS HOUSEKEEPING

I am a frank-hearted man, as perhaps you have by this time perceived, and you will not, therefore, be surprised to know that I read my last article on the carpet to my wife and the girls before I sent it to the "Atlantic," and we had a hearty laugh over it together. My wife and the girls, in fact, felt that they could afford to laugh, for they had carried their point, their reproach among women was taken away, they had become like other folks. Like other folks they had a parlor, an undeniable best parlor, shut up and darkened, with all proper carpets, curtains, lounges, and marble-topped tables, too good for human nature's daily food; and being sustained by this consciousness, they cheerfully went on receiving their friends in the study, and having good times in the old free-and-easy way; for did not everybody know that this room was not their best? and if the furniture was old-fashioned and a little the worse for antiquity, was it not certain that they had better, which they could use if they would?

"And supposing we wanted to give a party," said Jenny, "how nicely our parlor would light up! Not that we ever do give parties, but if we should,—and for a wedding-reception, you know."

I felt the force of the necessity; it was evident that the four or five hundred extra which we had expended was no more than such solemn possibilities required.

"Now, papa thinks we have been foolish," said Marianne, "and he has his own way of making a good story of it; but, after all, I desire to know if people are never to get a new carpet. Must we keep the old one till it actually wears to tatters?"

This is a specimen of the *reductio ad absurdum* which our fair antagonists of the other sex are fond of employing. They strip what we say of all delicate shadings and illusory phrases, and reduce it to some bare question of fact, with which they make a home-thrust at us.

"Yes, that's it; are people *never* to get a new carpet?" echoed Jenny.

"My dears," I replied, "it is a fact that to introduce anything new into an apartment hallowed by many home associations, where all things have grown old together, requires as much care and adroitness as for an architect to restore an arch or niche in a fine old ruin. The fault of our carpet was that it was in another style from everything in our room, and made everything in it look dilapidated. Its colors, material, and air belonged to another manner of life, and were a constant plea for alterations; and you see it actually drove out and expelled the whole furniture of the room, and I am not sure yet that it may not entail on us the necessity of refurnishing the whole house."

"My dear!" said my wife, in a tone of remonstrance; but Jane and Marianne laughed and colored.

"Confess, now," said I, looking at them; "have you not had secret designs on the hall and stair carpet?"

"Now, papa, how could you know it? I only said to Marianne that to have Brussels in the parlor and that old mean-looking ingrain carpet in the hall did not seem exactly the thing; and in fact you know, mamma, Messrs. Ketchem & Co. showed us such a lovely pattern, designed to harmonize with our parlor carpet."

"I know it, girls," said my wife; "but you know I said at once that such an expense was not to be thought of."

"Now, girls," said I, "let me tell you a story I heard once of a very sensible old New England minister, who lived, as our country ministers generally do, rather near to the bone, but still quite contentedly. It was in the days when knee-breeches and long stockings were worn, and this good man was offered a present of a very nice pair of black silk hose. He declined, saying he 'could not afford to wear them.'"

"'Not afford it?' said the friend; 'why, I *give* them to you.'

"'Exactly; but it will cost me not less than two hundred dollars to take them, and I cannot do it.'

"'How is that?'

"'Why, in the first place, I shall no sooner put them on than my wife will say, "My dear, you must have a new pair of knee-breeches," and I shall get them. Then my wife will say, "My dear, how shabby your coat is! You must have a new one," and I shall get a new coat. Then she will say, "Now, my dear, that hat will never do," and then I shall have a new hat; and then I shall say, "My dear, it will never do for me to be so fine and you to wear your old gown," and so my wife will get a new gown; and then the new gown will require a new shawl and a new bonnet; all of which we shall not feel the need of if I

14

don't take this pair of silk stockings, for, as long as we don't see them, our old things seem very well suited to each other.'"

The girls laughed at this story, and I then added, in my most determined manner, —

"But I must warn you, girls, that I have compromised to the utmost extent of my power, and that I intend to plant myself on the old stair carpet in determined resistance. I have no mind to be forbidden the use of the front stairs, or condemned to get up into my bedroom by a private ladder, as I should be immediately if there were a new carpet down."

"Why, papa!"

"Would it not be so? Can the sun shine in the parlor now for fear of fading the carpet? Can we keep a fire there for fear of making dust, or use the lounges and sofas for fear of wearing them out? If you got a new entry and stair carpet, as I said, I should have to be at the expense of another staircase to get up to our bedroom."

"Oh no, papa," said Jane innocently; "there are very pretty druggets now for covering stair carpets, so that they can be used without hurting them."

"Put one over the old carpet, then," said I, "and our acquaintance will never know but it is a new one."

All the female senate laughed at this proposal, and said it sounded just like a man.

"Well," said I, standing up resolutely for my sex, "a man's ideas on woman's matters may be worth some attention. I flatter myself that an intelligent, educated man doesn't think upon and observe with interest any particular subject for years of his life without gaining some ideas respecting it that are good for something; at all events, I have written another article for the 'Atlantic,' which I will read to you."

"Well, wait one minute, papa, till we get our work," said the girls, who, to say the truth, always exhibit a flattering interest in anything their papa writes, and who have the good taste never to interrupt his readings with any conversations in an undertone on cross-stitch and floss-silks, as the manner of some is. Hence the little feminine bustle of arranging all these matters beforehand. Jane, or Jenny, as I call her in my good-natured moods, put on a fresh clear stick of hickory, of that species denominated shagbark, which is full of most charming slivers, burning with such a clear flame, and emitting such a delicious perfume in burning, that I would not change it with the millionaire who kept up his fire with cinnamon.

You must know, my dear Mr. Atlantic, and you, my confidential friends of the reading public, that there is a certain magic or spiritualism which I have the knack of in regard to these mine articles, in virtue of which my wife and daughters never hear or see the little personalities respecting them which form parts of my papers. By a peculiar arrangement which I have made with the elves of the inkstand and the familiar spirits of the quill, a sort of glamour falls on their eyes and ears when I am reading, or when they read the parts personal to themselves; otherwise their sense of feminine propriety would be shocked at the free way in which they and their most internal affairs are confidentially spoken of between me and you, O loving readers.

Thus, in an undertone, I tell you that my little Jenny, as she is zealously and systematically arranging the fire, and trimly whisking every untidy particle of ashes from the hearth, shows in every movement of her little hands, in the cock of her head, in the knowing, observing glance of her eye, and in all her energetic movements, that her small person is endued and made up of the very expressed essence of housewifeliness, — she is the very attar, not of roses, but of housekeeping. Care-taking and thrift and neatness are a nature to her; she is as dainty and delicate in her person as a white cat, as everlastingly busy as a bee; and all the most needful faculties of time, weight, measure, and proportion ought to be fully developed in her skull, if there is any truth in phrenology. Besides all this, she has a sort of hard-grained little vein of common sense, against which my fanciful conceptions and poetical notions are apt to hit with just a little sharp grating, if they are not well put. In fact, this kind of woman needs carefully to be idealized in the process of education, or she will stiffen and dry, as she grows old, into a veritable household Pharisee, a sort of domestic tyrant. She needs to be trained in artistic values and artistic weights and measures, to study all the arts and sciences of the beautiful, and then she is charming. Most useful, most needful, these little women: they have the centripetal force which keeps all the domestic planets from gyrating and frisking in unseemly orbits, and, properly trained, they fill a house with the beauty of order, the harmony and consistency of proportion, the melody of things moving in time and tune, without violating the graceful appearance of ease which Art requires.

So I had an eye to Jenny's education in my article which I unfolded and read, and which was entitled

HOMEKEEPING VERSUS HOUSEKEEPING

There are many women who know how to keep a house, but there are but few that know how to keep a home. To keep a house may seem a complicated affair, but it is a thing that may be learned; it lies in the region of the material; in the region of weight, measure, color, and the positive forces of life. To keep a home lies not merely in the sphere of all these, but it takes in the intellectual, the social, the spiritual, the immortal.

Here the hickory stick broke in two, and the two brands fell controversially out and apart on the hearth, scattering the ashes and coals, and calling for Jenny and the hearth-brush. Your wood fire has this foible, that it needs something to be done to it every five minutes; but, after all, these little interruptions of our bright-faced genius are like the piquant sallies of a clever friend,—they do not strike us as unreasonable.

When Jenny had laid down her brush she said,—

"Seems to me, papa, you are beginning to soar into metaphysics."

"Everything in creation is metaphysical in its abstract terms," said I, with a look calculated to reduce her to a respectful condition. "Everything has a subjective and an objective mode of presentation."

"There papa goes with subjective and objective!" said Marianne. "For my part, I never can remember which is which."

"I remember," said Jenny; "it's what our old nurse used to call internal and *out*-ternal,—I always remember by that."

"Come, my dears," said my wife, "let your father read;" so I went on as follows:—

I remember in my bachelor days going with my boon companion, Bill Carberry, to look at the house to which he was in a few weeks to introduce his bride. Bill was a gallant, free-hearted, open-handed fellow, the life of our whole set, and we felt that natural aversion to losing him that bachelor friends would. How could we tell under what strange aspects he might look forth upon us, when once he had passed into "that undiscovered country" of matrimony? But Bill laughed to scorn our apprehensions.

"I'll tell you what, Chris," he said, as he sprang cheerily up the steps and unlocked the door of his future dwelling, "do you know what I chose this house for? Because it's a social-looking house. Look there, now," he said, as he ushered me into a pair of parlors, —"look at those long south windows, the sun lies there nearly all day long; see what a capital corner there is for a lounging-chair; fancy us, Chris, with our books or our paper, spread out loose and easy, and Sophie gliding in and out like a sunbeam. I'm getting poetical, you see. Then, did you ever see a better, wider, airier dining-room? What capital suppers and things we'll have there! the nicest times, — everything free and easy, you know, —just what I've always wanted a house for. I tell you, Chris, you and Tom Innis shall have latch-keys just like mine, and there is a capital chamber there at the head of the stairs, so that you can be free to come and go. And here now's the library, —fancy this full of books and engravings from the ceiling to the floor; here you shall come just as you please and ask no questions, —all the same as if it were your own, you know."

"And Sophie, what will she say to all this?"

"Why, you know Sophie is a prime friend to both of you, and a capital girl to keep things going. Oh, Sophie'll make a house of this, you may depend!"

A day or two after, Bill dragged me stumbling over boxes and through straw and wrappings to show me the glories of the parlor furniture, with which he seemed pleased as a child with a new toy.

"Look here," he said; "see these chairs, garnet-colored satin, with a pattern on each; well, the sofa's just like them, and the curtains to match, and the carpets made for the floor with centrepieces and borders. I never saw anything more magnificent in my life. Sophie's governor furnishes the house, and everything is to be A No. 1, and all that, you see. Messrs. Curtain & Collamore are coming to make the rooms up, and her mother is busy as a bee getting us in order."

"Why, Bill," said I, "you are going to be lodged like a prince. I hope you'll be able to keep it up; but law business comes in rather slowly at first, old fellow."

"Well, you know it isn't the way I should furnish, if my capital was the one to cash the bills; but then, you see, Sophie's people do it, and let them, —a girl doesn't want to come down out of the style she has always lived in."

I said nothing, but had an oppressive presentiment that social freedom would expire in that house, crushed under a weight of upholstery.

But there came in due time the wedding and the wedding-reception, and we all went to see Bill in his new house, splendidly lighted up and complete from top to toe, and everybody said what a lucky fellow he was; but that was about the end of it, so far as our visiting was concerned. The running in, and dropping in, and keeping latch-keys, and making informal calls, that had been forespoken, seemed about as likely as if Bill had lodged in the Tuileries.

Sophie, who had always been one of your snapping, sparkling, busy sort of girls, began at once to develop her womanhood and show her principles, and was as different from her former self as your careworn, mousing old cat is from your rollicking, frisky kitten. Not but that Sophie was a good girl. She had a capital heart, a good, true womanly one, and was loving and obliging; but still she was one of the desperately painstaking, conscientious sort of women whose very blood, as they grow older, is devoured with anxiety, and she came of a race of women in whom housekeeping was more than an art or a science,—it was, so to speak, a religion. Sophie's mother, aunts, and grandmothers, for nameless generations back, were known and celebrated housekeepers. They might have been genuine descendants of the inhabitants of that Hollandic town of Broeck, celebrated by Washington Irving, where the cows' tails are kept tied up with unsullied blue ribbons, and the ends of the fire-wood are painted white. He relates how a celebrated preacher, visiting this town, found it impossible to draw these housewives from their earthly views and employments, until he took to preaching on the neatness of the celestial city, the unsullied crystal of its walls and the polish of its golden pavement, when the faces of all the housewives were set Zionward at once.

Now this solemn and earnest view of housekeeping is onerous enough when a poor girl first enters on the care of a moderately furnished house, where the articles are not too expensive to be reasonably renewed as time and use wear them; but it is infinitely worse when a cataract of splendid furniture is heaped upon her care,—when splendid crystals cut into her conscience, and mirrors reflect her duties, and moth and rust stand ever ready to devour and sully in every room and passageway.

Sophie was solemnly warned and instructed by all the mothers and aunts,—she was warned of moths, warned of cockroaches, warned of flies, warned of dust; all the articles of furniture had their covers, made of cold Holland linen, in which they looked like bodies laid out,—even the curtain tassels had each its little shroud,—and bundles of receipts, and of rites and ceremonies necessary for the preservation and purification and care of all these articles, were stuffed into the poor girl's head, before guiltless of cares as the feathers that floated above it.

Poor Bill found very soon that his house and furniture were to be kept at such an ideal point of perfection that he needed another house to live in,—for, poor fellow, he found the difference between having a house and a home. It was only a year or two after that my wife and I started our ménage on very different principles, and Bill would often drop in upon us, wistfully lingering in the cosy armchair between my writing-table and my wife's sofa, and saying with a sigh how confoundedly pleasant things looked there,—so pleasant to have a bright, open fire, and geraniums and roses and birds, and all that sort of thing, and to dare to stretch out one's legs and move without thinking what one was going to hit. "Sophie is a good girl!" he would say, "and wants to have everything right, but you see they won't let her. They've loaded her with so many things that have to be kept in lavender that the poor girl is actually getting thin and losing her health; and then, you see, there's Aunt Zeruah, she mounts guard at our house, and keeps up such strict police regulations that a fellow can't do a thing. The parlors are splendid, but so lonesome and dismal!—not a ray of sunshine, in fact not a ray of light, except when a visitor is calling, and then they open a crack. They're afraid of flies, and yet, dear knows, they keep every looking-glass and picture-frame muffled to its throat from March to December. I'd like, for curiosity, to see what a fly would do in our parlors!"

"Well," said I, "can't you have some little family sitting-room where you can make yourselves cosy?"

"Not a bit of it. Sophie and Aunt Zeruah have fixed their throne up in our bedroom, and there they sit all day long, except at calling-hours, and then Sophie dresses herself and comes down. Aunt Zeruah insists upon it that the way is to put the whole house in order, and shut all the blinds, and sit in your bedroom, and then, she says, nothing gets out of place; and she tells poor Sophie the most hocus-pocus stories about her grandmothers and aunts, who always kept everything in their houses so that they could go and lay their hands on it in the darkest night. I'll bet they could in our house. From end to end it is kept looking as if we had shut it up and gone to

Europe,—not a book, not a paper, not a glove, or any trace of a human being in sight; the piano shut tight, the bookcases shut and locked, the engravings locked up, all the drawers and closets locked. Why, if I want to take a fellow into the library, in the first place it smells like a vault, and I have to unbarricade windows, and unlock and rummage for half an hour before I can get at anything; and I know Aunt Zeruah is standing tiptoe at the door, ready to whip everything back and lock up again. A fellow can't be social, or take any comfort in showing his books and pictures that way. Then there's our great, light dining-room, with its sunny south windows,—Aunt Zeruah got us out of that early in April, because she said the flies would speck the frescoes and get into the china-closet, and we have been eating in a little dingy den, with a window looking out on a back alley, ever since; and Aunt Zeruah says that now the dining-room is always in perfect order, and that it is such a care off Sophie's mind that I ought to be willing to eat down cellar to the end of the chapter. Now, you see, Chris, my position is a delicate one, because Sophie's folks all agree that, if there is anything in creation that is ignorant and dreadful and mustn't be allowed his way anywhere, it's 'a man.' Why, you'd think, to hear Aunt Zeruah talk, that we were all like bulls in a china-shop, ready to toss and tear and rend, if we are not kept down cellar and chained; and she worries Sophie, and Sophie's mother comes in and worries, and if I try to get anything done differently Sophie cries, and says she don't know what to do, and so I give it up. Now, if I want to ask a few of our set in sociably to dinner, I can't have them where we eat down cellar,—oh, that would never do! Aunt Zeruah and Sophie's mother and the whole family would think the family honor was forever ruined and undone. We mustn't ask them unless we open the dining-room, and have out all the best china, and get the silver home from the bank; and if we do that, Aunt Zeruah doesn't sleep for a week beforehand, getting ready for it, and for a week after, getting things put away; and then she tells me that, in Sophie's delicate state, it really is abominable for me to increase her cares, and so I invite fellows to dine with me at Delmonico's, and then Sophie cries, and Sophie's mother says it doesn't look respectable for a family man to be dining at public places; but, hang it, a fellow wants a home somewhere!"

My wife soothed the chafed spirit, and spake comfortably unto him, and told him that he knew there was the old lounging-chair always ready for him at our fireside. "And you know," she said, "our things are all so plain that we are never tempted to mount any guard over them; our carpets are nothing, and therefore we let the sun fade them, and live on the sunshine and the flowers."

"That's it," said Bill bitterly. "Carpets fading,—that's Aunt Zeruah's monomania. These women think that the great object of houses is to keep out sunshine. What a fool I was when I gloated over the prospect of our sunny south windows! Why, man, there are three distinct sets of fortifications against the sunshine in those windows: first, outside blinds; then solid, folding, inside shutters; and, lastly, heavy, thick, lined damask curtains, which loop quite down to the floor. What's the use of my pictures, I desire to know? They are hung in that room, and it's a regular campaign to get light enough to see what they are."

"But, at all events, you can light them up with gas in the evening."

"In the evening! Why, do you know my wife never wants to sit there in the evening? She says she has so much sewing to do that she and Aunt Zeruah must sit up in the bedroom, because it wouldn't do to bring work into the parlor. Didn't you know that? Don't you know there mustn't be such a thing as a bit of real work ever seen in a parlor? What if some threads should drop on the carpet? Aunt Zeruah would have to open all the fortifications next day, and search Jerusalem with candles to find them. No; in the evening the gas is lighted at half-cock, you know; and if I turn it up, and bring in my newspapers and spread about me, and pull down some books to read, I can feel the nervousness through the chamber floor. Aunt Zeruah looks in at eight, and at a quarter past, and at half past, and at nine, and at ten, to see if I am done, so that she may fold up the papers and put a book on them, and lock up the books in their cases. Nobody ever comes in to spend an evening. They used to try it when we were first married, but I believe the uninhabited appearance of our parlors discouraged them. Everybody has stopped coming now, and Aunt Zeruah says 'it is such a comfort, for now the rooms are always in order. How poor Mrs. Crowfield lives, with her house such a thoroughfare, she is sure she can't see. Sophie never would have strength for it; but then, to be sure, some folks ain't as particular as others. Sophie was brought up in a family of very particular housekeepers.'"

My wife smiled, with that calm, easy, amused smile that has brightened up her sofa for so many years.

Bill added bitterly,—

"Of course, I couldn't say that I wished the whole set and system of housekeeping women at the—what-'s-his-name?—because Sophie would have cried for a week, and been utterly forlorn and disconsolate. I know it's not the poor girl's fault; I try sometimes to reason with her, but you can't reason with the whole of your wife's family, to the third and fourth generation backwards; but I'm sure it's hurting her health,—wearing her out. Why, you know Sophie used to be the life of our set; and now she really seems eaten up with care from morning to night, there are so many things in the house that something dreadful is happening to all the while, and the servants we get are so clumsy. Why, when I sit with Sophie and Aunt Zeruah, it's nothing but a constant string of complaints about the girls in the kitchen. We keep changing our servants all the time, and they break and destroy so that now we are turned out of the use of all our things. We not only eat in the basement, but all our pretty table-things are put away, and we have all the cracked plates and cracked tumblers and cracked teacups and old buck-handled knives that can be raised out of chaos. I could use these things and be merry if I didn't know we had better ones; and I can't help wondering whether there isn't some way that our table could be set to look like a gentleman's table; but Aunt Zeruah says that 'it would cost thousands, and what difference does it make as long as nobody sees it but us?' You see, there is no medium in her mind between china and crystal and cracked earthenware. Well, I'm wondering how all these laws of the Medes and Persians are going to work when the children come along. I'm in hopes the children will soften off the old folks, and make the house more habitable."

Well, children did come, a good many of them, in time. There was Tom, a broad-shouldered, chubby-cheeked, active, hilarious son of mischief, born in the very image of his father; and there was Charlie, and Jim, and Louisa, and Sophie the second, and Frank,—and a better, brighter, more joy-giving household, as far as temperament and nature were concerned, never existed.

But their whole childhood was a long battle,—children versus furniture, and furniture always carried the day. The first step of the housekeeping powers was to choose the least agreeable and least available room in the house for the children's nursery, and to fit it up with all the old, cracked, rickety furniture a neighboring auction-shop could afford, and then to keep them in it. Now everybody knows that to bring up children to be upright, true, generous, and religious needs so much discipline, so much restraint and correction, and so many rules and regulations, that it is all that the parents can carry out, and all the children can bear. There is only a certain amount of the vital force for parents or children to use in this business of education, and one must choose what it shall be used for. The Aunt Zeruah faction chose to use it for keeping the house and furniture, and the children's education proceeded accordingly. The rules of right and wrong of which they heard most frequently were all of this sort: Naughty children were those who went up the front stairs, or sat on the best sofa, or fingered any of the books in the library, or got out one of the best teacups, or drank out of the cut-glass goblets.

Why did they ever want to do it? If there ever is a forbidden fruit in an Eden, will not our young Adams and Eves risk soul and body to find out how it tastes? Little Tom, the oldest boy, had the courage and enterprise and perseverance of a Captain Parry or Dr. Kane, and he used them all in voyages of discovery to forbidden grounds. He stole Aunt Zeruah's keys, unlocked her cupboards and closets, saw, handled, and tasted everything for himself, and gloried in his sins.

"Don't you know, Tom," said the nurse to him once, "if you are so noisy and rude, you'll disturb your dear mamma? She's sick, and she may die, if you're not careful."

"Will she die?" says Tom gravely.

"Why, she may."

"Then," said Tom, turning on his heel, — "then I'll go up the front stairs."

As soon as ever the little rebel was old enough, he was sent away to boarding-school, and then there was never found a time when it was convenient to have him come home again. He could not come in the spring, for then they were house-cleaning, nor in the autumn, because then they were house-cleaning; and so he spent his vacations at school, unless, by good luck, a companion who was so fortunate as to have a home invited him there. His associations, associates, habits, principles, were as little known to his mother as if she had sent him to China. Aunt Zeruah used to congratulate herself on the rest there was at home, now he was gone, and say she was only living in hopes of the time when Charlie and Jim would be big enough to send away, too; and meanwhile Charlie and Jim, turned out of the charmed circle which should hold growing boys to the father's and mother's side, detesting the dingy, lonely playroom, used to run the city streets, and hang round the railroad depots or docks. Parents may depend upon it that, if they do not make an attractive resort for their boys, Satan will. There are places enough, kept warm and light and bright and merry, where boys can go whose mothers' parlors are too fine for them to sit in. There are enough to be found to clap them on the back, and tell them stories that their mothers must not hear, and laugh when they compass with their little piping voices the dreadful litanies of sin and shame. In middle life, our poor Sophie, who as a girl was so gay and frolicsome, so full of spirits, had dried and sharpened into a hard-visaged, angular woman,—careful and troubled about many things, and forgetful that one thing is needful. One of the boys had run away to sea; I believe he has never been heard of. As to Tom, the eldest, he ran a career wild and hard enough for a time, first at school and then in college, and there came a time when he came home, in the full might of six feet two, and almost broke his mother's heart with his assertions of his home rights and privileges. Mothers who throw away the key of their children's hearts and childhood sometimes have a sad retribution. As the children never were considered when they were little and helpless, so they do not consider when they are strong and powerful. Tom spread wide desolation among the household gods, lounging on the sofas, spitting tobacco juice on the carpets, scattering books and engravings hither and thither, and throwing all the family traditions into wild disorder, as he would never have done had not all his childish remembrances of them been embittered by the association of restraint and privation. He actually seemed to hate any appearance of luxury or taste or order,—he was a perfect Philistine.

As for my friend Bill, from being the pleasantest and most genial of fellows, he became a morose, misanthropic man. Dr. Franklin has a significant proverb,—"Silks and satins put out the kitchen fire." Silks and satins—meaning by them the luxuries of housekeeping—often put out not only the parlor fire, but that more sacred flame, the fire of domestic love. It is the greatest possible misery to a man and to his children to be homeless; and many a man has a splendid house, but no home.

"Papa," said Jenny, "you ought to write and tell what are your ideas of keeping a home."

"Girls, you have only to think how your mother has brought you up."

Nevertheless, I think, being so fortunate a husband, I might reduce my wife's system to an analysis, and my next paper shall be, What is a Home, and How to Keep it.

III

WHAT IS A HOME

It is among the sibylline secrets which lie mysteriously between you and me, O reader, that these papers, besides their public aspect, have a private one proper to the bosom of mine own particular family. They are not merely an *ex post facto* protest in regard to that carpet and parlor of celebrated memory, but they are forth-looking towards other homes that may yet arise near us. For, among my other confidences, you may recollect I stated to you that our Marianne was busy in those interesting cares and details which relate to the preparing and ordering of another dwelling.

Now, when any such matter is going on in a family, I have observed that every feminine instinct is in a state of fluttering vitality,—every woman, old or young, is alive with womanliness to the tips of her fingers; and it becomes us of the other sex, however consciously respected, to walk softly and put forth our sentiments discreetly, and with due reverence for the mysterious powers that reign in the feminine breast.

I had been too well advised to offer one word of direct counsel on a subject where there were such charming voices, so able to convict me of absurdity at every turn. I had merely so arranged my affairs as to put into the hands of my bankers, subject to my wife's order, the very modest marriage portion which I could place at my girl's disposal; and Marianne and Jenny, unused to the handling of money, were incessant in their discussions with ever patient mamma as to what was to be done with it. I say Marianne and Jenny, for, though the case undoubtedly is Marianne's, yet, like everything else in our domestic proceedings, it seems to fall, somehow or other, into Jenny's hands, through the intensity and liveliness of her domesticity of nature. Little Jenny is so bright and wide awake, and with so many active plans and fancies touching anything in the housekeeping world, that, though the youngest sister and second party in this affair, a stranger, hearkening to the daily discussions, might listen a half-hour at a time without finding out that it was not Jenny's future establishment that was in question. Marianne is a soft, thoughtful, quiet girl, not given to many words; and though, when you come fairly at it, you will find that, like most quiet girls, she has a will five times as inflexible as one who talks more, yet in all family counsels it is Jenny and mamma that do the discussion, and her own little well-considered "Yes" or "No" that finally settles each case.

I must add to this family tableau the portrait of the excellent Bob Stephens, who figured as future proprietor and householder in these consultations. So far as the question of financial possibilities is concerned, it is important to remark that Bob belongs to the class of young Edmunds celebrated by the poet: —

"Wisdom and worth were all he had."

He is, in fact, an excellent-hearted and clever fellow, with a world of agreeable talents, a good tenor in a parlor duet, a good actor at a charade, a lively, off-hand conversationist, well up in all the current literature of the day, and what is more, in my eyes, a well-read lawyer, just admitted to the bar, and with as fair business prospects as usually fall to the lot of young aspirants in that profession.

Of course, he and my girl are duly and truly in love, in all the proper moods and tenses; but as to this work they have in hand of being householders, managing fuel, rent, provision, taxes, gas and water rates, they seem to my older eyes about as sagacious as a pair of this year's robins. Nevertheless, as the robins of each year do somehow learn to build nests as well as their ancestors, there is reason to hope as much for each new pair of human creatures. But it is one of the fatalities of our ill-jointed life that houses are usually furnished for future homes by young people in just this state of blissful ignorance of what they are really wanted for, or what is likely to be done with the things in them.

Now, to people of large incomes, with ready wealth for the rectification of mistakes, it doesn't much matter how the ménage is arranged at first; they will, if they have good sense, soon rid themselves of the little infelicities and absurdities of their first arrangements, and bring their establishment to meet their more instructed tastes.

But to that greater class who have only a modest investment for this first start in domestic life, mistakes are far more serious. I have known people go on for years groaning under the weight of domestic possessions they did not want, and pining in vain for others which they did, simply from the fact that all their first purchases were made in this time of blissful ignorance.

I had been a quiet auditor to many animated discussions among the young people as to what they wanted and were to get, in which the subject of prudence and economy was discussed, with quotations of advice thereon given in serious good faith by various friends and relations who lived easily on incomes four or five times larger than our own. Who can show the ways of elegant economy more perfectly than people thus at ease in their possessions? From what serene heights do they instruct the inexperienced beginners! Ten thousand a year gives one leisure for reflection, and elegant leisure enables one to view household economies dispassionately; hence the unction with which these gifted daughters of upper air delight to exhort young neophytes.

"Depend upon it, my dear," Aunt Sophia Easygo had said, "it's always the best economy to get the best things. They cost more in the beginning, but see how they last! These velvet carpets on my floor have been in constant wear for ten years, and look how they wear! I never have an ingrain carpet in my house,—not even on the chambers. Velvet and Brussels cost more to begin with, but then they last. Then I cannot recommend the fashion that is creeping in of having plate instead of solid silver. Plate wears off, and has to be renewed, which comes to about the same thing in the end as if you bought all solid at first. If I were beginning as Marianne is, I should just set aside a thousand dollars for my silver, and be content with a few plain articles. She should buy all her furniture at Messrs. David & Saul's. People call them dear, but their work will prove cheapest in the end, and there is an air and style about their things that can be told anywhere. Of course, you won't go to any extravagant lengths,—simplicity is a grace of itself."

The waters of the family council were troubled when Jenny, flaming with enthusiasm, brought home the report of this conversation. When my wife proceeded, with her well-trained business knowledge, to compare the prices of the simplest elegancies recommended by Aunt Easygo with the sum total to be drawn on, faces lengthened perceptibly.

"How *are* people to go to housekeeping," said Jenny, "if everything costs so much?"

My wife quietly remarked that we had had great comfort in our own home,—had entertained unnumbered friends, and had only ingrain carpets on our chambers and a three-ply on our parlor, and she doubted if any guest had ever thought of it,—if the rooms had been a shade less pleasant; and as to durability, Aunt Easygo had renewed her carpets oftener than we. Such as ours were, they had worn longer than hers.

"But, mamma, you know everything has gone on since your day. Everybody must at least approach a certain style nowadays. One can't furnish so far behind other people."

My wife answered in her quiet way, setting forth her doctrine of a plain average to go through the whole establishment, placing parlors, chambers, kitchen, pantries, and the unseen depths of linen-closets in harmonious relations of just proportion, and showed by calm estimates how far the sum given could go towards this result. *There* the limits were inexorable. There is nothing so damping to the ardor of youthful economies as the hard, positive logic of figures. It is so delightful to think in some airy way that the things we like best are the cheapest, and that a sort of rigorous duty compels us to get them at any sacrifice. There is no remedy for this illusion but to show by the multiplication and addition tables what things are and are not possible. My wife's figures met Aunt Easygo's assertions, and there was a lull among the high contracting parties for a season; nevertheless, I could see Jenny was secretly uneasy. I began to hear of journeys made to far places, here and there, where expensive articles of luxury were selling at reduced prices. Now a gilded mirror was discussed, and now a velvet carpet which chance had brought down temptingly near the sphere of financial possibility. I thought of our parlor, and prayed the good fairies to avert the advent of ill-assorted articles.

"Pray keep common sense uppermost in the girls' heads, if you can," said I to Mrs. Crowfield, "and don't let the poor little puss spend her money for what she won't care a button about by and by."

"I shall try," she said; "but you know Marianne is inexperienced, and Jenny is so ardent and active, and so confident, too. Then they both, I think, have the impression that we are a little behind the age. To say the truth, my dear, I think your papers afford a good opportunity of dropping a thought now and then in their minds. Jenny was asking last night when you were going to write your next paper. The girl has a bright, active mind, and thinks of what she hears."

So flattered, by the best of flatterers, I sat down to write on my theme; and that evening, at firelight time, I read to my little senate as follows: —

WHAT IS A HOME, AND HOW TO KEEP IT

I have shown that a dwelling, rented or owned by a man, in which his own wife keeps house, is not always, or of course, a home. What is it, then, that makes a home? All men and women have the indefinite knowledge of what they want and long for when that word is spoken. "Home!" sighs the disconsolate bachelor, tired of boarding-house fare and buttonless shirts. "Home!" says the wanderer in foreign lands, and thinks of mother's love, of wife and sister and child. Nay, the word has in it a higher meaning hallowed by religion; and when the Christian would express the highest of his hopes for a better life, he speaks of his *home* beyond the grave. The word "home" has in it the elements of love, rest, permanency, and liberty; but, besides these, it has in it the idea of an education by which all that is purest within us is developed into nobler forms, fit for a higher life. The little child by the home-fireside was taken on the Master's knee when he would explain to his disciples the mysteries of the kingdom.

Of so great dignity and worth is this holy and sacred thing, that the power to create a HOME ought to be ranked above all creative faculties. The sculptor who brings out the breathing statue from cold marble, the painter who warms the canvas into a deathless glow of beauty, the architect who built cathedrals and hung the world-like dome of St. Peter's in midair, is not to be compared, in sanctity and worthiness, to the humblest artist who, out of the poor materials afforded by this shifting, changing, selfish world, creates the secure Eden of a home.

A true home should be called the noblest work of art possible to human creatures, inasmuch as it is the very image chosen to represent the last and highest rest of the soul, the consummation of man's blessedness.

Not without reason does the oldest Christian church require of those entering on marriage the most solemn review of all the past life, the confession and repentance of every sin of thought, word, and deed, and the reception of the holy sacrament; for thus the man and woman who approach the august duty of creating a home are reminded of the sanctity and beauty of what they undertake.

In this art of homemaking I have set down in my mind certain first principles, like the axioms of Euclid, and the first is, —

No home is possible without love.

All business marriages and marriages of convenience, all mere culinary marriages and marriages of mere animal passion, make the creation of a true home impossible in the outset. Love is the jeweled foundation of this New Jerusalem descending from God out of heaven, and takes as many bright forms as the amethyst, topaz, and sapphire of that mysterious vision. In this range of creative art all

31

things are possible to him that loveth, but without love nothing is possible.

We hear of most convenient marriages in foreign lands, which may better be described as commercial partnerships. The money on each side is counted; there is enough between the parties to carry on the firm, each having the appropriate sum allotted to each. No love is pretended, but there is great politeness. All is so legally and thoroughly arranged that there seems to be nothing left for future quarrels to fasten on. Monsieur and Madame have each their apartments, their carriages, their servants, their income, their friends, their pursuits,—understand the solemn vows of marriage to mean simply that they are to treat each other with urbanity in those few situations where the path of life must necessarily bring them together.

We are sorry that such an idea of marriage should be gaining foothold in America. It has its root in an ignoble view of life,—an utter and pagan darkness as to all that man and woman are called to do in that highest relation where they act as one. It is a mean and low contrivance on both sides, by which all the grand work of home-building, all the noble pains and heroic toils of home education— that education where the parents learn more than they teach—shall be (let us use the expressive Yankee idiom) *shirked*.

It is a curious fact that, in those countries where this system of marriages is the general rule, there is no word corresponding to our English word "home." In many polite languages of Europe it would be impossible neatly to translate the sentiment with which we began this essay, that a man's house is not always his home.

Let any one try to render the song, "Sweet Home," into French, and one finds how Anglo-Saxon is the very genius of the word. The structure of life, in all its relations, in countries where marriages are matter of arrangement and not of love, excludes the idea of home.

How does life run in such countries? The girl is recalled from her convent or boarding-school, and told that her father has found a husband for her. No objection on her part is contemplated or provided for; none generally occurs, for the child is only too happy to obtain the fine clothes and the liberty which she has been taught come only with marriage. Be the man handsome or homely, interesting or stupid, still he brings these.

How intolerable such a marriage! we say, with the close intimacies of Anglo-Saxon life in our minds. They are not intolerable, because they are provided for by arrangements which make it possible for each to go his or her several way, seeing very little of the other. The son or daughter, which in due time makes its appearance in this ménage, is sent out to nurse in infancy, sent to boarding-school in youth, and in maturity portioned and married, to repeat the same process for another generation. Meanwhile father and mother keep a quiet establishment and pursue their several pleasures. Such is the system.

Houses built for this kind of life become mere sets of reception-rooms, such as are the greater proportion of apartments to let in Paris, where a hearty English or American family, with their children about them, could scarcely find room to establish themselves. Individual character, it is true, does something to modify this programme. There are charming homes in France and Italy, where warm and noble natures, thrown together perhaps by accident, or mated by wise paternal choice, infuse warmth into the coldness of the system under which they live. There are in all states of society some of such domesticity of nature that they will create a home around themselves under any circumstances, however barren. Besides, so kindly is human nature, that Love, uninvited before marriage, often becomes a guest after, and with Love always comes a home.

My next axiom is, —

There can be no true home without liberty.

The very idea of home is of a retreat where we shall be free to act out personal and individual tastes and peculiarities, as we cannot do before the wide world. We are to have our meals at what hour we will, served in what style suits us. Our hours of going and coming are to be as we please. Our favorite haunts are to be here or there; our pictures and books so disposed as seems to us good; and our whole arrangements the expression, so far as our means can compass it, of our own personal ideas of what is pleasant and desirable in life. This element of liberty, if we think of it, is the chief charm of home. "Here I can do as I please," is the thought with which the tempest-tossed earth-pilgrim blesses himself or herself, turning inward from the crowded ways of the world. This thought blesses the man of business, as he turns from his day's care and crosses the sacred threshold. It is as restful to him as the slippers and gown and easy-chair by the fireside. Everybody understands him here. Everybody is well content that he should take his ease in his own way. Such is the case in the ideal home. That such is not always the case in the real home comes often from the mistakes in the house-furnishing. Much house-furnishing is too fine for liberty.

In America there is no such thing as rank and station which impose a sort of prescriptive style on people of certain income. The consequence is that all sorts of furniture and belongings, which in the Old World have a recognized relation to certain possibilities of income, and which require certain other accessories to make them in good keeping, are thrown in the way of all sorts of people.

Young people who cannot expect by any reasonable possibility to keep more than two or three servants, if they happen to have the means in the outset furnish a house with just such articles as in England would suit an establishment of sixteen. We have seen houses in England having two or three housemaids, and tables served by a butler and two waiters, where the furniture, carpets, china, crystal, and silver were in one and the same style with some establishments in America where the family was hard pressed to keep three Irish servants.

This want of servants is the one thing that must modify everything in American life; it is, and will long continue to be, a leading feature in the life of a country so rich in openings for man and woman that domestic service can be only the stepping-stone to something higher. Nevertheless we Americans are great travelers; we are sensitive, appreciative, fond of novelty, apt to receive and incorporate into our own life what seems fair and graceful in that of other people. Our women's wardrobes are made elaborate with the thousand elegancies of French toilet,—our houses filled with a thousand knick-knacks of which our plain ancestors never dreamed. Cleopatra did not set sail on the Nile in more state and beauty than that in which our young American bride is often ushered into her new home,—her wardrobe all gossamer lace and quaint frill and crimp and embroidery, her house a museum of elegant and costly gewgaws, and, amid the whole collection of elegancies and fragilities, she, perhaps, the frailest.

Then comes the tug of war. The young wife becomes a mother, and while she is retired to her chamber, blundering Biddy rusts the elegant knives, or takes off the ivory handles by soaking in hot water; the silver is washed in greasy soapsuds, and refreshed now and then with a thump, which cocks the nose of the teapot awry, or makes the handle assume an air of drunken defiance. The fragile china is chipped here and there around its edges with those minute gaps so vexatious to a woman's soul; the handles fly hither and thither in the wild confusion of Biddy's washing-day hurry, when cook wants her to help hang out the clothes. Meanwhile Bridget sweeps the parlor with a hard broom, and shakes out showers of ashes from the grate, forgetting to cover the damask lounges, and they directly look as rusty and time-worn as if they had come from an auction-store; and all together unite in making such havoc of the delicate ruffles and laces of the bridal outfit and baby *layette* that, when the poor young wife comes out of her chamber after her nurse has left her, and, weakened and embarrassed with the demands of the newcomer, begins to look once more into the affairs of her little world, she is ready to sink with vexation and discouragement. Poor little princess! Her clothes are made as princesses wear them, her baby's clothes like a young duke's, her house furnished like a lord's, and only Bridget and Biddy and Polly to do the work of cook, scullery-maid, butler, footman, laundress, nursery-maid, housemaid, and lady's maid. Such is the array that in the Old Country would be deemed necessary to take care of an establishment got up like hers. Everything in it is too fine, — not too fine to be pretty, not in bad taste in itself, but too fine for the situation, too fine for comfort or liberty.

What ensues in a house so furnished? Too often, ceaseless fretting of the nerves, in the wife's despairing, conscientious efforts to keep things as they should be. There is no freedom in a house where things are too expensive and choice to be freely handled and easily replaced. Life becomes a series of petty embarrassments and restrictions, something is always going wrong, and the man finds his fireside oppressive, — the various articles of his parlor and table seem like so many temper-traps and spring-guns, menacing explosion and disaster.

There may be, indeed, the most perfect home-feeling, the utmost cosiness and restfulness, in apartments crusted with gilding, carpeted with velvet, and upholstered with satin. I have seen such, where the home-like look and air of free use was as genuine as in a Western log cabin; but this was in a range of princely income that made all these things as easy to be obtained or replaced as the most ordinary of our domestic furniture. But so long as articles must be shrouded from use, or used with fear and trembling, because their cost is above the general level of our means, we had better be without them, even though the most lucky of accidents may put their possession in our power.

But it is not merely by the effort to maintain too much elegance that the sense of home liberty is banished from a house. It is sometimes expelled in another way, with all painstaking and conscientious strictness, by the worthiest and best of human beings, the blessed followers of Saint Martha. Have we not known them, the deaf, worthy creatures, up before daylight, causing most scrupulous lustrations of every pane of glass and inch of paint in our parlors, in consequence whereof every shutter and blind must be kept closed for days to come, lest the flies should speck the freshly washed windows and wainscoting? Dear shade of Aunt Mehitabel, forgive our boldness! Have we not been driven for days, in our youth, to read our newspaper in the front veranda, in the kitchen, out in the barn,—anywhere, in fact, where sunshine could be found,—because there was not a room in the house that was not cleaned, shut up, and darkened? Have we not shivered with cold, all the glowering, gloomy month of May, because, the august front parlor having undergone the spring cleaning, the andirons were snugly tied up in the tissue-paper, and an elegant frill of the same material was trembling before the mouth of the once glowing fireplace? Even so, dear soul, full of loving-kindness and hospitality as thou wast, yet ever making our house seem like a tomb! And with what patience wouldst thou sit sewing by a crack in the shutters an inch wide, rejoicing in thy immaculate paint and clear glass! But was there ever a thing of thy spotless and unsullied belongings which a boy might use? How I trembled to touch thy scoured tins, that hung in appalling brightness! with what awe I asked for a basket to pick strawberries! and where in the house could I find a place to eat a piece of gingerbread? How like a ruffian, a Tartar, a pirate, I always felt when I entered thy domains! and how, from day to day, I wondered at the immeasurable depths of depravity which were always leading me to upset something, or break or tear or derange something, in thy exquisitely kept premises! Somehow the impression was burned with overpowering force into my mind that houses and furniture, scrubbed floors, white curtains, bright tins and brasses, were the great, awful, permanent facts of existence; and that men and women, and particularly children, were the meddlesome intruders upon this divine order, every trace of whose intermeddling must be scrubbed out and obliterated in the quickest way possible. It seemed evident to me that houses would be far more perfect if nobody lived in them at all, but that, as men had really and absurdly taken to living in them, they must live as little as possible. My only idea of a house was a place full of traps and pitfalls for boys, a deadly temptation to sins which beset one every moment; and when I read about a sailor's free life on the ocean, I felt an untold longing to go forth and be free in like manner.

But a truce to these fancies, and back again to our essay.

If liberty in a house is a comfort to a husband, it is a necessity to children. When we say liberty, we do not mean license. We do not mean that Master Johnny be allowed to handle elegant volumes with bread-and-butter fingers, or that little Miss be suffered to drum on the piano, or practice line-drawing with a pin on varnished furniture. Still it is essential that the family parlors be not too fine for the family to sit in,—too fine for the ordinary accidents, haps and mishaps of reasonably well-trained children. The elegance of the parlor where papa and mamma sit and receive their friends should wear an inviting, not a hostile and bristling, aspect to little people. Its beauty and its order gradually form in the little mind a love of beauty and order, and the insensible carefulness of regard.

Nothing is worse for a child than to shut him up in a room which he understands is his, *because* he is disorderly,—where he is expected, of course, to maintain and keep disorder. We have sometimes pitied the poor little victims who show their faces longingly at the doors of elegant parlors, and are forthwith collared by the domestic police and consigned to some attic apartment, called a playroom, where chaos continually reigns. It is a mistake to suppose, because children derange a well-furnished apartment, that they like confusion. Order and beauty are always pleasant to them as to grown people, and disorder and defacement are painful; but they know neither how to create the one nor to prevent the other,—their little lives are a series of experiments, often making disorder by aiming at some new form of order. Yet, for all this, I am not one of those who feel that in a family everything should bend to the sway of these little people. They are the worst of tyrants in such houses: still, where children are, though the fact must not appear to them, *nothing must be done without a wise thought of them.*

Here, as in all high art, the old motto is in force, "*Ars est celare artem.*" Children who are taught too plainly, by every anxious look and word of their parents, by every family arrangement, by the impressment of every chance guest into the service, that their parents consider their education as the one important matter in creation, are apt to grow up fantastical, artificial, and hopelessly self-conscious. The stars cannot stop in their courses, even for our personal improvement, and the sooner children learn this the better. The great art is to organize a home which shall move on with a strong, wide, generous movement, where the little people shall act themselves out as freely and impulsively as can consist with the comfort of the whole, and where the anxious watching and planning for them shall be kept as secret from them as possible.

It is well that one of the sunniest and airiest rooms in the house be the children's nursery. It is good philosophy, too, to furnish it attractively, even if the sum expended lower the standard of parlor luxuries. It is well that the children's chamber, which is to act constantly on their impressible natures for years, should command a better prospect, a sunnier aspect, than one which serves for a day's occupancy of the transient guest. It is well that journeys should be made or put off in view of the interests of the children; that guests should be invited with a view to their improvement; that some intimacies should be chosen and some rejected on their account. But it is not well that all this should, from infancy, be daily talked out before the child, and he grow up in egotism from moving in a sphere where everything from first to last is calculated and arranged with reference to himself. A little appearance of wholesome neglect combined with real care and never ceasing watchfulness has often seemed to do wonders in this work of setting human beings on their own feet for the life journey.

Education is the highest object of home, but education in the widest sense,—education of the parents no less than of the children. In a true home the man and the woman receive, through their cares, their watchings, their hospitality, their charity, the last and highest finish that earth can put upon them. From that they must pass upward, for earth can teach them no more.

The home education is incomplete unless it include the idea of hospitality and charity. Hospitality is a Biblical and apostolic virtue, and not so often recommended in Holy Writ without reason. Hospitality is much neglected in America for the very reasons touched upon above. We have received our ideas of propriety and elegance of living from old countries, where labor is cheap, where domestic service is a well-understood, permanent occupation, adopted cheerfully for life, and where of course there is such a subdivision of labor as insures great thoroughness in all its branches. We are ashamed or afraid to conform honestly and hardily to a state of things purely American. We have not yet accomplished what our friend the Doctor calls "our weaning," and learned that dinners with circuitous courses and divers other Continental and English refinements, well enough in their way, cannot be accomplished in families with two or three untrained servants, without an expense of care and anxiety which makes them heart-withering to the delicate wife, and too severe a trial to occur often. America is the land of subdivided fortunes, of a general average of wealth and comfort, and there ought to be, therefore, an understanding in the social basis far more simple than in the Old World.

Many families of small fortunes know this,—they are quietly living so,—but they have not the steadiness to share their daily average living with a friend, a traveler, or guest, just as the Arab shares his tent and the Indian his bowl of succotash. They cannot have company, they say. Why? Because it is such a fuss to get out the best things, and then to put them back again. But why get out the best things! Why not give your friend what he would like a thousand times better,—a bit of your average home life, a seat at any time at your board, a seat at your fire? If he sees that there is a handle off your teacup, and that there is a crack across one of your plates, he only thinks, with a sigh of relief, "Well, mine aren't the only things that meet with accidents," and he feels nearer to you ever after; he will let you come to his table and see the cracks in his teacups, and you will condole with each other on the transient nature of earthly possessions. If it become apparent in these entirely undressed rehearsals that your children are sometimes disorderly, and that your cook sometimes overdoes the meat, and that your second girl sometimes is awkward in waiting, or has forgotten a table propriety, your friend only feels, "Ah, well, other people have trials as well as I," and he thinks, if you come to see him, he shall feel easy with you.

"Having company" is an expense that may always be felt; but easy daily hospitality, the plate always on your table for a friend, is an expense that appears on no accounts book, and a pleasure that is daily and constant.

Under this head of hospitality, let us suppose a case. A traveler comes from England; he comes in good faith and good feeling to see how Americans live. He merely wants to penetrate into the interior of domestic life, to see what there is genuinely and peculiarly American about it. Now here is Smilax, who is living, in a small, neat way, on his salary from the daily press. He remembers hospitalities received from our traveler in England, and wants to return them. He remembers, too, with dismay, a well-kept establishment, the well-served table, the punctilious, orderly servants. Smilax keeps two, a cook and chambermaid, who divide the functions of his establishment between them. What shall he do? Let him say, in a fair, manly way, "My dear fellow, I'm delighted to see you. I live in a small way, but I'll do my best for you, and Mrs. Smilax will be delighted. Come and dine with us, so and so, and we'll bring in one or two friends." So the man comes, and Mrs. Smilax serves up such a dinner as lies within the limits of her knowledge and the capacities of her servants. All plain, good of its kind, unpretending, without an attempt to do anything English or French,—to do anything more than if she were furnishing a gala dinner for her father or returned brother. Show him your house freely, just as it is, talk to him freely of it, just as he in England showed you his larger house and talked to you of his finer things. If the man is a true man, he will thank you for such unpretending, sincere welcome; if he is a man of straw, then he is not worth wasting Mrs. Smilax's health and spirits for, in unavailing efforts to get up a foreign dinner-party.

A man who has any heart in him values a genuine, little bit of home more than anything else you can give him. He can get French cooking at a restaurant; he can buy expensive wines at first-class hotels, if he wants them; but the traveler, though ever so rich and ever so well-served at home, is, after all, nothing but a man as you are, and he is craving something that doesn't seem like an hotel,— some bit of real, genuine heart life. Perhaps he would like better than anything to show you the last photograph of his wife, or to read to you the great, round-hand letter of his ten-year-old which he has got to-day. He is ready to cry when he thinks of it. In this mood he goes to see you, hoping for something like, home, and you first receive him in a parlor opened only on state occasions, and that has been circumstantially and exactly furnished, as the upholsterer assures you, as every other parlor of the kind in the city is furnished. You treat him to a dinner got up for the occasion, with hired waiters,—a dinner which it has taken Mrs. Smilax a week to prepare for, and will take her a week to recover from,—for which the baby has been snubbed and turned off, to his loud indignation, and your young four-year-old sent to his aunts. Your traveler eats your dinner, and finds it inferior, as a work of art, to other dinners,—a poor imitation. He goes away and criticises; you hear of it, and resolve never to invite a foreigner again. But if you had given him a little of your heart, a little home warmth and feeling,—if you had shown him your baby, and let him romp with your four-year-old, and eat a genuine dinner with you,—would he have been false to that? Not so likely. He wanted something real and human,—you gave him a bad dress rehearsal, and dress rehearsals always provoke criticism.

Besides hospitality, there is, in a true home, a mission of charity. It is a just law which regulates the possession of great or beautiful works of art in the Old World, that they shall in some sense be considered the property of all who can appreciate. Fine grounds have hours when the public may be admitted; pictures and statues may be shown to visitors: and this is a noble charity. In the same manner the fortunate individuals who have achieved the greatest of all human works of art should employ it as a sacred charity. How many, morally wearied, wandering, disabled, are healed and comforted by the warmth of a true home! When a mother has sent her son to the temptations of a distant city, what news is so glad to her heart as that he has found some quiet family where he visits often and is made to feel at HOME? How many young men have good women saved from temptation and shipwreck by drawing them often to the sheltered corner by the fireside! The poor artist; the wandering genius who has lost his way in this world, and stumbles like a child among hard realities; the many men and women who, while they have houses, have no homes, see from afar, in their distant, bleak life journey, the light of a true home fire, and, if made welcome there, warm their stiffened limbs, and go forth stronger to their pilgrimage. Let those who have accomplished this beautiful and perfect work of divine art be liberal of its influence. Let them not seek to bolt the doors and draw the curtains; for they know not, and will never know till the future life, of the good they may do by the ministration of this great charity of home.

We have heard much lately of the restricted sphere of woman. We have been told how many spirits among women are of a wider, stronger, more heroic mould than befits the mere routine of housekeeping. It may be true that there are many women far too great, too wise, too high, for mere housekeeping. But where is the woman in any way too great, or too high, or too wise, to spend herself in creating a home? What can any woman make diviner, higher, better? From such homes go forth all heroisms, all inspirations, all great deeds. Such mothers and such homes have made the heroes and martyrs, faithful unto death, who have given their precious lives to us during these three years of our agony!

Homes are the work of art peculiar to the genius of woman. Man helps in this work, but woman leads; the hive is always in confusion without the queen bee. But what a woman must she be who does this work perfectly! She comprehends all, she balances and arranges all; all different tastes and temperaments find in her their rest, and she can unite at one hearthstone the most discordant elements. In her is order, yet an order ever veiled and concealed by indulgence. None are checked, reproved, abridged of privileges by her love of system; for she knows that order was made for the family, and not the family for order. Quietly she takes on herself what all others refuse or overlook. What the unwary disarrange she silently rectifies. Everybody in her sphere breathes easy, feels free; and the driest twig begins in her sunshine to put out buds and blossoms. So quiet are her operations and movements that none sees that it is she who holds all things in harmony; only, alas, when she is gone, how many things suddenly appear disordered, inharmonious, neglected! All these threads have been smilingly held in her weak hand. Alas, if that is no longer there!

Can any woman be such a housekeeper without inspiration? No. In the words of the old church service, "her soul must ever have affiance in God." The New Jerusalem of a perfect home cometh down from God out of heaven. But to make such a home is ambition high and worthy enough for any woman, be she what she may.

One thing more. Right on the threshold of all perfection lies the cross to be taken up. No one can go over or around that cross in science or in art. Without labor and self-denial neither Raphael nor Michel Angelo nor Newton was made perfect. Nor can man or woman create a true home who is not willing in the outset to embrace life heroically to encounter labor and sacrifice. Only to such shall this divinest power be given to create on earth that which is the nearest image of heaven.

IV

THE ECONOMY OF THE BEAUTIFUL

Talking to you in this way once a month, O my confidential reader, there seems to be danger, as in all intervals of friendship, that we shall not readily be able to take up our strain of conversation just where we left off. Suffer me, therefore, to remind you that the month past left us seated at the fireside, just as we had finished reading of what a home was, and how to make one.

The fire had burned low, and great, solid hickory coals were winking dreamily at us from out their fluffy coats of white ashes, —just as if some household sprite there were opening now one eye and then the other, and looking in a sleepy, comfortable way at us.

The close of my piece about the good house mother had seemed to tell on my little audience. Marianne had nestled close to her mother, and laid her head on her knee; and though Jenny sat up straight as a pin, yet her ever busy knitting was dropped in her lap, and I saw the glint of a tear in her quick, sparkling eye, —yes, actually a little bright bead fell upon her work; whereupon she started up actively, and declared that the fire wanted just one more stick to make a blaze before bedtime; and then there was such a raking among the coals, such an adjusting of the andirons, such vigorous arrangement of the wood, and such a brisk whisking of the hearth-brush, that it was evident Jenny had something on her mind. When all was done, she sat down again and looked straight into the blaze, which went dancing and crackling up, casting glances and flecks of light on our pictures and books, and making all the old, familiar furniture seem full of life and motion.

"I think that's a good piece," she said decisively. "I think those are things that should be thought about."

Now Jenny was the youngest of our flock, and therefore, in a certain way, regarded by my wife and me as perennially "the baby;" and these little, old-fashioned, decisive ways of announcing her opinions seemed so much a part of her nature, so peculiarly "Jennyish," as I used to say, that my wife and I only exchanged amused glances over her head when they occurred.

In a general way, Jenny, standing in the full orb of her feminine instincts like Diana in the moon, rather looked down on all masculine views of women's matters as *tolerabiles ineptiæ*; but towards her papa she had gracious turns of being patronizing to the last degree; and one of these turns was evidently at its flood-tide, as she proceeded to say, —

"I think papa is right, — that keeping house and having a home, and all that, is a very serious thing, and that people go into it with very little thought about it. I really think those things papa has been saying there ought to be thought about."

"Papa," said Marianne, "I wish you would tell me exactly how you would spend that money you gave me for house-furnishing. I should like just your views."

"Precisely," said Jenny with eagerness; "because it is just as papa says, — a sensible man, who has thought and had experience, can't help having some ideas, even about women's affairs, that are worth attending to. I think so, decidedly."

I acknowledged the compliment for my sex and myself with my best bow.

"But then, papa," said Marianne, "I can't help feeling sorry that one can't live in such a way as to have beautiful things around one. I'm sorry they must cost so much, and take so much care, for I am made so that I really want them. I do so like to see pretty things! I do like rich carpets and elegant carved furniture, and fine china and cut-glass and silver. I can't bear mean, common-looking rooms. I should so like to have my house look beautiful!"

"Your house ought not to look mean and common, — your house ought to look beautiful," I replied. "It would be a sin and a shame to have it otherwise. No house ought to be fitted up for a future home without a strong and a leading reference to beauty in all its arrangements. If I were a Greek, I should say that the first household libation should be made to beauty; but, being an old-fashioned Christian, I would say that he who prepares a home with no eye to beauty neglects the example of the great Father who has filled our earth home with such elaborate ornament."

"But then, papa, there's the money!" said Jenny, shaking her little head wisely. "You men don't think of that. You want us girls, for instance, to be patterns of economy, but we must always be wearing fresh, nice things; you abhor soiled gloves and worn shoes; and yet how is all this to be done without money? And it's just so in housekeeping. You sit in your armchairs, and conjure up visions of all sorts of impossible things to be done; but when mamma there takes out that little account-book, and figures away on the cost of things, where do the visions go?"

"You are mistaken, my little dear, and you talk just like a woman," — this was my only way of revenging myself; "that is to say, you jump to conclusions, without sufficient knowledge. I maintain that in house-furnishing, as well as woman-furnishing, there's nothing so economical as beauty."

"There's one of papa's paradoxes!" said Jenny.

"Yes," said I, "that is my thesis, which I shall nail up over the mantelpiece there, as Luther nailed his to the church door. It is time to rake up the fire now; but to-morrow night I will give you a paper on the Economy of the Beautiful."

"Come, now we are to have papa's paradox," said Jenny, as soon as the tea-things had been carried out.

Entre nous, I must tell you that insensibly we had fallen into the habit of taking our tea by my study fire. Tea, you know, is a mere nothing in itself, its only merit being its social and poetic associations, its warmth and fragrance; and the more socially and informally it can be dispensed, the more in keeping with its airy and cheerful nature.

Our circle was enlightened this evening by the cheery visage of Bob Stephens, seated, as of right, close to Marianne's work-basket.

"You see, Bob," said Jenny, "papa has undertaken to prove that the most beautiful things are always the cheapest."

"I'm glad to hear that," said Bob; "for there's a carved antique bookcase and study-table that I have my eye on, and if this can in any way be made to appear" —

"Oh, it won't be made to appear," said Jenny, settling herself at her knitting, "only in some transcendental, poetic sense, such as papa can always make out. Papa is more than half a poet, and his truths turn out to be figures of rhetoric when one comes to apply them to matters of fact."

"Now, Miss Jenny, please remember my subject and thesis," I replied, —"that in house-furnishing there is nothing so economical as beauty; and I will make it good against all comers, not by figures of rhetoric, but by figures of arithmetic. I am going to be very matter-of-fact and commonplace in my details, and keep ever in view the addition table. I will instance a case which has occurred under my own observation."

THE ECONOMY OF THE BEAUTIFUL

Two of the houses lately built on the new land in Boston were bought by two friends, Philip and John. Philip had plenty of money, and paid the cash down for his house, without feeling the slightest vacancy in his pocket. John, who was an active, rising young man, just entering on a flourishing business, had expended all his moderate savings for years in the purchase of his dwelling, and still had a mortgage remaining, which he hoped to clear off by his future successes. Philip begins the work of furnishing as people do with whom money is abundant, and who have simply to go from shop to shop and order all that suits their fancy and is considered "the thing" in good society. John begins to furnish with very little money. He has a wife and two little ones, and he wisely deems that to insure to them a well-built house, in an open, airy situation, with conveniences for warming, bathing, and healthy living, is a wise beginning in life; but it leaves him little or nothing beyond.

Behold, then, Philip and his wife, well pleased, going the rounds of shops and stores in fitting up their new dwelling, and let us follow step by step. To begin with the wall-paper. Imagine a front and back parlor, with folding-doors, with two south windows on the front, and two looking on a back court, after the general manner of city houses. We will suppose they require about thirty rolls of wall-paper. Philip buys the heaviest French velvet, with gildings and traceries, at four dollars a roll. This, by the time it has been put on, with gold mouldings, according to the most established taste of the best paper-hangers, will bring the wall-paper of the two rooms to a figure something like two hundred dollars. Now they proceed to the carpet stores, and there are thrown at their feet by obsequious clerks velvets and Axminsters, with flowery convolutions and medallion centres, as if the flower gardens of the tropics were whirling in waltzes, with graceful lines of arabesque,—roses, callas, lilies, knotted, wreathed, twined, with blue and crimson and golden ribbons, dazzling marvels of color and tracery. There is no restraint in price,—four or six dollars a yard, it is all the same to them,—and soon a magic flower garden blooms on the floors, at a cost of five hundred dollars. A pair of elegant rugs, at fifty dollars apiece, complete the inventory, and bring our rooms to the mark of eight hundred dollars for papering and carpeting alone. Now come the great mantel-mirrors for four hundred more, and our rooms progress. Then comes the upholsterer, and measures our four windows, that he may skillfully barricade them from air and sunshine. The fortifications against heaven, thus prepared, cost, in the shape of damask, cord, tassels, shades, laces, and cornices, about two hundred dollars per window. To be sure, they make the rooms close and sombre as the grave, but they are of the most splendid stuffs; and if the sun would only reflect, he would see, himself, how foolish it was for him to try to force himself into a window guarded by his betters. If there is anything cheap and plebeian, it is sunshine and fresh air! Behold us, then, with our two rooms papered, carpeted, and curtained for two thousand dollars; and now are to be put in them sofas, lounges, étagères, centre-tables, screens, chairs of every pattern and device, for which it is but moderate to allow a thousand more. We have now two parlors furnished at an outlay of three thousand dollars, without a single picture, a single article of statuary, a single object of art of any kind, and without any light to see them by if they were there. We must say for our Boston upholsterers and furniture-makers that such good taste generally reigns in their establishments that rooms furnished at haphazard from them cannot fail of a certain air of good taste, so far as the individual things are concerned. But the different articles we have supposed, having been ordered without reference to one another or the rooms, have, when brought together, no unity of effect, and the general result is scattering and confused. If asked how Philip's parlors look, your reply is, "Oh, the usual way of such parlors,—everything that such people usually get,—medallion carpets, carved furniture, great mirrors, bronze mantel ornaments, and so on." The only impression a stranger receives, while waiting in the dim twilight of these rooms, is that their owner is rich, and able to get good, handsome things, such as all other rich people get.

Now our friend John, as often happens in America, is moving in the same social circle with Philip, visiting the same people,—his house is the twin of the one Philip has been furnishing,—and how shall he, with a few hundred dollars, make his rooms even presentable beside those which Philip has fitted up elegantly at three thousand?

Now for the economy of beauty. Our friend must make his prayer to the Graces,—for, if they cannot save him, nobody can. One thing John has to begin with, that rare gift to man, a wife with the magic cestus of Venus,—not around her waist, but, if such a thing could be, in her finger-ends. All that she touches falls at once into harmony and proportion. Her eye for color and form is intuitive: let her arrange a garret, with nothing but boxes, barrels, and cast-off furniture in it, and ten to one she makes it seem the most attractive place in the house. It is a veritable "gift of good faërie," this tact of beautifying and arranging, that some women have; and, on the present occasion, it has a real, material value, that can be estimated in dollars and cents. Come with us and you can see the pair taking their survey of the yet unfurnished parlors, as busy and happy as a couple of bluebirds picking up the first sticks and straws for their nest.

"There are two sunny windows to begin with," says the good fairy, with an appreciative glance. "That insures flowers all winter."

"Yes," says John; "I never would look at a house without a good sunny exposure. Sunshine is the best ornament of a house, and worth an extra thousand a year."

"Now for our wall-paper," says she. "Have you looked at wall-papers, John?"

"Yes; we shall get very pretty ones for thirty-seven cents a roll; all you want of a paper, you know, is to make a ground-tint to throw out your pictures and other matters, and to reflect a pleasant tone of light."

"Well, John, you know Uncle James says that a stone color is the best, but I can't bear those cold blue grays."

"Nor I," says John. "If we must have gray, let it at least be a gray suffused with gold or rose color, such as you see at evening in the clouds."

"So I think," responds she; "but, better, I should like a paper with a tone of buff,—something that produces warm yellowish reflections, and will almost make you think the sun is shining in cold gray weather; and then there is nothing that lights up so cheerfully in the evening. In short, John, I think the color of a *zafferano* rose will be just about the shade we want."

"Well, I can find that, in good American paper, as I said before, at from thirty-seven to forty cents a roll. Then our bordering: there's an important question, for that must determine the carpet, the chairs, and everything else. Now what shall be the ground-tint of our rooms?"

"There are only two to choose between," says the lady,—"green and maroon: which is the best for the picture?"

"I think," says John, looking above the mantelpiece, as if he saw a picture there,—"I think a border of maroon velvet, with maroon furniture, is the best for the picture."

"I think so, too," said she; "and then we will have that lovely maroon and crimson carpet that I saw at Lowe's; it is an ingrain, to be sure, but has a Brussels pattern, a mossy, mixed figure, of different shades of crimson; it has a good warm, strong color, and when I come to cover the lounges and our two old armchairs with maroon rep, it will make such a pretty effect."

"Yes," said John; "and then, you know, our picture is so bright, it will light up the whole. Everything depends on the picture."

Now as to "the picture," it has a story which must be told. John, having been all his life a worshiper and adorer of beauty and beautiful things, had never passed to or from his business without stopping at the print-shop windows, and seeing a little of what was there.

On one of these occasions he was smitten to the heart with the beauty of an autumn landscape, where the red maples and sumachs, the purple and crimson oaks, all stood swathed and harmonized together in the hazy Indian summer atmosphere. There was a great yellow chestnut tree, on a distant hill, which stood out so naturally that John instinctively felt his fingers tingling for a basket, and his heels alive with a desire to bound over on to the rustling hillside and pick up the glossy brown nuts. Everything was there of autumn, even to the goldenrod and purple asters and scarlet creepers in the foreground.

John went in and inquired. It was by an unknown French artist, without name or patrons, who had just come to our shores to study our scenery, and this was the first picture he had exposed for sale. John had just been paid a quarter's salary; he bethought him of board-bill and washerwoman, sighed, and faintly offered fifty dollars.

To his surprise he was taken up at once, and the picture became his. John thought himself dreaming. He examined his treasure over and over, and felt sure that it was the work of no amateur beginner, but of a trained hand and a true artist soul. So he found his way to the studio of the stranger, and apologized for having got such a gem for so much less than its worth. "It was all I could give, though," he said; "and one who paid four times as much could not value it more." And so John took one and another of his friends, with longer purses than his own, to the studio of the modest stranger; and now his pieces command their full worth in the market, and he works with orders far ahead of his ability to execute, giving to the canvas the trails of American scenery as appreciated and felt by the subtile delicacy of the French mind,—our rural summer views, our autumn glories, and the dreamy, misty delicacy of our snowy winter landscapes. Whoso would know the truth of the same, let him inquire for the modest studio of Morvillier, at Maiden, scarce a bowshot from our Boston.

This picture had always been the ruling star of John's house, his main dependence for brightening up his bachelor apartments; and when he came to the task of furbishing those same rooms for a fair occupant, the picture was still his mine of gold. For a picture painted by a real artist, who studies Nature minutely and conscientiously, has something of the charm of the good Mother herself,—something of her faculty of putting on different aspects under different lights. John and his wife had studied their picture at all hours of the day: they had seen how it looked when the morning sun came aslant the scarlet maples and made a golden shimmer over the blue mountains, how it looked toned down in the cool shadows of afternoon, and how it warmed up in the sunset and died off mysteriously into the twilight; and now, when larger parlors were to be furnished, the picture was still the tower of strength, the rallying-point of their hopes.

"Do you know, John," said the wife, hesitating, "I am really in doubt whether we shall not have to get at least a few new chairs and a sofa for our parlors? They are putting in such splendid things at the other door that I am positively ashamed of ours; the fact is, they look almost disreputable,—like a heap of rubbish."

"Well," said John, laughing, "I don't suppose all together sent to an auction-room would bring us fifty dollars, and yet, such as they are, they answer the place of better things for us; and the fact is, Mary, the hard impassable barrier in the case is that there really is no money to get any more."

"Ah, well, then, if there isn't, we must see what we can do with these, and summon all the good fairies to our aid," said Mary. "There's your little cabinet-maker, John, will look over the things and furbish them up; there's that broken arm of the chair must be mended, and everything re-varnished; then I have found such a lovely rep, of just the richest shade of maroon, inclining to crimson, and when we come to cover the lounges and armchairs and sofas and ottomans all alike, you know they will be quite another thing."

"Trust you for that, Mary! By the bye, I've found a nice little woman, who has worked on upholstery, who will come in by the day, and be the hands that shall execute the decrees of your taste."

"Yes, I am sure we shall get on capitally. Do you know that I'm almost glad we can't get new things? It's a sort of enterprise to see what we can do with old ones."

"Now, you see, Mary," said John, seating himself on a lime-cask which the plasterers had left, and taking out his memorandum-book,—"you see, I've calculated this thing all over; I've found a way by which I can make our rooms beautiful and attractive without a cent expended on new furniture."

"Well, let's hear."

"Well, my way is short and simple. We must put things into our rooms that people will look at, so that they will forget to look at the furniture, and never once trouble their heads about it. People never look at furniture so long as there is anything else to look at; just as Napoleon, when away on one of his expeditions, being told that the French populace were getting disaffected, wrote back, 'Gild the *dome des Invalides*,' and so they gilded it, and the people, looking at that, forgot everything else."

"But I'm not clear yet," said Mary, "what is coming of this rhetoric."

"Well, then, Mary, I'll tell you. A suit of new carved black-walnut furniture, severe in taste and perfect in style, such as I should choose at David & Saul's, could not be got under three hundred dollars, and I haven't the three hundred to give. What, then, shall we do? We must fall back on our resources; we must look over our treasures. We have our proof cast of the great glorious head of the Venus di Milo; we have those six beautiful photographs of Rome, that Brown brought to us; we have the great German lithograph of the San Sisto Mother and Child, and we have the two angel heads, from the same; we have that lovely golden twilight sketch of Heade's; we have some sea photographs of Bradford's; we have an original pen-and-ink sketch by Billings; and then, as before, we have 'our picture.' What has been the use of our watching at the gates and waiting at the doors of Beauty all our lives, if she hasn't thrown us out a crust now and then, so that we might have it for time of need? Now, you see, Mary, we must make the toilet of our rooms just as a pretty woman makes hers when money runs low, and she sorts and freshens her

51

ribbons, and matches them to her hair and eyes, and, with a bow here and a bit of fringe there, and a button somewhere else, dazzles us into thinking that she has an infinity of beautiful attire. Our rooms are new and pretty of themselves, to begin with; the tint of the paper, and the rich coloring of the border, corresponding with the furniture and carpets, will make them seem prettier. And now for arrangement. Take this front room. I propose to fill those two recesses each side of the fireplace with my books, in their plain pine cases, just breast-high from the floor: they are stained a good dark color, and nobody need stick a pin in them to find out that they are not rosewood. The top of these shelves on either side to be covered with the same stuff as the furniture, finished with a crimson fringe. On top of the shelves on one side of the fireplace I shall set our noble Venus di Milo, and I shall buy at Cicci's the lovely Clytie, and put it the other side. Then I shall get of Williams & Everett two of their chromo lithographs, which give you all the style and charm of the best English watercolor school. I will have the lovely Bay of Amalfi over my Venus, because she came from those suns and skies of southern Italy, and I will hang Lake Como over my Clytie. Then, in the middle, over the fireplace, shall be 'our picture.' Over each door shall hang one of the lithographed angel heads of the San Sisto, to watch our going out and coming in; and the glorious Mother and Child shall hang opposite the Venus di Milo, to show how Greek and Christian unite in giving the noblest type to womanhood. And then, when we have all our sketches and lithographs framed and hung here and there, and your flowers blooming as they always do, and your ivies wandering and rambling as they used to, and hanging in the most graceful ways and places, and all those little shells and ferns and vases, which you are always conjuring with, tastefully arranged, I'll venture to say that our rooms will be not only pleasant, but beautiful, and that people will oftener say, 'How beautiful!' when they enter, than if we spent three times the money on new furniture."

In the course of a year after this conversation, one and another of my acquaintances were often heard speaking of John Morton's house. "Such beautiful rooms,—so charmingly furnished,—you must go and see them. What does make them so much pleasanter than those rooms in the other house, which have everything in them that money can buy?" So said the folk; for nine people out of ten only feel the effect of a room, and never analyze the causes from which it flows: they know that certain rooms seem dull and heavy and confused, but they don't know why; that certain others seem cheerful, airy, and beautiful, but they know not why. The first exclamation, on entering

John's parlors, was so often "How beautiful!" that it became rather a byword in the family. Estimated by their mere money value, the articles in the rooms were of very trifling worth; but, as they stood arranged and combined, they had all the effect of a lovely picture. Although the statuary was only plaster, and the photographs and lithographs such as were all within the compass of limited means, yet every one of them was a good thing of its own kind, or a good reminder of some of the greatest works of art. A good plaster cast is a daguerreotype, so to speak, of a great statue, though it may be bought for five or six dollars, while its original is not to be had for any namable sum. A chromo lithograph of the best sort gives all the style and manner and effect of Turner or Stanfield, or any of the best of modern artists, though you buy it for five or ten dollars, and though the original would command a thousand guineas. The lithographs from Raphael's immortal picture give you the results of a whole age of artistic culture, in a form within the compass of very humble means. There is now selling for five dollars at Williams & Everett's a photograph of Cheney's crayon drawing of the San Sisto Madonna and Child, which has the very spirit of the glorious original. Such a picture, hung against the wall of a child's room, would train its eye from infancy; and yet how many will freely spend five dollars in embroidery on its dress, that say they cannot afford works of art!

There was one advantage which John and his wife found, in the way in which they furnished their house, that I have hinted at before: it gave freedom to their children. Though their rooms were beautiful, it was not with the tantalizing beauty of expensive and frail knick-knacks. Pictures hung against the wall, and statuary safely lodged on brackets, speak constantly to the childish eye, but are out of the reach of childish fingers, and are not upset by childish romps. They are not, like china and crystal, liable to be used and abused by servants; they do not wear out; they are not spoiled by dust, nor consumed by moths. The beauty once there is always there; though the mother be ill and in her chamber, she has no fears that she shall find it all wrecked and shattered. And this style of beauty, inexpensive as it is, compared with luxurious furniture, is a means of cultivation. No child is ever stimulated to draw or to read by an Axminster carpet or a carved centre-table; but a room surrounded with photographs and pictures and fine casts suggests a thousand inquiries, stimulates the little eye and hand. The child is found with its pencil, drawing, or he asks for a book on Venice, or wants to hear the history of the Roman Forum.

But I have made my article too long. I will write another on the moral and intellectual effects of house-furnishing.

"I have proved my point, Miss Jenny, have I not? *In house-furnishing nothing is more economical than beauty.*"

"Yes, papa," said Jenny; "I give it up."

V

RAKING UP THE FIRE

We have a custom at our house which we call *raking up the fire*. That is to say, the last half hour before bedtime, we draw in, shoulder to shoulder, around the last brands and embers of our hearth, which we prick up and brighten, and dispose for a few farewell flickers and glimmers. This is a grand time for discussion. Then we talk over parties, if the young people have been out of an evening, —a book, if we have been reading one; we discuss and analyze characters, —give our views on all subjects, æsthetic, theological, and scientific, in a way most wonderful to hear; and, in fact, we sometimes get so engaged in our discussions that every spark of the fire burns out, and we begin to feel ourselves shivering around the shoulders, before we can remember that it is bedtime.

So, after the reading of my last article, we had a "raking-up talk," — to wit, Jenny, Marianne, and I, with Bob Stephens: my wife, still busy at her work-basket, sat at the table a little behind us. Jenny, of course, opened the ball in her usual incisive manner.

"But now, papa, after all you say in your piece there, I cannot help feeling that, if I had the taste and the money too, it would be better than the taste alone with no money. I like the nice arrangements and the books and the drawings, but I think all these would appear better still with really elegant furniture."

"Who doubts that?" said I. "Give me a large tub of gold coin to dip into, and the furnishing and beautifying of a house is a simple affair. The same taste that could make beauty out of cents and dimes could make it more abundantly out of dollars and eagles. But I have been speaking for those who have not and cannot get riches, and who wish to have agreeable houses; and I begin in the outset by saying that beauty is a thing to be respected, reverenced, and devoutly cared for, and then I say that BEAUTY IS CHEAP, —nay, to put it so that the shrewdest Yankee will understand it, —BEAUTY IS THE CHEAPEST THING YOU CAN HAVE, because in many ways it is a substitute for expense. A few vases of flowers in a room, a few blooming, well-kept plants, a few prints framed in fanciful frames of cheap domestic fabric, a statuette, a bracket, an engraving, a pencil-sketch, —above all, a few choice books, —all these arranged by a woman who has the gift in her finger-ends, often produce such an illusion on the mind's eye that one goes away without once having noticed that the cushion of the armchair was worn out, and that some veneering had fallen off the centre-table.

"I have a friend, a schoolmistress, who lives in a poor little cottage enough, which, let alone of the Graces, might seem mean and sordid, but a few flower-seeds and a little weeding in the spring make it, all summer, an object which everybody stops to look at. Her æsthetic soul was at first greatly tried with the water-barrel which stood under the eaves spout,—a most necessary evil, since only thus could her scanty supply of soft water for domestic purposes be secured. One of the Graces, however, suggested to her a happy thought. She planted a row of morning-glories round the bottom of her barrel, and drove a row of tacks around the top, and strung her water-butt with twine, like a great harpsichord. A few weeks covered the twine with blossoming plants, which every morning were a mass of many-colored airy blooms, waving in graceful sprays, and looking at themselves in the water. The water-barrel, in fact, became a celebrated stroke of ornamental gardening, which the neighbors came to look at."

"Well, but," said Jenny, "everybody hasn't mamma's faculty with flowers. Flowers will grow for some people, and for some they won't. Nobody can see what mamma does so very much, but her plants always look fresh and thriving and healthy,—her things blossom just when she wants them, and do anything else she wishes them to; and there are other people that fume and fuss and try, and their things won't do anything at all. There's Aunt Easygo has plant after plant brought from the greenhouse, and hanging-baskets, and all sorts of things; but her plants grow yellow and drop their leaves, and her hanging-baskets get dusty and poverty-stricken, while mamma's go on flourishing as heart could desire."

"I can tell you what your mother puts into her plants," said I,—"just what she has put into her children, and all her other home-things,— her *heart*. She loves them; she lives in them; she has in herself a plant-life and a plant-sympathy. She feels for them as if she herself were a plant; she anticipates their wants,—always remembers them without an effort, and so the care flows to them daily and hourly. She hardly knows when she does the things that make them grow, but she gives them a minute a hundred times a day. She moves this nearer the glass,—draws that back,—detects some thief of a worm on one,— digs at the root of another, to see why it droops,—washes these leaves and sprinkles those,—waters, and refrains from watering, all with the habitual care of love. Your mother herself doesn't know why her plants grow; it takes a philosopher and a writer for the 'Atlantic' to tell her what the cause is."

Here I saw my wife laughing over her work-basket as she answered,—

"Girls, one of these days *I* will write an article for the 'Atlantic,' that your papa need not have *all* the say to himself; however, I believe he has hit the nail on the head this time."

"Of course he has," said Marianne. "But, mamma, I am afraid to begin to depend much on plants for the beauty of my rooms, for fear I should not have your gift,—and, of all forlorn and hopeless things in a room, ill-kept plants are the most so."

"I would not recommend," said I, "a young housekeeper, just beginning, to rest much for her home ornament on plant-keeping, unless she has an experience of her own love and talent in this line which makes her sure of success; for plants will not thrive if they are forgotten or overlooked, and only tended in occasional intervals; and, as Marianne says, neglected plants are the most forlorn of all things."

"But, papa," said Marianne anxiously, "there, in those patent parlors of John's that you wrote of, flowers acted a great part."

"The charm of those parlors of John's may be chemically analyzed," I said. "In the first place, there is sunshine, a thing that always affects the human nerves of happiness. Why else is it that people are always so glad to see the sun after a long storm? why are bright days matters of such congratulation? Sunshine fills a house with a thousand beautiful and fanciful effects of light and shade,—with soft, luminous, reflected radiances, that give picturesque effects to the pictures, books, statuettes of an interior. John, happily, had no money to buy brocatelle curtains, and, besides this, he loved sunshine too much to buy them, if he could. He had been enough with artists to know that heavy damask curtains darken precisely that part of the window where the light proper for pictures and statuary should come in, namely, the upper part. The fashionable system of curtains lights only the legs of the chairs and the carpets, and leaves all the upper portion of the room in shadow. John's windows have shades which can at pleasure be drawn down from the top or up from the bottom, so that the best light to be had may always be arranged for his little interior."

"Well, papa," said Marianne, "in your chemical analysis of John's rooms, what is the next thing to the sunshine?"

"The next," said I, "is harmony of color. The wall-paper, the furniture, the carpets, are of tints that harmonize with one another. This is a grace in rooms always, and one often neglected. The French have an expressive phrase with reference to articles which are out of accord,—they say that they swear at each other, I have been in rooms where I seemed to hear the wall-paper swearing at the carpet, and the carpet swearing back at the wall-paper, and each article of furniture swearing at the rest. These appointments may all of them be of the most expensive kind, but with such dis-harmony no arrangement can ever produce anything but a vulgar and disagreeable effect. On the other hand, I have been in rooms where all the material was cheap and the furniture poor, but where, from some instinctive knowledge of the reciprocal effect of colors, everything was harmonious, and produced a sense of elegance.

"I recollect once traveling on a Western canal through a long stretch of wilderness, and stopping to spend the night at an obscure settlement of a dozen houses. We were directed to lodgings in a common frame house at a little distance, where, it seemed, the only hotel was kept. When we entered the parlor, we were struck with utter amazement at its prettiness, which affected us before we began to ask ourselves how it came to be pretty. It was, in fact, only one of the miracles of harmonious color working with very simple materials. Some woman had been busy there, who had both eyes and fingers. The sofa, the common wooden rocking-chairs, and some ottomans, probably made of old soap-boxes, were all covered with American nankeen of a soft yellowish-brown, with a bordering of blue print. The window-shades, the table-cover, and the piano-cloth all repeated the same colors, in the same cheap material. A simple straw matting was laid over the floor, and, with a few books, a vase of flowers, and one or two prints, the room had a home-like and even elegant air, that struck us all the more forcibly from its contrast with the usual tawdry, slovenly style of such parlors.

"The means used for getting up this effect were the most inexpensive possible,—simply the following out, in cheap material, a law of uniformity and harmony, which always will produce beauty. In the same manner, I have seen a room furnished, whose effect was really gorgeous in color, where the only materials used were Turkey-red cotton and a simple ingrain carpet of corresponding color.

"Now, you girls have been busy lately in schemes for buying a velvet carpet for the new parlor that is to be, and the only points that have seemed to weigh in the council were that it was velvet, that it was cheaper than velvets usually are, and that it was a genteel pattern."

"Now, papa," said Jenny, "what ears you have! We thought you were reading all the time!"

"I see what you are going to say," said Marianne. "You think that we have not once mentioned the consideration which should determine the carpet, whether it will harmonize with our other things. But you see, papa, we don't really know what our other things are to be."

"Yes," said Jenny, "and Aunt Easygo said it was an unusually good chance to get a velvet carpet."

"Yet, good as the chance is, it costs just twice as much as an ingrain."

"Yes, papa, it does."

"And you are not sure that the effect of it, after you get it down, will be as good as a well-chosen ingrain one."

"That's true," said Marianne reflectively.

"But then, papa," said Jenny, "Aunt Easygo said she never heard of such a bargain; only think, two dollars a yard for a *velvet*!"

"And why is it two dollars a yard? Is the man a personal friend, that he wishes to make you a present of a dollar on the yard, or is there some reason why it is undesirable?" said I.

"Well, you know, papa, he said those large patterns were not so salable."

"To tell the truth," said Marianne, "I never did like the pattern exactly; as to uniformity of tint, it might match with anything, for there's every color of the rainbow in it."

"You see, papa, it's a gorgeous flower-pattern," said Jenny.

"Well, Marianne, how many yards of this wonderfully cheap carpet do you want?"

"We want sixty yards for both rooms," said Jenny, always primed with statistics.

"That will be a hundred and twenty dollars," I said.

"Yes," said Jenny; "and we went over the figures together, and thought we could make it out by economizing in other things. Aunt Easygo said that the carpet was half the battle, — that it gave the air to everything else."

"Well, Marianne, if you want a man's advice in the case, mine is at your service."

"That is just what I want, papa."

"Well, then, my dear, choose your wall-papers and borderings, and, when they are up, choose an ingrain carpet to harmonize with them, and adapt your furniture to the same idea. The sixty dollars that you save on your carpet spend on engravings, chromo lithographs, or photographs of some good works of art, to adorn your walls."

"Papa, I'll do it," said Marianne.

"My little dear," said I, "your papa may seem to be a sleepy old book-worm, yet he has his eyes open. Do you think I don't know why my girls have the credit of being the best-dressed girls on the street?"

"Oh papa!" cried out both girls in a breath.

"Fact, that!" said Bob, with energy, pulling at his mustache. "Everybody talks about your dress, and wonders how you make it out."

"Well," said I, "I presume you do not go into a shop and buy a yard of ribbon because it is selling at half price, and put it on without considering complexion, eyes, hair, and shade of the dress, do you?"

"Of course we don't!" chimed in the duo with energy.

"Of course you don't. Haven't I seen you mincing downstairs, with all your colors harmonized, even to your gloves and gaiters? Now, a room must be dressed as carefully as a lady."

"Well, I'm convinced," said Jenny, "that papa knows how to make rooms prettier than Aunt Easygo; but then she said this was cheap, because it would outlast two common carpets."

"But, as you pay double price," said I, "I don't see that. Besides, I would rather, in the course of twenty years, have two nice, fresh ingrain carpets, of just the color and pattern that suited my rooms, than labor along with one ill-chosen velvet that harmonized with nothing."

"I give it up," said Jenny; "I give it up."

"Now, understand me," said I; "I am not traducing velvet or Brussels or Axminster. I admit that more beautiful effects can be found in those goods than in the humbler fabrics of the carpet rooms. Nothing would delight me more than to put an unlimited credit to

Marianne's account, and let her work out the problems of harmonious color in velvet and damask. All I have to say is, that certain unities of color, certain general arrangements, will secure very nearly as good general effects in either material. A library with a neat, mossy green carpet on the floor, harmonizing with wall-paper and furniture, looks generally as well, whether the mossy green is made in Brussels or in ingrain. In the carpet stores, these two materials stand side by side in the very same pattern, and one is often as good for the purpose as the other. A lady of my acquaintance, some years since, employed an artist to decorate her parlors. The walls being frescoed and tinted to suit his ideal, he immediately issued his decree that her splendid velvet carpets must be sent to auction, and others bought of certain colors harmonizing with the walls. Unable to find exactly the color and pattern he wanted, he at last had the carpets woven in a neighboring factory, where, as yet, they had only the art of weaving ingrains. Thus was the material sacrificed at once to the harmony."

I remarked, in passing, that this was before Bigelow's mechanical genius had unlocked for America the higher secrets of carpet-weaving, and made it possible to have one's desires accomplished in Brussels or velvet. In those days, English carpet-weavers did not send to America for their looms, as they now do.

"But now to return to my analysis of John's rooms.

"Another thing which goes a great way towards giving them their agreeable air is the books in them. Some people are fond of treating books as others do children. One room in the house is selected, and every book driven into it and kept there. Yet nothing makes a room so home-like, so companionable, and gives it such an air of refinement, as the presence of books. They change the aspect of a parlor from that of a mere reception-room, where visitors perch for a transient call, and give it the air of a room where one feels like taking off one's things to stay. It gives the appearance of permanence and repose and quiet fellowship; and, next to pictures on the walls, the many-colored bindings and gildings of books are the most agreeable adornment of a room."

"Then, Marianne," said Bob, "we have something to start with, at all events. There are my English Classics and English Poets, and my uniform editions of Scott and Thackeray and Macaulay and Prescott and Irving and Longfellow and Lowell and Hawthorne and Holmes and a host more. We really have something pretty there."

"You are a lucky girl," I said, "to have so much secured. A girl brought up in a house full of books, always able to turn to this or that author and look for any passage or poem when she thinks of it, doesn't know what a blank a house without books might be."

"Well," said Marianne, "mamma and I were counting over my treasures the other day. Do you know, I have one really fine old engraving, that Bob says is quite a genuine thing; and then there is that pencil-sketch that poor Schöne made for me the month before he died,—it is truly artistic."

"And I have a couple of capital things of Landseer's," said Bob.

"There's no danger that your rooms will not be pretty," said I, "now you are fairly on the right track."

"But, papa," said Marianne, "I am troubled about one thing. My love of beauty runs into everything. I want pretty things for my table; and yet, as you say, servants are so careless, one cannot use such things freely without great waste."

"For my part," said my wife, "I believe in best china, to be kept carefully on an upper shelf, and taken down for high-days and holidays; it may be a superstition, but I believe in it. It must never be taken out except when the mistress herself can see that it is safely cared for. My mother always washed her china herself; and it was a very pretty social ceremony, after tea was over, while she sat among us washing her pretty cups, and wiping them on a fine damask towel."

"With all my heart," said I; "have your best china and venerate it,—it is one of the loveliest of domestic superstitions; only do not make it a bar to hospitality, and shrink from having a friend to tea with you, unless you feel equal to getting up to the high shelf where you keep it, getting it down, washing, and putting it up again.

"But in serving a table, I say, as I said of a house, beauty is a necessity, and beauty is cheap. Because you cannot afford beauty in one form, it does not follow that you cannot have it in another. Because one cannot afford to keep up a perennial supply of delicate china and crystal, subject to the accidents of raw, untrained servants, it does not follow that the every-day table need present a sordid assortment of articles chosen simply for cheapness, while the whole capacity of the purse is given to the set forever locked away for state occasions.

"A table-service all of simple white, of graceful forms, even though not of china, if arranged with care, with snowy, well-kept table-linen, clear glasses, and bright American plate in place of solid silver, may be made to look inviting; add a glass of flowers every day, and your table may look pretty: and it is far more important that it should look pretty for the family every day than for company once in two weeks."

"I tell my girls," said my wife, "as the result of my experience, you may have your pretty china and your lovely fanciful articles for the table only so long as you can take all the care of them yourselves. As soon as you get tired of doing this, and put them into the hands of the trustiest servants, some good, well-meaning creature is sure to break her heart and your own and your very pet darling china pitcher all in one and the same minute, and then her frantic despair leaves you not even the relief of scolding."

"I have become perfectly sure," said I "that there are spiteful little brownies, intent on seducing good women to sin, who mount guard over the special idols of the china closet. If you hear a crash, and a loud Irish wail from the inner depths, you never think of its being a yellow pie-plate, or that dreadful one-handled tureen that you have been wishing were broken these five years; no, indeed, — it is sure to be the lovely painted china bowl, wreathed with morning-glories and sweet-peas, or the engraved glass goblet, with quaint Old English initials. China sacrificed must be a great means of saintship to women. Pope, I think, puts it as the crowning grace of his perfect woman that she is

"'Mistress of herself though china fall.'"

"I ought to be a saint by this time, then," said mamma; "for in the course of my days I have lost so many idols by breakage, and peculiar accidents that seemed by a special fatality to befall my prettiest and most irreplaceable things, that in fact it has come to be a superstitious feeling now with which I regard anything particularly pretty of a breakable nature."

"Well," said Marianne, "unless one has a great deal of money, it seems to me that the investment in these pretty fragilities is rather a poor one."

"Yet," said I, "the principle of beauty is never so captivating as when it presides over the hour of daily meals. I would have the room where they are served one of the pleasantest and sunniest in the house. I would have its coloring cheerful, and there should be companionable pictures and engravings on the walls. Of all things, I dislike a room that seems to be kept, like a restaurant, merely to eat in. I like to see in a dining-room something that betokens a pleasant sitting-room at other hours. I like there some books, a comfortable sofa or lounge, and all that should make it cosy and inviting. The custom in some families, of adopting for the daily meals one of the two parlors which a city house furnishes, has often seemed to me a particularly happy one. You take your meals, then, in an agreeable place, surrounded by the little pleasant arrangements of your daily sitting-room; and after the meal, if the lady of the house does the honors of her own pretty china herself, the office may be a pleasant and social one.

"But in regard to your table-service I have my advice at hand. Invest in pretty table-linen, in delicate napkins, have your vase of flowers, and be guided by the eye of taste in the choice and arrangement of even the every-day table articles, and have no ugly things when you can have pretty ones by taking a little thought. If you are sore tempted with lovely china and crystal, too fragile to last, too expensive to be renewed, turn away to a print-shop and comfort yourself by hanging around the walls of your dining-room beauty that will not break or fade, that will meet your eye from year to year, though plates, tumblers, and teasets successively vanish. There is my advice for you, Marianne."

At the same time let me say, in parenthesis, that my wife, whose weakness is china, informed me that night, when we were by ourselves, that she was ordering secretly a teaset as a bridal gift for Marianne every cup of which was to be exquisitely painted with the wild flowers of America, from designs of her own,—a thing, by the by, that can now be very nicely executed in our country, as one may find by looking in at our friend Briggs's on School Street. "It will last her all her life," she said, "and always be such a pleasure to look at; and a pretty tea-table is such a pretty sight!" So spoke Mrs. Crowfield, "unweaned from china by a thousand falls." She spoke even with tears in her eyes. Verily these women are harps of a thousand strings!

But to return to my subject.

"Finally and lastly," I said, "in my analysis and explication of the agreeableness of those same parlors, comes the growing grace,— their *homeliness*. By 'homeliness' I mean not ugliness, as the word is apt to be used, but the air that is given to a room by being really at home in it. Not the most skillful arrangement can impart this charm.

"It is said that a king of France once remarked, 'My son, you must seem to love your people.'

"'Father, how shall I *seem* to love them?'

"'My son, you *must* love them.'

"So, to make rooms seem home-like, you must be at home in them. Human light and warmth are so wanting in some rooms, it is so evident that they are never used, that you can never be at ease there. In vain the housemaid is taught to wheel the sofa and turn chair toward chair; in vain it is attempted to imitate a negligent arrangement of the centre-table.

"Books that have really been read and laid down, chairs that have really been moved here and there in the animation of social contact, have a sort of human vitality in them; and a room in which people really live and enjoy is as different from a shut-up apartment as a live woman from a wax image.

"Even rooms furnished without taste often become charming from this one grace, that they seem to let you into the home life and home current. You seem to understand in a moment that you are taken into the family, and are moving in its inner circles, and not revolving at a distance in some outer court of the gentiles.

"How many people do we call on from year to year and know no more of their feelings, habits, tastes, family ideas and ways, than if they lived in Kamtschatka! And why? Because the room which they call a front parlor is made expressly so that you never shall know. They sit in a back room,—work, talk, read, perhaps. After the servant has let you in and opened a crack of the shutters, and while you sit waiting for them to change their dress and come in, you speculate as to what they may be doing. From some distant region, the laugh of a child, the song of a canary-bird reaches you, and then a door claps hastily to. Do they love plants? Do they write letters, sew, embroider, crochet? Do they ever romp and frolic? What books do they read? Do they sketch or paint? Of all these possibilities the mute and muffled room says nothing. A sofa and six chairs, two ottomans fresh from the upholsterer's, a Brussels carpet, a centre-table with four gilt Books of Beauty on it, a mantel-clock from Paris, and two bronze vases,—all those tell you only in frigid tones, 'This is the best room,'—only that, and nothing more,—and soon *she* trips in in her best clothes, and apologizes for keeping you waiting, asks how your mother is, and you remark that it is a pleasant day, and thus the acquaintance progresses from year to year. One hour in the back room, where the plants and canary-bird and children are, might have made you fast friends for life; but, little as it is, you care no more for them than for the gilt clock on the mantel.

"And now, girls," said I, pulling a paper out of my pocket, "you must know that your father is getting to be famous by means of these 'House and Home Papers.' Here is a letter I have just received: —

"MOST EXCELLENT MR. CROWFIELD, — Your thoughts have lighted into our family circle and echoed from our fireside. We all feel the force of them, and are delighted with the felicity of your treatment of the topic you have chosen. You have taken hold of a subject that lies deep in our hearts, in a genial, temperate, and convincing spirit. All must acknowledge the power of your sentiments upon their imaginations; if they could only trust to them in actual life! There is the rub.

"Omitting further upon these points, there is a special feature of your articles upon which we wish to address you. You seem as yet (we do not know, of course, what you may hereafter do) to speak only of homes whose conduct depends upon the help of servants. Now your principles apply, as some of us well conceive, to nearly all classes of society; yet most people, to take an impressive hint, must have their portraits drawn out more exactly. We therefore hope that you will give a reasonable share of your attention to us who do not employ servants, so that you may ease us of some of our burdens, which, in spite of common sense, we dare not throw off. For instance, we have company, — a friend from afar (perhaps wealthy), or a minister, or some other man of note. What do we do? Sit down and receive our visitor with all good will and the freedom of a home? No; we (the lady of the house) flutter about to clear up things, apologizing about this, that, and the other condition of unpreparedness, and, having settled the visitor in the parlor, set about marshaling the elements of a grand dinner or supper, such as no person but a gourmand wants to sit down to, when at home and comfortable; and in getting up this meal, clearing away and washing the dishes, we use up a good half of the time which our guest spends with us. We have spread ourselves, and shown him what we could do; but what a paltry, heart-sickening achievement! Now, good Mr. Crowfield, thou friend of the robbed and despairing, wilt thou not descend into our purgatorial circle, and tell the world what thou hast seen there of doleful remembrance? Tell us how we, who must do and desire to do our own work, can show forth in our homes a homely yet genial hospitality, and entertain our guests without making a fuss and hurlyburly, and seeming to be anxious for their sake about many things, and spending too much time getting meals, as if eating were the chief social pleasure. Won't you do this, Mr. Crowfield?

"Yours beseechingly,

"R. H. A."

"That's a good letter," said Jenny.

"To be sure it is," said I.

"And shall you answer it, papa?"

"In the very next 'Atlantic,' you may be sure I shall. The class that do their own work are the strongest, the most numerous, and, taking one thing with another, quite as well cultivated a class as any other. They are the anomaly of our country,—the distinctive feature of the new society that we are building up here; and, if we are to accomplish our national destiny, that class must increase rather than diminish. I shall certainly do my best to answer the very sensible and pregnant questions of that letter."

Here Marianne shivered and drew up a shawl, and Jenny gaped; my wife folded up the garment in which she had set the last stitch, and the clock struck twelve.

Bob gave a low whistle. "Who knew it was so late?"

"We have talked the fire fairly out," said Jenny.

VI

THE LADY WHO DOES HER OWN WORK

"My dear Chris," said my wife, "isn't it time to be writing the next 'House and Home Paper'?"

I was lying back in my study-chair, with my heels luxuriously propped on an ottoman, reading for the two-hundredth time Hawthorne's "Mosses from an Old Manse," or his "Twice-Told Tales," I forget which, —I only know that these books constitute my cloud-land, where I love to sail away in dreamy quietude, forgetting the war, the price of coal and flour, the rates of exchange, and the rise and fall of gold. What do all these things matter, as seen from those enchanted gardens in Padua where the weird Rappaccini tends his enchanted plants, and his gorgeous daughter fills us with the light and magic of her presence, and saddens us with the shadowy allegoric mystery of her preternatural destiny? But my wife represents the positive forces of time, place, and number in our family, and, having also a chronological head, she knows the day of the month, and therefore gently reminded me that by inevitable dates the time drew near for preparing my—which is it, now, May or June number?

"Well, my dear, you are right," I said, as by an exertion I came head-uppermost, and laid down the fascinating volume. "Let me see, what was I to write about?"

"Why, you remember you were to answer that letter from the lady who does her own work."

"Enough!" said I, seizing the pen with alacrity; "you have hit the exact phrase:—

"'The *lady* who *does her own work*.'"

America is the only country where such a title is possible, —the only country where there is a class of women who may be described as *ladies* who do their own work. By a lady we mean a woman of education, cultivation, and refinement, of liberal tastes and ideas, who, without any very material additions or changes, would be recognized as a lady in any circle of the Old World or the New.

What I have said is, that the existence of such a class is a fact peculiar to American society, a clear, plain result of the new principles involved in the doctrine of universal equality.

When the colonists first came to this country, of however mixed ingredients their ranks might have been composed, and however imbued with the spirit of feudal and aristocratic ideas, the discipline of the wilderness soon brought them to a democratic level; the gentleman felled the wood for his log-cabin side by side with the ploughman, and thews and sinews rose in the market. "A man was deemed honorable in proportion as he lifted his hand upon the high trees of the forest." So in the interior domestic circle. Mistress and maid, living in a log-cabin together, became companions, and sometimes the maid, as the more accomplished and stronger, took precedence of the mistress. It became natural and unavoidable that children should begin to work as early as they were capable of it. The result was a generation of intelligent people brought up to labor from necessity, but turning on the problem of labor the acuteness of a disciplined brain. The mistress, outdone in sinews and muscles by her maid, kept her superiority by skill and contrivance. If she could not lift a pail of water she could invent methods which made lifting the pail unnecessary; if she could not take a hundred steps without weariness, she could make twenty answer the purpose of a hundred.

Slavery, it is true, was to some extent introduced into New England, but it never suited the genius of the people, never struck deep root, or spread so as to choke the good seed of self-helpfulness. Many were opposed to it from conscientious principle, — many from far-sighted thrift, and from a love of thoroughness and well-doing which despised the rude, unskilled work of barbarians. People, having once felt the thorough neatness and beauty of execution which came of free, educated, and thoughtful labor, could not tolerate the clumsiness of slavery. Thus it came to pass that for many years the rural population of New England, as a general rule, did their own work, both out doors and in. If there were a black man or black woman or bound girl, they were emphatically only the *helps*, following humbly the steps of master and mistress, and used by them as instruments of lightening certain portions of their toil. The master and mistress with their children were the head workers.

Great merriment has been excited in the Old Country because years ago the first English travelers found that the class of persons by them denominated servants were in America denominated help or helpers. But the term was the very best exponent of the state of society. There were few servants in the European sense of the word;

there was a society of educated workers, where all were practically equal, and where, if there was a deficiency in one family and an excess in another, a *helper*, not a servant, was hired. Mrs. Brown, who has six sons and no daughters, enters into agreement with Mrs. Jones, who has six daughters and no sons. She borrows a daughter, and pays her good wages to help in her domestic toil, and sends a son to help the labors of Mr. Jones. These two young people go into the families in which they are to be employed in all respects as equals and companions, and so the work of the community is equalized. Hence arose, and for many years continued, a state of society more nearly solving than any other ever did the problem of combining the highest culture of the mind with the highest culture of the muscles and the physical faculties.

Then were to be seen families of daughters, handsome, strong females, rising each day to their indoor work with cheerful alertness, — one to sweep the room, another to make the fire, while a third prepared the breakfast for the father and brothers who were going out to manly labor; and they chatted meanwhile of books, studies, embroidery, discussed the last new poem, or some historical topic started by graver reading, or perhaps a rural ball that was to come off the next week. They spun with the book tied to the distaff; they wove; they did all manner of fine needlework; they made lace, painted flowers, and, in short, in the boundless consciousness of activity, invention, and perfect health, set themselves to any work they had ever read or thought of. A bride in those days was married with sheets and tablecloths of her own weaving, with counterpanes and toilet-covers wrought in divers embroidery by her own and her sisters' hands. The amount of fancy work done in our days by girls who have nothing else to do will not equal what was done by these, who performed besides, among them, the whole work of the family.

For many years these habits of life characterized the majority of our rural towns. They still exist among a class respectable in numbers and position, though perhaps not as happy in perfect self-satisfaction and a conviction of the dignity and desirableness of its lot as in former days. Human nature is above all things — lazy. Every one confesses in the abstract that exertion which brings out all the powers of body and mind is the best thing for us all; but practically most people do all they can to get rid of it, and as a general rule nobody does much more than circumstances drive him to do. Even I would not write this article were not the publication-day hard on my heels. I should read Hawthorne and Emerson and Holmes, and dream in my armchair, and project in the clouds those lovely unwritten stories that curl and veer and change like mist-wreaths in the sun. So also, however dignified, however invigorating, however really desirable, are habits of life involving daily physical toil, there is a constant evil demon at every one's elbow, seducing him to evade it, or to bear its weight with sullen, discontented murmurs.

I will venture to say that there are at least, to speak very moderately, a hundred houses where these humble lines will be read and discussed, where there are no servants except the ladies of the household. I will venture to say, also, that these households, many of them, are not inferior in the air of cultivation and refined elegance to many which are conducted by the ministration of domestics. I will venture to assert furthermore that these same ladies who live thus find quite as much time for reading, letter-writing, drawing, embroidery, and fancy work as the women of families otherwise arranged. I am quite certain that they would be found on an average to be in the enjoyment of better health, and more of that sense of capability and vitality which gives one confidence in one's ability to look into life and meet it with cheerful courage, than three quarters of the women who keep servants; and that, on the whole, their domestic establishment is regulated more exactly to their mind, their food prepared and served more to their taste. And yet, with all this, I will *not* venture to assert that they are satisfied with this way of living, and that they would not change it forthwith if they could. They have a secret feeling all the while that they are being abused, that they are working harder than they ought to, and that women who live in their houses like boarders, who have only to speak and it is done, are the truly enviable ones. One after another of their associates, as opportunity offers and means increase, deserts the ranks, and commits her domestic affairs to the hands of hired servants. Self-respect takes the alarm. Is it altogether genteel to live as we do? To be sure, we are accustomed to it; we have it all systematized and arranged; the work of our own hands suits us better than any we can hire; in fact, when we do hire, we are discontented and uncomfortable, for who will do for us what we will do for ourselves? But when we have company! there's the rub, to get out all our best things and put them back,—to cook the meals and wash the dishes ingloriously,—and to make all appear as if we didn't do it, and had servants like other people.

There, after all, is the rub. A want of hardy self-respect, an unwillingness to face with dignity the actual facts and necessities of our situation in life,—this, after all, is the worst and most dangerous feature of the case. It is the same sort of pride which makes Smilax think he must hire a waiter in white gloves, and get up a circuitous dinner party on English principles, to entertain a friend from England. Because the friend in England lives in such and such a style, he must make believe for a day that he lives so, too, when in fact it is a whirlwind in his domestic establishment equal to a removal or a fire, and threatens the total extinction of Mrs. Smilax. Now there are two principles of hospitality that people are very apt to overlook. One is, that their guests like to be made at home, and treated with confidence; and another is, that people are always interested in the details of a way of life that is new to them. The Englishman comes to America as weary of his old, easy, family-coach life as you can be of yours: he wants to see something new under the sun,—something American; and forthwith we all bestir ourselves to give him something as near as we can fancy exactly like what he is already tired of. So city people come to the country, not to sit in the best parlor and to see the nearest imitation of city life, but to lie on the haymow, to swing in the barn, to form intimacy with the pigs, chickens, and ducks, and to eat baked potatoes, exactly on the critical moment when they are done, from the oven of the cooking-stove,—and we remark, *en passant*, that nobody has ever truly eaten a baked potato unless he has seized it at that precise and fortunate moment.

I fancy you now, my friends, whom I have in my eye. You are three happy women together. You are all so well that you know not how it feels to be sick. You are used to early rising, and would not lie in bed if you could. Long years of practice have made you familiar with the shortest, neatest, most expeditious method of doing every household office, so that really, for the greater part of the time in your house, there seems to a looker-on to be nothing to do. You rise in the morning and dispatch your husband, father, and brothers to the farm or wood-lot; you go sociably about chatting with each other, while you skim the milk, make the butter, turn the cheeses. The forenoon is long; it's ten to one that all the so-called morning work is over, and you have leisure for an hour's sewing or reading before it is time to start the dinner preparations. By two o'clock your housework is done, and you have the long afternoon for books, needlework, or drawing,—for perhaps there is among you one with a gift at her pencil. Perhaps one of you reads aloud while the others sew, and you manage in that way to keep up with a great deal of reading. I see on your bookshelves Prescott, Macaulay, Irving, besides the lighter fry of poems and novels, and, if I mistake not, the friendly covers of the "Atlantic." When you have company, you invite Mrs. Smith or Brown or Jones to tea: you have no trouble—

they come early, with their knitting or sewing; your particular crony sits with you by your polished stove while you watch the baking of those light biscuits and tea rusks for which you are so famous, and Mrs. Somebodyelse chats with your sister, who is spreading the table with your best china in the best room. When tea is over, there is plenty of volunteering to help you wash your pretty India teacups, and get them back into the cupboard. There is no special fatigue or exertion in all this, though you have taken down the best things and put them back, because you have done all without anxiety or effort, among those who would do precisely the same if you were their visitors.

But now comes down pretty Mrs. Simmons and her pretty daughter to spend a week with you, and forthwith you are troubled. Your youngest, Fanny, visited them in New York last fall, and tells you of their cook and chambermaid, and the servant in white gloves that waits on the table. You say in your soul, "What shall we do? they never can be contented to live as we do; how shall we manage?" And now you long for servants.

This is the very time that you should know that Mrs. Simmons is tired to death of her fine establishment, and weighed down with the task of keeping the peace among her servants. She is a quiet soul, dearly loving her ease and hating strife; and yet last week she had five quarrels to settle between her invaluable cook and the other members of her staff, because invaluable cook, on the strength of knowing how to get up state dinners and to manage all sorts of mysteries which her mistress knows nothing about, asserts the usual right of spoiled favorites to insult all her neighbors with impunity, and rule with a rod of iron over the whole house. Anything that is not in the least like her own home and ways of living will be a blessed relief and change to Mrs. Simmons. Your clean, quiet house, your delicate cookery, your cheerful morning tasks, if you will let her follow you about, and sit and talk with you while you are at your work, will all seem a pleasant contrast to her own life. Of course, if it came to the case of offering to change lots in life, she would not do it; but very likely she *thinks* she would, and sighs over and pities herself, and thinks sentimentally how fortunate you are, how snugly and securely you live, and wishes she were as untrammeled and independent as you. And she is more than half right; for, with her helpless habits, her utter ignorance of the simplest facts concerning the reciprocal relations of milk, eggs, butter, saleratus, soda, and yeast, she is completely the victim and slave of the person she pretends to rule.

Only imagine some of the frequent scenes and rehearsals in her family. After many trials, she at last engages a seamstress who promises to prove a perfect treasure,—neat, dapper, nimble, skillful, and spirited. The very soul of Mrs. Simmons rejoices in heaven. Illusive bliss! The newcomer proves to be no favorite with Madam Cook, and the domestic fates evolve the catastrophe, as follows. First, low murmur of distant thunder in the kitchen; then a day or two of sulky silence, in which the atmosphere seems heavy with an approaching storm. At last comes the climax. The parlor door flies open during breakfast. Enter seamstress in tears, followed by Mrs. Cook, with a face swollen and red with wrath, who tersely introduces the subject-matter of the drama in a voice trembling with rage.

"Would you be plased, ma'am, to suit yerself with another cook? Me week will be up next Tuesday, and I want to be going."

"Why, Bridget, what's the matter?"

"Matter enough, ma'am! I niver could live with them Cork girls in a house, nor I won't; them as likes the Cork girls is welcome for all me; but it's not for the likes of me to live with them, and she been in the kitchen a-upsettin' of me gravies with her flatirons and things."

Here bursts in the seamstress with a whirlwind of denial, and the altercation wages fast and furious, and poor, little, delicate Mrs. Simmons stands like a kitten in a thunderstorm in the midst of a regular Irish row.

Cook, of course, is sure of her victory. She knows that a great dinner is to come off Wednesday, and that her mistress has not the smallest idea how to manage it, and that therefore, whatever happens, she must be conciliated.

Swelling with secret indignation at the tyrant, poor Mrs. Simmons dismisses her seamstress with longing looks. She suited her mistress exactly, but she didn't suit cook!

Now, if Mrs. Simmons had been brought up in early life with the experience that you have, she would be mistress in her own house. She would quietly say to Madam Cook, "If my family arrangements do not suit you, you can leave. I can see to the dinner myself." And she could do it. Her well-trained muscles would not break down under a little extra work; her skill, adroitness, and perfect familiarity with everything that is to be done would enable her at once to make cooks of any bright girls of good capacity who might still be in her establishment; and, above all, she would feel herself mistress in her own house. This is what would come of an experience in doing her own work as you do. She who can at once put her own trained hand to the machine in any spot where a hand is needed never comes to be the slave of a coarse, vulgar Irishwoman.

So, also, in forming a judgment of what is to be expected of servants in a given time, and what ought to be expected of a given amount of provisions, poor Mrs. Simmons is absolutely at sea. If even for one six months in her life she had been a practical cook, and had really had the charge of the larder, she would not now be haunted, as she constantly is, by an indefinite apprehension of an immense wastefulness, perhaps of the disappearance of provisions through secret channels of relationship and favoritism. She certainly could not be made to believe in the absolute necessity of so many pounds of sugar, quarts of milk, and dozens of eggs, not to mention spices and wine, as are daily required for the accomplishment of Madam Cook's purposes. But though now she does suspect and apprehend, she cannot speak with certainty. She cannot say, "*I* have made these things. I know exactly what they require. I have done this and that myself, and know it can be done, and done well, in a certain time." It is said that women who have been accustomed to doing their own work become hard mistresses. They are certainly more sure of the ground they stand on,—they are less open to imposition,—they can speak and act in their own houses more as those "having authority," and therefore are less afraid to exact what is justly their due, and less willing to endure impertinence and unfaithfulness. Their general error lies in expecting that any servant ever will do as well for them as they will do for themselves, and that an untrained, undisciplined human being ever *can* do housework, or any other work, with the neatness and perfection that a person of trained intelligence can. It has been remarked in our armies that the men of cultivation, though bred in delicate and refined spheres, can bear up under the hardships of camp-life better and longer than rough laborers. The reason is, that an educated mind knows how to use and save its body, to work it and spare it, as an uneducated mind cannot; and so the college-bred youth brings himself safely through fatigues which kill the unreflective laborer. Cultivated, intelligent women, who are brought up to do the work of their own families, are labor-saving institutions. They make the head save the wear of the muscles. By forethought, contrivance, system, and arrangement, they lessen the amount to be done, and do it with less expense of time and strength than others. The old New England motto, *Get your work done up in the forenoon,* applied to an amount of work which would keep a common Irish servant toiling from daylight to sunset.

A lady living in one of our obscure New England towns, where there were no servants to be hired, at last by sending to a distant city succeeded in procuring a raw Irish maid of all work, a creature of immense bone and muscle, but of heavy, unawakened brain. In one fortnight she established such a reign of Chaos and old Night in the kitchen and through the house that her mistress, a delicate woman, incumbered with the care of young children, began seriously to think that she made more work each day than she performed, and dismissed her. What was now to be done? Fortunately, the daughter of a neighboring farmer was going to be married in six months, and wanted a little ready money for her trousseau. The lady was informed that Miss So-and-so would come to her, not as a servant, but as hired "help." She was fain to accept any help with gladness. Forthwith came into the family circle a tall, well-dressed young person, grave, unobtrusive, self-respecting, yet not in the least presuming, who sat at the family table and observed all its decorums with the modest self-possession of a lady. The newcomer took a survey of the labors of a family of ten members, including four or five young children, and, looking, seemed at once to throw them into system, matured her plans, arranged her hours of washing, ironing, baking, cleaning, rose early, moved deftly, and in a single day the slatternly and littered kitchen assumed that neat, orderly appearance that so often strikes one in New England farmhouses. The work seemed to be all gone. Everything was nicely washed, brightened, put in place, and stayed in place: the floors, when cleaned, remained clean; the work was always done, and not doing; and every afternoon the young lady sat neatly dressed in her own apartment, either writing letters to her betrothed, or sewing on her bridal outfit. Such is the result of employing those who have been brought up to do their own work. That tall, fine-looking girl, for aught we know, may yet be mistress of a fine house on Fifth Avenue; and, if she is, she will, we fear, prove rather an exacting mistress to Irish Biddy and Bridget; but she will never be threatened by her cook and chambermaid, after the first one or two have tried the experiment.

Having written thus far on my article I laid it aside till evening, when, as usual, I was saluted by the inquiry, "Has papa been writing anything to-day?" and then followed loud petitions to hear it; and so I read as far, reader, as you have.

"Well, papa," said Jenny, "what are you meaning to make out there? Do you really think it would be best for us all to try to go back to that old style of living you describe? After all, you have shown only the dark side of an establishment with servants, and the bright side of the other way of living. Mamma does not have such trouble with her servants; matters have always gone smoothly in our family; and, if we are not such wonderful girls as those you describe, yet we may make pretty good housekeepers on the modern system, after all."

"You don't know all the troubles your mamma has had in your day," said my wife. "I have often, in the course of my family history, seen the day when I have heartily wished for the strength and ability to manage my household matters as my grandmother of notable memory managed hers. But I fear that those remarkable women of the olden times are like the ancient painted glass,—the art of making them is lost; my mother was less than her mother, and I am less than my mother."

"And Marianne and I come out entirely at the little end of the horn," said Jenny, laughing; "yet I wash the breakfast cups and dust the parlors, and have always fancied myself a notable housekeeper."

"It is just as I told you," I said. "Human nature is always the same. Nobody ever is or does more than circumstances force him to be and do. Those remarkable women of old were made by circumstances. There were, comparatively speaking, no servants to be had, and so children were trained to habits of industry and mechanical adroitness from the cradle, and every household process was reduced to the very minimum of labor. Every step required in a process was counted, every movement calculated; and she who took ten steps, when one would do, lost her reputation for 'faculty.' Certainly such an early drill was of use in developing the health and the bodily powers, as well as in giving precision to the practical mental faculties. All household economies were arranged with equal niceness in those thoughtful minds. A trained housekeeper knew just how many sticks of hickory of a certain size were required to heat her oven, and how many of each different kind of wood. She knew by a sort of intuition just what kind of food would yield the most palatable nutriment with the least outlay of accessories in cooking. She knew to a minute the time when each article must go into and be withdrawn from her oven; and, if she could only lie in her chamber and direct, she could guide an intelligent child through the processes with mathematical certainty. It is impossible, however, that anything but early training and long experience can produce these results, and it is earnestly to be wished that the grandmothers of New England had only written down their experiences for our children; they would have been a mine of maxims and traditions, better than any other traditions of the elders which we know of."

"One thing I know," said Marianne, "and that is, I wish I had been brought up so, and knew all that I should, and had all the strength and adroitness that those women had. I should not dread to begin housekeeping, as I now do. I should feel myself independent. I should feel that I knew how to direct my servants, and what it was reasonable and proper to expect of them; and then, as you say, I shouldn't be dependent on all their whims and caprices of temper. I dread those household storms, of all things."

Silently pondering these anxieties of the young expectant housekeeper, I resumed my pen, and concluded my paper as follows:—

In this country, our democratic institutions have removed the superincumbent pressure which in the Old World confines the servants to a regular orbit. They come here feeling that this is somehow a land of liberty, and with very dim and confused notions of what liberty is. They are for the most part the raw, untrained Irish peasantry, and the wonder is, that, with all the unreasoning heats and prejudices of the Celtic blood, all the necessary ignorance and rawness, there should be the measure of comfort and success there is in our domestic arrangements. But, so long as things are so, there will be constant changes and interruptions in every domestic establishment, and constantly recurring interregnums when the mistress must put her own hand to the work, whether the hand be a trained or an untrained one. As matters now are, the young housekeeper takes life at the hardest. She has very little strength,— no 100 experience to teach her how to save her strength. She knows nothing experimentally of the simplest processes necessary to keep her family comfortably fed and clothed; and she has a way of looking at all these things which makes them particularly hard and distasteful to her. She does not escape being obliged to do housework at intervals, but she does it in a weak, blundering, confused way, that makes it twice as hard and disagreeable as it need be.

Now what I have to say is, that, if every young woman learned to do housework and cultivated her practical faculties in early life, she would, in the first place, be much more likely to keep her servants, and, in the second place, if she lost them temporarily, would avoid all that wear and tear of the nervous system which comes from constant ill-success in those departments on which family health and temper mainly depend. This is one of the peculiarities of our American life which require a peculiar training. Why not face it sensibly?

The second thing I have to say is, that our land is now full of motorpathic institutions to which women are sent at great expense to have hired operators stretch and exercise their inactive muscles. They lie for hours to have their feet twigged, their arms flexed, and all the different muscles of the body worked for them, because they are so flaccid and torpid that the powers of life do not go on. Would it not be quite as cheerful and less expensive a process if young girls from early life developed the muscles in sweeping, dusting, ironing, rubbing furniture, and all the multiplied domestic processes which our grandmothers knew of? A woman who did all these, and diversified the intervals with spinning on the great and little wheel, never came to need the gymnastics of Dio Lewis or of the Swedish motorpathist, which really are a necessity now. Does it not seem poor economy to pay servants for letting our muscles grow feeble, and then to pay operators to exercise them for us? I will venture to say that our grandmothers in a week went over every movement that any gymnast has invented, and went over them to some productive purpose, too.

Lastly, my paper will not have been in vain if those ladies who have learned and practice the invaluable accomplishment of doing their own work will know their own happiness and dignity, and properly value their great acquisition, even though it may have been forced upon them by circumstances.

VII

WHAT CAN BE GOT IN AMERICA

While I was preparing my article for the "Atlantic," our friend Bob Stephens burst in upon us, in some considerable heat, with a newspaper in his hand.

"Well, girls, your time is come now! You women have been preaching heroism and sacrifice to us, —'so splendid to go forth and suffer and die for our country,'—and now comes the test of feminine patriotism."

"Why, what's the matter now?" said Jenny, running eagerly to look over his shoulder at the paper.

"No more foreign goods," said he, waving it aloft, —"no more gold shipped to Europe for silks, laces, jewels, kid gloves, and what not. Here it is,—great movement, headed by senators' and generals' wives, Mrs. General Butler, Mrs. John P. Hale, Mrs. Henry Wilson, and so on, a long string of them, to buy no more imported articles during the war."

"But I don't see how it *can* be done," said Jenny.

"Why," said I, "do you suppose that 'nothing to wear' is made in America?"

"But, dear Mr. Crowfield," said Miss Featherstone, a nice girl, who was just then one of our family circle, "there is not, positively, much that is really fit to use or wear made in America, —is there now? Just think: how is Marianne to furnish her house here without French papers and English carpets?—those American papers are so very ordinary, and, as to American carpets, everybody knows their colors don't hold; and then, as to dress, a lady must have gloves, you know,—and everybody knows no such things are made in America as gloves."

"I think," I said, "that I have heard of certain fair ladies wishing that they were men, that they might show with what alacrity they would sacrifice everything on the altar of their country: life and limb would be nothing; they would glory in wounds and bruises, they would enjoy losing a right arm, they wouldn't mind limping about on a lame leg the rest of their lives, if they were John or Peter, if only they might serve their dear country."

"Yes," said Bob, "that's female patriotism! Girls are always ready to jump off from precipices, or throw themselves into abysses, but as to wearing an unfashionable hat or thread gloves, that they can't do, — not even for their dear country. No matter whether there's any money left to pay for the war or not, the dear souls must have twenty yards of silk in a dress, — it's the fashion, you know."

"Now, isn't he too bad?" said Marianne. "As if we'd ever been asked to make these sacrifices and refused! I think I have seen women ready to give up dress and fashion and everything else for a good cause."

"For that matter," said I, "the history of all wars has shown women ready to sacrifice what is most intimately feminine in times of peril to their country. The women of Carthage not only gave up their jewels in the siege of their city, but, in the last extremity, cut off their hair for bowstrings. The women of Hungary and Poland, in their country's need, sold their jewels and plate and wore ornaments of iron and lead. In the time of our own Revolution, our women dressed in plain homespun and drank herb-tea, — and certainly nothing is more feminine than a cup of tea. And in this very struggle, the women of the Southern States have cut up their carpets for blankets, have borne the most humiliating retrenchments and privations of all kinds without a murmur. So let us exonerate the female sex of want of patriotism, at any rate."

"Certainly," said my wife; "and if our Northern women have not retrenched and made sacrifices, it has been because it has not been impressed on them that there is any particular call for it. Everything has seemed to be so prosperous and plentiful in the Northern States, money has been so abundant and easy to come by, that it has really been difficult to realize that a dreadful and destructive war was raging. Only occasionally, after a great battle, when the lists of the killed and wounded have been sent through the country, have we felt that we were making a sacrifice. The women who have spent such sums for laces and jewels and silks have not had it set clearly before them why they should not do so. The money has been placed freely in their hands, and the temptation before their eyes."

"Yes," said Jenny, "I am quite sure that there are hundreds who have been buying foreign goods who would not do it if they could see any connection between their not doing it and the salvation of the country; but when I go to buy a pair of gloves, I naturally want the best pair I can find, the pair that will last the longest and look the best, and these always happen to be French gloves."

"Then," said Miss Featherstone, "I never could clearly see why people should confine their patronage and encouragement to works of their own country. I'm sure the poor manufacturers of England have shown the very noblest spirit with relation to our cause, and so have the silk weavers and artisans of France,—at least, so I have heard; why should we not give them a fair share of encouragement, particularly when they make things that we are not in circumstances to make, have not the means to make?"

"Those are certainly sensible questions," I replied, "and ought to meet a fair answer, and I should say that, were our country in a fair ordinary state of prosperity, there would be no reason why our wealth should not flow out for the encouragement of well-directed industry in any part of the world; from this point of view we might look on the whole world as our country, and cheerfully assist in developing its wealth and resources. But our country is now in the situation of a private family whose means are absorbed by an expensive sickness, involving the life of its head: just now it is all we can do to keep the family together; all our means are swallowed up by our own domestic wants; we have nothing to give for the encouragement of other families, we must exist ourselves; we must get through this crisis and hold our own, and, that we may do it, all the family expenses must be kept within ourselves as far as possible. If we drain off all the gold of the country to send to Europe to encourage her worthy artisans, we produce high prices and distress among equally worthy ones at home, and we lessen the amount of our resources for maintaining the great struggle for national existence. The same amount of money which we pay for foreign luxuries, if passed into the hands of our own manufacturers and producers, becomes available for the increasing expenses of the war."

"But, papa," said Jenny, "I understood that a great part of our governmental income was derived from the duties on foreign goods, and so I inferred that the more foreign goods were imported the better it would be."

"Well, suppose," said I, "that for every hundred thousand dollars we send out of the country we pay the government ten thousand; that is about what our gain as a nation would be: we send our gold abroad in a great stream, and give our government a little driblet."

"Well, but," said Miss Featherstone, "what can be got in America? Hardly anything, I believe, except common calicoes."

"Begging your pardon, my dear lady," said I, "there is where you and multitudes of others are greatly mistaken. Your partiality for foreign things has kept you ignorant of what you have at home. Now I am not blaming the love of foreign things: it is not peculiar to us Americans; all nations have it. It is a part of the poetry of our nature to love what comes from afar, and reminds us of lands distant and different from our own. The English belles seek after French laces; the French beauty enumerates English laces among her rarities; and the French dandy piques himself upon an English tailor. We Americans are great travelers, and few people travel, I fancy, with more real enjoyment than we; our domestic establishments, as compared with those of the Old World, are less cumbrous and stately, and so our money is commonly in hand as pocket-money, to be spent freely and gayly in our tours abroad.

"We have such bright and pleasant times in every country that we conceive a kindliness for its belongings. To send to Paris for our dresses and our shoes and our gloves may not be a mere bit of foppery, but a reminder of the bright, pleasant hours we have spent in that city of boulevards and fountains. Hence it comes, in a way not very blamable, that many people have been so engrossed with what can be got from abroad that they have neglected to inquire what can be found at home: they have supposed, of course, that to get a decent watch they must send to Geneva or to London; that to get thoroughly good carpets they must have the English manufacture; that a really tasteful wall-paper could be found only in Paris; and that flannels and broadcloths could come only from France, Great Britain, or Germany."

"Well, isn't it so?" said Miss Featherstone. "I certainly have always thought so; I never heard of American watches, I'm sure."

"Then," said I, "I'm sure you can't have read an article that you should have read on the Waltham watches, written by our friend George W. Curtis, in the 'Atlantic' for January of last year. I must refer you to that to learn that we make in America watches superior to those of Switzerland or England, bringing into the service machinery and modes of workmanship unequaled for delicacy and precision; as I said before, you must get the article and read it, and, if some sunny day you could make a trip to Waltham and see the establishment, it would greatly assist your comprehension."

"Then, as to men's clothing," said Bob, "I know to my entire satisfaction that many of the most popular cloths for men's wear are actually American fabrics baptized with French and English names to make them sell."

"Which shows," said I, "the use of a general community movement to employ American goods. It will change the fashion. The demand will create the supply. When the leaders of fashion are inquiring for American instead of French and English fabrics, they will be surprised to find what nice American articles there are. The work of our own hands will no more be forced to skulk into the market under French and English names, and we shall see, what is really true, that an American gentleman need not look beyond his own country for a wardrobe befitting him. I am positive that we need not seek broadcloth or other woolen goods from foreign lands, — that *better* hats are made in America than in Europe, and better boots and shoes; and I should be glad to send an American gentleman to the World's Fair dressed from top to toe in American manufactures, with an American watch in his pocket, and see if he would suffer in comparison with the gentlemen of any other country."

"Then, as to house-furnishing," began my wife, "American carpets are getting to be every way equal to the English."

"Yes," said I, "and, what is more, the Brussels carpets of England are woven on looms invented by an American, and bought of him. Our countryman, Bigelow, went to England to study carpet-weaving in the English looms, supposing that all arts were generously open for the instruction of learners. He was denied the opportunity of studying the machinery and watching the processes by a shortsighted jealousy. He immediately sat down with a yard of carpeting, and, patiently unraveling it thread by thread, combined and calculated till he invented the machinery on which the best carpets of the Old and the New World are woven. No pains which such ingenuity and energy can render effective are spared to make our fabrics equal those of the British market, and we need only to be disabused of the old prejudice, and to keep up with the movement of our own country, and find out our own resources. The fact is, every year improves our fabrics. Our mechanics, our manufacturers, are working with an energy, a zeal, and a skill that carry things forward faster than anybody dreams of; and nobody can predicate the character of American articles in any department now by their character even five years ago."

"Well, as to wall-papers," said Miss Featherstone, "there you must confess the French are and must be unequaled."

"I do not confess any such thing," said I hardily. "I grant you that, in that department of paper-hangings which exhibits floral decoration, the French designs and execution are, and must be for some time to come, far ahead of all the world: their drawing of flowers, vines, and foliage has the accuracy of botanical studies and the grace of finished works of art, and we cannot as yet pretend in America to do anything equal to it. But for satin finish, and for a variety of exquisite tints of plain colors, American papers equal any in the world: our gilt papers even surpass in the heaviness and polish of the gilding those of foreign countries; and we have also gorgeous velvets. All I have to say is, let people who are furnishing houses inquire for articles of American manufacture, and they will be surprised at what they will see. We need go no farther than our Cambridge glassworks to see that the most dainty devices of cut-glass, crystal, ground and engraved glass of every color and pattern, may be had of American workmanship, every way equal to the best European make, and for half the price. And American painting on china is so well executed, both in Boston and New York, that deficiencies in the finest French or English sets can be made up in a style not distinguishable from the original, as one may easily see by calling on our worthy next neighbor, Briggs, who holds the opposite corner to our 'Atlantic Monthly.' No porcelain, it is true, is yet made in America, these decorative arts being exercised on articles imported from Europe. Our tables must, therefore, perforce, be largely indebted to foreign lands for years to come. Exclusive of this item, however, I believe it would require very little self-denial to paper, carpet, and furnish a house entirely from the manufactures of America. I cannot help saying one word here in favor of the cabinet-makers of Boston. There is so much severity of taste, such a style and manner about the best-made Boston furniture, as raises it really quite into the region of the fine arts. Our artisans have studied foreign models with judicious eyes, and so transferred to our country the spirit of what is best worth imitating that one has no need to import furniture from Europe."

"Well," said Miss Featherstone, "there is one point you cannot make out,—gloves; certainly the French have the monopoly of that article."

"I am not going to ruin my cause by asserting too much," said I. "I haven't been with nicely dressed women so many years not to speak with proper respect of Alexander's gloves; and I confess honestly that to forego them must be a fair, square sacrifice to patriotism. But then, on the other hand, it is nevertheless true that gloves have long been made in America and surreptitiously brought into market as

French. I have lately heard that very nice kid gloves are made at Watertown and in Philadelphia. I have only heard of them and not seen. A loud demand might bring forth an unexpected supply from these and other sources. If the women of America were bent on having gloves made in their own country, how long would it be before apparatus and factories would spring into being? Look at the hoop-skirt factories; women wanted hoop-skirts,—would have them or die,—and forthwith factories arose, and hoop-skirts became as the dust of the earth for abundance."

"Yes," said Miss Featherstone, "and, to say the truth, the American hoop-skirts are the only ones fit to wear. When we were living on the Champs Élysées, I remember we searched high and low for something like them, and finally had to send home to America for some."

"Well," said I, "that shows what I said. Let there be only a hearty call for an article and it will come. These spirits of the vasty deep are not so very far off, after all, as we may imagine, and women's unions and leagues will lead to inquiries and demands which will as infallibly bring supplies as a vacuum will create a draught of air."

"But, at least, there are no ribbons made in America," said Miss Featherstone.

"Pardon, my lady, there is a ribbon factory now in operation in Boston, and ribbons of every color are made in New York; there is also in the vicinity of Boston a factory which makes Roman scarfs. This shows that the faculty of weaving ribbons is not wanting to us Americans, and a zealous patronage would increase the supply.

"Then, as for a thousand and one little feminine needs, I believe our manufacturers can supply them. The Portsmouth Steam Company makes white spool-cotton equal to any in England, and colored spool-cotton, of every shade and variety, such as is not made either in England or France. Pins are well made in America; so are hooks and eyes, and a variety of buttons. Straw bonnets of American manufacture are also extensively in market, and quite as pretty ones as the double-priced ones which are imported.

"As to silks and satins, I am not going to pretend that they are to be found here. It is true, there are silk manufactories, like that of the Cheneys in Connecticut, where very pretty foulard dress-silks are made, together with sewing-silk enough to supply a large demand. Enough has been done to show that silks might be made in America;

but at present, as compared with Europe, we claim neither silks nor thread laces among our manufactures.

"But what then? These are not necessaries of life. Ladies can be very tastefully dressed in other fabrics besides silks. There are many pretty American dress-goods which the leaders of fashion might make fashionable, and certainly no leader of fashion could wish to dress for a nobler object than to aid her country in deadly peril.

"It is not a life-pledge, not a total abstinence, that is asked,—only a temporary expedient to meet a stringent crisis. We only ask a preference for American goods where they can be found. Surely, women whose exertions in Sanitary Fairs have created an era in the history of the world will not shrink from so small a sacrifice for so obvious a good.

"Here is something in which every individual woman can help. Every woman who goes into a shop and asks for American goods renders an appreciable aid to our cause. She expresses her opinion and her patriotism, and her voice forms a part of that demand which shall arouse and develop the resources of her country. We shall learn to know our own country. We shall learn to respect our own powers, and every branch of useful labor will spring and flourish under our well-directed efforts. We shall come out of our great contest, not bedraggled, ragged, and poverty-stricken, but developed, instructed, and rich. Then will we gladly join with other nations in the free interchange of manufactures, and gratify our eye and taste with what is foreign, while we can in turn send abroad our own productions in equal ratio."

"Upon my word," said Miss Featherstone, "I should think it was the Fourth of July; but I yield the point. I am convinced; and henceforth you will see me among the most stringent of the leaguers."

"Right!" said I.

And, fair lady reader, let me hope you will say the same. You can do something for your country,—it lies right in your hand. Go to the shops, determined on supplying your family and yourself with American goods. Insist on having them; raise the question of origin over every article shown to you. In the Revolutionary times, some of the leading matrons of New England gave parties where the ladies were dressed in homespun and drank sage tea. Fashion makes all things beautiful, and you, my charming and accomplished friend, can create beauty by creating fashion. What makes the beauty of half the Cashmere shawls? Not anything in the shawls themselves, for they often look coarse and dingy and barbarous. It is the association with style and fashion. Fair lady, give style and fashion to the products of your own country,—resolve that the money in your hand shall go to your brave brothers, to your co-Americans, now straining every nerve to uphold the nation and cause it to stand high in the earth. What are you without your country? As Americans you can hope for no rank but the rank of your native land, no badge of nobility but her beautiful stars. It rests with this conflict to decide whether those stars shall be badges of nobility to you and your children in all lands. Women of America, your country expects every woman to do her duty!

VIII

ECONOMY

"The fact is," said Jenny, as she twirled a little hat on her hand, which she had been making over, with nobody knows what of bows and pompons, and other matters for which the women have curious names,—"the fact is, American women and girls must learn to economize; it isn't merely restricting one's self to American goods, it is general economy, that is required. Now here's this hat,—costs me only three dollars, all told; and Sophie Page bought an English one this morning at Madam Meyer's for which she gave fifteen. And I really don't think hers has more of an air than mine. I made this over, you see, with things I had in the house, bought nothing but the ribbon, and paid for altering and pressing, and there you see what a stylish hat I have!"

"Lovely! admirable!" said Miss Featherstone. "Upon my word, Jenny, you ought to marry a poor parson; you would be quite thrown away upon a rich man."

"Let me see," said I. "I want to admire intelligently. That isn't the hat you were wearing yesterday?"

"Oh no, papa! This is just done. The one I wore yesterday was my waterfall-hat, with the green feather; this, you see, is an oriole."

"A what?"

"An oriole. Papa, how can you expect to learn about these things?"

"And that plain little black one, with the stiff crop of scarlet feathers sticking straight up?"

"That's my jockey, papa, with a plume *en militaire*."

"And did the waterfall and the jockey cost anything?"

"They were very, very cheap, papa, all things considered. Miss Featherstone will remember that the waterfall was a great bargain, and I had the feather from last year; and as to the jockey, that was made out of my last year's white one, dyed over. You know, papa, I always take care of my things, and they last from year to year."

"I do assure you, Mr. Crowfield," said Miss Featherstone, "I never saw such little economists as your daughters; it is perfectly wonderful what they contrive to dress on. How they manage to do it I'm sure I can't see. I never could, I'm convinced."

"Yes," said Jenny, "I've bought but just one new hat. I only wish you could sit in church where we do, and see those Miss Fielders. Marianne and I have counted six new hats apiece of those girls',—*new*, you know, just out of the milliner's shop; and last Sunday they came out in such lovely puffed tulle bonnets! Weren't they lovely, Marianne? And next Sunday, I don't doubt, there'll be something else."

"Yes," said Miss Featherstone,—"their father, they say, has made a million dollars lately on government contracts."

"For my part," said Jenny, "I think such extravagance, at such a time as this, is shameful."

"Do you know," said I, "that I'm quite sure the Misses Fielder think they are practicing rigorous economy?"

"Papa! Now there you are with your paradoxes! How can you say so?"

"I shouldn't be afraid to bet a pair of gloves, now," said I, "that Miss Fielder thinks herself half ready for translation, because she has bought only six new hats and a tulle bonnet so far in the season. If it were not for her dear bleeding country, she would have had thirty-six, like the Misses Sibthorpe. If we were admitted to the secret councils of the Fielders, doubtless we should perceive what temptations they daily resist; how perfectly rubbishy and dreadful they suffer themselves to be, because they feel it important now, in this crisis, to practice economy; how they abuse the Sibthorpes, who have a new hat every time they drive out, and never think of wearing one more than two or three times; how virtuous and self-denying they feel when they think of the puffed tulle, for which they only gave eighteen dollars, when Madame Caradori showed them those lovely ones, like the Misses Sibthorpe's, for forty-five; and how they go home descanting on virgin simplicity, and resolving that they will not allow themselves to be swept into the vortex of extravagance, whatever other people may do."

"Do you know," said Miss Featherstone, "I believe your papa is right? I was calling on the oldest Miss Fielder the other day, and she told me that she positively felt ashamed to go looking as she did, but that she really did feel the necessity of economy. 'Perhaps we might afford to spend more than some others,' she said; 'but it's so much better to give the money to the Sanitary Commission!'"

"Furthermore," said I, "I am going to put forth another paradox, and say that very likely there are some people looking on my girls, and commenting on them for extravagance in having three hats, even though made over, and contrived from last year's stock."

"They can't know anything about it, then," said Jenny decisively; "for, certainly, nobody can be decent and invest less in millinery than Marianne and I do."

"When I was a young lady," said my wife, "a well-dressed girl got her a new bonnet in the spring, and another in the fall; that was the extent of her purchases in this line. A second-best bonnet, left of last year, did duty to relieve and preserve the best one. My father was accounted well-to-do, but I had no more, and wanted no more. I also bought myself, every spring, two pair of gloves, a dark and a light pair, and wore them through the summer, and another two through the winter; one or two pair of white kids, carefully cleaned, carried me through all my parties. Hats had not been heard of, and the great necessity which requires two or three new ones every spring and fall had not arisen. Yet I was reckoned a well-appearing girl, who dressed liberally. Now, a young lady who has a waterfall-hat, an oriole-hat, and a jockey must still be troubled with anxious cares for her spring and fall and summer and winter bonnets,—all the variety will not take the place of them. Gloves are bought by the dozen; and as to dresses, there seems to be no limit to the quantity of material and trimming that may be expended upon them. When I was a young lady, seventy-five dollars a year was considered by careful parents a liberal allowance for a daughter's wardrobe. I had a hundred, and was reckoned rich; and I sometimes used a part to make up the deficiencies in the allowance of Sarah Evans, my particular friend, whose father gave her only fifty. We all thought that a very scant allowance; yet she generally made a very pretty and genteel appearance, with the help of occasional presents from friends."

"How could a girl dress for fifty dollars?" said Marianne.

"She could get a white muslin and a white cambric, which, with different sortings of ribbons, served her for all dress occasions. A silk, in those days, took only ten yards in the making, and one dark silk was considered a reasonable allowance to a lady's wardrobe. Once made, it stood for something,—always worn carefully, it lasted for years. One or two calico morning-dresses, and a merino for winter wear, completed the list. Then, as to collars, capes, cuffs, etc., we all did our own embroidering, and very pretty things we wore, too. Girls looked as prettily then as they do now, when four or five hundred dollars a year is insufficient to clothe them."

"But, mamma, you know our allowance isn't anything like that,—it is quite a slender one, though not so small as yours was," said Marianne. "Don't you think the customs of society make a difference? Do you think, as things are, we could go back and dress for the sum you did?"

"You cannot," said my wife, "without a greater sacrifice of feeling than I wish to impose on you. Still, though I don't see how to help it, I cannot but think that the requirements of fashion are becoming needlessly extravagant, particularly in regard to the dress of women. It seems to me, it is making the support of families so burdensome that young men are discouraged from marriage. A young man, in a moderately good business, might cheerfully undertake the world with a wife who could make herself pretty and attractive for seventy-five dollars a year, when he might sigh in vain for one who positively could not get through, and be decent, on four hundred. Women, too, are getting to be so attached to the trappings and accessories of life that they cannot think of marriage without an amount of fortune which few young men possess."

"You are talking in very low numbers about the dress of women," said Miss Featherstone. "I do assure you that it is the easiest thing in the world for a girl to make away with a thousand dollars a year, and not have so much to show for it, either, as Marianne and Jenny."

"To be sure," said I. "Only establish certain formulas of expectation, and it is the easiest thing in the world. For instance, in your mother's day girls talked of a pair of gloves,—now they talk of a pack; then it was a bonnet summer and winter,—now it is a bonnet spring, summer, autumn, and winter, and hats like monthly roses,—a new blossom every few weeks."

"And then," said my wife, "every device of the toilet is immediately taken up and varied and improved on, so as to impose an almost monthly necessity for novelty. The jackets of May are outshone by the jackets of June; the buttons of June are antiquated in July; the trimmings of July are *passées* by September; side-combs, back-combs, puffs, rats, and all sorts of such matters, are in a distracted race of improvement; every article of feminine toilet is on the move towards perfection. It seems to me that an infinity of money must be spent in these trifles by those who make the least pretension to keep in the fashion."

"Well, papa," said Jenny, "after all, it's just the way things always have been since the world began. You know the Bible says, 'Can a maid forget her ornaments?' It's clear she can't. You see, it's a law of nature; and you remember all that long chapter in the Bible that we had read in church last Sunday about the curls and veils and tinkling ornaments and crimping-pins, and all that, of those wicked daughters of Zion in old times. Women always have been too much given to dress, and they always will be."

"The thing is," said Marianne, "how can any woman, I, for example, know what is too much or too little? In mamma's day, it seems, a girl could keep her place in society, by hard economy, and spend only fifty dollars a year on her dress. Mamma found a hundred dollars ample. I have more than that, and find myself quite straitened to keep myself looking well. I don't want to live for dress, to give all my time and thoughts to it; I don't wish to be extravagant: and yet I wish to be lady-like—it annoys and makes me unhappy not to be fresh and neat and nice, shabbiness and seediness are my aversion. I don't see where the fault is. Can one individual resist the whole current of society? It certainly is not strictly necessary for us girls to have half the things we do. We might, I suppose, live without many of them, and, as mamma says, look just as well, because girls did so before these things were invented. Now I confess I flatter myself, generally, that I am a pattern of good management and economy, because I get so much less than other girls I associate with. I wish you could see Miss Thorne's fall dresses that she showed me last year when she was visiting here. She had six gowns, and no one of them could have cost less than seventy or eighty dollars, and some of them must have been even more expensive, and yet I don't doubt that this fall she will feel that she must have just as many more. She runs through and wears out these expensive things, with all their velvet and thread lace, just as I wear my commonest ones; and at the end of the season they are really gone,—spotted, stained, frayed, the lace all pulled to pieces,—nothing left to save or make over. I feel as if Jenny and I were patterns of economy when I see such things. I really don't know what economy is. What is it?"

"There is the same difficulty in my housekeeping," said my wife. "I think I am an economist. I mean to be one. All our expenses are on a modest scale, and yet I can see much that really is not strictly necessary; but if I compare myself with some of my neighbors, I feel as if I were hardly respectable. There is no subject on which all the world are censuring one another so much as this. Hardly any one but thinks her neighbors extravagant in some one or more particulars, and takes for granted that she herself is an economist."

"I'll venture to say," said I, "that there isn't a woman of my acquaintance that does not think she is an economist."

"Papa is turned against us women, like all the rest of them," said Jenny. "I wonder if it isn't just so with the men?"

"Yes," said Marianne, "it's the fashion to talk as if all the extravagance of the country was perpetrated by women. For my part, I think young men are just as extravagant. Look at the sums they spend for cigars and meerschaums,—an expense which hasn't even the pretense of usefulness in any way; it's a purely selfish, nonsensical indulgence. When a girl spends money in making herself look pretty, she contributes something to the agreeableness of society; but a man's cigars and pipes are neither ornamental nor useful."

"Then look at their dress," said Jenny: "they are to the full as fussy and particular about it as girls; they have as many fine, invisible points of fashion, and their fashions change quite as often; and they have just as many knick-knacks, with their studs and their sleeve buttons and waistcoat buttons, their scarfs and scarf pins, their watch chains and seals and seal rings, and nobody knows what. Then they often waste and throw away more than women, because they are not good judges of material, nor saving in what they buy, and have no knowledge of how things should be cared for, altered, or mended. If their cap is a little too tight, they cut the lining with a penknife, or slit holes in a new shirt-collar because it does not exactly fit to their mind. For my part, I think men are naturally twice as wasteful as women. A pretty thing, to be sure, to have all the waste of the country laid to us!"

"You are right, child," said I; "women are by nature, as compared with men, the care-taking and saving part of creation,—the authors and conservators of economy. As a general rule, man earns and woman saves and applies. The wastefulness of woman is commonly the fault of man."

"I don't see into that," said Bob Stevens.

"In this way. Economy is the science of proportion. Whether a particular purchase is extravagant depends mainly on the income it is taken from. Suppose a woman has a hundred and fifty a year for her dress, and gives fifty dollars for a bonnet, she gives a third of her income,—it is a horrible extravagance; while for the woman whose income is ten thousand it may be no extravagance at all. The poor clergyman's wife, when she gives five dollars for a bonnet, may be giving as much in proportion to her income as the woman who gives fifty. Now the difficulty with the greater part of women is, that the men, who make the money and hold it, give them no kind of standard by which to measure their expenses. Most women and girls are in this matter entirely at sea, without chart or compass. They don't know in the least what they have to spend. Husbands and fathers often pride themselves about not saying a word on business matters to their wives and daughters. They don't wish them to understand them, or to inquire into them, or to make remarks or suggestions concerning them. 'I want you to have everything that is suitable and proper,' says Jones to his wife, 'but don't be extravagant.'

"'But, my dear,' says Mrs. Jones, 'what is suitable and proper depends very much on our means; if you could allow me any specific sum for dress and housekeeping, I could tell better.'

"'Nonsense, Susan! I can't do that,—it's too much trouble. Get what you need, and avoid foolish extravagances; that's all I ask.'

"By and by Mrs. Jones's bills are sent in, in an evil hour, when Jones has heavy notes to meet, and then comes a domestic storm.

"'I shall just be ruined, madam, if that's the way you are going on. I can't afford to dress you and the girls in the style you have set up: look at this milliner's bill!'

"'I assure you,' says Mrs. Jones, 'we haven't got any more than the Stebbinses, nor so much.'

"'Don't you know that the Stebbinses are worth five times as much as ever I was?'

"No, Mrs. Jones did not know it: how should she, when her husband makes it a rule never to speak of his business to her, and she has not the remotest idea of his income?

"Thus multitudes of good, conscientious women and girls are extravagant from pure ignorance. The male provider allows bills to be run up in his name, and they have no earthly means of judging whether they are spending too much or too little, except the semi-annual hurricane which attends the coming in of these bills.

"The first essential in the practice of economy is a knowledge of one's income, and the man who refuses to accord to his wife and children this information has never any right to accuse them of extravagance, because he himself deprives them of that standard of comparison which is an indispensable requisite in economy. As early as possible in the education of children, they should pass from that state of irresponsible waiting to be provided for by parents, and be trusted with the spending of some fixed allowance, that they may learn prices and values, and have some notion of what money is actually worth and what it will bring. The simple fact of the possession of a fixed and definite income often suddenly transforms a giddy, extravagant girl into a care-taking, prudent little woman. Her allowance is her own; she begins to plan upon it,—to add, subtract, multiply, divide, and do numberless sums in her little head. She no longer buys everything she fancies; she deliberates, weighs, compares. And now there is room for self-denial and generosity to come in. She can do without this article; she can furbish up some older possession to do duty a little longer, and give this money to some friend poorer than she; and ten to one the girl whose bills last year were four or five hundred finds herself bringing through this year creditably on a hundred and fifty. To be sure, she goes without numerous things which she used to have. From the standpoint of a fixed income she sees that these are impossible, and no more wants them than the green cheese of the moon. She learns to make her own taste and skill take the place of expensive purchases. She refits her hats and bonnets, retrims her dresses, and in a thousand busy, earnest, happy little ways sets herself to make the most of her small income.

"So the woman who has her definite allowance for housekeeping finds at once a hundred questions set at rest. Before it was not clear to her why she should not 'go and do likewise' in relation to every purchase made by her next neighbor. Now, there is a clear logic of proportion. Certain things are evidently not to be thought of, though next neighbors do have them; and we must resign ourselves to find some other way of living."

"My dear," said my wife, "I think there is a peculiar temptation in a life organized as ours is in America. There are here no settled classes, with similar ratios of income. Mixed together in the same society, going to the same parties, and blended in daily neighborly intercourse, are families of the most opposite extremes in point of fortune. In England there is a very well understood expression, that people should not dress or live above their station; in America none will admit that they have any particular station, or that they can live above it. The principle of democratic equality unites in society people of the most diverse positions and means.

"Here, for instance, is a family like Dr. Selden's: an old and highly respected one, with an income of only two or three thousand; yet they are people universally sought for in society, and mingle in all the intercourse of life with merchant millionaires whose incomes are from ten to thirty thousand. Their sons and daughters go to the same schools, the same parties, and are thus constantly meeting upon terms of social equality.

"Now it seems to me that our danger does not lie in the great and evident expenses of our richer friends. We do not expect to have pineries, graperies, equipages, horses, diamonds,—we say openly and of course that we do not. Still, our expenses are constantly increased by the proximity of these things, unless we understand ourselves better than most people do. We don't, of course, expect to get a fifteen-hundred-dollar Cashmere, like Mrs. So-and-so, but we begin to look at hundred-dollar shawls and nibble about the hook. We don't expect sets of diamonds, but a diamond ring, a pair of solitaire diamond ear-rings, begin to be speculated about among the young people as among possibilities. We don't expect to carpet our house with Axminster and hang our windows with damask, but at least we must have Brussels and brocatelle,—it *would not* do not to. And so we go on getting hundreds of things that we don't need, that have no real value except that they soothe our self-love; and for these inferior articles we pay a higher proportion of our income than our rich neighbor does for his better ones. Nothing is uglier than low-priced Cashmere shawls; and yet a young man just entering business will spend an eighth of a year's income to put one on his wife, and when he has put it there it only serves as a constant source of disquiet, for, now that the door is opened and Cashmere shawls are possible, she is consumed with envy at the superior ones constantly sported around her. So, also, with point-lace, velvet dresses, and hundreds of things of that sort, which belong to a certain rate of income, and are absurd below it."

"And yet, mamma, I heard Aunt Easygo say that velvet, point-lace, and Cashmere were the cheapest finery that could be bought, because they lasted a lifetime."

"Aunt Easygo speaks from an income of ten thousand a year: they may be cheap for her rate of living; but for us, for example, by no magic of numbers can it be made to appear that it is cheaper to have the greatest bargain in the world in Cashmere, lace, and diamonds than not to have them at all. I never had a diamond, never wore a piece of point-lace, never had a velvet dress, and have been perfectly happy, and just as much respected as if I had. Who ever thought of objecting to me for not having them? Nobody, that I ever heard."

"Certainly not, mamma," said Marianne.

"The thing I have always said to you girls is, that you were not to expect to live like richer people, not to begin to try, not to think or inquire about certain rates of expenditure, or take the first step in certain directions. We have moved on all our life after a very antiquated and old-fashioned mode. We have had our little, old-fashioned house, our little old-fashioned ways."

"Except the parlor carpet, and what came of it, my dear," said I mischievously.

"Yes, except the parlor carpet," said my wife, with a conscious twinkle, "and the things that came of it; there was a concession there, but one can't be wise always."

"*We* talked mamma into that," said Jenny.

"But one thing is certain," said my wife,—"that, though I have had an antiquated, plain house, and plain furniture, and plain dress, and not the beginning of a thing such as many of my neighbors have possessed, I have spent more money than many of them for real comforts. While I had young children, I kept more and better servants than many women who wore Cashmere and diamonds. I thought it better to pay extra wages to a really good, trusty woman who lived with me from year to year, and relieved me of some of my heaviest family cares, than to have ever so much lace locked away in my drawers. We always were able to go into the country to spend our summers, and to keep a good family horse and carriage for daily driving,—by which means we afforded, as a family, very poor patronage to the medical profession. Then we built our house, and, while we left out a great many expensive commonplaces that other people think they must have, we put in a profusion of bathing accommodations such as very few people think of having. There never was a time when we did not feel able to afford to do what was necessary to preserve or to restore health; and for this I always drew on the surplus fund laid up by my very unfashionable housekeeping and dressing."

"Your mother has had," said I, "what is the great want in America, perfect independence of mind to go her own way without regard to the way others go. I think there is, for some reason, more false shame among Americans about economy than among Europeans. 'I cannot afford it' is more seldom heard among us. A young man beginning life, whose income may be from five to eight hundred a year, thinks it elegant and gallant to affect a careless air about money, especially among ladies,—to hand it out freely, and put back his change without counting it,—to wear a watch chain and studs and shirt-fronts like those of some young millionaire. None but the most expensive tailors, shoemakers, and hatters will do for him; and then he grumbles at the dearness of living, and declares that he cannot get along on his salary. The same is true of young girls, and of married men and women, too,—the whole of them are ashamed of economy. The cares that wear out life and health in many households are of a nature that cannot be cast on God, or met by any promise from the Bible: it is not care for 'food convenient,' or for comfortable raiment, but care to keep up false appearances, and to stretch a narrow income over the space that can be covered only by a wider one.

"The poor widow in her narrow lodgings, with her monthly rent staring her hourly in the face, and her bread and meat and candles and meal all to be paid for on delivery or not obtained at all, may find comfort in the good old Book, reading of that other widow whose wasting measure of oil and last failing handful of meal were of such account before her Father in heaven that a prophet was sent to recruit them; and when customers do not pay, or wages are cut down, she can enter into her chamber, and, when she hath shut her door, present to her Father in heaven His sure promise that with the fowls of the air she shall be fed and with the lilies of the field she shall be clothed: but what promises are there for her who is racking her brains on the ways and means to provide as sumptuous an entertainment of oysters and champagne at her next party as her richer neighbor, or to compass that great bargain which shall give her a point-lace set almost as handsome as that of Mrs. Crœsus, who has ten times her income?"

"But, papa," said Marianne, with a twinge of that exacting sensitiveness by which the child is characterized, "I think I am an economist, thanks to you and mamma, so far as knowing just what my income is, and keeping within it; but that does not satisfy me, and it seems that isn't all of economy; the question that haunts me is, Might I not make my little all do more and better than I do?"

"There," said I, "you have hit the broader and deeper signification of economy, which is, in fact, the science of *comparative values*. In its highest sense, economy is a just judgment of the comparative value of things,—money only the means of enabling one to express that value. This is the reason why the whole matter is so full of difficulty,—why every one criticises his neighbor in this regard. Human beings are so various, the necessities of each are so different, they are made comfortable or uncomfortable by such opposite means, that the spending of other people's incomes must of necessity often look unwise from our standpoint. For this reason multitudes of people who cannot be accused of exceeding their incomes often seem to others to be spending them foolishly and extravagantly."

"But is there no standard of value?" said Marianne.

"There are certain things upon which there is a pretty general agreement, verbally, at least, among mankind. For instance, it is generally agreed that *health* is an indispensable good, — that money is well spent that secures it, and worse than ill spent that ruins it.

"With this standard in mind, how much money is wasted even by people who do not exceed their income! Here a man builds a house, and pays, in the first place, ten thousand more than he need, for a location in a fashionable part of the city, though the air will be closer and the chances of health less; he spends three or four thousand more on a stone front, on marble mantels imported from Italy, on plate-glass windows, plated hinges, and a thousand nice points of finish, and has perhaps but one bath-room for a whole household, and that so connected with his own apartment that nobody but himself and his wife can use it.

"Another man buys a lot in an open, airy situation, which fashion has not made expensive, and builds without a stone front, marble mantels, or plate-glass windows, but has a perfect system of ventilation through his house, and bathing-rooms in every story, so that the children and guests may all, without inconvenience, enjoy the luxury of abundant water.

"The first spends for fashion and show, the second for health and comfort.

"Here is a man that will buy his wife a diamond bracelet and a lace shawl, and take her yearly to Washington to show off her beauty in ball dresses, who yet will not let her pay wages which will command any but the poorest and most inefficient domestic service. The woman is worn out, her life made a desert by exhaustion consequent on a futile attempt to keep up a showy establishment with only half the hands needed for the purpose. Another family will give brilliant parties, have a gay season every year at the first hotels at Newport, and not be able to afford the wife a fire in her chamber in midwinter, or the servants enough food to keep them from constantly deserting. The damp, mouldy, dingy cellar-kitchen, the cold, windy, desolate attic, devoid of any comfort, where the domestics are doomed to pass their whole time, are witnesses to what such families consider economy. Economy in the view of some is undisguised slipshod slovenliness in the home circle for the sake of fine clothes to be shown abroad; it is undisguised hard selfishness to servants and dependants, counting their every approach to comfort a needless waste, — grudging the Roman Catholic cook her cup of tea at dinner on Friday, when she must not eat meat,—and murmuring that a cracked, second-hand looking-glass must be got for the servants' room: what business have they to want to know how they look?

"Some families will employ the cheapest physician, without regard to his ability to kill or cure; some will treat diseases in their incipiency with quack medicines, bought cheap, hoping thereby to fend off the doctor's bill. Some women seem to be pursued by an evil demon of economy, which, like an *ignis fatuus* in a bog, delights constantly to tumble them over into the mire of expense. They are dismayed at the quantity of sugar in the recipe for preserves, leave out a quarter, and the whole ferments and is spoiled. They cannot by any means be induced at any one time to buy enough silk to make a dress, and the dress finally, after many convulsions and alterations, must be thrown by altogether as too scanty. They get poor needles, poor thread, poor sugar, poor raisins, poor tea, poor coal. One wonders, in looking at their blackened, smouldering grates in a freezing day, what the fire is there at all for,—it certainly warms nobody. The only thing they seem likely to be lavish in is funeral expenses, which come in the wake of leaky shoes and imperfect clothing. These funeral expenses at last swallow all, since nobody can dispute an undertaker's bill. One pities these joyless beings. Economy, instead of a rational act of the judgment, is a morbid monomania, eating the pleasure out of life, and haunting them to the grave.

"Some people's ideas of economy seem to run simply in the line of eating. Their flour is of an extra brand, their meat the first cut; the delicacies of every season, in their dearest stages, come home to their table with an apologetic smile,—'It was scandalously dear, my love, but I thought we must just treat ourselves.' And yet these people cannot afford to buy books, and pictures they regard as an unthought-of extravagance. Trudging home with fifty dollars' worth of delicacies on his arm, Smith meets Jones, who is exulting with a bag of crackers under one arm and a choice little bit of an oil painting under the other, which he thinks a bargain at fifty dollars. 'I can't afford to buy pictures,' Smith says to his spouse, 'and I don't know how Jones and his wife manage.' Jones and his wife will live on bread and milk for a month, and she will turn her best gown the third time, but they will have their picture, and they are happy. Jones's picture remains, and Smith's fifty dollars' worth of oysters and canned fruit to-morrow will be gone forever. Of all modes of spending money, the swallowing of expensive dainties brings the least return. There is one step lower than this,—the consuming of luxuries that are injurious to the health. If all the money spent on tobacco and liquors could be spent in books and pictures, I predict that nobody's health would be a whit less sound, and houses would be vastly more attractive. There is enough money spent in smoking, drinking, and over-eating to give every family in the community a good library, to hang everybody's parlor walls with lovely pictures, to set up in every house a conservatory which should bloom all winter with choice flowers, to furnish every dwelling with ample bathing and warming accommodations, even down to the dwellings of the poor; and in the millennium I believe this is the way things are to be.

"In these times of peril and suffering, if the inquiry arises, How shall there be retrenchment? I answer, First and foremost, retrench things needless, doubtful, and positively hurtful, as rum, tobacco, and all the meerschaums of divers colors that do accompany the same. Second, retrench all eating not necessary to health and comfort. A French family would live in luxury on the leavings that are constantly coming from the tables of those who call themselves in middling circumstances. There are superstitions of the table that ought to be broken through. Why must you always have cake in your closet? why need you feel undone to entertain a guest with no cake on your tea-table? Do without it a year, and ask yourselves if you or your children, or any one else, have suffered materially in consequence.

"Why is it imperative that you should have two or three courses at every meal? Try the experiment of having but one, and that a very good one, and see if any great amount of suffering ensues. Why must social intercourse so largely consist in eating? In Paris there is a very pretty custom. Each family has one evening in the week when it stays at home and receives friends. Tea, with a little bread and butter and cake, served in the most informal way, is the only refreshment. The rooms are full, busy, bright,—everything as easy and joyous as if a monstrous supper, with piles of jelly and mountains of cake, were waiting to give the company a nightmare at the close.

"Said a lady, pointing to a gentleman and his wife in a social circle of this kind, 'I ought to know them well,—I have seen them every week for twenty years.' It is certainly pleasant and confirmative of social enjoyment for friends to eat together; but a little enjoyed in this way answers the purpose as well as a great deal, and better, too."

"Well, papa," said Marianne, "in the matter of dress, now,—how much ought one to spend just to look as others do?"

"I will tell you what I saw the other night, girls, in the parlor of one of our hotels. Two middle-aged Quaker ladies came gliding in, with calm, cheerful faces, and lustrous dove-colored silks. By their conversation I found that they belonged to that class of women among the Friends who devote themselves to traveling on missions of benevolence. They had just completed a tour of all the hospitals for wounded soldiers in the country, where they had been carrying comforts, arranging, advising, and soothing by their cheerful, gentle presence. They were now engaged on another mission, to the lost and erring of their own sex; night after night, guarded by a policeman, they had ventured after midnight into the dance-houses where girls are being led to ruin, and with gentle words of tender, motherly counsel sought to win them from their fatal ways,—telling them where they might go the next day to find friends who would open to them an asylum and aid them to seek a better life.

"As I looked upon these women, dressed with such modest purity, I began secretly to think that the Apostle was not wrong when he spoke of women adorning themselves with the *ornament* of a meek and quiet spirit; for the habitual gentleness of their expression, the calmness and purity of the lines in their faces, the delicacy and simplicity of their apparel, seemed of themselves a rare and peculiar beauty. I could not help thinking that fashionable bonnets, flowing lace sleeves, and dresses elaborately trimmed could not have improved even their outward appearance. Doubtless their simple wardrobe needed but a small trunk in traveling from place to place, and hindered but little their prayers and ministrations.

"Now, it is true, all women are not called to such a life as this; but might not all women take a leaf at least from their book? I submit the inquiry humbly. It seems to me that there are many who go monthly to the sacrament, and receive it with sincere devotion, and who give thanks each time sincerely that they are thus made 'members incorporate in the mystical body of Christ,' who have never thought of this membership as meaning that they should share Christ's sacrifices for lost souls, or abridge themselves of one ornament or encounter one inconvenience for the sake of those wandering sheep for whom he died. Certainly there is a higher economy which we need to learn,—that which makes all things subservient to the spiritual and immortal, and that not merely to the good of our own souls and those of our family, but of all who are knit with us in the great bonds of human brotherhood.

"There have been from time to time, among well-meaning Christian people, retrenchment societies on high moral grounds, which have failed for want of knowledge how to manage the complicated question of necessaries and luxuries. These words have a signification in the case of different people as varied as the varieties of human habit and constitution. It is a department impossible to be bound by external rules, but none the less should every high-minded Christian soul in this matter have a law unto itself. It may safely be laid down as a general rule, that no income, however large or however small, should be unblessed by the divine touch of self-sacrifice. Something for the poor, the sorrowing, the hungry, the tempted, and the weak should be taken from *what is our own* at the expense of some personal sacrifice, or we suffer more morally than the brother from whom we withdraw it. Even the Lord of all, when dwelling among men, out of that slender private purse which he accepted for his little family of chosen ones, had ever something reserved to give to the poor. It is easy to say, 'It is but a drop in the bucket. I cannot remove the great mass of misery in the world. What little I could save or give does nothing.' It does this, if no more, — it prevents one soul, and that soul your own, from drying and hardening into utter selfishness and insensibility; it enables you to say, I have done something; taken one atom from the great heap of sins and miseries and placed it on the side of good.

"The Sisters of Charity and the Friends, each with their different costume of plainness and self-denial, and other noble-hearted women of no particular outward order, but kindred in spirit, have shown to womanhood, on the battlefield and in the hospital, a more excellent way, — a beauty and nobility before which all the common graces and ornaments of the sex fade, appear like dim candles by the pure, eternal stars."

IX

SERVANTS

In the course of my papers various domestic revolutions have occurred. Our Marianne has gone from us with a new name to a new life, and a modest little establishment not many squares off claims about as much of my wife's and Jenny's busy thoughts as those of the proper mistress.

Marianne, as I always foresaw, is a careful and somewhat anxious housekeeper. Her tastes are fastidious; she is made for exactitude: the smallest departures from the straight line appear to her shocking deviations. She had always lived in a house where everything had been formed to quiet and order under the ever-present care and touch of her mother; nor had she ever participated in those cares more than to do a little dusting of the parlor ornaments, or wash the best china, or make sponge-cake or chocolate-caramels. Certain conditions of life had always appeared so to be matters of course that she had never conceived of a house without them. It never occurred to her that such bread and biscuit as she saw at the home table would not always and of course appear at every table, — that the silver would not always be as bright, the glass as clear, the salt as fine and smooth, the plates and dishes as nicely arranged, as she had always seen them, apparently without the thought or care of any one; for my wife is one of those housekeepers whose touch is so fine that no one feels it. She is never heard scolding or reproving, — never entertains her company with her recipes for cookery or the faults of her servants. She is so unconcerned about receiving her own personal share of credit for the good appearance of her establishment that even the children of the house have not supposed that there is any particular will of hers in the matter: it all seems the natural consequence of having very good servants.

One phenomenon they had never seriously reflected on, — that, under all the changes of the domestic cabinet which are so apt to occur in American households, the same coffee, the same bread and biscuit, the same nicely prepared dishes and neatly laid table, always gladdened their eyes; and from this they inferred only that good servants were more abundant than most people had supposed. They were somewhat surprised when these marvels were wrought by professedly green hands, but were given to suppose that these green hands must have had some remarkable quickness or aptitude for acquiring. That sparkling jelly, well-flavored ice-creams, clear soups, and delicate biscuits could be made by a raw Irish girl, fresh from her native Erin, seemed to them a proof of the genius of the race; and my wife, who never felt it important to attain to the reputation of a cook, quietly let it pass.

For some time, therefore, after the inauguration of the new household, there was trouble in the camp. Sour bread had appeared on the table; bitter, acrid coffee had shocked and astonished the palate; lint had been observed on tumblers, and the spoons had sometimes dingy streaks on the brightness of their first bridal polish; beds were detected made shockingly awry: and Marianne came burning with indignation to her mother.

"Such a little family as we have, and two strong girls," said she,— "everything ought to be perfect; there is really nothing to do. Think of a whole batch of bread absolutely sour! and when I gave that away, then this morning another exactly like it! and when I talked to cook about it, she said she had lived in this and that family, and her bread had always been praised as equal to the baker's!"

"I don't doubt she is right," said I. "Many families never have anything but sour bread from one end of the year to the other, eating it unperceiving, and with good cheer; and they buy also sour bread of the baker, with like approbation,—lightness being in their estimation the only virtue necessary in the article."

"Could you not correct her fault?" suggested my wife.

"I have done all I can. I told her we could not have such bread, that it was dreadful; Bob says it would give him the dyspepsia in a week; and then she went and made exactly the same! It seems to me mere willfulness."

"But," said I, "suppose, instead of such general directions, you should analyze her proceedings and find out just where she makes her mistake: is the root of the trouble in the yeast, or in the time she begins it, letting it rise too long?—the time, you know, should vary so much with the temperature of the weather."

"As to that," said Marianne, "I know nothing. I never noticed; it never was my business to make bread; it always seemed quite a simple process, mixing yeast and flour and kneading it; and our bread at home was always good."

"It seems, then, my dear, that you have come to your profession without even having studied it."

My wife smiled and said,—

"You know, Marianne, I proposed to you to be our family bread-maker for one month of the year before you married."

"Yes, mamma, I remember; but I was like other girls: I thought there was no need of it. I never liked to do such things; perhaps I had better have done it."

"You certainly had," said I, "for the first business of a housekeeper in America is that of a teacher. She can have a good table only by having practical knowledge, and tact in imparting it. If she understands her business practically and experimentally, her eye detects at once the weak spot; it requires only a little tact, some patience, some clearness in giving directions, and all comes right. I venture to say that your mother would have exactly such bread as always appears on our table, and have it by the hands of your cook, because she could detect and explain to her exactly her error."

"Do you know," said my wife, "what yeast she uses?"

"I believe," said Marianne, "it's a kind she makes herself. I think I heard her say so. I know she makes a great fuss about it, and rather values herself upon it. She is evidently accustomed to being praised for her bread, and feels mortified and angry, and I don't know how to manage her."

"Well," said I, "if you carry your watch to a watchmaker, and undertake to show him how to regulate the machinery, he laughs and goes on his own way; but if a brother-machinist makes suggestions, he listens respectfully. So, when a woman who knows nothing of woman's work undertakes to instruct one who knows more than she does, she makes no impression; but a woman who has been trained experimentally, and shows she understands the matter thoroughly, is listened to with respect."

"I think," said my wife, "that your Bridget is worth teaching. She is honest, well-principled, and tidy. She has good recommendations from excellent families, whose ideas of good bread, it appears, differ from ours; and with a little good-nature, tact, and patience, she will come into your ways."

"But the coffee, mamma,—you would not imagine it to be from the same bag with your own, so dark and so bitter; what do you suppose she has done to it?"

"Simply this," said my wife. "She has let the berries stay a few moments too long over the fire,—they are burnt, instead of being roasted; and there are people who think it essential to good coffee that it should look black, and have a strong, bitter flavor. A very little change in the preparing will alter this."

"Now," said I, "Marianne, if you want my advice, I'll give it to you gratis: make your own bread for one month. Simple as the process seems, I think it will take as long as that to give you a thorough knowledge of all the possibilities in the case; but after that you will never need to make any more,—you will be able to command good bread by the aid of all sorts of servants; you will, in other words, be a thoroughly prepared teacher."

"I did not think," said Marianne, "that so simple a thing required so much attention."

"It is simple," said my wife, "and yet requires a delicate care and watchfulness. There are fifty ways to spoil good bread; there are a hundred little things to be considered and allowed for that require accurate observation and experience. The same process that will raise good bread in cold weather will make sour bread in the heat of summer; different qualities of flour require variations in treatment, as also different sorts and conditions of yeast; and when all is done, the baking presents another series of possibilities which require exact attention."

"So it appears," said Marianne gayly, "that I must begin to study my profession at the eleventh hour."

"Better late than never," said I. "But there is this advantage on your side: a well-trained mind, accustomed to reflect, analyze, and generalize, has an advantage over uncultured minds even of double experience. Poor as your cook is, she now knows more of her business than you do. After a very brief period of attention and experiment you will not only know more than she does, but you will convince her that you do, which is quite as much to the purpose."

"In the same manner," said my wife, "you will have to give lessons to your other girl on the washing of silver and the making of beds. Good servants do not often come to us: they must be *made* by patience and training; and if a girl has a good disposition and a reasonable degree of handiness, and the housekeeper understands her profession, she may make a good servant out of an indifferent one. Some of my best girls have been those who came to me directly from the ship, with no preparation but docility and some natural quickness. The hardest cases to be managed are not of those who have been taught nothing, but of those who have been taught wrongly,—who come to you self-opinionated, with ways which are distasteful to you, and contrary to the genius of your housekeeping. Such require that their mistress shall understand at least so much of the actual conduct of affairs as to prove to the servant that there are better ways than those in which she has hitherto been trained."

"Don't you think, mamma," said Marianne, "that there has been a sort of reaction against woman's work in our day? So much has been said of the higher sphere of woman, and so much has been done to find some better work for her, that insensibly, I think, almost everybody begins to feel that it is rather degrading for a woman in good society to be much tied down to family affairs."

"Especially," said my wife, "since in these Woman's Rights Conventions there is so much indignation expressed at those who would confine her ideas to the kitchen and nursery."

"There is reason in all things," said I. "Woman's Rights Conventions are a protest against many former absurd, unreasonable ideas, — the mere physical and culinary idea of womanhood as connected only with puddings and shirt-buttons, the unjust and unequal burdens which the laws of harsher ages had cast upon the sex. Many of the women connected with these movements are as superior in everything properly womanly as they are in exceptional talent and culture. There is no manner of doubt that the sphere of woman is properly to be enlarged, and that republican governments in particular are to be saved from corruption and failure only by allowing to woman this enlarged sphere. Every woman has rights as a human being first, which belong to no sex, and ought to be as freely conceded to her as if she were a man, — and, first and foremost, the great right of doing anything which God and Nature evidently have fitted her to excel in. If she be made a natural orator, like Miss Dickinson, or an astronomer, like Mrs. Somerville, or a singer, like Grisi, let not the technical rules of womanhood be thrown in the way of her free use of her powers. Nor can there be any reason shown why a woman's vote in the state should not be received with as much respect as in the family. A state is but an association of families, and laws relate to the rights and immunities which touch woman's most private and immediate wants and dearest hopes; and there is no reason why sister, wife, and mother should be more powerless in the state than in the home. Nor does it make a woman unwomanly to express an opinion by dropping a slip of paper into a box, more than to express that same opinion by conversation. In fact, there is no doubt that, in all matters relating to the interests of education, temperance, and religion, the state would be a material gainer by receiving the votes of women.

"But, having said all this, I must admit, *per contra*, not only a great deal of crude, disagreeable talk in these conventions, but a too great tendency of the age to make the education of women anti-domestic. It seems as if the world never could advance except like ships under a head wind, tacking and going too far, now in this direction and now in the opposite. Our common-school system now rejects sewing from the education of girls, which very properly used to occupy many hours daily in school a generation ago. The daughters of laborers and artisans are put through algebra, geometry, trigonometry, and the higher mathematics, to the entire neglect of that learning which belongs distinctively to woman. A girl cannot keep pace with her class if she gives any time to domestic matters, and accordingly she is excused from them all during the whole term of her education. The boy of a family, at an early age, is put to a trade, or the labors of a farm; the father becomes impatient of his support, and requires of him to care for himself. Hence an interrupted education,—learning coming by snatches in the winter months, or in the intervals of work. As the result, the females in our country towns are commonly, in mental culture, vastly in advance of the males of the same household; but with this comes a physical delicacy, the result of an exclusive use of the brain and a neglect of the muscular system, with great inefficiency in practical domestic duties. The race of strong, hardy, cheerful girls, that used to grow up in country places, and made the bright, neat, New England kitchens of old times,—the girls that could wash, iron, brew, bake, harness a horse and drive him, no less than braid straw, embroider, draw, paint, and read innumerable books,—this race of women, pride of olden time, is daily lessening; and in their stead come the fragile, easily fatigued, languid girls of a modern age, drilled in book-learning, ignorant of common things. The great danger of all this, and of the evils that come from it, is that society by and by will turn as blindly against female intellectual culture as it now advocates it, and, having worked disproportionately one way, will work disproportionately in the opposite direction."

"The fact is," said my wife, "that domestic service is the great problem of life here in America; the happiness of families, their thrift, well-being, and comfort, are more affected by this than by any one thing else. Our girls, as they have been brought up, cannot perform the labor of their own families, as in those simpler, old-fashioned days you tell of; and, what is worse, they have no practical skill with which to instruct servants, and servants come to us, as a class, raw and untrained; so what is to be done? In the present state of prices, the board of a domestic costs double her wages, and the waste she makes is a more serious matter still. Suppose you give us an article upon this subject in your 'House and Home Papers.' You could not have a better one."

So I sat down, and wrote thus on

SERVANTS AND SERVICE

Many of the domestic evils in America originate in the fact that, while society here is professedly based on new principles which ought to make social life in every respect different from the life of the Old World, yet these principles have never been so thought out and applied as to give consistency and harmony to our daily relations. America starts with a political organization based on a declaration of the primitive freedom and equality of all men. Every human being, according to this principle, stands on the same natural level with every other, and has the same chance to rise, according to the degree of power or capacity given by the Creator. All our civil institutions are designed to preserve this equality, as far as possible, from generation to generation: there is no entailed property, there are no hereditary titles, no monopolies, no privileged classes,—all are to be as free to rise and fall as the waves of the sea.

The condition of domestic service, however, still retains about it something of the influences from feudal times, and from the near presence of slavery in neighboring States. All English literature, all the literature of the world, describes domestic service in the old feudal spirit and with the old feudal language, which regarded the master as belonging to a privileged class and the servant to an inferior one. There is not a play, not a poem, not a novel, not a history, that does not present this view. The master's rights, like the rights of kings, were supposed to rest in his being born in a superior rank. The good servant was one who, from childhood, had learned "to order himself lowly and reverently to all his betters." When New England brought to these shores the theory of democracy, she brought, in the persons of the first pilgrims, the habits of thought and of action formed in aristocratic communities. Winthrop's Journal, and all the old records of the earlier colonists, show households where masters and mistresses stood on the "right divine" of the privileged classes, howsoever they might have risen up against authorities themselves.

111

The first consequence of this state of things was a universal rejection of domestic service in all classes of American-born society. For a generation or two, there was, indeed, a sort of interchange of family strength,—sons and daughters engaging in the service of neighboring families, in default of a sufficient working force of their own, but always on conditions of strict equality. The assistant was to share the table, the family sitting-room, and every honor and attention that might be claimed by son or daughter. When families increased in refinement and education so as to make these conditions of close intimacy with more uncultured neighbors disagreeable, they had to choose between such intimacies and the performance of their own domestic toil. No wages could induce a son or daughter of New England to take the condition of a servant on terms which they thought applicable to that of a slave. The slightest hint of a separate table was resented as an insult; not to enter the front door, and not to sit in the front parlor on state occasions, was bitterly commented on as a personal indignity.

The well-taught, self-respecting daughters of farmers, the class most valuable in domestic service, gradually retired from it. They preferred any other employment, however laborious. Beyond all doubt, the labors of a well-regulated family are more healthy, more cheerful, more interesting, because less monotonous, than the mechanical toils of a factory; yet the girls of New England, with one consent, preferred the factory, and left the whole business of domestic service to a foreign population; and they did it mainly because they would not take positions in families as an inferior laboring class by the side of others of their own age who assumed as their prerogative to live without labor.

"I can't let you have one of my daughters," said an energetic matron to her neighbor from the city, who was seeking for a servant in her summer vacation; "if you hadn't daughters of your own, maybe I would; but my girls ain't going to work so that your girls may live in idleness."

It was vain to offer money. "We don't need your money, ma'am, we can support ourselves in other ways; my girls can braid straw and bind shoes, but they ain't going to be slaves to anybody."

In the Irish and German servants who took the place of Americans in families, there was, to begin with, the tradition of education in favor of a higher class; but even the foreign population became more or less infected with the spirit of democracy. They came to this country with vague notions of freedom and equality, and in ignorant and uncultivated people such ideas are often more unreasonable for being vague. They did not, indeed, claim a seat at the table and in the parlor, but they repudiated many of those habits of respect and courtesy which belonged to their former condition, and asserted their own will and way in the round, unvarnished phrase which they supposed to be their right as republican citizens. Life became a sort of domestic wrangle and struggle between the employers, who secretly confessed their weakness, but endeavored openly to assume the air and bearing of authority, and the employed, who knew their power and insisted on their privileges. From this cause domestic service in America has had less of mutual kindliness than in old countries. Its terms have been so ill understood and defined that both parties have assumed the defensive; and a common topic of conversation in American female society has often been the general servile war which in one form or another was going on in their different families,—a war as interminable as would be a struggle between aristocracy and common people, undefined by any bill of rights or constitution, and therefore opening fields for endless disputes. In England, the class who go to service *are* a class, and service is a profession; the distance between them and their employers is so marked and defined, and all the customs and requirements of the position are so perfectly understood, that the master or mistress has no fear of being compromised by condescension, and no need of the external voice or air of authority. The higher up in the social scale one goes, the more courteous seems to become the intercourse of master and servant; the more perfect and real the power, the more is it veiled in outward expression,— commands are phrased as requests, and gentleness of voice and manner covers an authority which no one would think of offending without trembling.

But in America all is undefined. In the first place, there is no class who mean to make domestic service a profession to live and die in. It is universally an expedient, a stepping-stone to something higher; your best servants always have something else in view as soon as they have laid by a little money; some form of independence which shall give them a home of their own is constantly in mind. Families look forward to the buying of landed homesteads, and the scattered brothers and sisters work awhile in domestic service to gain the common fund for the purpose; your seamstress intends to become a dressmaker, and take in work at her own house; your cook is pondering a marriage with the baker, which shall transfer her toils from your cooking-stove to her own. Young women are eagerly rushing into every other employment, till female trades and callings are all overstocked. We are continually harrowed with tales of the sufferings of distressed needlewomen, of the exactions and extortions practiced on the frail sex in the many branches of labor and trade at which they try their hands; and yet women will encounter all these chances of ruin and starvation rather than make up their minds to permanent domestic service. Now what is the matter with domestic service? One would think, on the face of it, that a calling which gives a settled home, a comfortable room, rent-free, with fire and lights, good board and lodging, and steady, well-paid wages, would certainly offer more attractions than the making of shirts for tenpence, with all the risks of providing one's own sustenance and shelter.

I think it is mainly from the want of a definite idea of the true position of a servant under our democratic institutions that domestic service is so shunned and avoided in America, that it is the very last thing which an intelligent young woman will look to for a living. It is more the want of personal respect toward those in that position than the labors incident to it which repels our people from it. Many would be willing to perform these labors, but they are not willing to place themselves in a situation where their self-respect is hourly wounded by *the implication of a degree of inferiority which does not follow any kind of labor or service in this country but that of the family.*

There exists in the minds of employers an unsuspected spirit of superiority, which is stimulated into an active form by the resistance which democracy inspires in the working class. Many families think of servants only as a necessary evil, their wages as exactions, and all that is allowed them as so much taken from the family; and they seek in every way to get from them as much and to give them as little as possible. Their rooms are the neglected, ill-furnished, incommodious ones,—and the kitchen is the most cheerless and comfortless place in the house. Other families, more good-natured and liberal, provide their domestics with more suitable accommodations, and are more indulgent; but there is still a latent spirit of something like contempt for the position. That they treat their servants with so much consideration seems to them a merit entitling them to the most prostrate gratitude; and they are constantly disappointed and shocked at that want of sense of inferiority on the part of these people which leads them to appropriate pleasant rooms, good furniture, and good living as mere matters of common justice.

It seems to be a constant surprise to some employers that servants should insist on having the same human wants as themselves. Ladies who yawn in their elegantly furnished parlors, among books and pictures, if they have not company, parties, or opera to diversify the evening, seem astonished and half indignant that cook and chambermaid are more disposed to go out for an evening gossip than to sit on hard chairs in the kitchen where they have been toiling all day. The pretty chambermaid's anxieties about her dress, the time she spends at her small and not very clear mirror, are sneeringly noticed by those whose toilet-cares take up serious hours; and the question has never apparently occurred to them why a serving-maid should not want to look pretty as well as her mistress. She is a woman as well as they, with all a woman's wants and weaknesses; and her dress is as much to her as theirs to them.

A vast deal of trouble among servants arises from impertinent interferences and petty tyrannical exactions on the part of employers. Now the authority of the master and mistress of a house in regard to their domestics extends simply to the things they have contracted to do and the hours during which they have contracted to serve; otherwise than this, they have no more right to interfere with them in the disposal of their time than with any mechanic whom they employ. They have, indeed, a right to regulate the hours of their own household, and servants can choose between conformity to these hours and the loss of their situation; but, within reasonable limits, their right to come and go at their own discretion, in their own time, should be unquestioned.

If employers are troubled by the fondness of their servants for dancing, evening company, and late hours, the proper mode of proceeding is to make these matters a subject of distinct contract in hiring. The more strictly and perfectly the business matters of the first engagement of domestics are conducted, the more likelihood there is of mutual quiet and satisfaction in the relation. It is quite competent to every housekeeper to say what practices are or are not consistent with the rules of her family, and what will be inconsistent with the service for which she agrees to pay. It is much better to regulate such affairs by cool contract in the outset than by warm altercations and protracted domestic battles.

As to the terms of social intercourse, it seems somehow to be settled in the minds of many employers that their servants owe them and their family more respect than they and the family owe to the servants. But do they? What is the relation of servant to employer in a democratic country? Precisely that of a person who for money performs any kind of service for you. The carpenter comes into your house to put up a set of shelves,—the cook comes into your kitchen to cook your dinner. You never think that the carpenter owes you any more respect than you owe to him because he is in your house doing your behests; he is your fellow-citizen, you treat him with respect, you expect to be treated with respect by him. You have a claim on him that he shall do your work according to your directions,—no more. Now I apprehend that there is a very common notion as to the position and rights of servants which is quite different from this. Is it not a common feeling that a servant is one who may be treated with a degree of freedom by every member of the family which he or she may not return? Do not people feel at liberty to question servants about their private affairs, to comment on their dress and appearance, in a manner which they would feel to be an impertinence if reciprocated? Do they not feel at liberty to express dissatisfaction with their performances in rude and unceremonious terms, to reprove them in the presence of company, while yet they require that the dissatisfaction of servants shall be expressed only in terms of respect? A woman would not feel herself at liberty to talk to her milliner or her dressmaker in language as devoid of consideration as she will employ towards her cook or chambermaid. Yet both are rendering her a service which she pays for in money, and one is no more made her inferior thereby than the other. Both have an equal right to be treated with courtesy. The master and mistress of a house have a right to require respectful treatment from all whom their roof shelters, but they have no more right to exact it of servants than of every guest and every child, and they themselves owe it as much to servants as to guests.

In order that servants may be treated with respect and courtesy, it is not necessary, as in simpler patriarchal days, that they sit at the family table. Your carpenter or plumber does not feel hurt that you do not ask him to dine with you, nor your milliner and mantua-maker that you do not exchange ceremonious calls and invite them to your parties. It is well understood that your relations with them are of a mere business character. They never take it as an assumption of superiority on your part that you do not admit them to relations of private intimacy. There may be the most perfect respect and esteem and even friendship between them and you, notwithstanding. So it may be in the case of servants. It is easy to make any person understand that there are quite other reasons than the assumption of personal superiority for not wishing to admit servants to the family privacy. It was not, in fact, to sit in the parlor or at the table, in themselves considered, that was the thing aimed at by New England girls,—these were valued only as signs that they were deemed worthy of respect and consideration, and, where freely conceded, were often in point of fact declined.

Let servants feel, in their treatment by their employers, and in the atmosphere of the family, that their position is held to be a respectable one, let them feel in the mistress of the family the charm of unvarying consideration and good manners, let their work rooms be made convenient and comfortable, and their private apartments bear some reasonable comparison in point of agreeableness to those of other members of the family, and domestic service will be more frequently sought by a superior and self-respecting class. There are families in which such a state of things prevails; and such families, amid the many causes which unite to make the tenure of service uncertain, have generally been able to keep good permanent servants.

There is an extreme into which kindly disposed people often run with regard to servants, which may be mentioned here. They make pets of them. They give extravagant wages and indiscreet indulgences, and, through indolence and easiness of temper, tolerate neglect of duty. Many of the complaints of the ingratitude of servants come from those who have spoiled them in this way; while many of the longest and most harmonious domestic unions have sprung from a simple, quiet course of Christian justice and benevolence, a recognition of servants as fellow-beings and fellow-Christians, and a doing to them as we would in like circumstances that they should do to us.

The mistresses of American families, whether they like it or not, have the duties of missionaries imposed upon them by that class from which our supply of domestic servants is drawn. They may as well accept the position cheerfully, and, as one raw, untrained hand after another passes through their family, and is instructed by them in the mysteries of good housekeeping, comfort themselves with the reflection that they are doing something to form good wives and mothers for the Republic.

The complaints made of Irish girls are numerous and loud; the failings of green Erin, alas! are but too open and manifest; yet, in arrest of judgment, let us move this consideration: let us imagine our own daughters between the ages of sixteen and twenty-four, untaught and inexperienced in domestic affairs as they commonly are, shipped to a foreign shore to seek service in families. It may be questioned whether as a whole they would do much better. The girls that fill our families and do our housework are often of the age of our own daughters, standing for themselves, without mothers to guide them, in a foreign country, not only bravely supporting themselves, but sending home in every ship remittances to impoverished friends left behind. If our daughters did as much for us, should we not be proud of their energy and heroism?

When we go into the houses of our country, we find a majority of well-kept, well-ordered, and even elegant establishments where the only hands employed are those of the daughters of Erin. True, American women have been their instructors, and many a weary hour of care have they had in the discharge of this office; but the result on the whole is beautiful and good, and the end of it, doubtless, will be peace.

In speaking of the office of the American mistress as being a missionary one, we are far from recommending any controversial interference with the religious faith of our servants. It is far better to incite them to be good Christians in their own way than to run the risk of shaking their faith in all religion by pointing out to them the errors of that in which they have been educated. The general purity of life and propriety of demeanor of so many thousands of undefended young girls cast yearly upon our shores, with no home but their church, and no shield but their religion, are a sufficient proof that this religion exerts an influence over them not to be lightly trifled with. But there is a real unity even in opposite Christian forms; and the Roman Catholic servant and the Protestant mistress, if alike possessed by the spirit of Christ, and striving to conform to the Golden Rule, cannot help being one in heart, though one go to mass and the other to meeting.

Finally, the bitter baptism through which we are passing, the life blood dearer than our own which is drenching distant fields, should remind us of the preciousness of distinctive American ideas. They who would seek in their foolish pride to establish the pomp of liveried servants in America are doing that which is simply absurd. A servant can never in our country be the mere appendage to another man, to be marked like a sheep with the color of his owner; he must be a fellow-citizen, with an established position of his own, free to make contracts, free to come and go, and having in his sphere titles to consideration and respect just as definite as those of any trade or profession whatever.

Moreover, we cannot in this country maintain to any great extent large retinues of servants. Even with ample fortunes they are forbidden by the general character of society here, which makes them cumbrous and difficult to manage. Every mistress of a family knows that her cares increase with every additional servant. Two keep the peace with each other and their employer; three begin a possible discord, which possibility increases with four, and becomes certain with five or six. Trained housekeepers, such as regulate the complicated establishments of the Old World, form a class that are not, and from the nature of the case never will be, found in any great numbers in this country. All such women, as a general thing, are keeping, and prefer to keep, houses of their own.

A moderate style of housekeeping, small, compact, and simple domestic establishments, must necessarily be the general order of life in America. So many openings of profit are to be found in this country that domestic service necessarily wants the permanence which forms so agreeable a feature of it in the Old World. This being the case, it should be an object in America to exclude from the labors of the family all that can, with greater advantage, be executed out of it by combined labor.

Formerly, in New England, soap and candles were to be made in each separate family; now, comparatively few take this toil upon them. We buy soap of the soap-maker, and candles of the candle-factor. This principle might be extended much further. In France no family makes its own bread, and better bread cannot be eaten than what can be bought at the appropriate shops. No family does its own washing; the family's linen is all sent to women who, making this their sole profession, get it up with a care and nicety which can seldom be equaled in any family.

How would it simplify the burdens of the American housekeeper to have washing and ironing day expunged from her calendar! How much more neatly and compactly could the whole domestic system be arranged! If all the money that each separate family spends on the outfit and accommodations for washing and ironing, on fuel, soap, starch, and the other et ceteras, were united in a fund to create a laundry for every dozen families, one or two good women could do in firstrate style what now is very indifferently done by the disturbance and disarrangement of all other domestic processes in these families. Whoever sets neighborhood laundries on foot will do much to solve the American housekeeper's hardest problem.

Finally, American women must not try with three servants to carry on life in the style which in the Old World requires sixteen: they must thoroughly understand, and be prepared *to teach*, every branch of housekeeping; they must study to make domestic service desirable by treating their servants in a way to lead them to respect themselves and to feel themselves respected; and there will gradually be evolved from the present confusion a solution of the

119

domestic problem which shall be adapted to the life of a new and growing world.

X

COOKERY

My wife and I were sitting at the open bow-window of my study, watching the tuft of bright-red leaves on our favorite maple, which warned us that summer was over. I was solacing myself, like all the world in our days, with reading the "Schönberg Cotta Family," when my wife made her voice heard through the enchanted distance, and dispersed the pretty vision of German cottage life.

"Chris!"

"Well, my dear."

"Do you know the day of the month?"

Now my wife knows this is a thing that I never do know, that I can't know, and in fact that there is no need I should trouble myself about, since she always knows, and, what is more, always tells me. In fact, the question, when asked by her, meant more than met the ear. It was a delicate way of admonishing me that another paper for the "Atlantic" ought to be in train; and so I answered, not to the external form, but to the internal intention, —

"Well, you see, my dear, I haven't made up my mind what my next paper shall be about."

"Suppose, then, you let me give you a subject."

"Sovereign lady, speak on! Your slave hears!"

"Well, then, take *Cookery*. It may seem a vulgar subject, but I think more of health and happiness depends on that than on any other one thing. You may make houses enchantingly beautiful, hang them with pictures, have them clean and airy and convenient; but if the stomach is fed with sour bread and burnt coffee, it will raise such rebellions that the eyes will see no beauty anywhere. Now, in the little tour that you and I have been taking this summer, I have been thinking of the great abundance of splendid material we have in America, compared with the poor cooking. How often, in our stoppings, we have sat down to tables loaded with material, originally of the very best kind, which had been so spoiled in the treatment that there was really nothing to eat! Green biscuits with acrid spots of alkali; sour yeast-bread; meat slowly simmered in fat till it seemed like grease itself, and slowly congealing in cold grease; and, above all, that unpardonable enormity, strong butter! How

121

often I have longed to show people what might have been done with the raw material out of which all these monstrosities were concocted!"

"My dear," said I, "you are driving me upon delicate ground. Would you have your husband appear in public with that most opprobrious badge of the domestic furies, a dishcloth, pinned to his coat-tail? It is coming to exactly the point I have always predicted, Mrs. Crowfield: you must write yourself. I always told you that you could write far better than I, if you would only try. Only sit down and write as you sometimes talk to me, and I might hang up my pen by the side of 'Uncle Ned's' fiddle and bow."

"Oh, nonsense!" said my wife. "I never could write. I know what ought to be said, and I could *say* it to any one; but my ideas freeze in the pen, cramp in my fingers, and make my brain seem like heavy bread. I was born for extemporary speaking. Besides, I think the best things on all subjects in this world of ours are said, not by the practical workers, but by the careful observers."

"Mrs. Crowfield, that remark is as good as if I had made it myself," said I. "It is true that I have been all my life a speculator and observer in all domestic matters, having them so confidentially under my eye in our own household; and so, if I write on a pure woman's matter, it must be understood that I am only your pen and mouthpiece,—only giving tangible form to wisdom which I have derived from you."

So down I sat and scribbled, while my sovereign lady quietly stitched by my side. And here I tell my reader that I write on such a subject under protest,—declaring again my conviction that, if my wife only believed in herself as firmly as I do, she would write so that nobody would ever want to listen to me again.

COOKERY

We in America have the raw material of provision in greater abundance than any other nation. There is no country where an ample, well-furnished table is more easily spread, and for that reason, perhaps, none where the bounties of Providence are more generally neglected. I do not mean to say that the traveler through the length and breadth of our land could not, on the whole, find an average of comfortable subsistence; yet, considering that our resources are greater than those of any other civilized people, our results are comparatively poorer.

It is said that, a list of the summer vegetables which are exhibited on New York hotel tables being shown to a French *artiste*, he declared that to serve such a dinner properly would take till midnight. I recollect how I was once struck with our national plenteousness on returning from a Continental tour, and going directly from the ship to a New York hotel, in the bounteous season of autumn. For months I had been habituated to my neat little bits of chop or poultry garnished with the inevitable cauliflower or potato, which seemed to be the sole possibility after the reign of green peas was over. Now I sat down all at once to a carnival of vegetables,—ripe, juicy tomatoes, raw or cooked; cucumbers in brittle slices; rich, yellow sweet potatoes; broad Lima-beans, and beans of other and various names; tempting ears of Indian corn steaming in enormous piles, and great smoking tureens of the savory succotash, an Indian gift to the table for which civilization need not blush; sliced egg-plant in delicate fritters; and marrow squashes, of creamy pulp and sweetness: a rich variety, embarrassing to the appetite, and perplexing to the choice. Verily, the thought has often impressed itself on my mind that the vegetarian doctrine preached in America left a man quite as much as he had capacity to eat or enjoy, and that in the midst of such tantalizing abundance he really lost the apology which elsewhere bears him out in preying upon his less gifted and accomplished animal neighbors.

But with all this, the American table, taken as a whole, is inferior to that of England or France. It presents a fine abundance of material, carelessly and poorly treated. The management of food is nowhere in the world, perhaps, more slovenly and wasteful. Everything betokens that want of care that waits on abundance; there are great capabilities and poor execution. A tourist through England can seldom fail, at the quietest country inn, of finding himself served with the essentials of English table comfort,—his mutton-chop done to a turn, his steaming little private apparatus for concocting his own tea, his choice pot of marmalade or slice of cold ham, and his delicate rolls and creamy butter, all served with care and neatness. In France, one never asks in vain for delicious *café-au-lait*, good bread and butter, a nice omelet, or some savory little portion of meat with a French name. But to a tourist taking like chance in American country fare, what is the prospect? What is the coffee? what the tea? and the meat? and, above all, the butter?

In lecturing on cookery, as on housebuilding, I divide the subject into, not four, but five grand elements: first, Bread; second, Butter; third, Meat; fourth, Vegetables; and fifth, Tea,—by which I mean, generically, all sorts of warm, comfortable drinks served out in teacups, whether they be called tea, coffee, chocolate, broma, or what not.

I affirm that, if these five departments are all perfect, the great ends of domestic cookery are answered, so far as the comfort and well-being of life are concerned. I am aware that there exists another department, which is often regarded by culinary amateurs and young aspirants as the higher branch and very collegiate course of practical cookery; to wit, confectionery, by which I mean to designate all pleasing and complicated compounds of sweets and spices, devised not for health and nourishment, and strongly suspected of interfering with both,—mere tolerated gratifications of the palate, which we eat, not with the expectation of being benefited, but only with the hope of not being injured by them. In this large department rank all sorts of cakes, pies, preserves, ices, etc. I shall have a word or two to say under this head before I have done. I only remark now that, in my tours about the country, I have often had a virulent ill-will excited towards these works of culinary supererogation, because I thought their excellence was attained by treading under foot and disregarding the five grand essentials. I have sat at many a table garnished with three or four kinds of well-made cake, compounded with citron and spices and all imaginable good things, where the meat was tough and greasy, the bread some hot preparation of flour, lard, saleratus, and acid, and the butter unutterably detestable. At such tables I have thought that, if the mistress of the feast had given the care, time, and labor to preparing the simple items of bread, butter, and meat that she evidently had given to the preparation of these extras, the lot of a traveler might be much more comfortable. Evidently she never had thought of these common articles as constituting a good table. So long as she had puff pastry, rich black cake, clear jelly, and preserves, she seemed to consider that such unimportant matters as bread, butter, and meat could take care of themselves. It is the same inattention to common things as that which leads people to build houses with stone fronts and window-caps and expensive front-door trimmings, without bathing-rooms or fireplaces or ventilators.

Those who go into the country looking for summer board in farmhouses know perfectly well that a table where the butter is always fresh, the tea and coffee of the best kinds and well made, and the meats properly kept, dressed, and served, is the one table of a hundred, the fabulous enchanted island. It seems impossible to get the idea into the minds of people that what is called common food, carefully prepared, becomes, in virtue of that very care and attention, a delicacy, superseding the necessity of artificially compounded dainties.

To begin, then, with the very foundation of a good table, — *Bread*: What ought it to be? It should be light, sweet, and tender.

This matter of lightness is the distinctive line between savage and civilized bread. The savage mixes simple flour and water into balls of paste, which he throws into boiling water, and which come out solid, glutinous masses, of which his common saying is, "Man eat dis, he no die," — which a facetious traveler who was obliged to subsist on it interpreted to mean, "Dis no kill you, nothing will." In short, it requires the stomach of a wild animal or of a savage to digest this primitive form of bread, and of course more or less attention in all civilized modes of bread making is given to producing lightness. By lightness is meant simply that the particles are to be separated from each other by little holes or air-cells; and all the different methods of making light bread are neither more nor less than the formation in bread of these air-cells.

So far as we know, there are four practicable methods of aerating bread, namely, by fermentation; by effervescence of an acid and an alkali; by aerated egg, or egg which has been filled with air by the process of beating; and, lastly, by pressure of some gaseous substance into the paste, by a process much resembling the impregnation of water in a soda fountain. All these have one and the same object, — to give us the cooked particles of our flour separated by such permanent air-cells as will enable the stomach more readily to digest them.

A very common mode of aerating bread in America is by the effervescence of an acid and an alkali in the flour. The carbonic acid gas thus formed produces minute air-cells in the bread, or, as the cook says, makes it light. When this process is performed with exact attention to chemical laws, so that the acid and alkali completely neutralize each other, leaving no overplus of either, the result is often very palatable. The difficulty is, that this is a happy conjunction of circumstances which seldom occurs. The acid most commonly employed is that of sour milk, and, as milk has many degrees of sourness, the rule of a certain quantity of alkali to the pint must necessarily produce very different results at different times. As an actual fact, where this mode of making bread prevails, as we lament to say it does to a great extent in this country, one finds five cases of failure to one of success. It is a woful thing that the daughters of

New England have abandoned the old respectable mode of yeast brewing and bread raising for this specious substitute, so easily made, and so seldom well made. The green, clammy, acrid substance called biscuit, which many of our worthy republicans are obliged to eat in these days, is wholly unworthy of the men and women of the Republic. Good patriots ought not to be put off in that way,—they deserve better fare.

As an occasional variety, as a household convenience for obtaining bread or biscuit at a moment's notice, the process of effervescence may be retained; but we earnestly entreat American housekeepers, in Scriptural language, to stand in the way and ask for the old paths, and return to the good yeast-bread of their sainted grandmothers.

If acid and alkali must be used, by all means let them be mixed in due proportions. No cook should be left to guess and judge for herself about this matter. There is an article, called "Preston's Infallible Yeast Powder," which is made by chemical rule, and produces very perfect results. The use of this obviates the worst dangers in making bread by effervescence.

Of all processes of aeration in bread-making, the oldest and most time-honored is by fermentation. That this was known in the days of our Saviour is evident from the forcible simile in which he compares the silent permeating force of truth in human society to the very familiar household process of raising bread by a little yeast.

There is, however, one species of yeast, much used in some parts of the country, against which I have to enter my protest. It is called salt-risings, or milk-risings, and is made by mixing flour, milk, and a little salt together and leaving them to ferment. The bread thus produced is often very attractive, when new and made with great care. It is white and delicate, with fine, even air-cells. It has, however, when kept, some characteristics which remind us of the terms in which our old English Bible describes the effect of keeping the manna of the ancient Israelites, which we are informed, in words more explicit than agreeable, "stank, and bred worms." If salt-rising bread does not fulfill the whole of this unpleasant description, it certainly does emphatically a part of it. The smell which it has in baking, and when more than a day old, suggests the inquiry whether it is the saccharine or the putrid fermentation with which it is raised. Whoever breaks a piece of it after a day or two will often see minute filaments or clammy strings drawing out from the fragments, which, with the unmistakable smell, will cause him to pause before consummating a nearer acquaintance.

The fermentation of flour by means of brewer's or distiller's yeast produces, if rightly managed, results far more palatable and wholesome. The only requisites for success in it are, first, good materials, and, second, great care in a few small things. There are certain low-priced or damaged kinds of flour which can never by any kind of domestic chemistry be made into good bread; and to those persons whose stomachs forbid them to eat gummy, glutinous paste, under the name of bread, there is no economy in buying these poor brands, even at half the price of good flour.

But good flour and good yeast being supposed, with a temperature favorable to the development of fermentation, the whole success of the process depends on the thorough diffusion of the proper proportion of yeast through the whole mass, and on stopping the subsequent fermentation at the precise and fortunate point. The true housewife makes her bread the sovereign of her kitchen, —its behests must be attended to in all critical points and moments, no matter what else be postponed. She who attends to her bread when she has done this, and arranged that, and performed the other, very often finds that the forces of nature will not wait for her. The snowy mass, perfectly mixed, kneaded with care and strength, rises in its beautiful perfection till the moment comes for fixing the air-cells by baking. A few minutes now, and the acetous fermentation will begin, and the whole result be spoiled. Many bread-makers pass in utter carelessness over this sacred and mysterious boundary. Their oven has cake in it, or they are skimming jelly, or attending to some other of the so-called higher branches of cookery, while the bread is quickly passing into the acetous stage. At last, when they are ready to attend to it, they find that it has been going its own way, —it is so sour that the pungent smell is plainly perceptible. Now the saleratus-bottle is handed down, and a quantity of the dissolved alkali mixed with the paste, —an expedient sometimes making itself too manifest by greenish streaks or small acrid spots in the bread. As the result, we have a beautiful article spoiled, —bread without sweetness, if not absolutely sour.

In the view of many, lightness is the only property required in this article. The delicate, refined sweetness which exists in carefully kneaded bread, baked just before it passes to the extreme point of fermentation, is something of which they have no conception; and thus they will even regard this process of spoiling the paste by the acetous fermentation, and then rectifying that acid by effervescence with an alkali, as something positively meritorious. How else can they value and relish baker's loaves, such as some are, drugged with ammonia and other disagreeable things, light indeed, so light that they seem to have neither weight nor substance, but with no more sweetness or taste than so much white cotton?

Some persons prepare bread for the oven by simply mixing it in the mass, without kneading, pouring it into pans, and suffering it to rise there. The air-cells in bread thus prepared are coarse and uneven; the bread is as inferior in delicacy and nicety to that which is well kneaded as a raw Irish servant to a perfectly educated and refined lady. The process of kneading seems to impart an evenness to the minute air-cells, a fineness of texture, and a tenderness and pliability to the whole substance, that can be gained in no other way.

The divine principle of beauty has its reign over bread as well as over all other things; it has its laws of æsthetics; and that bread which is so prepared that it can be formed into separate and well-proportioned loaves, each one carefully worked and moulded, will develop the most beautiful results. After being moulded, the loaves should stand a little while, just long enough to allow the fermentation going on in them to expand each little air-cell to the point at which it stood before it was worked down, and then they should be immediately put into the oven.

Many a good thing, however, is spoiled in the oven. We cannot but regret, for the sake of bread, that our old steady brick ovens have been almost universally superseded by those of ranges and cooking-stoves, which are infinite in their caprices, and forbid all general rules. One thing, however, may be borne in mind as a principle, — that the excellence of bread in all its varieties, plain or sweetened, depends on the perfection of its air-cells, whether produced by yeast, egg, or effervescence; that one of the objects of baking is to fix these air-cells, and that the quicker this can be done through the whole mass, the better will the result be. When cake or bread is made heavy by baking too quickly, it is because the immediate formation of the top crust hinders the exhaling of the moisture in the centre, and prevents the air-cells from cooking. The weight also of the crust pressing down on the doughy air-cells below destroys them, producing that horror of good cooks, a heavy streak. The problem in baking, then, is the quick application of heat rather below than above the loaf, and its steady continuance till all the air-cells are thoroughly dried into permanent consistency. Every housewife must watch her own oven to know how this can be best accomplished.

Bread-making can be cultivated to any extent as a fine art; and the various kinds of biscuit, tea-rusks, twists, rolls, into which bread may be made, are much better worth a housekeeper's ambition than the getting up of rich and expensive cake or confections. There are also varieties of material which are rich in good effects. Unbolted flour, altogether more wholesome than the fine wheat, and when properly prepared more palatable, rye-flour and corn-meal, each affording a thousand attractive possibilities,—each and all of these come under the general laws of breadstuffs, and are worth a careful attention.

A peculiarity of our American table, particularly in the Southern and Western States, is the constant exhibition of various preparations of hot bread. In many families of the South and West, bread in loaves to be eaten cold is an article quite unknown. The effect of this kind of diet upon the health has formed a frequent subject of remark among travelers; but only those know the full mischiefs of it who have been compelled to sojourn for a length of time in families where it is maintained. The unknown horrors of dyspepsia from bad bread are a topic over which we willingly draw a veil.

Next to bread comes *butter*,—on which we have to say that, when we remember what butter is in civilized Europe, and compare it with what it is in America, we wonder at the forbearance and lenity of travelers in their strictures on our national commissariat.

Butter in England, France, and Italy is simply solidified cream, with all the sweetness of the cream in its taste, freshly churned each day, and unadulterated by salt. At the present moment, when salt is five cents a pound and butter fifty, we Americans are paying, I should judge from the taste, for about one pound of salt to every ten of butter, and those of us who have eaten the butter of France and England do this with rueful recollections.

There is, it is true, an article of butter made in the American style with salt, which, in its own kind and way, has a merit not inferior to that of England and France. Many prefer it, and it certainly takes a rank equally respectable with the other. It is yellow, hard, and worked so perfectly free from every particle of buttermilk that it might make the voyage of the world without spoiling. It is salted, but salted with care and delicacy, so that it may be a question whether even a fastidious Englishman might not prefer its golden solidity to the white, creamy freshness of his own. Now I am not for universal imitation of foreign customs, and where I find this butter made perfectly I call it our American style, and am not ashamed of it.

I only regret that this article is the exception, and not the rule, on our tables. When I reflect on the possibilities which beset the delicate stomach in this line, I do not wonder that my venerated friend Dr. Mussey used to close his counsels to invalids with the direction, "And don't eat grease on your bread."

America must, I think, have the credit of manufacturing and putting into market more bad butter than all that is made in all the rest of the world together. The varieties of bad tastes and smells which prevail in it are quite a study. This has a cheesy taste, that a mouldy, — this is flavored with cabbage, and that again with turnip; and another has the strong, sharp savor of rancid animal fat. These varieties, I presume, come from the practice of churning only at long intervals, and keeping the cream meanwhile in unventilated cellars or dairies, the air of which is loaded with the effluvia of vegetable substances. No domestic articles are so sympathetic as those of the milk tribe: they readily take on the smell and taste of any neighboring substance, and hence the infinite variety of flavors on which one mournfully muses who has late in autumn to taste twenty firkins of butter in hopes of finding one which will simply not be intolerable on his winter table.

A matter for despair as regards bad butter is that, at the tables where it is used, it stands sentinel at the door to bar your way to every other kind of food. You turn from your dreadful half-slice of bread, which fills your mouth with bitterness, to your beefsteak, which proves virulent with the same poison; you think to take refuge in vegetable diet, and find the butter in the string-beans, and polluting the innocence of early peas; it is in the corn, in the succotash, in the squash; the beets swim in it, the onions have it poured over them. Hungry and miserable, you think to solace yourself at the dessert; but the pastry is cursed, the cake is acrid with the same plague. You are ready to howl with despair, and your misery is great upon you, especially if this is a table where you have taken board for three months with your delicate wife and four small children. Your case is dreadful, — and it is hopeless, because long usage and habit have rendered your host perfectly incapable of discovering what is the matter. "Don't like the butter, sir? I assure you I paid an extra price for it, and it's the very best in the market. I looked over as many as a hundred tubs, and picked out this one." You are dumb, but not less despairing.

Yet the process of making good butter is a very simple one. To keep the cream in a perfectly pure, cool atmosphere, to churn while it is yet sweet, to work out the buttermilk thoroughly, and to add salt with such discretion as not to ruin the fine, delicate flavor of the fresh cream,—all this is quite simple, so simple that one wonders at thousands and millions of pounds of butter yearly manufactured which are merely a hobgoblin-bewitchment of cream into foul and loathsome poisons.

The third head of my discourse is that of *Meat*, of which America furnishes, in the gross material, enough to spread our tables royally, were it well cared for and served.

The faults in the meat generally furnished to us are, first, that it is too new. A beefsteak, which three or four days of keeping might render practicable, is served up to us palpitating with freshness, with all the toughness of animal muscle yet warm. In the Western country, the traveler, on approaching an hotel, is often saluted by the last shrieks of the chickens which half an hour afterward are presented to him à la spread-eagle for his dinner. The example of the Father of the Faithful, most wholesome to be followed in so many respects, is imitated only in the celerity with which the young calf, tender and good, was transformed into an edible dish for hospitable purposes. But what might be good housekeeping in a nomadic Emir, in days when refrigerators were yet in the future, ought not to be so closely imitated as it often is in our own land.

In the next place, there is a woful lack of nicety in the butcher's work of cutting and preparing meat. Who that remembers the neatly trimmed mutton-chop of an English inn, or the artistic little circle of lamb-chop fried in bread-crumbs coiled around a tempting centre of spinach which can always be found in France, can recognize any family resemblance to these dapper civilized preparations in those coarse, roughly hacked strips of bone, gristle, and meat which are commonly called mutton-chop in America? There seems to be a large dish of something resembling meat, in which each fragment has about two or three edible morsels, the rest being composed of dry and burnt skin, fat, and ragged bone.

Is it not time that civilization should learn to demand somewhat more care and nicety in the modes of preparing what is to be cooked and eaten? Might not some of the refinement and trimness which characterize the preparations of the European market be with advantage introduced into our own? The housekeeper who wishes to garnish her table with some of those nice things is stopped in the outset by the butcher. Except in our large cities, where some foreign travel may have created the demand, it seems impossible to get much in this line that is properly prepared.

I am aware that, if this is urged on the score of æsthetics, the ready reply will be, "Oh, we can't give time here in America to go into niceties and French whim-whams!" But the French mode of doing almost all practical things is based on that true philosophy and utilitarian good sense which characterize that seemingly thoughtless people. Nowhere is economy a more careful study, and their market is artistically arranged to this end. The rule is so to cut their meats that no portion designed to be cooked in a certain manner shall have wasteful appendages which that mode of cooking will spoil. The French soup kettle stands ever ready to receive the bones, the thin fibrous flaps, the sinewy and gristly portions, which are so often included in our roasts or broilings, which fill our plates with unsightly débris, and finally make an amount of blank waste for which we pay our butcher the same price that we pay for what we have eaten.

The dead waste of our clumsy, coarse way of cutting meats is immense. For example, at the beginning of the present season, the part of a lamb denominated leg and loin, or hind-quarter, sold for thirty cents a pound. Now this includes, besides the thick, fleshy portions, a quantity of bone, sinew, and thin fibrous substance, constituting full one third of the whole weight. If we put it into the oven entire, in the usual manner, we have the thin parts overdone, and the skinny and fibrous parts utterly dried up, by the application of the amount of heat necessary to cook the thick portion. Supposing the joint to weigh six pounds, at thirty cents, and that one third of the weight is so treated as to become perfectly useless, we throw away sixty cents. Of a piece of beef at twenty-five cents a pound, fifty cents' worth is often lost in bone, fat, and burnt skin.

The fact is, this way of selling and cooking meat in large, gross portions is of English origin, and belongs to a country where all the customs of society spring from a class who have no particular occasion for economy. The practice of minute and delicate division comes from a nation which acknowledges the need of economy, and has made it a study. A quarter of lamb in this mode of division would be sold in three nicely prepared portions. The thick part would be sold by itself, for a neat, compact little roast; the rib-bones would be artistically separated, and all the edible matters scraped away would form those delicate dishes of lamb-chop which, fried in bread-crumbs to a golden brown, are so ornamental and so palatable a side-dish; the trimmings which remain after this division would be destined to the soup kettle or stew pan. In a French market is a little portion for every purse, and the far-famed and delicately flavored soups and stews which have arisen out of French economy are a study worth a housekeeper's attention. Not one atom of food is wasted in the French modes of preparation; even tough animal cartilages and sinews, instead of appearing burnt and blackened in company with the roast meat to which they happen to be related, are treated according to their own laws, and come out either in savory soups, or those fine, clear meat-jellies which form a garnish no less agreeable to the eye than palatable to the taste.

Whether this careful, economical, practical style of meat cooking can ever to any great extent be introduced into our kitchens now is a question. Our butchers are against it; our servants are wedded to the old wholesale wasteful ways, which seem to them easier because they are accustomed to them. A cook who will keep and properly tend a soup kettle which shall receive and utilize all that the coarse preparations of the butcher would require her to trim away, who understands the art of making the most of all these remains, is a treasure scarcely to be hoped for. If such things are to be done, it must be primarily through the educated brain of cultivated women who do not scorn to turn their culture and refinement upon domestic problems.

When meats have been properly divided—so that each portion can receive its own appropriate style of treatment—next comes the consideration of the modes of cooking. These may be divided into two great general classes: those where it is desired to keep the juices within the meat, as in baking, broiling, and frying; and those whose object is to extract the juice and dissolve the fibre, as in the making of soups and stews. In the first class of operations, the process must be as rapid as may consist with the thorough cooking of all the particles. In this branch of cookery, doing quickly is doing well. The fire must be brisk, the attention alert. The introduction of cooking-stoves offers to careless domestics facilities for gradually drying up meats, and despoiling them of all flavor and nutriment,—facilities which appear to be very generally laid hold of. They have almost banished the genuine, old-fashioned roast meat from our tables, and left in its stead dried meats with their most precious and nutritive juices evaporated. How few cooks, unassisted, are competent to the simple process of broiling a beefsteak or mutton-chop! how very generally one has to choose between these meats gradually dried away, or burned on the outside and raw within! Yet in England these articles *never* come on table done amiss; their perfect cooking is as absolute a certainty as the rising of the sun.

No one of these rapid processes of cooking, however, is so generally abused as frying. The frying-pan has awful sins to answer for. What untold horrors of dyspepsia have arisen from its smoky depths, like the ghosts from witches' caldrons! The fizzle of frying meat is as a warning knell on many an ear, saying, "Touch not, taste not, if you would not burn and writhe!"

Yet those who have traveled abroad remember that some of the lightest, most palatable, and most digestible preparations of meat have come from this dangerous source. But we fancy quite other rites and ceremonies inaugurated the process, and quite other hands performed its offices, than those known to our kitchens. Probably the delicate *côte-lettes* of France are not flopped down into half-melted grease, there gradually to warm and soak and fizzle, while Biddy goes in and out on her other ministrations, till finally, when thoroughly saturated and dinner-hour impends, she bethinks herself, and crowds the fire below to a roaring heat, and finishes the process by a smart burn, involving the kitchen and surrounding precincts in volumes of Stygian gloom.

From such preparations has arisen the very current medical opinion that fried meats are indigestible. They are indigestible if they are greasy; but French cooks have taught us that a thing has no more need to be greasy because emerging from grease than Venus had to be salt because she rose from the sea.

There are two ways of frying employed by the French cook. One is, to immerse the article to be cooked in *boiling* fat, with an emphasis on the present participle,—and the philosophical principle is, so immediately to crisp every pore at the first moment or two of immersion as effectually to seal the interior against the intrusion of greasy particles; it can then remain as long as may be necessary thoroughly to cook it, without imbibing any more of the boiling fluid than if it were enclosed in an eggshell. The other method is, to rub a perfectly smooth iron surface with just enough of some oily substance to prevent the meat from adhering, and cook it with a quick heat, as cakes are baked on a griddle. In both these cases there must be the most rapid application of heat that can be made without burning, and by the adroitness shown in working out this problem the skill of the cook is tested. Any one whose cook attains this important secret will find fried things quite as digestible and often more palatable than any other.

In the second department of meat cookery, to wit, the slow and gradual application of heat for the softening and dissolution of its fibre and the extraction of its juices, common cooks are equally untrained. Where is the so-called cook who understands how to prepare soups and stews? These are precisely the articles in which a French kitchen excels. The soup kettle, made with a double bottom to prevent burning, is a permanent, ever-present institution, and the coarsest and most impracticable meats distilled through that alembic come out again in soups, jellies, or savory stews. The toughest cartilage, even the bones, being first cracked, are here made to give forth their hidden virtues, and to rise in delicate and appetizing forms. One great law governs all these preparations: the application of heat must be gradual, steady, long protracted, never reaching the point of active boiling. Hours of quiet simmering dissolve all dissoluble parts, soften the sternest fibre, and unlock every minute cell in which Nature has stored away her treasures of nourishment. This careful and protracted application of heat and the skillful use of flavors constitute the two main points in all those nice preparations of meat for which the French have so many names,—processes by which a delicacy can be imparted to the coarsest and cheapest food superior to that of the finest articles under less philosophic treatment.

French soups and stews are a study, and they would not be an unprofitable one to any person who wishes to live with comfort and even elegance on small means.

John Bull looks down from the sublime of ten thousand a year on French kickshaws, as he calls them: "Give me my meat cooked so I may know what it is!" An ox roasted whole is dear to John's soul, and his kitchen arrangements are Titanic. What magnificent rounds and sirloins of beef, revolving on self-regulating spits, with a rich click of satisfaction, before grates piled with roaring fires! Let us do justice to the royal cheer. Nowhere are the charms of pure, unadulterated animal food set forth in more imposing style. For John is rich, and what does he care for odds and ends and parings? Has he not all the beasts of the forest, and the cattle on a thousand hills? What does he want of economy? But his brother Jean has not ten thousand pounds a year,—nothing like it; but he makes up for the slenderness of his purse by boundless fertility of invention and delicacy of practice. John began sneering at Jean's soups and ragouts, but all John's modern sons and daughters send to Jean for their cooks, and the sirloins of England rise up and do obeisance to this Joseph with a white apron who comes to rule in their kitchens.

There is no animal fibre that will not yield itself up to long-continued, steady heat. But the difficulty with almost any of the common servants who call themselves cooks is, that they have not the smallest notion of the philosophy of the application of heat. Such a one will complacently tell you, concerning certain meats, that the harder you boil them the harder they grow,—an obvious fact, which, under her mode of treatment by an indiscriminate galloping boil, has frequently come under her personal observation. If you tell her that such meat must stand for six hours in a heat just below the boiling-point, she will probably answer, "Yes, ma'am," and go on her own way. Or she will let it stand till it burns to the bottom of the kettle,—a most common termination of the experiment. The only way to make sure of the matter is either to import a French kettle, or to fit into an ordinary kettle a false bottom, such as any tinman may make, that shall leave a space of an inch or two between the meat and the fire. This kettle may be maintained as a constant *habitué* of the range, and into it the cook may be instructed to throw all the fibrous trimmings of meat, all the gristle, tendons, and bones, having previously broken up these last with a mallet.

Such a kettle will furnish the basis for clear, rich soups or other palatable dishes. Clear soup consists of the dissolved juices of the meat and gelatine of the bones, cleared from the fat and fibrous portions by straining when cold. The grease, which rises to the top of the fluid, may thus be easily removed. In a stew, on the contrary, you boil down this soup till it permeates the fibre which long exposure to heat has softened. All that remains, after the proper preparation of the fibre and juices, is the flavoring, and it is in this, particularly, that French soups excel those of America and England and all the world.

English and American soups are often heavy and hot with spices. There are appreciable tastes in them. They burn your mouth with cayenne or clove or allspice. You can tell at once what is in them, oftentimes to your sorrow. But a French soup has a flavor which one recognises at once as delicious, yet not to be characterized as due to any single condiment; it is the just blending of many things. The same remark applies to all their stews, ragouts, and other delicate preparations. No cook will ever study these flavors; but perhaps many cooks' mistresses may, and thus be able to impart delicacy and comfort to economy.

As to those things called hashes, commonly manufactured by unwatched, untaught cooks, out of the remains of yesterday's repast, let us not dwell too closely on their memory,—compounds of meat, gristle, skin, fat, and burnt fibre, with a handful of pepper and salt flung at them, dredged with lumpy flour, watered from the spout of the tea-kettle, and left to simmer at the cook's convenience while she is otherwise occupied. Such are the best performances a housekeeper can hope for from an untrained cook.

But the cunningly devised minces, the artful preparations choicely flavored, which may be made of yesterday's repast,—by these is the true domestic artist known. No cook untaught by an educated brain ever makes these, and yet economy is a great gainer by them.

As regards the department of *Vegetables*, their number and variety in America are so great that a table might almost be furnished by these alone. Generally speaking, their cooking is a more simple art, and therefore more likely to be found satisfactorily performed, than that of meats. If only they are not drenched with rancid butter, their own native excellence makes itself known in most of the ordinary modes of preparation.

There is, however, one exception.

Our stanch old friend the potato is to other vegetables what bread is on the table. Like bread, it is held as a sort of *sine qua non*; like that, it may be made invariably palatable by a little care in a few plain particulars, through neglect of which it often becomes intolerable. The soggy, waxy, indigestible viand that often appears in the potato-dish is a downright sacrifice of the better nature of this vegetable.

The potato, nutritive and harmless as it appears, belongs to a family suspected of very dangerous traits. It is a family connection of the deadly nightshade and other ill-reputed gentry, and sometimes shows strange proclivities to evil,—now breaking out uproariously, as in the noted potato rot, and now more covertly in various evil affections. For this reason, scientific directors bid us beware of the water in which potatoes are boiled,—into which, it appears, the evil principle is drawn off; and they caution us not to shred them into stews without previously suffering the slices to lie for an hour or so in salt and water. These cautions are worth attention.

The most usual modes of preparing the potato for the table are by roasting or boiling. These processes are so simple that it is commonly supposed every cook understands them without special directions, and yet there is scarcely an uninstructed cook who can boil or roast a potato.

A good roasted potato is a delicacy worth a dozen compositions of the cook-book; yet when we ask for it, what burnt, shriveled abortions are presented to us! Biddy rushes to her potato-basket and pours out two dozen of different sizes, some having in them three times the amount of matter of others. These being washed, she tumbles them into her oven at a leisure interval, and there lets them lie till it is time to serve breakfast, whenever that may be. As a result, if the largest are cooked, the smallest are presented in cinders, and the intermediate sizes are withered and watery. Nothing is so utterly ruined by a few moments of overdoing. That which at the right moment was plump with mealy richness, a quarter of an hour later shrivels and becomes watery,—and it is in this state that roast potatoes are most frequently served.

In the same manner we have seen boiled potatoes from an untaught cook coming upon the table like lumps of yellow wax,—and the same article, the day after, under the directions of a skillful mistress, appearing in snowy balls of powdery lightness. In the one case, they were thrown in their skins into water and suffered to soak or boil, as the case might be, at the cook's leisure, and, after they were boiled, to stand in the water till she was ready to peel them. In the other case, the potatoes being first peeled were boiled as quickly as possible in salted water, which, the moment they were done, was drained off, and then they were gently shaken for a minute or two over the fire to dry them still more thoroughly. We have never yet seen the potato so depraved and given over to evil that could not be reclaimed by this mode of treatment.

As to fried potatoes, who that remembers the crisp, golden slices of the French restaurant, thin as wafers and light as snowflakes, does not speak respectfully of them? What cousinship with these have those coarse, greasy masses of sliced potato, wholly soggy and partly burnt, to which we are treated under the name of fried potatoes à la America? In our cities the restaurants are introducing the French article to great acceptance, and to the vindication of the fair fame of this queen of vegetables.

Finally, I arrive at the last great head of my subject, to wit, *Tea*,—meaning thereby, as before observed, what our Hibernian friend did in the inquiry, "Will y'r Honor take 'tay tay' or 'coffee tay'?"

I am not about to enter into the merits of the great tea and coffee controversy, or say whether these substances are or are not wholesome. I treat of them as actual existences, and speak only of the modes of making the most of them.

The French coffee is reputed the best in the world; and a thousand voices have asked, What is it about the French coffee? In the first place, then, the French coffee is coffee, and not chicory, or rye, or beans, or peas. In the second place, it is freshly roasted, whenever made,—roasted with great care and evenness in a little revolving cylinder which makes part of the furniture of every kitchen, and which keeps in the aroma of the berry. It is never overdone, so as to destroy the coffee flavor, which is in nine cases out of ten the fault of the coffee we meet with. Then it is ground, and placed in a coffee-pot with a filter, through which it percolates in clear drops—the coffee-pot standing on a heated stove to maintain the temperature. The nose of the coffee-pot is stopped up to prevent the escape of the aroma during this process. The extract thus obtained is a perfectly clear, dark fluid, know as *café noir*, or black coffee. It is black only because of its strength, being in fact almost the very essential oil of coffee. A tablespoonful of this in boiled milk would make what is ordinarily called a strong cup of coffee. The boiled milk is prepared with no less care. It must be fresh and new, not merely warmed or even brought to the boiling point, but slowly simmered till it attains a thick, creamy richness. The coffee mixed with this, and sweetened with that sparkling beet-root sugar which ornaments a French table, is the celebrated *café-au-lait*, the name of which has gone round the world.

As we look to France for the best coffee, so we must look to England for the perfection of tea. The tea-kettle is as much an English institution as aristocracy or the Prayer Book; and when one wants to know exactly how tea should be made, one has only to ask how a fine old English housekeeper makes it.

The first article of her faith is, that the water must not merely be hot, not merely *have boiled* a few moments since, but be actually *boiling* at the moment it touches the tea. Hence, though servants in England are vastly better trained than with us, this delicate mystery is seldom left to their hands. Tea making belongs to the drawing-room, and high-born ladies preside at "the bubbling and loud-hissing urn," and see that all due rites and solemnities are properly performed,—that the cups are hot, and that the infused tea waits the exact time before the libations commence. Oh, ye dear old English tea-tables, resorts of the kindest-hearted hospitality in the world! we still cherish your memory, even though you do not say pleasant things of us there. One of these days you will think better of us. Of late, the introduction of English breakfast tea has raised a new sect among the tea drinkers, reversing some of the old canons. Breakfast tea must be boiled! Unlike the delicate article of olden time, which required only a momentary infusion to develop its richness, this requires a longer and severer treatment to bring out its strength,—thus confusing all the established usages, and throwing the work into the hands of the cook in the kitchen.

The faults of tea, as too commonly found at our hotels and boarding-houses, are that it is made in every way the reverse of what it should be. The water is hot, perhaps, but not boiling; the tea has a general flat, stale, smoky taste, devoid of life or spirit; and it is served, usually, with thin milk instead of cream. Cream is as essential to the richness of tea as of coffee. We could wish that the English fashion might generally prevail, of giving the traveler his own kettle of boiling water and his own tea-chest, and letting him make tea for himself. At all events he would then be sure of one merit in his tea,— it would be hot, a very simple and obvious virtue, but one very seldom obtained.

Chocolate is a French and Spanish article, and one seldom served on American tables. We in America, however, make an article every way equal to any which can be imported from Paris, and he who buys Baker's best vanilla-chocolate may rest assured that no foreign land can furnish anything better. A very rich and delicious beverage may be made by dissolving this in milk slowly boiled down after the French fashion.

I have now gone over all the ground I laid out, as comprising the great first principles of cookery; and I would here modestly offer the opinion that a table where all these principles are carefully observed would need few dainties. The struggle after so-called delicacies comes from the poorness of common things. Perfect bread and butter would soon drive cake out of the field; it has done so in many families. Nevertheless, I have a word to say under the head of *Confectionery*, meaning by this the whole range of ornamental cookery,—or pastry, ices, jellies, preserves, etc. The art of making all these very perfectly is far better understood in America than the art of common cooking.

There are more women who know how to make good cake than good bread,—more who can furnish you with a good ice-cream than a well-cooked mutton-chop; a fair charlotte-russe is easier to come by than a perfect cup of coffee; and you shall find a sparkling jelly to your dessert where you sighed in vain for so simple a luxury as a well-cooked potato.

Our fair countrywomen might rest upon their laurels in these higher fields, and turn their great energy and ingenuity to the study of essentials. To do common things perfectly is far better worth our endeavor than to do uncommon things respectably. We Americans in many things as yet have been a little inclined to begin making our shirt at the ruffle; but nevertheless, when we set about it, we can make the shirt as nicely as anybody, — it needs only that we turn our attention to it, resolved that, ruffle or no ruffle, the shirt we will have.

I have also a few words to say as to the prevalent ideas in respect to French cookery. Having heard much of it, with no very distinct idea what it is, our people have somehow fallen into the notion that its forte lies in high spicing, — and so, when our cooks put a great abundance of clove, mace, nutmeg, and cinnamon into their preparations, they fancy that they are growing up to be French cooks. But the fact is, that the Americans and English are far more given to spicing than the French. Spices in our made dishes are abundant, and their taste is strongly pronounced. In living a year in France I forgot the taste of nutmeg, clove, and allspice, which had met me in so many dishes in America.

The thing may be briefly defined. The English and Americans deal in *spices*, the French in *flavors*, —flavors many and subtle, imitating often in their delicacy those subtle blendings which Nature produces in high-flavored fruits. The recipes of our cookery-books are most of them of English origin, coming down from the times of our phlegmatic ancestors, when the solid, burly, beefy growth of the foggy island required the heat of fiery condiments, and could digest heavy sweets. Witness the national recipe for plum-pudding, which may be rendered: Take a pound of every indigestible substance you can think of, boil into a cannon-ball, and serve in flaming brandy. So of the Christmas mince-pie and many other national dishes. But in America, owing to our brighter skies and more fervid climate, we have developed an acute, nervous delicacy of temperament far more akin to that of France than of England.

Half of the recipes in our cook-books are mere murder to such constitutions and stomachs as we grow here. We require to ponder these things, and think how we in our climate and under our circumstances ought to live, and, in doing so, we may, without accusation of foreign foppery, take some leaves from many foreign books.

But Christopher has prosed long enough. I must now read this to my wife, and see what she says.

XI

OUR HOUSE

Our gallant Bob Stephens, into whose lifeboat our Marianne has been received, has lately taken the mania of housebuilding into his head. Bob is somewhat fastidious, difficult to please, fond of domesticities and individualities; and such a man never can fit himself into a house built by another, and accordingly housebuilding has always been his favorite mental recreation. During all his courtship, as much time was taken up in planning a future house as if he had money to build one; and all Marianne's patterns, and the backs of half their letters, were scrawled with ground-plans and elevations. But latterly this chronic disposition has been quickened into an acute form by the falling-in of some few thousands to their domestic treasury,—left as the sole residuum of a painstaking old aunt, who took it into her head to make a will in Bob's favor, leaving, among other good things, a nice little bit of land in a rural district half an hour's railroad ride from Boston.

So now ground-plans thicken, and my wife is being consulted morning, noon, and night; and I never come into the room without finding their heads close together over a paper, and hearing Bob expatiate on his favorite idea of a library. He appears to have got so far as this, that the ceiling is to be of carved oak, with ribs running to a boss overhead, and finished mediævally with ultramarine blue and gilding,—and then away he goes sketching Gothic patterns of bookshelves which require only experienced carvers, and the wherewithal to pay them, to be the divinest things in the world.

Marianne is exercised about china-closets and pantries, and about a bedroom on the ground-floor,—for, like all other women of our days, she expects not to have strength enough to run upstairs oftener than once or twice a week; and my wife, who is a native genius in this line, and has planned in her time dozens of houses for acquaintances, wherein they are at this moment living happily, goes over every day with her pencil and ruler the work of rearranging the plans, according as the ideas of the young couple veer and vary.

One day Bob is importuned to give two feet off from his library for a closet in the bedroom, but resists like a Trojan. The next morning, being mollified by private domestic supplications, Bob yields, and my wife rubs out the lines of yesterday, two feet come off the library, and a closet is constructed. But now the parlor proves too narrow,—

the parlor wall must be moved two feet into the hall. Bob declares this will spoil the symmetry of the latter; and, if there is anything he wants, it is a wide, generous, ample hall to step into when you open the front door.

"Well, then," says Marianne, "let's put two feet more into the width of the house."

"Can't on account of the expense, you see," says Bob. "You see every additional foot of outside wall necessitates so many more bricks, so much more flooring, so much more roofing, etc."

And my wife, with thoughtful brow, looks over the plans, and considers how two feet more are to be got into the parlor without moving any of the walls.

"I say," says Bob, bending over her shoulder, "here, take your two feet in the parlor, and put two more feet on to the other side of the hall stairs;" and he dashes heavily with his pencil.

"Oh, Bob!" exclaims Marianne, "there are the kitchen pantries! you ruin them,—and no place for the cellar stairs!"

"Hang the pantries and cellar stairs!" says Bob. "Mother must find a place for them somewhere else. I say the house must be roomy and cheerful, and pantries and those things may take care of themselves; they can be put *somewhere* well enough. No fear but you will find a place for them somewhere. What do you women always want such a great enormous kitchen for?"

"It is not any larger than is necessary," said my wife, thoughtfully; "nothing is gained by taking off from it."

"What if you should put it all down into a basement," suggests Bob, "and so get it all out of sight together?"

"Never, if it can be helped," said my wife. "Basement kitchens are necessary evils, only to be tolerated in cities where land is too dear to afford any other."

So goes the discussion till the trio agree to sleep over it. The next morning an inspiration visits my wife's pillow. She is up and seizes plans and paper, and, before six o'clock, has enlarged the parlor very cleverly by throwing out a bow-window. So waxes and wanes the prospective house, innocently battered down and rebuilt with India-rubber and black-lead. Doors are cut out to-night and walled up to-morrow; windows knocked out here and put in there, as some observer suggests possibilities of too much or too little draught. Now all seems finished, when, lo! a discovery! There is no fireplace nor stove-flue in my lady's bedroom, and can be none without moving the bathing-room. Pencil and India-rubber are busy again, and for a while the whole house seems to threaten to fall to pieces with the confusion of the moving; the bath-room wanders like a ghost, now invading a closet, now threatening the tranquillity of the parlor, till at last it is laid, by some unheard-of calculations of my wife's, and sinks to rest in a place so much better that everybody wonders it never was thought of before.

"Papa," said Jenny, "it appears to me people don't exactly know what they want when they build; why don't you write a paper on housebuilding?"

"I have thought of it," said I, with the air of a man called to settle some great reform. "It must be entirely because Christopher has not written that our young people and mamma are tangling themselves daily in webs which are untangled the next day."

"You see," said Jenny, "they have only just so much money, and they want everything they can think of under the sun. There's Bob been studying architectural antiquities, and nobody knows what, and sketching all sorts of curly-whorlies; and Marianne has her notions about a parlor and boudoir and china closets and bedroom closets; and Bob wants a baronial hall; and mamma stands out for linen closets and bathing-rooms and all that; and so, among them all it will just end in getting them head over ears in debt."

The thing struck me as not improbable.

"I don't know, Jenny, whether my writing an article is going to prevent all this; but as my time in the 'Atlantic' is coming round, I may as well write on what I am obliged to think of, and so I will give a paper on the subject to enliven our next evening's session."

So that evening, when Bob and Marianne had dropped in as usual, and while the customary work of drawing and rubbing out was going on at Mrs. Crowfield's sofa, I produced my paper and read as follows:—

OUR HOUSE

There is a place, called "our house," which everybody knows of. The sailor talks of it in his dreams at sea. The wounded soldier, turning in his uneasy hospital-bed, brightens at the word; it is like the dropping of cool water in the desert, like the touch of cool fingers on a burning brow. "Our house," he says feebly, and the light comes back into his dim eyes; for all homely charities, all fond thoughts, all purities, all that man loves on earth or hopes for in heaven, rise with the word.

"Our house" may be in any style of architecture, low or high. It may be the brown old farmhouse, with its tall wellsweep, or the one-story gambrel-roofed cottage, or the large, square, white house, with green blinds, under the wind-swung elms of a century; or it may be the log-cabin of the wilderness, with its one room, —still there is a spell in the memory of it beyond all conjurations. Its stone and brick and mortar are like no other; its very clapboards and shingles are dear to us, powerful to bring back the memories of early days and all that is sacred in home love.

"Papa is getting quite sentimental," whispered Jenny, loud enough for me to hear. I shook my head at her impressively, and went on undaunted.

There is no one fact of our human existence that has a stronger influence upon us than the house we dwell in, especially that in which our earlier and more impressible years are spent. The building and arrangement of a house influence the health, the comfort, the morals, the religion. There have been houses built so devoid of all consideration for the occupants, so rambling and haphazard in the disposal of rooms, so sunless and cheerless and wholly without snugness or privacy, as to make it seem impossible to live a joyous, generous, rational, religious family life in them.

There are, we shame to say, in our cities *things* called houses, built and rented by people who walk erect and have the general air and manner of civilized and Christianized men, which are so inhuman in their building that they can only be called snares and traps for souls,—places where children cannot well escape growing up filthy and impure; places where to form a home is impossible, and to live a decent, Christian life would require miraculous strength.

A celebrated British philanthropist, who had devoted much study to the dwellings of the poor, gave it as his opinion that the temperance societies were a hopeless undertaking in London unless these dwellings underwent a transformation. They were so squalid, so dark, so comfortless, so constantly pressing upon the senses foulness, pain, and inconvenience, that it was only by being drugged with gin and opium that their miserable inhabitants could find heart to drag on life from day to day. He had himself tried the experiment of reforming a drunkard by taking him from one of these loathsome dens, and enabling him to rent a tenement in a block of model lodging-houses which had been built under his supervision. The young man had been a designer of figures for prints; he was of a delicate frame, and a nervous, susceptible temperament. Shut in one miserable room with his wife and little children, without the possibility of pure air, with only filthy, fetid water to drink, with the noise of other miserable families resounding through the thin partitions, what possibility was there of doing anything except by the help of stimulants, which for a brief hour lifted him above the perception of these miseries? Changed at once to a neat flat, where, for the same rent as his former den, he had three good rooms, with water for drinking, house-service, and bathing freely supplied, and the blessed sunshine and air coming in through windows well arranged for ventilation, he became in a few weeks a new man. In the charms of the little spot which he could call home, its quiet, its order, his former talent came back to him, and he found strength, in pure air and pure water and those purer thoughts of which they are the emblems, to abandon burning and stupefying stimulants.

The influence of dwelling-houses for good or for evil—their influence on the brain, the nerves, and, through these, on the heart and life—is one of those things that cannot be enough pondered by those who build houses to sell or rent.

Something more generous ought to inspire a man than merely the percentage which he can get for his money. He who would build houses should think a little on the subject. He should reflect what houses are for, what they may be made to do for human beings. The great majority of houses in cities are not built by the indwellers themselves; they are built for them by those who invest their money in this way, with little other thought than the percentage which the investment will return.

For persons of ample fortune there are, indeed, palatial residences, with all that wealth can do to render life delightful. But in that class of houses which must be the lot of the large majority, those which must be chosen by young men in the beginning of life, when means are comparatively restricted, there is yet wide room for thought and the judicious application of money.

In looking over houses to be rented by persons of moderate means, one cannot help longing to build,—one sees so many ways in which the same sum which built an inconvenient and unpleasant house might have been made to build a delightful one.

"That's so!" said Bob with emphasis. "Don't you remember, Marianne, how many dismal, commonplace, shabby houses we trailed through?"

"Yes," said Marianne. "You remember those houses with such little squeezed rooms and that flourishing staircase, with the colored-glass china-closet window, and no butler's sink?"

"Yes," said Bob; "and those astonishing, abominable stone abortions that adorned the doorsteps. People do lay out a deal of money to make houses look ugly, it must be confessed."

"One would willingly," said Marianne, "dispense with frightful stone ornaments in front, and with heavy mouldings inside, which are of no possible use or beauty, and with showy plaster cornices and centrepieces in the parlor ceilings, and even with marble mantels, for the luxury of hot and cold water in each chamber, and a couple of comfortable bath-rooms. Then, the disposition of windows and doors is so wholly without regard to convenience! How often we find rooms, meant for bedrooms, where really there is no good place for either bed or dressing-table!"

Here my wife looked up, having just finished redrawing the plans to the latest alteration.

"One of the greatest reforms that could be, in these reforming days," she observed, "would be to have women architects. The mischief with houses built to rent is that they are all mere male contrivances. No woman would ever plan chambers where there is no earthly place to set a bed except against a window or door, or waste the room in entries that might be made into closets. I don't see, for my part, apropos to the modern movement for opening new professions to the female sex, why there should not be well-educated female architects. The planning and arrangement of houses, and the laying-out of grounds, are a fair subject of womanly knowledge and taste. It is the teaching of Nature. What would anybody think of a bluebird's nest that had been built entirely by Mr. Blue, without the help of his wife?"

"My dear," said I, "you must positively send a paper on this subject to the next Woman's Rights Convention."

"I am of Sojourner Truth's opinion," said my wife,—"that the best way to prove the propriety of one's doing anything is to go and *do it*. A woman who should have energy to grow through the preparatory studies and set to work in this field would, I am sure, soon find employment."

"If she did as well as you would do, my dear," said I. "There are plenty of young women in our Boston high schools who are going through higher fields of mathematics than are required by the architect, and the schools for design show the flexibility and fertility of the female pencil. The thing appears to me altogether more feasible than many other openings which have been suggested to woman."

"Well," said Jenny, "isn't papa ever to go on with his paper?"

I continued:—

What ought "our house" to be? Could any other question be asked admitting in its details of such varied answers,—answers various as the means, the character, and situation of different individuals? But there are great wants, pertaining to every human being, into which all lesser ones run. There are things in a house that every one, high or low, rich or poor, ought, according to his means, to seek. I think I shall class them according to the elemental division of the old philosophers: Fire, Air, Earth, and Water. These form the groundwork of this *need-be*,—the *sine-qua-nons* of a house.

"Fire, air, earth, and water! I don't understand," said Jenny.

"Wait a little till you do, then," said I. "I will try to make my meaning plain."

The first object of a house is shelter from the elements. This object is effected by a tent or wigwam which keeps off rain and wind. The first disadvantage of this shelter is, that the vital air which you take into your lungs, and on the purity of which depends the purity of blood and brain and nerves, is vitiated. In the wigwam or tent you are constantly taking in poison, more or less active, with every inspiration. Napoleon had his army sleep without tents. He stated that from experience he found it more healthy, and wonderful have been the instances of delicate persons gaining constantly in rigor from being obliged, in the midst of hardships, to sleep constantly in the open air. Now the first problem in housebuilding is to combine the advantage of shelter with the fresh elasticity of outdoor air. I am not going to give here a treatise on ventilation, but merely to say, in general terms, that the first object of a house builder or contriver should be to make a healthy house; and the first requisite of a healthy house is a pure, sweet, elastic air.

I am in favor, therefore, of those plans of housebuilding which have wide central spaces, whether halls or courts, into which all the rooms open, and which necessarily preserve a body of fresh air for the use of them all. In hot climates this is the object of the central court which cuts into the body of the house, with its fountain and flowers, and its galleries, into which the various apartments open. When people are restricted for space, and cannot afford to give up wide central portions of the house for the mere purposes of passage, this central hall can be made a pleasant sitting-room. With tables, chairs, bookcases, and sofas comfortably disposed, this ample central room above and below is, in many respects, the most agreeable lounging room of the house; while the parlors below and the chambers above, opening upon it, form agreeable withdrawing rooms for purposes of greater privacy.

It is customary with many persons to sleep with bedroom windows open,—a very imperfect and often dangerous mode of procuring that supply of fresh air which a sleeping-room requires. In a house constructed in the manner indicated, windows might be freely left open in these central halls, producing there a constant movement of air, and the doors of the bedrooms placed ajar, when a very slight opening in the windows would create a free circulation through the apartments.

In the planning of a house, thought should be had as to the general disposition of the windows, and the quarters from which favoring breezes may be expected should be carefully considered. Windows should be so arranged that draughts of air can be thrown quite through and across the house. How often have we seen pale mothers and drooping babes fanning and panting during some of our hot days on the sunny side of a house, while the breeze that should have cooled them beat in vain against a dead wall! One longs sometimes to knock holes through partitions, and let in the air of heaven.

No other gift of God so precious, so inspiring, is treated with such utter irreverence and contempt in the calculations of us mortals as this same air of heaven. A sermon on oxygen, if one had a preacher who understood the subject, might do more to repress sin than the most orthodox discourse to show when and how and why sin came. A minister gets up in a crowded lecture-room, where the mephitic air almost makes the candles burn blue, and bewails the deadness of the church,—the church the while, drugged by the poisoned air, growing sleepier and sleepier, though they feel dreadfully wicked for being so.

Little Jim, who, fresh from his afternoon's ramble in the fields, last evening said his prayers dutifully, and lay down to sleep in a most Christian frame, this morning sits up in bed with his hair bristling with crossness, strikes at his nurse, and declares he won't say his prayers,—that he don't want to be good. The simple difference is, that the child, having slept in a close box of a room, his brain all night fed by poison, is in a mild state of moral insanity. Delicate women remark that it takes them till eleven or twelve o'clock to get up their strength in the morning. Query: Do they sleep with closed windows and doors, and with heavy bed-curtains?

The houses built by our ancestors were better ventilated in certain respects than modern ones, with all their improvements. The great central chimney, with its open fireplaces in the different rooms, created a constant current which carried off foul and vitiated air. In these days, how common is it to provide rooms with only a flue for a stove! This flue is kept shut in summer, and in winter opened only to admit a close stove, which burns away the vital portion of the air quite as fast as the occupants breathe it away. The sealing up of fireplaces and introduction of air-tight stoves may, doubtless, be a saving of fuel; it saves, too, more than that,—in thousands and thousands of cases it has saved people from all further human wants, and put an end forever to any needs short of the six feet of narrow earth which are man's only inalienable property. In other words, since the invention of air-tight stoves, thousands have died of slow poison. It is a terrible thing to reflect upon, that our Northern winters last from November to May, six long months, in which many families confine themselves to one room, of which every window-crack has been carefully calked to make it air-tight, where an air-tight stove keeps the atmosphere at a temperature between eighty and ninety, and the inmates sitting there, with all their winter clothes on, become enervated both by the heat and by the poisoned air, for which there is no escape but the occasional opening of a door.

It is no wonder that the first result of all this is such a delicacy of skin and lungs that about half the inmates are obliged to give up going into the open air during the six cold months, because they invariably catch cold if they do so. It is no wonder that the cold caught about the first of December has by the first of March become a fixed consumption, and that the opening of the spring, which ought to bring life and health, in so many cases brings death.

We hear of the lean condition in which the poor bears emerge from their six months' wintering, during which they subsist on the fat which they have acquired the previous summer. Even so, in our long winters, multitudes of delicate people subsist on the daily waning strength which they acquired in the season when windows and doors were open, and fresh air was a constant luxury. No wonder we hear of spring fever and spring biliousness, and have thousands of nostrums for clearing the blood in the spring. All these things are the pantings and palpitations of a system run down under slow poison, unable to get a step farther. Better, far better, the old houses of the olden time, with their great roaring fires, and their bedrooms where the snow came in and the wintry winds whistled. Then, to be sure, you froze your back while you burned your face; your water froze nightly in your pitcher; your breath congealed in ice-wreaths on the blankets; and you could write your name on the pretty snow-wreath that had sifted in through the window-cracks. But you woke full of life and vigor,—you looked out into the whirling snowstorms without a shiver, and thought nothing of plunging through drifts as high as your head on your daily way to school. You jingled in sleighs, you snowballed, you lived in snow like a snowbird, and your blood coursed and tingled, in full tide of good, merry, real life, through your veins,—none of the slow-creeping, black blood which clogs the brain and lies like a weight on the vital wheels!

"Mercy upon us, papa!" said Jenny, "I hope we need not go back to such houses?"

"No, my dear," I replied. "I only said that such houses were better than those which are all winter closed by double windows and burnt-out air-tight stoves."

The perfect house is one in which there is a constant escape of every foul and vitiated particle of air through one opening, while a constant supply of fresh outdoor air is admitted by another. In winter, this outdoor air must pass through some process by which it is brought up to a temperate warmth.

Take a single room, and suppose on one side a current of outdoor air which has been warmed by passing through the air chamber of a modern furnace. Its temperature need not be above sixty-five,—it answers breathing purposes better at that. On the other side of the room let there be an open wood or coal fire. One cannot conceive the purposes of warmth and ventilation more perfectly combined.

Suppose a house with a great central hall, into which a current of fresh, temperately warmed air is continually pouring. Each chamber opening upon this hall has a chimney up whose flue the rarefied air is constantly passing, drawing up with it all the foul and poisonous gases. That house is well ventilated, and in a way that need bring no dangerous draughts upon the most delicate invalid. For the better securing of privacy in sleeping-rooms, we have seen two doors employed, one of which is made with slats, like a window-blind, so that air is freely transmitted without exposing the interior.

When we speak of fresh air, we insist on the full rigor of the term. It must not be the air of a cellar, heavily laden with the poisonous nitrogen of turnips and cabbages, but good, fresh, outdoor air from a cold-air pipe, so placed as not to get the lower stratum near the ground, where heavy damps and exhalations collect, but high up, in just the clearest and most elastic region.

The conclusion of the whole matter is, that as all of man's and woman's peace and comfort, all their love, all their amiability, all their religion, have got to come to them, while they live in this world, through the medium of the brain,—and as black, uncleansed blood acts on the brain as a poison, and as no other than black, uncleansed blood can be got by the lungs out of impure air,—the first object of the man who builds a house is to secure a pure and healthy atmosphere therein.

Therefore, in allotting expenses, set this down as a *must-be*: "Our house must have fresh air,—everywhere, at all times, winter and summer." Whether we have stone facings or no; whether our parlor has cornices or marble mantles or no; whether our doors are machine-made or hand-made. All our fixtures shall be of the plainest and simplest, but we will have fresh air. We will open our door with a latch and string, if we cannot afford lock and knob and fresh air too; but in our house we will live cleanly and Christianly. We will no more breathe the foul air rejected from a neighbor's lungs than we will use a neighbor's tooth-brush and hair-brush. Such is the first essential of "our house,"—the first great element of human health and happiness,—AIR.

"I say, Marianne," said Bob, "have we got fireplaces in our chambers?"

"Mamma took care of that," said Marianne.

"You may be quite sure," said I, "if your mother has had a hand in planning your house, that the ventilation is cared for."

It must be confessed that Bob's principal idea in a house had been a Gothic library, and his mind had labored more on the possibility of adapting some favorite bits from the baronial antiquities to modern needs than on anything so terrestrial as air. Therefore he awoke as from a dream, and taking two or three monstrous inhalations, he seized the plans and began looking over them with new energy. Meanwhile I went on with my prelection.

The second great vital element for which provision must be made in "our house" is FIRE. By which I do not mean merely artificial fire, but fire in all its extent and branches,—the heavenly fire which God sends us daily on the bright wings of sunbeams, as well as the mimic fires by which we warm our dwellings, cook our food, and light our nightly darkness.

To begin, then, with heavenly fire or sunshine. If God's gift of vital air is neglected and undervalued, His gift of sunshine appears to be hated. There are many houses where not a cent has been expended on ventilation, but where hundreds of dollars have been freely lavished to keep out the sunshine. The chamber, truly, is tight as a box; it has no fireplace, not even a ventilator opening into the stove-flue; but, oh, joy and gladness! it has outside blinds and inside folding-shutters, so that in the brightest of days we may create there a darkness that may be felt. To observe the generality of New England houses, a spectator might imagine they were planned for the torrid zone, where the great object is to keep out a furnace draught of burning air.

But let us look over the months of our calendar. In which of them do we not need fires on our hearths? We will venture to say that from October to June all families, whether they actually have it or not, would be the more comfortable for a morning and evening fire. For eight months in the year the weather varies on the scale of cool, cold, colder, and freezing; and for all the four other months what is the number of days that really require the torrid-zone system of shutting up houses? We all know that extreme heat is the exception, and not the rule.

Yet let anybody travel, as I did last year, through the valley of the Connecticut, and observe the houses. All clean and white and neat and well-to-do, with their turfy yards and their breezy great elms, but all shut up from basement to attic, as if the inmates had all sold out and gone to China. Not a window-blind open above or below. Is the house inhabited? No,—yes,—there is a faint stream of blue smoke from the kitchen chimney, and half a window-blind open in some distant back part of the house. They are living there in the dim shadows, bleaching like potato-sprouts in the cellar.

"I can tell you why they do it, papa," said Jenny. "It's the flies, and flies are certainly worthy to be one of the plagues of Egypt. I can't myself blame people that shut up their rooms and darken their houses in fly-time,—do you, mamma?"

"Not in extreme cases; though I think there is but a short season when this is necessary; yet the habit of shutting up lasts the year round, and gives to New England villages that dead, silent, cold, uninhabited look which is so peculiar."

"The one fact that a traveler would gather in passing through our villages would be this," said I, "that the people live in their houses and in the dark. Barely do you see doors and windows open, people sitting at them, chairs in the yard, and signs that the inhabitants are living out-of-doors."

"Well," said Jenny, "I have told you why, for I have been at Uncle Peter's in summer, and aunt does her spring-cleaning in May, and then she shuts all the blinds and drops all the curtains, and the house stays clean till October. That's the whole of it. If she had all her windows open, there would be paint and windows to be cleaned every week; and who is to do it? For my part, I can't much blame her."

"Well," said I, "I have my doubts about the sovereign efficacy of living in the dark, even if the great object of existence were to be rid of flies. I remember, during this same journey, stopping for a day or two at a country boarding-house, which was dark as Egypt from cellar to garret. The long, dim, gloomy dining-room was first closed by outside blinds, and then by impenetrable paper curtains, notwithstanding which it swarmed and buzzed like a beehive. You found where the cake plate was by the buzz which your hand made, if you chanced to reach in that direction. It was disagreeable, because in the darkness flies could not always be distinguished from huckleberries; and I couldn't help wishing, that, since we must have the flies, we might at last have the light and air to console us under them. People darken their rooms and shut up every avenue of outdoor enjoyment, and sit and think of nothing but flies; in fact, flies are all they have left. No wonder they become morbid on the subject."

"Well now, papa talks just like a man, doesn't he?" said Jenny. "He hasn't the responsibility of keeping things clean. I wonder what he would do, if he were a housekeeper."

"Do? I will tell you. I would do the best I could. I would shut my eyes on fly-specks, and open them on the beauties of Nature. I would let the cheerful sun in all day long, in all but the few summer days when coolness is the one thing needful: those days may be soon numbered every year. I would make a calculation in the spring how much it would cost to hire a woman to keep my windows and paint clean, and I would do with one less gown and have her; and when I had spent all I could afford on cleaning windows and paint, I would harden my heart and turn off my eyes, and enjoy my sunshine and my fresh air, my breezes, and all that can be seen through the picture windows of an open, airy house, and snap my fingers at the flies. There you have it."

"Papa's hobby is sunshine," said Marianne.

"Why shouldn't it be? Was God mistaken, when He made the sun? Did He make him for us to hold a life's battle with? Is that vital power which reddens the cheek of the peach and pours sweetness through the fruits and flowers of no use to us? Look at plants that grow without sun,—wan, pale, long-visaged, holding feeble, imploring hands of supplication towards the light. Can human beings afford to throw away a vitalizing force so pungent, so exhilarating? You remember the experiment of a prison where one row of cells had daily sunshine and the others none. With the same regimen, the same cleanliness, the same care, the inmates of the sunless cells were visited with sickness and death in double measure. Our whole population in New England are groaning and suffering under afflictions, the result of a depressed vitality, — neuralgia, with a new ache for every day of the year, rheumatism, consumption, general debility; for all these a thousand nostrums are daily advertised, and money enough is spent on them to equip an army, while we are fighting against, wasting, and throwing away with both hands, that blessed influence which comes nearest to pure vitality of anything God has given.

"Who is it that the Bible describes as a sun, arising with healing in his wings? Surely, that sunshine which is the chosen type and image of His love must be healing through all the recesses of our daily life, drying damp and mould, defending from moth and rust, sweetening ill smells, clearing from the nerves the vapors of melancholy, making life cheery. If I did not know Him, I should certainly adore and worship the sun, the most blessed and beautiful image of Him among things visible! In the land of Egypt, in the day of God's wrath, there was darkness, but in the land of Goshen there was light. I am a Goshenite, and mean to walk in the light, and forswear the works of darkness. But to proceed with our reading."

"Our house" shall be set on a southeast line, so that there shall not be a sunless room in it, and windows shall be so arranged that it can be traversed and transpierced through and through with those bright shafts of light which come straight from God.

"Our house" shall not be blockaded with a dank, dripping mass of shrubbery set plumb against the windows, keeping out light and air. There shall be room all round it for breezes to sweep, and sunshine to sweeten and dry and vivify; and I would warn all good souls who begin life by setting out two little evergreen-trees within a foot of each of their front-windows, that these trees will grow and increase till their front-rooms will be brooded over by a sombre, stifling shadow fit only for ravens to croak in.

One would think, by the way some people hasten to convert a very narrow front-yard into a dismal jungle, that the only danger of our New England climate was sunstroke. Ah, in those drizzling months which form at least one half of our life here, what sullen, censorious, uncomfortable, unhealthy thoughts are bred of living in dark, chilly rooms, behind such dripping thickets? Our neighbors' faults assume a deeper hue, life seems a dismal thing, our very religion grows mouldy.

My idea of a house is, that, as far as is consistent with shelter and reasonable privacy, it should give you on first entering an open, breezy, outdoor freshness of sensation. Every window should be a picture—sun and trees and clouds and green grass should seem never to be far from us. "Our house" may shade but not darken us. "Our house" shall have bow-windows, many, sunny, and airy,—not for the purpose of being cleaned and shut up, but to be open and enjoyed. There shall be long verandas above and below, where invalids may walk dry-shod, and enjoy open-air recreation in wettest weather. In short, I will try to have "our house" combine as far as possible the sunny, joyous, fresh life of a gypsy in the fields and woods with the quiet and neatness and comfort and shelter of a roof, rooms, floors, and carpets.

After heavenly fire, I have a word to say of earthly, artificial fires. Furnaces, whether of hot water, steam, or hot air, are all healthy and admirable provisions for warming our houses during the eight or nine months of our year that we must have artificial heat, if only, as I have said, fireplaces keep up a current of ventilation.

The kitchen-range with its water-back I humbly salute. It is a great throbbing heart, and sends its warm tides of cleansing, comforting fluid all through the house. One could wish that this friendly dragon could be in some way moderated in his appetite for coal,—he does consume without mercy, it must be confessed,—but then great is the work he has to do. At any hour of day or night, in the most distant part of your house, you have but to turn a stop-cock and your red dragon sends you hot water for your need; your washing-day becomes a mere play-day; your pantry has its ever-ready supply; and then, by a little judicious care in arranging apartments and economizing heat, a range may make two or three chambers comfortable in winter weather. A range with a water-back is among the *must-be's* in "our house."

Then, as to the evening light,—I know nothing as yet better than gas, where it can be had. I would certainly not have a house without it. The great objection to it is the danger of its escape through imperfect fixtures. But it must not do this: a fluid that kills a tree or a plant with one breath must certainly be a dangerous ingredient in the atmosphere, and if admitted into houses, must be introduced with every safeguard.

There are families living in the country who make their own gas by a very simple process. This is worth an inquiry from those who build. There are also contrivances now advertised, with good testimonials, of domestic machines for generating gas, said to be perfectly safe, simple to be managed, and producing a light superior to that of the city gas works. This also is worth an inquiry when "our house" is to be in the country.

And now I come to the next great vital element for which "our house" must provide, — WATER. "Water, water, everywhere," — it must be plentiful, it must be easy to get at, it must be pure. Our ancestors had some excellent ideas in home living and housebuilding. Their houses were, generally speaking, very sensibly contrived, — roomy, airy, and comfortable; but in their water arrangements they had little mercy on womankind. The well was out in the yard; and in winter one must flounder through snow and bring up the ice-bound bucket, before one could fill the tea-kettle for breakfast. For a sovereign princess of the republic, this was hardly respectful or respectable. Wells have come somewhat nearer in modern times; but the idea of a constant supply of fresh water by the simple turning of a stop-cock has not yet visited the great body of our houses. Were we free to build "our house" just as we wish it, there should be a bath-room to every two or three inmates, and the hot and cold water should circulate to every chamber.

Among our *must-be's*, we would lay by a generous sum for plumbing. Let us have our bath-rooms, and our arrangements for cleanliness and health in kitchen and pantry; and afterwards let the quality of our lumber and the style of our finishing be according to the sum we have left. The power to command a warm bath in a house at any hour of day or night is better in bringing up a family of children than any amount of ready medicine. In three quarters of childish ailments the warm bath is an almost immediate remedy. Bad colds, incipient fevers, rheumatisms, convulsions, neuralgias innumerable, are washed off in their first beginnings, and run down the lead pipes into oblivion. Have, then, O friend, all the water in your house that you can afford, and enlarge your ideas of the worth of it, that you *may* afford a great deal. A bathing-room is nothing to you that requires an hour of lifting and fire-making to prepare it for use. The apparatus is too cumbrous, — you do not turn to it. But when your chamber opens upon a neat, quiet little nook, and you have only to turn your stop-cocks and all is ready, your remedy is at hand, you use it constantly. You are waked in the night by a scream, and find little Tom sitting up, wild with burning fever. In three minutes he is in the bath, quieted and comfortable; you get him back, cooled and tranquil, to his little crib, and in the morning he wakes as if nothing had happened.

Why should not so invaluable and simple a remedy for disease, such a preservative of health, such a comfort, such a stimulus, be considered as much a matter-of-course in a house as a kitchen-chimney? At least there should be one bath-room always in order, so arranged that all the family can have access to it, if one cannot afford the luxury of many.

A house in which water is universally and skillfully distributed is so much easier to take care of as almost to verify the saying of a friend, that his house was so contrived that it did its own work: one had better do without carpets on the floors, without stuffed sofas and rocking-chairs, and secure this.

"Well, papa," said Marianne, "you have made out all your four elements in your house, except one. I can't imagine what you want of *earth*."

"I thought," said Jenny, "that the less of our common mother we had in our houses, the better housekeepers we were."

"My dears," said I, "we philosophers must give an occasional dip into the mystical, and say something apparently absurd for the purpose of explaining that we mean nothing in particular by it. It gives common people an idea of our sagacity, to find how clear we come out of our apparent contradictions and absurdities. Listen."

For the fourth requisite of "our house," EARTH, let me point you to your mother's plant-window, and beg you to remember the fact that through our long, dreary winters we are never a month without flowers, and the vivid interest which always attaches to growing things. The perfect house, as I conceive it, is to combine as many of the advantages of living out of doors as may be consistent with warmth and shelter, and one of these is the sympathy with green and growing things. Plants are nearer in their relations to human health and vigor than is often imagined. The cheerfulness that well-kept plants impart to a room comes not merely from gratification of the eye,—there is a healthful exhalation from them, they are a corrective of the impurities of the atmosphere. Plants, too, are valuable as tests of the vitality of the atmosphere; their drooping and failure convey to us information that something is amiss with it. A lady once told me that she could never raise plants in her parlors on account of the gas and anthracite coal. I answered, "Are you not afraid to live and bring up your children in an atmosphere which blights your plants?" If the gas escape from the pipes, and the red-hot anthracite coal or the red-hot air-tight stove burns out all the vital part of the air, so that healthy plants in a few days wither and begin to drop their leaves, it is sign that the air must be looked to and reformed. It is a fatal augury for a room that plants cannot be made to thrive in it. Plants should not turn pale, be long-jointed, long-leaved, and spindling; and where they grow in this way, we may be certain that there is a want of vitality for human beings. But where plants appear as they do in the open air, with vigorous, stocky growth, and short-stemmed, deep-green leaves, we may believe the conditions of that atmosphere are healthy for human lungs.

It is pleasant to see how the custom of plant growing has spread through our country. In how many farmhouse windows do we see petunias and nasturtiums vivid with bloom, while snows are whirling without, and how much brightness have those cheap enjoyments shed on the lives of those who cared for them! We do not believe there is a human being who would not become a passionate lover of plants, if circumstances once made it imperative to tend upon and watch the growth of one. The history of Picciola for substance has been lived over and over by many a man and woman who once did not know that there was a particle of plant-love in their souls. But to the proper care of plants in pots there are many hindrances and drawbacks. The dust chokes the little pores of their green lungs, and they require constant showering; and to carry all one's plants to a sink or porch for this purpose is a labor which many will not endure. Consequently plants often do not get a showering once a month! We should try to imitate more closely the action of Mother Nature, who washes every green child of hers nightly with dews, which lie glittering on its leaves till morning.

"Yes, there it is!" said Jenny. "I think I could manage with plants, if it were not for this eternal showering and washing they seem to require to keep them fresh. They are always tempting one to spatter the carpet and surrounding furniture, which are not equally benefited by the libation."

"It is partly for that very reason," I replied, "that the plan of 'our house' provides for the introduction of Mother Earth, as you will see."

A perfect house, according to my idea, should always include in it a little compartment where plants can be kept, can be watered, can be defended from the dust, and have the sunshine and all the conditions of growth.

People have generally supposed a conservatory to be one of the last trappings of wealth,—something not to be thought of for those in modest circumstances. But is this so? You have a bow-window in your parlor. Leave out the flooring, fill the space with rich earth, close it from the parlor by glass doors, and you have room for enough plants and flowers to keep you gay and happy all winter. If on the south side, where the sunbeams have power, it requires no heat but that which warms the parlor; and the comfort of it is incalculable, and the expense a mere trifle greater than that of the bow-window alone.

In larger houses a larger space might be appropriated in this way. We will not call it a conservatory, because that name suggests ideas of gardeners, and mysteries of culture and rare plants, which bring all sorts of care and expense in their train. We would rather call it a greenery, a room floored with earth, with glass sides to admit the sun,—and let it open on as many other rooms of the house as possible.

Why should not the dining-room and parlor be all winter connected by a spot of green and flowers, with plants, mosses, and ferns for the shadowy portions, and such simple blooms as petunias and nasturtiums garlanding the sunny portion near the windows? If near the water-works, this greenery might be enlivened by the play of a fountain, whose constant spray would give that softness to the air which is so often burned away by the dry heat of the furnace.

"And do you really think, papa, that houses built in this way are a practical result to be aimed at?" said Jenny. "To me it seems like a dream of the Alhambra."

"Yet I happen to have seen real people in our day living in just such a house," said I. "I could point you, this very hour, to a cottage, which in style of building is the plainest possible, which unites many of the best ideas of a true house. My dear, can you sketch the ground plan of that house we saw in Brighton?"

"Here it is," said my wife, after a few dashes with her pencil, "an inexpensive house, yet one of the pleasantest I ever saw."

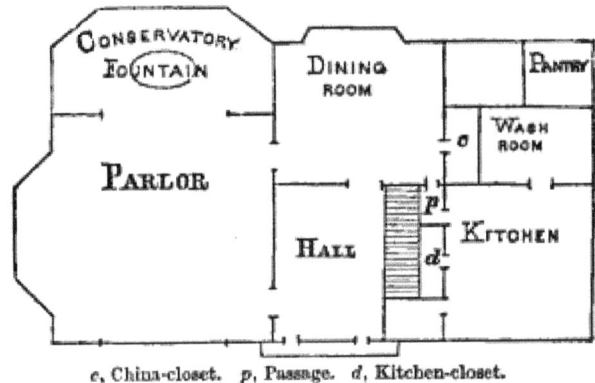

c, China-closet.   p, Passage.   d, Kitchen-closet.

"This cottage, which might, at the rate of prices before the war, have been built for five thousand dollars, has many of the requirements which I seek for a house. It has two stories, and a tier of very pleasant attic-rooms, two bathing-rooms, and the water carried into each story. The parlor and dining-room both look into a little bower, where a fountain is ever playing into a little marble basin, and which all the year through has its green and bloom. It is heated simply from the furnace by a register, like any other room of the house, and requires no more care than a delicate woman could easily give. The brightness and cheerfulness it brings during our long, dreary winters is incredible."

But one caution is necessary in all such appendages. The earth must be thoroughly underdrained to prevent the vapors of stagnant water, and have a large admixture of broken charcoal to obviate the consequences of vegetable decomposition. Great care must be taken that there be no leaves left to fall and decay on the ground, since vegetable exhalations poison the air. With these precautions such a plot will soften and purify the air of a house.

Where the means do not allow even so small a conservatory, a recessed window might be fitted with a deep box, which should have a drain-pipe at the bottom, and a thick layer of broken charcoal and gravel, with a mixture of fine wood-soil and sand, for the top stratum. Here ivies may be planted, which will run and twine and strike their little tendrils here and there, and give the room in time the aspect of a bower; the various greenhouse nasturtiums will make winter gorgeous with blossoms. In windows unblessed by sunshine—and, alas! such are many—one can cultivate ferns and mosses; the winter-growing ferns, of which there are many varieties, can be mixed with mosses and woodland flowers.

Early in February, when the cheerless frosts of winter seem most wearisome, the common blue violet, wood anemone, hepatica, or rock-columbine, if planted in this way, will begin to bloom. The common partridge-berry, with its brilliant scarlet fruit and dark-green leaves, will also grow finely in such situations, and have a beautiful effect. These things require daily showering to keep them fresh, and the moisture arising from them will soften and freshen the too dry air of heated winter rooms.

Thus I have been through my four essential elements in housebuilding,—air, fire, water, and earth. I would provide for these before anything else. After they are secured, I would gratify my taste and fancy as far as possible in other ways. I quite agree with Bob in hating commonplace houses, and longing for some little bit of architectural effect! and I grieve profoundly that every step in that direction must cost so much. I have also a taste for niceness of finish. I have no objection to silver-plated door-locks and hinges, none to windows which are an entire plate of clear glass. I congratulate neighbors who are so fortunate as to be able to get them; and after I have put all the essentials into a house, I would have these too, if I had the means.

But if all my wood work were to be without groove or moulding, if my mantels were to be of simple wood, if my doors were all to be machine-made, and my lumber of the second quality, I would have my bath-rooms, my conservatory, my sunny bow-windows, and my perfect ventilation; and my house would then be so pleasant, and every one in it in such a cheerful mood, that it would verily seem to be ceiled with cedar.

Speaking of ceiling with cedar, I have one thing more to say. We Americans have a country abounding in beautiful timber, of whose beauties we know nothing, on account of the pernicious and stupid habit of covering it with white paint.

The celebrated zebra wood with its golden stripes cannot exceed in quaint beauty the grain of unpainted chestnut, prepared simply with a coat or two of oil. The butternut has a rich golden brown, the very darling color of painters, a shade so rich, and grain so beautiful, that it is of itself as charming to look at as a rich picture. The black-walnut, with its heavy depth of tone, works in well as an adjunct; and as to oak, what can we say enough of its quaint and many shadings? Even common pine, which has been considered not decent to look upon till hastily shrouded in a friendly blanket of white paint, has, when oiled and varnished, the beauty of satin-wood. The second quality of pine, which has what are called *shakes* in it, under this mode of treatment often shows clouds and veins equal in beauty to the choicest woods. The cost of such a finish is greatly less than that of the old method; and it saves those days and weeks of cleaning which are demanded by white paint, while its general tone is softer and more harmonious. Experiments in color may be tried in the combinations of these woods, which at small expense produce the most charming effects.

As to paper hangings, we are proud to say that our American manufacturers now furnish all that can be desired. There are some branches of design where artistic, ingenious France must still excel us; but whoso has a house to fit up, let him first look at what his own country has to show, and he will be astonished.

There is one topic in housebuilding on which I would add a few words. The difficulty of procuring and keeping good servants, which must long be one of our chief domestic troubles, warns us so to arrange our houses that we shall need as few as possible. There is the greatest conceivable difference in the planning and building of houses as to the amount of work which will be necessary to keep them in respectable condition. Some houses require a perfect staff of housemaids: there are plated hinges to be rubbed, paint to be cleaned, with intricacies of moulding and carving which daily consume hours of dusting to preserve them from a slovenly look. Simple finish, unpainted wood, a general distribution of water through the dwelling, will enable a very large house to be cared for by one pair of hands, and yet maintain a creditable appearance.

In kitchens one servant may perform the work of two by a close packing of all the conveniences for cooking and such arrangements as shall save time and steps. Washing-day may be divested of its terrors by suitable provisions for water, hot and cold; by wringers, which save at once the strength of the linen and of the laundress; and by drying-closets connected with ranges, where articles can in a few moments be perfectly dried. These, with the use of a small mangle, such as is now common in America, reduce the labors of the laundry one half.

There are many more things which might be said of "our house," and Christopher may, perhaps, find some other opportunity to say them. For the present his pen is tired and ceaseth.

XII

HOME RELIGION

It was Sunday evening, and our little circle were convened by my study fireside, where a crackling hickory fire proclaimed the fall of the year to be coming on, and cold weather impending. Sunday evenings, my married boys and girls are fond of coming home and gathering round the old hearthstone, and "making believe" that they are children again. We get out the old-fashioned music-books, and sing old hymns to very old tunes, and my wife and her matron daughters talk about the babies in the intervals; and we discourse of the sermon, and of the choir, and all the general outworks of good pious things which Sunday suggests.

"Papa," said Marianne, "you are closing up your 'House and Home Papers,' are you not?"

"Yes, —I am come to the last one, for this year at least."

"My dear," said my wife, "there is one subject you haven't touched on yet; you ought not to close the year without it; no house and home can be complete without Religion: you should write a paper on Home Religion."

My wife, as you may have seen in these papers, is an old-fashioned woman, something of a conservative. I am, I confess, rather given to progress and speculation; but I feel always as if I were going on in these ways with a string round my waist, and my wife's hand steadily pulling me back into the old paths. My wife is a steady, Bible-reading, Sabbath-keeping woman, cherishing the memory of her fathers, and loving to do as they did, —believing, for the most part, that the paths well beaten by righteous feet are safest, even though much walking therein has worn away the grass and flowers. Nevertheless, she has an indulgent ear for all that gives promise of bettering anybody or anything, and therefore is not severe on any new methods that may arise in our progressive days of accomplishing old good objects.

"There must be a home religion," said my wife.

"I believe in home religion," said Bob Stephens, —"but not in the outward show of it. The best sort of religion is that which one keeps at the bottom of his heart, and which goes up thence quietly through all his actions, and not the kind that comes through a certain routine of forms and ceremonies. Do you suppose family prayers, now, and a blessing at meals, make people any better?"

"Depend upon it, Robert," said my wife,—she always calls him Robert on Sunday evenings,—"depend upon it, we are not so very much wiser than our fathers were, that we need depart from their good old ways. Of course I would have religion in the heart, and spreading quietly through the life; but does this interfere with those outward, daily acts of respect and duty which we owe to our Creator? It is too much the slang of our day to decry forms, and to exalt the excellency of the spirit in opposition to them; but tell me, are you satisfied with friendship that has none of the outward forms of friendship, or love that has none of the outward forms of love? Are you satisfied of the existence of a sentiment that has no outward mode of expression? Even the old heathen had their pieties; they would not begin a feast without a libation to their divinities, and there was a shrine in every well-regulated house for household gods."

"The trouble with all these things," said Bob, "is that they get to be mere forms. I never could see that family worship amounted to much more in most families."

"The outward expression of all good things is apt to degenerate into mere form," said I. "The outward expression of social good feeling becomes a mere form; but for that reason must we meet each other like oxen? not say, 'Good morning,' or 'Good evening,' or 'I am happy to see you'? Must we never use any of the forms of mutual good will, except in those moments when we are excited by a real, present emotion? What would become of society? Forms are, so to speak, a daguerreotype of a past good feeling, meant to take and keep the impression of it when it is gone. Our best and most inspired moments are crystallized in them; and even when the spirit that created them is gone, they help to bring it back. Every one must be conscious that the use of the forms of social benevolence, even towards those who are personally unpleasant to us, tends to ameliorate prejudices. We see a man entering our door who is a weary bore, but we use with him those forms of civility which society prescribes, and feel far kinder to him than if we had shut the door in his face and said, 'Go along, you tiresome fellow!' Now why does not this very obvious philosophy apply to better and higher feelings? The forms of religion are as much more necessary than the forms of politeness and social good will as religion is more important than all other things."

"Besides," said my wife, "a form of worship kept up from year to year in a family—the assembling of parents and children for a few sacred moments each day, though it may be a form many times, especially in the gay and thoughtless hours of life—often becomes invested with deep sacredness in times of trouble, or in those crises that rouse our deeper feelings. In sickness, in bereavement, in separation, the daily prayer at home has a sacred and healing power. Then we remember the scattered and wandering ones; and the scattered and wandering think tenderly of that hour when they know they are remembered. I know, when I was a young girl, I was often thoughtless and careless about family prayers; but now that my father and mother are gone forever, there is nothing I recall more often. I remember the great old Family Bible, the hymn-book, the chair where father used to sit. I see him as he looked bending over that Bible more than in any other way; and expressions and sentences in his prayers which fell unheeded on my ears in those days have often come back to me like comforting angels. We are not aware of the influence things are having on us till we have left them far behind in years. When we have summered and wintered them, and look back on them from changed times and other days, we find that they were making their mark upon us, though we knew it not."

"I have often admired," said I, "the stateliness and regularity of family worship in good old families in England,—the servants, guests, and children all assembled,—the reading of the Scriptures and the daily prayers by the master or mistress of the family, ending with the united repetition of the Lord's Prayer by all."

"No such assemblage is possible in our country," said Bob. "Our servants are for the most part Roman Catholics, and forbidden by their religion to join with us in acts of worship."

"The greater the pity," said I. "It is a pity that all Christians who can conscientiously repeat the Apostles' Creed and the Lord's Prayer together should for any reason be forbidden to do so. It would do more to harmonize our families, and promote good feeling between masters and servants, to meet once a day on the religious ground common to both, than many sermons on reciprocal duties."

"But, while the case is so," said Marianne, "we can't help it. Our servants cannot unite with us; our daily prayers are something forbidden to them."

"We cannot in this country," said I, "give to family prayer that solemn stateliness which it has in a country where religion is a civil institution, and masters and servants, as a matter of course, belong to one church. Our prayers must resemble more a private interview with a father than a solemn act of homage to a king. They must be more intimate and domestic. The hour of family devotion should be the children's hour,—held dear as the interval when the busy father drops his business and cares, and, like Jesus of old, takes the little ones in his arms and blesses them. The child should remember it as the time when the father always seemed most accessible and loving. The old family worship of New England lacked this character of domesticity and intimacy,—it was stately and formal, distant and cold; but, whatever were its defects, I cannot think it an improvement to leave it out altogether, as too many good sort of people in our day are doing. There may be practical religion where its outward daily forms are omitted, but there is assuredly no more of it for the omission. No man loves God and his neighbor *less*, is a *less* honest and good man, for daily prayers in his household,—the chances are quite the other way; and if the spirit of love rules the family hour, it may prove the source and spring of all that is good through the day. It seems to be a solemn duty in the parents thus to make the Invisible Fatherhood real to their children, who can receive this idea at first only through outward forms and observances. The little one thus learns that his father has a Father in heaven, and that the earthly life he is living is only a sacrament and emblem,—a type of the eternal life which infolds it, and of more lasting relations there. Whether, therefore, it be the silent grace and silent prayer of the Friends, or the form of prayer of ritual churches, or the extemporaneous outpouring of those whose habits and taste lead them to extempore prayer, in one of these ways there should be daily outward and visible acts of worship in every family."

"Well, now," said Bob, "about this old question of Sunday-keeping, Marianne and I are much divided. I am always for doing something that she thinks isn't the thing."

"Well, you see," said Marianne, "Bob is always talking against our old Puritan fathers, and saying all manner of hard things about them. He seems to think that all their ways and doings must of course have been absurd. For my part, I don't think we are in any danger of being too strict about anything. It appears to me that in this country there is a general tendency to let all sorts of old forms and observances float down-stream, and yet nobody seems quite to have made up his mind what shall come next."

"The fact is," said I, "that we realize very fully all the objections and difficulties of the experiments in living that we have tried; but the difficulties in others that we are intending to try have not yet come to light. The Puritan Sabbath had great and very obvious evils. Its wearisome restraints and over-strictness cast a gloom on religion, and arrayed against the day itself the active prejudices that now are undermining it and threatening its extinction. But it had great merits and virtues, and produced effects on society that we cannot well afford to dispense with. The clearing of a whole day from all possibilities of labor and amusement necessarily produced a grave and thoughtful people, and a democratic republic can be carried on by no other. In lands which have Sabbaths of mere amusement, mere gala days, republics rise and fall as quick as children's card-houses; and the reason is, they are built by those whose political and religious education has been childish. The common people of Europe have been sedulously nursed on amusements by the reigning powers, to keep them from meddling with serious matters; their religion has been sensuous and sentimental, and their Sabbaths thoughtless holidays. The common people of New England are educated to think, to reason, to examine all questions of politics and religion for themselves; and one deeply thoughtful day every week baptizes and strengthens their reflective and reasoning faculties. The Sunday-schools of Paris are whirligigs where Young France rides round and round on little hobby-horses till his brain spins even faster than Nature made it to spin; and when he grows up, his political experiments are as whirligig as his Sunday education. If I were to choose between the Sabbath of France and the old Puritan Sabbath, I should hold up both hands for the latter, with all its objectionable features."

"Well," said my wife, "cannot we contrive to retain all that is really valuable of the Sabbath, and to ameliorate and smooth away what is forbidding?"

"That is the problem of our day," said I. "We do not want the Sabbath of Continental Europe: it does not suit democratic institutions; it cannot be made even a quiet or a safe day, except by means of that ever-present armed police that exists there. If the Sabbath of America is simply to be a universal loafing, picnicking, dining-out day, as it is now with all our foreign population, we shall need what they have in Europe, the gendarmes at every turn, to protect the fruit on our trees and the melons in our fields. People who live a little out from great cities see enough, and more than enough, of this sort of Sabbath-keeping, with our loose American police.

"The fact is, our system of government was organized to go by moral influences as much as mills by water, and Sunday was the great day for concentrating these influences and bringing them to bear; and we might just as well break down all the dams and let out all the water of the Lowell mills, and expect still to work the looms, as to expect to work our laws and constitution with European notions of religion.

"It is true the Puritan Sabbath had its disagreeable points. So have the laws of Nature. They are of a most uncomfortable sternness and rigidity; yet for all that, we would hardly join in a petition to have them repealed, or made wavering and uncertain for human convenience. We can bend to them in a thousand ways, and live very comfortably under them."

"But," said Bob, "Sabbath-keeping is the iron rod of bigots; they don't allow a man any liberty of his own. One says it's wicked to write a letter Sunday; another holds that you must read no book but the Bible; and a third is scandalized if you take a walk, ever so quietly, in the fields. There are all sorts of quips and turns. We may fasten things with pins of a Sunday, but it's wicked to fasten with needle and thread, and so on, and so on; and each one, planting himself on his own individual mode of keeping Sunday, points his guns and frowns severely over the battlements on his neighbors whose opinions and practice are different from his."

"Yet," said I, "Sabbath days are expressly mentioned by Saint Paul as among those things concerning which no man should judge another. It seems to me that the error as regards the Puritan Sabbath was in representing it, not as a gift from God to man, but as a tribute of man to God. Hence all these hagglings and nice questions and exactions to the uttermost farthing. The holy time must be weighed and measured. It must begin at twelve o'clock of one night, and end at twelve o'clock of another; and from beginning to end, the mind must be kept in a state of tension by the effort not to think any of its usual thoughts or do any of its usual works. The fact is, that the metaphysical, defining, hair-splitting mind of New England, turning its whole powers on this one bit of ritual, this one only day of divine service, which was left of all the feasts and fasts of the old churches, made of it a thing straiter and stricter than ever the old Jews dreamed of.

"The old Jewish Sabbath entered only into the physical region, merely enjoining cessation from physical toil. 'Thou shalt not *labor* nor do any *work*,' covered the whole ground. In other respects than this it was a joyful festival, resembling, in the mode of keeping it, the Christmas of the modern church. It was a day of social hilarity, — the Jewish law strictly forbidding mourning and gloom during festivals.

The people were commanded on feast days to rejoice before the Lord their God with all their might. We fancy there were no houses where children were afraid to laugh, where the voice of social cheerfulness quavered away in terror lest it should awake a wrathful God. The Jewish Sabbath was instituted, in the absence of printing, of books, and of all the advantages of literature, to be the great means of preserving sacred history,—a day cleared from all possibility of other employment than social and family communion, when the heads of families and the elders of tribes might instruct the young in those religious traditions which have thus come down to us.

"The Christian Sabbath is meant to supply the same moral need in that improved and higher state of society which Christianity introduced. Thus it was changed from the day representing the creation of the world to the resurrection day of Him who came to make all things new. The Jewish Sabbath was buried with Christ in the sepulchre, and arose with Him, not a Jewish, but a Christian festival, still holding in itself that provision for man's needs which the old institution possessed, but with a wider and more generous freedom of application. It was given to the Christian world as a day of rest, of refreshment, of hope and joy, and of worship. The manner of making it such a day was left open and free to the needs and convenience of the varying circumstances and characters of those for whose benefit it was instituted."

"Well," said Bob, "don't you think there is a deal of nonsense about Sabbath-keeping?"

"There is a deal of nonsense about everything human beings have to deal with," I said.

"And," said Marianne, "how to find out what is nonsense?" —

"By clear conceptions," said I, "of what the day is for. I should define the Sabbath as a divine and fatherly gift to man,—a day expressly set apart for the cultivation of his moral nature. Its object is not merely physical rest and recreation, but moral improvement. The former are proper to the day only so far as they are subservient to the latter. The whole human race have the conscious need of being made better, purer, and more spiritual; the whole human race have one common danger of sinking to a mere animal life under the pressure of labor or in the dissipations of pleasure; and of the whole human race the proverb holds good, that what may be done any time is done at no time. Hence the Heavenly Father appoints one day as a special season for the culture of man's highest faculties. Accordingly, whatever ways and practices interfere with the purpose of the

173

Sabbath as a day of worship and moral culture should be avoided, and all family arrangements for the day should be made with reference thereto."

"Cold dinners on Sunday, for example," said Bob. "Marianne holds these as prime articles of faith."

"Yes,—they doubtless are most worthy and merciful, in giving to the poor cook one day she may call her own, and rest from the heat of range and cooking-stove. For the same reason, I would suspend as far as possible all traveling, and all public labor, on Sunday. The hundreds of hands that these things require to carry them on are the hands of human beings, whose right to this merciful pause of rest is as clear as their humanity. Let them have their day to look upward."

"But the little ones," said my oldest matron daughter, who had not as yet spoken,—"they are the problem. Oh, this weary labor of making children keep Sunday! If I try it, I have no rest at all myself. If I must talk to them or read to them to keep them from play, my Sabbath becomes my hardest working day."

"And, pray, what commandment of the Bible ever said children should not play on Sunday?" said I. "We are forbidden to work, and we see the reason why; but lambs frisk and robins sing on Sunday; and little children, who are as yet more than half animals, must not be made to keep the day in the manner proper to our more developed faculties. As much cheerful, attractive religious instruction as they can bear without weariness may be given, and then they may simply be restrained from disturbing others. Say to the little one, 'This day we have noble and beautiful things to think of that interest us deeply: you are a child; you cannot read and think and enjoy such things as much as we can; you may play softly and quietly, and remember not to make a disturbance.' I would take a child to public worship at least once of a Sunday; it forms a good habit in him. If the sermon be long and unintelligible, there are the little Sabbath-school books in every child's hands; and while the grown people are getting what they understand, who shall forbid a child's getting what is suited to him in a way that interests him and disturbs nobody? The Sabbath-school is the child's church and happily it is yearly becoming a more and more attractive institution. I approve the custom of those who beautify the Sabbath school-room with plants, flowers, and pictures, thus making it an attractive place to the childish eye. The more this custom prevails, the more charming in after years will be the memories of Sunday.

"It is most especially to be desired that the whole air and aspect of the day should be one of cheerfulness. Even the new dresses, new bonnets, and new shoes, in which children delight of a Sunday, should not be despised. They have their value in marking the day as a festival; and it is better for the child to long for Sunday, for the sake of his little new shoes, than that he should hate and dread it as a period of wearisome restraint. All the latitude should be given to children that can be, consistently with fixing in their minds the idea of a sacred season. I would rather that the atmosphere of the day should resemble that of a weekly Thanksgiving than that it should make its mark on the tender mind only by the memory of deprivations and restrictions."

"Well," said Bob, "here's Marianne always breaking her heart about my reading on Sunday. Now I hold that what is bad on Sunday is bad on Monday, — and what is good on Monday is good on Sunday."

"We cannot abridge other people's liberty," said I. "The generous, confiding spirit of Christianity has imposed not a single restriction upon us in reference to Sunday. The day is put at our disposal as a good Father hands a piece of money to his child, — 'There it is; take it and spend it well.' The child knows from his father's character what he means by spending it well, but he is left free to use his own judgment as to the mode.

"If a man conscientiously feels that reading of this or that description is the best for him as regards his moral training and improvement, let him pursue it, and let no man judge him. It is difficult, with the varying temperaments of men, to decide what are or are not religious books. One man is more religiously impressed by the reading of history or astronomy than he would be by reading a sermon. There may be overwrought and wearied states of the brain and nerves which require and make proper the diversions of light literature; and if so, let it be used. The mind must have its recreations as well as the body."

"But for children and young people," said my daughter, — "would you let them read novels on Sunday?"

"That is exactly like asking, Would you let them talk with people on Sunday? Now people are different; it depends, therefore, on who they are. Some are trifling and flighty, some are positively bad-principled, some are altogether good in their influence. So of the class of books called novels. Some are merely frivolous, some are absolutely noxious and dangerous, others again are written with a strong moral and religious purpose, and, being vivid and interesting, produce far more religious effect on the mind than dull treatises and sermons. The parables of Christ sufficiently establish the point that there is no inherent objection to the use of fiction in teaching religious truth. Good religious fiction, thoughtfully read, may be quite as profitable as any other reading."

"But don't you think," said Marianne, "that there is danger in too much fiction?"

"Yes," said I. "But the chief danger of all that class of reading is its *easiness*, and the indolent, careless mental habits it induces. A great deal of the reading of young people on all days is really reading to no purpose, its object being merely present amusement. It is a listless yielding of the mind to be washed over by a stream which leaves no fertilizing properties, and carries away by constant wear the good soil of thought. I should try to establish a barrier against this kind of reading, not only on Sunday, but on Monday, on Tuesday, and on all days. Instead, therefore, of objecting to any particular class of books for Sunday reading, I should say in general that reading merely for pastime, without any moral aim, is the thing to be guarded against. That which inspires no thought, no purpose, which steals away all our strength and energy, and makes the Sabbath a day of dreams, is the reading I would object to.

"So of music. I do not see the propriety of confining one's self to technical sacred music. Any grave, solemn, thoughtful, or pathetic music has a proper relation to our higher spiritual nature, whether it be printed in a church service-book or on secular sheets. On me, for example, Beethoven's Sonatas have a far more deeply religious influence than much that has religious names and words. Music is to be judged of by its effects."

"Well," said Bob, "if Sunday is given for our own individual improvement, I for one should not go to church. I think I get a great deal more good in staying at home and reading."

"There are two considerations to be taken into account in reference to this matter of church-going," I replied. "One relates to our duty as members of society in keeping up the influence of the Sabbath, and causing it to be respected in the community; the other, to the proper disposition of our time for our own moral improvement. As members of the community, we should go to church, and do all in our power to support the outward ordinances of religion. If a conscientious man makes up his mind that Sunday is a day for outward acts of worship and reverence, he should do his own part as an individual towards sustaining these observances. Even though he may have such mental and moral resources that as an individual he could gain much more in solitude than in a congregation, still he owes to the congregation the influence of his presence and sympathy. But I have never yet seen the man, however finely gifted morally and intellectually, whom I thought in the long run a gainer in either of these respects by the neglect of public worship. I have seen many who in their pride kept aloof from the sympathies and communion of their brethren, who lost strength morally, and deteriorated in ways that made themselves painfully felt. Sunday is apt in such cases to degenerate into a day of mere mental idleness and reverie, or to become a sort of waste-paper box for scraps, odds and ends of secular affairs.

"As to those very good people—and many such there are—who go straight on with the work of life on Sunday, on the plea that 'to labor is to pray,' I simply think they are mistaken. In the first place, to labor is *not* the same thing as to pray. It may sometimes be as good a thing to do, and in some cases even a better thing; but it is not the same thing. A man might as well never write a letter to his wife, on the plea that making money for her is writing to her. It may possibly be quite as great a proof of love to work for a wife as to write to her, but few wives would not say that both were not better than either alone. Furthermore, there is no doubt that the intervention of one day of spiritual rest and aspiration so refreshes a man's whole nature, and oils the many wheels of existence, that he who allows himself a weekly Sabbath does more work in the course of his life for the omission of work on that day.

"A young student in a French college, where the examinations are rigidly severe, found by experience that he succeeded best in his examination by allowing one day of entire rest just before it. His brain and nervous system refreshed in this way carried him through the work better than if taxed to the last moment. There are men transacting a large and complicated business who can testify to the same influence from the repose of the Sabbath.

"I believe those Christian people who from conscience and principle turn their thoughts most entirely out of the current of worldly cares on Sunday fulfill unconsciously a great law of health; and that, whether their moral nature be thereby advanced or not, their brain will work more healthfully and actively for it, even in physical and worldly matters. It is because the Sabbath thus harmonizes the physical and moral laws of our being that the injunction concerning it is placed among the ten great commandments, each of which represents some one of the immutable needs of humanity."

"There is yet another point of family religion that ought to be thought of," said my wife: "I mean the customs of mourning. If there is anything that ought to distinguish Christian families from Pagans, it should be their way of looking at and meeting those inevitable events that must from time to time break the family chain. It seems to be the peculiarity of Christianity to shed hope on such events. And yet it seems to me as if it were the very intention of many of the customs of society to add tenfold to their gloom and horror,—such swathings of black crape, such funereal mufflings of every pleasant object, such darkening of rooms, and such seclusion from society and giving up to bitter thoughts and lamentation. How can little children that look on such things believe that there is a particle of truth in all they hear about the joyous and comforting doctrines which the Bible holds forth for such times?"

"That subject is a difficult one," I rejoined. "Nature seems to indicate a propriety in some outward expressions of grief when we lose our friends. All nations agree in these demonstrations. In a certain degree they are soothing to sorrow; they are the language of external life made to correspond to the internal. Wearing mourning has its advantages. It is a protection to the feelings of the wearer, for whom it procures sympathetic and tender consideration; it saves grief from many a hard jostle in the ways of life; it prevents the necessity of many a trying explanation, and is the ready apology for many an omission of those tasks to which sorrow is unequal. For all these reasons I never could join the crusade which some seem disposed to wage against it. Mourning, however, ought not to be continued for years. Its uses are more for the first few months of sorrow, when it serves the mourner as a safeguard from intrusion, insuring quiet and leisure in which to reunite the broken threads of life, and to gather strength for a return to its duties. But to wear mourning garments and forego society for two or three years after the loss of any friend, however dear, I cannot but regard as a morbid, unhealthy nursing of sorrow, unworthy of a Christian."

"And yet," said my wife, "to such an unhealthy degree does this custom prevail, that I have actually known young girls who have never worn any other dress than mourning, and consequently never been into society, during the entire period of their girlhood. First, the death of a father necessitated three years of funereal garments and abandonment of social relations; then the death of a brother added two years more; and before that mourning was well ended, another of a wide circle of relatives being taken, the habitual seclusion was still protracted. What must a child think of the Christian doctrine of life and death who has never seen life except through black crape? We profess to believe in a better life to which the departed good are called,—to believe in the shortness of our separation, the certainty of reunion, and that all these events are arranged in all their relations by an infinite tenderness which cannot err. Surely, Christian funerals too often seem to say that affliction 'cometh of the dust,' and not from above."

"But," said Bob, "after all, death is a horror; you can make nothing less of it. You can't smooth it over, nor dress it with flowers; it is what Nature shudders at."

"It is precisely for this reason," said I, "that Christians should avoid those customs which aggravate and intensify this natural dread. Why overpower the senses with doleful and funereal images in the hour of weakness and bereavement, when the soul needs all her force to rise above the gloom of earth, and to realize the mysteries of faith? Why shut the friendly sunshine from the mourner's room? Why muffle in a white shroud every picture that speaks a cheerful household word to the eye? Why make a house look stiff and ghastly and cold as a corpse? In some of our cities, on the occurrence of a death in the family, all the shutters on the street are closed and tied with black crape, and so remain for months. What an oppressive gloom must this bring on a house! how like the very shadow of death! It is enlisting the nerves and the senses against our religion, and making more difficult the great duty of returning to life and its interests. I would have flowers and sunshine in the deserted rooms, and make them symbolical of the cheerful mansions above, to which our beloved ones are gone. Home ought to be so religiously cheerful, so penetrated by the life of love and hope and Christian faith, that the other world may be made real by it. Our home life should be a type of the higher life. Our home should be so sanctified, its joys and its sorrows so baptized and hallowed, that it shall not be sacrilegious to think of heaven as a higher form of the same thing,—a Father's house in the better country, whose mansions are many, whose love is perfect, whose joy is eternal."

THE CHIMNEY-CORNER

I

WHAT WILL YOU DO WITH HER? OR, THE WOMAN QUESTION

"Well, what will you do with her?" said I to my wife.

My wife had just come down from an interview with a pale, faded-looking young woman in rusty black attire, who had called upon me on the very common supposition that I was an editor of the "Atlantic Monthly."

By the by, this is a mistake that brings me, Christopher Crowfield, many letters that do not belong to me, and which might with equal pertinency be addressed, "To the Man in the Moon." Yet these letters often make my heart ache,—they speak so of people who strive and sorrow and want help; and it is hard to be called on in plaintive tones for help which you know it is perfectly impossible for you to give.

For instance, you get a letter in a delicate hand, setting forth the old distress,—she is poor, and she has looking to her for support those that are poorer and more helpless than herself: she has tried sewing, but can make little at it; tried teaching, but cannot now get a school,—all places being filled, and more than filled; at last has tried literature, and written some little things, of which she sends you a modest specimen, and wants your opinion whether she can gain her living by writing. You run over the articles, and perceive at a glance that there is no kind of hope or use in her trying to do anything at literature; and then you ask yourself mentally, "What is to be done with her? What can she do?"

Such was the application that had come to me this morning,—only, instead of by note, it came, as I have said, in the person of the applicant, a thin, delicate, consumptive-looking being, wearing that rusty mourning which speaks sadly at once of heart bereavement and material poverty.

My usual course is to turn such cases over to Mrs. Crowfield; and it is to be confessed that this worthy woman spends a large portion of her time, and wears out an extraordinary amount of shoe-leather, in performing the duties of a self-constituted intelligence office. Talk of giving money to the poor! what is that, compared to giving sympathy, thought, time, taking their burdens upon you, sharing their perplexities? They who are able to buy off every application at the door of their heart with a five or ten dollar bill are those who free themselves at least expense.

My wife had communicated to our friend, in the gentlest tones and in the blandest manner, that her poor little pieces, however interesting to her own household circle, had nothing in them wherewith to enable her to make her way in the thronged and crowded thoroughfare of letters,—that they had no more strength or adaptation to win bread for her than a broken-winged butterfly to draw a plough; and it took some resolution in the background of her tenderness to make the poor applicant entirely certain of this. In cases like this, absolute certainty is the very greatest, the only true kindness.

It was grievous, my wife said, to see the discouraged shade which passed over her thin, tremulous features when this certainty forced itself upon her. It is hard, when sinking in the waves, to see the frail bush at which the hand clutches uprooted; hard, when alone in the crowded thoroughfare of travel, to have one's last bank-note declared a counterfeit. I knew I should not be able to see her face, under the shade of this disappointment; and so, coward that I was, I turned this trouble, where I have turned so many others, upon my wife.

"Well, what shall we do with her?" said I.

"I really don't know," said my wife musingly.

"Do you think we could get that school in Taunton for her?"

"Impossible; Mr. Herbert told me he had already twelve applicants for it."

"Couldn't you get her plain sewing? Is she handy with her needle?"

"She has tried that, but it brings on a pain in her side, and cough; and the doctor has told her it will not do for her to confine herself."

"How is her handwriting? Does she write a good hand?"

"Only passable."

"Because," said I, "I was thinking if I could get Steele and Simpson to give her law papers to copy."

"They have more copyists than they need now; and, in fact, this woman does not write the sort of hand at all that would enable her to get on as a copyist."

"Well," said I, turning uneasily in my chair, and at last hitting on a bright masculine expedient, "I'll tell you what must be done. She must get married."

"My dear," said my wife, "marrying for a living is the very hardest way a woman can take to get it. Even marrying for love often turns out badly enough. Witness poor Jane."

Jane was one of the large number of people whom it seemed my wife's fortune to carry through life on her back. She was a pretty, smiling, pleasing daughter of Erin, who had been in our family originally as nursery-maid. I had been greatly pleased in watching a little idyllic affair growing up between her and a joyous, good-natured young Irishman, to whom at last we married her. Mike soon after, however, took to drinking and unsteady courses; and the result has been to Jane only a yearly baby, with poor health and no money.

"In fact," said my wife, "if Jane had only kept single, she could have made her own way well enough, and might have now been in good health and had a pretty sum in the savings bank. As it is, I must carry not only her, but her three children, on my back."

"You ought to drop her, my dear. You really ought not to burden yourself with other people's affairs as you do," said I inconsistently.

"How can I drop her? Can I help knowing that she is poor and suffering? And if I drop her, who will take her up?"

Now there is a way of getting rid of cases of this kind, spoken of in a quaint old book, which occurred strongly to me at this moment: —

"If a brother or sister be naked, and destitute of daily food, and one of you say unto them, 'Depart in peace, be ye warmed and filled,' notwithstanding ye give them not those things which are needful to the body, what doth it profit?"

I must confess, notwithstanding the strong point of the closing question, I looked with an evil eye of longing on this very easy way of disposing of such cases. A few sympathizing words, a few expressions of hope that I did not feel, a line written to turn the case into somebody else's hands, —any expedient, in fact, to hide the longing eyes and imploring hands from my sight, —was what my carnal nature at this moment greatly craved.

"Besides," said my wife, resuming the thread of her thoughts in regard to the subject just now before us, "as to marriage, it's out of the question at present for this poor child; for the man she loved and would have married lies low in one of the graves before Richmond. It's a sad story,—one of a thousand like it. She brightened for a few moments, and looked almost handsome, when she spoke of his bravery and goodness. Her father and lover have both died in this war. Her only brother has returned from it a broken-down cripple, and she has him and her poor old mother to care for, and so she seeks work. I told her to come again to-morrow, and I would look about for her a little to-day."

"Let me see, how many are now down on your list to be looked about for, Mrs. Crowfield?—some twelve or thirteen, are there not? You've got Tom's sister disposed of finally, I hope,—that's a comfort!"

"Well, I'm sorry to say she came back on my hands yesterday," said my wife patiently. "She is a foolish young thing, and said she didn't like living out in the country. I'm sorry, because the Morrises are an excellent family, and she might have had a life home there, if she had only been steady, and chosen to behave herself properly. But yesterday I found her back on her mother's hands again; and the poor woman told me that the dear child never could bear to be separated from her, and that she hadn't the heart to send her back."

"And in short," said I, "she gave you notice that you must provide for Miss O'Connor in some more agreeable way. Cross that name off your list, at any rate. That woman and girl need a few hard raps in the school of experience before you can do anything for them."

"I think I shall," said my long-suffering wife; "but it's a pity to see a young thing put in the direct road to ruin."

"It is one of the inevitables," said I, "and we must save our strength for those that are willing to help themselves."

"What's all this talk about?" said Bob, coming in upon us rather brusquely.

"Oh, as usual, the old question," said I,—"'What's to be done with her?'"

"Well," said Bob, "it's exactly what I've come to talk with mother about. Since she keeps a distressed women's agency office, I've come to consult her about Marianne. That woman will die before six months are out, a victim to high civilization and the Paddies. There we are, twelve miles out from Boston, in a country villa so convenient that every part of it might almost do its own work, — everything arranged in the most convenient, contiguous, self-adjusting, self-acting, patent-right, perfective manner, — and yet I tell you Marianne will die of that house. It will yet be recorded on her tombstone, 'Died of conveniences.' For myself, what I languish for is a log-cabin, with a bed in one corner, a trundle-bed underneath for the children, a fireplace only six feet off, a table, four chairs, one kettle, a coffee-pot, and a tin baker, — that's all. I lived deliciously in an establishment of this kind last summer, when I was up at Lake Superior; and I am convinced, if I could move Marianne into it at once, that she would become a healthy and a happy woman. Her life is smothered out of her with comforts; we have too many rooms, too many carpets, too many vases and knick-knacks, too much china and silver; she has too many laces and dresses and bonnets; the children all have too many clothes: in fact, to put it scripturally, our riches are corrupted, our garments are moth-eaten, our gold and our silver is cankered, and, in short, Marianne is sick in bed, and I have come to the agency office for distressed women to take you out to attend to her.

"The fact is," continued Bob, "that since our cook married, and Alice went to California, there seems to be no possibility of putting our domestic cabinet upon any permanent basis. The number of female persons that have been through our house, and the ravages they have wrought on it for the last six months, pass belief. I had yesterday a bill of sixty dollars' plumbing to pay for damages of various kinds which had had to be repaired in our very convenient water-works; and the blame of each particular one had been bandied like a shuttlecock among our three household divinities. Biddy privately assured my wife that Kate was in the habit of emptying dustpans of rubbish into the main drain from the chambers, and washing any little extra bits down through the bowls; and, in fact, when one of the bathing-room bowls had overflowed so as to damage the frescoes below, my wife, with great delicacy and precaution, interrogated Kate as to whether she had followed her instructions in the care of the water-pipes. Of course she protested the most immaculate care and circumspection. 'Sure, and she knew how careful one ought to be, and wasn't of the likes of thim as wouldn't mind what throuble they made, — like Biddy, who would throw trash and hair in the pipes, and niver listen to her tellin'; sure, and hadn't she broken the pipes in the kitchen, and lost the stoppers, as it was a shame to see in a Christian house?' Ann, the third girl, being privately questioned, blamed Biddy on Monday, and Kate on

Tuesday; on Wednesday, however, she exonerated both; but on Thursday, being in a high quarrel with both, she departed, accusing them severally, not only of all the evil practices aforesaid, but of lying and stealing, and all other miscellaneous wickednesses that came to hand. Whereat the two thus accused rushed in, bewailing themselves and cursing Ann in alternate strophes, averring that she had given the baby laudanum, and, taking it out riding, had stopped for hours with it in a filthy lane where the scarlet fever was said to be rife,—in short, made so fearful a picture that Marianne gave up the child's life at once, and has taken to her bed. I have endeavored all I could to quiet her, by telling her that the scarlet fever story was probably an extemporaneous work of fiction, got up to gratify the Hibernian anger at Ann; and that it wasn't in the least worth while to believe one thing more than another from the fact that any of the tribe said it. But she refuses to be comforted, and is so Utopian as to lie there crying, 'Oh, if I only could get one that I could trust,—one that would really speak the truth to me,—one that I might know really went where she said she went, and really did as she said she did!' To have to live so, she says, and bring up little children with those she can't trust out of her sight, whose word is good for nothing,—to feel that her beautiful house and her lovely things are all going to rack and ruin, and she can't take care of them, and can't see where or when or how the mischief is done,—in short, the poor child talks as women do who are violently attacked with housekeeping fever tending to congestion of the brain. She actually yesterday told me that she wished, on the whole, she never had got married, which I take to be the most positive indication of mental alienation."

"Here," said I, "we behold at this moment two women dying for the want of what they can mutually give one another,—each having a supply of what the other needs, but held back by certain invisible cobwebs, slight but strong, from coming to each other's assistance. Marianne has money enough, but she wants a helper in her family, such as all her money has been hitherto unable to buy; and here, close at hand, is a woman who wants home shelter, healthy, varied, active, cheerful labor, with nourishing food, kind care, and good wages. What hinders these women from rushing to the help of one another, just as two drops of water on a leaf rush together and make one? Nothing but a miserable prejudice,—but a prejudice so strong that women will starve in any other mode of life rather than accept competency and comfort in this."

"You don't mean," said my wife, "to propose that our protégée should go to Marianne as a servant?"

"I do say it would be the best thing for her to do,—the only opening that I see, and a very good one, too, it is. Just look at it. Her bare living at this moment cannot cost her less than five or six dollars a week,—everything at the present time is so very dear in the city. Now by what possible calling open to her capacity can she pay her board and washing, fuel and lights, and clear a hundred and some odd dollars a year? She could not do it as a district school teacher; she certainly cannot, with her feeble health, do it by plain sewing; she could not do it as a copyist. A robust woman might go into a factory and earn more; but factory work is unintermitted, twelve hours daily, week in and out, in the same movement, in close air, amid the clatter of machinery; and a person delicately organized soon sinks under it. It takes a stolid, enduring temperament to bear factory labor. Now look at Marianne's house and family, and see what is insured to your protégée there.

"In the first place, a home,—a neat, quiet chamber, quite as good as she has probably been accustomed to,—the very best of food, served in a pleasant, light, airy kitchen, which is one of the most agreeable rooms in the house, and the table and table service quite equal to those of most farmers and mechanics. Then her daily tasks would be light and varied,—some sweeping, some dusting, the washing and dressing of children, the care of their rooms and the nursery,—all of it the most healthful, the most natural work of a woman,—work alternating with rest, and diverting thought from painful subjects by its variety, and, what is more, a kind of work in which a good Christian woman might have satisfaction, as feeling herself useful in the highest and best way; for the child's nurse, if she be a pious, well-educated woman, may make the whole course of nursery life an education in goodness. Then, what is far different from any other modes of gaining a livelihood, a woman in this capacity can make and feel herself really and truly beloved. The hearts of little children are easily gained, and their love is real and warm, and no true woman can become the object of it without feeling her own life made brighter. Again, she would have in Marianne a sincere, warm-hearted friend, who would care for her tenderly, respect her sorrows, shelter her feelings, be considerate of her wants, and in every way aid her in the cause she has most at heart,—the succor of her family. There are many ways besides her wages in which she would infallibly be assisted by Marianne, so that the probability would be that she could send her little salary almost untouched to those for whose support she was toiling,—all this on her part."

"But," added my wife, "on the other hand, she would be obliged to associate and be ranked with common Irish servants."

"Well," I answered, "is there any occupation, by which any of us gain our living, which has not its disagreeable side? Does not the lawyer spend all his days either in a dusty office or in the foul air of a court-room? Is he not brought into much disagreeable contact with the lowest class of society? Are not his labors dry and hard and exhausting? Does not the blacksmith spend half his life in soot and grime, that he may gain a competence for the other half? If this woman were to work in a factory, would she not often be brought into associations distasteful to her? Might it not be the same in any of the arts and trades in which a living is to be got? There must be unpleasant circumstances about earning a living in any way, only I maintain that those which a woman would be likely to meet with as a servant in a refined, well-bred Christian family would be less than in almost any other calling. Are there no trials to a woman, I beg to know, in teaching a district school, where all the boys, big and little, of a neighborhood congregate? For my part, were it my daughter or sister who was in necessitous circumstances, I would choose for her a position such as I name, in a kind, intelligent, Christian family, before many of those to which women do devote themselves."

"Well," said Bob, "all this has a good sound enough, but it's quite impossible. It's true, I verily believe, that such a kind of servant in our family would really prolong Marianne's life years,—that it would improve her health, and be an unspeakable blessing to her, to me, and the children,—and I would almost go down on my knees to a really well-educated, good American woman who would come into our family and take that place; but I know it's perfectly vain and useless to expect it. You know we have tried the experiment two or three times of having a person in our family who should be on the footing of a friend, yet do the duties of a servant, and that we never could make it work well. These half-and-half people are so sensitive, so exacting in their demands, so hard to please, that we have come to the firm determination that we will have no sliding-scale in our family, and that whoever we are to depend on must come with bona fide willingness to take the position of a servant, such as that position is in our house; and that, I suppose, your protégée would never do, even if she could thereby live easier, have less hard work, better health, and quite as much money as she could earn in any other way."

"She would consider it a personal degradation, I suppose," said my wife.

"And yet, if she only knew it," said Bob, "I should respect her far more profoundly for her willingness to take that position, when adverse fortune has shut other doors."

"Well, now," said I, "this woman is, as I understand, the daughter of a respectable stone-mason, and the domestic habits of her early life have probably been economical and simple. Like most of our mechanics' daughters, she has received in one of our high schools an education which has cultivated and developed her mind far beyond those of her parents and the associates of her childhood. This is a common fact in our American life. By our high schools the daughters of plain workingmen are raised to a state of intellectual culture which seems to make the disposition of them in any kind of industrial calling a difficult one. They all want to teach school, —and schoolteaching, consequently, is an overcrowded profession, —and, failing that, there is only millinery and dressmaking. Of late, it is true, efforts have been made in various directions to widen their sphere. Typesetting and bookkeeping are in some instances beginning to be open to them.

"All this time there is lying, neglected and despised, a calling to which womanly talents and instincts are peculiarly fitted, —a calling full of opportunities of the most lasting usefulness; a calling which insures a settled home, respectable protection, healthful exercise, good air, good food, and good wages; a calling in which a woman may make real friends, and secure to herself warm affection: and yet this calling is the one always refused, shunned, contemned, left to the alien and the stranger, and that simply and solely because it bears the name of *servant*. A Christian woman, who holds the name of Christ in her heart in true devotion, would think it the greatest possible misfortune and degradation to become like him in taking upon her 'the form of a servant.' The founder of Christianity says: 'Whether is greater, he that sitteth at meat or he that serveth? But *I* am among you as he that serveth.' But notwithstanding these so plain declarations of Jesus, we find that scarce any one in a Christian land will accept real advantages of position and employment that come with that name and condition."

"I suppose," said my wife, "I could prevail upon this woman to do all the duties of the situation, if she could be, as they phrase it, 'treated as one of the family.'"

188

"That is to say," said Bob, "if she could sit with us at the same table, be introduced to our friends, and be in all respects as one of us. Now, as to this, I am free to say that I have no false aristocratic scruples. I consider every well-educated woman as fully my equal, not to say my superior; but it does not follow from this that she would be one whom I should wish to make a third party with me and my wife at meal-times. Our meals are often our seasons of privacy,—the times when we wish in perfect unreserve to speak of matters that concern ourselves and our family alone. Even invited guests and family friends would not be always welcome, however agreeable at times. Now a woman may be perfectly worthy of respect, and we may be perfectly respectful to her, whom nevertheless we do not wish to take into the circle of intimate friendship. I regard the position of a woman who comes to perform domestic service as I do any other business relation. We have a very respectable young lady in our employ who does legal copying for us, and all is perfectly pleasant and agreeable in our mutual relations; but the case would be far otherwise were she to take it into her head that we treated her with contempt, because my wife did not call on her, and because she was not occasionally invited to tea. Besides, I apprehend that a woman of quick sensibilities, employed in domestic service, and who was so far treated as a member of the family as to share our table, would find her position even more painful and embarrassing than if she took once for all the position of a servant. We could not control the feelings of our friends; we could not always insure that they would be free from aristocratic prejudice, even were we so ourselves. We could not force her upon their acquaintance, and she might feel far more slighted than she would in a position where no attentions of any kind were to be expected. Besides which, I have always noticed that persons standing in this uncertain position are objects of peculiar antipathy to the servants in full; that they are the cause of constant and secret cabals and discontents; and that a family where the two orders exist has always raked up in it the smouldering embers of a quarrel ready at any time to burst out into open feud."

"Well," said I, "here lies the problem of American life. Half our women, like Marianne, are being faded and made old before their time by exhausting endeavors to lead a life of high civilization and refinement with only such untrained help as is washed up on our shores by the tide of emigration. Our houses are built upon a plan that precludes the necessity of much hard labor, but requires rather careful and nice handling. A well-trained, intelligent woman, who had vitalized her finger-ends by means of a well-developed brain, could do all the work of such a house with comparatively little physical fatigue. So stands the case as regards our houses. Now, over against the women that are perishing in them from too much care, there is another class of American women that are wandering up and down, perishing for lack of some remunerating employment. That class of women, whose developed brains and less developed muscles mark them as peculiarly fitted for the performance of the labors of a high civilization, stand utterly aloof from paid domestic service. Sooner beg, sooner starve, sooner marry for money, sooner hang on as dependents in families where they know they are not wanted, than accept of a quiet home, easy, healthful work, and certain wages, in these refined and pleasant modern dwellings of ours."

"What is the reason of this?" said Bob.

"The reason is, that we have not yet come to the full development of Christian democracy. The taint of old aristocracies is yet pervading all parts of our society. We have not yet realized fully the true dignity of labor, and the surpassing dignity of domestic labor. And I must say that the valuable and courageous women who have agitated the doctrines of Woman's Rights among us have not in all things seen their way clear in this matter."

"Don't talk to me of those creatures," said Bob, "those men-women, those anomalies, neither flesh nor fish, with their conventions, and their cracked woman-voices strained in what they call public speaking, but which I call public squeaking! No man reverences true women more than I do. I hold a real, true, thoroughly good *woman*, whether in my parlor or my kitchen, as my superior. She can always teach me something that I need to know. She has always in her somewhat of the divine gift of prophecy; but in order to keep it, she must remain a woman. When she crops her hair, puts on pantaloons, and strides about in conventions, she is an abortion, and not a woman."

"Come! come!" said I, "after all, speak with deference. We that choose to wear soft clothing and dwell in kings' houses must respect the Baptists, who wear leathern girdles, and eat locusts and wild honey. They are the voices crying in the wilderness, preparing the way for a coming good. They go down on their knees in the mire of life to lift up and brighten and restore a neglected truth; and we that have not the energy to share their struggle should at least refrain from criticising their soiled garments and ungraceful action. There have been excrescences, eccentricities, peculiarities, about the camp of these reformers; but the body of them have been true and noble women, and worthy of all the reverence due to such. They have already in many of our States reformed the laws relating to woman's position, and placed her on a more just and Christian basis. It is through their movements that in many of our States a woman can hold the fruits of her own earnings, if it be her ill luck to have a worthless, drunken spendthrift for a husband. It is owing to their exertions that new trades and professions are opening to woman; and all that I have to say to them is, that in the suddenness of their zeal for opening new paths for her feet, they have not sufficiently considered the propriety of straightening, widening, and mending the one broad, good old path of domestic labor, established by God himself. It does appear to me, that, if at least a portion of their zeal could be spent in removing the stones out of this highway of domestic life, and making it pleasant and honorable, they would effect even more. I would not have them leave undone what they are doing; but I would, were I worthy to be considered, humbly suggest to their prophetic wisdom and enthusiasm, whether, in this new future of women which they wish to introduce, women's natural, God-given employment of *domestic service* is not to receive a new character, and rise in a new form.

"'To love and serve' is a motto worn with pride on some aristocratic family shields in England. It ought to be graven on the Christian shield. *Servant* is the name which Christ gives to the *Christian*; and in speaking of his kingdom as distinguished from earthly kingdoms, he distinctly said, that rank there should be conditioned, not upon desire to command, but on willingness to serve.

"'Ye know that the princes of the Gentiles exercise dominion over them, and they that are great exercise authority upon them. But it shall not be so among you: but whosoever will be great among you, let him be your minister; and whosoever will be chief among you, let him be your *servant*.'

"Why is it, that this name of servant, which Christ says is the highest in the kingdom of heaven, is so dishonored among us professing Christians, that good women will beg or starve, will suffer almost any extreme of poverty and privation, rather than accept home, competence, security, with this honored name?"

"The fault with many of our friends of the Woman's Rights order," said my wife, "is the depreciatory tone in which they have spoken of the domestic labors of a family as being altogether below the scope of the faculties of woman. '*Domestic drudgery*' they call it,—an expression that has done more harm than any two words that ever were put together.

"Think of a woman's calling clear-starching and ironing domestic drudgery, and to better the matter turning to typesetting in a grimy printing office! Call the care of china and silver, the sweeping of carpets, the arrangement of parlors and sitting-rooms, drudgery; and go into a factory and spend the day amid the whir and clatter and thunder of machinery, inhaling an atmosphere loaded with wool and machine grease, and keeping on the feet for twelve hours, nearly continuously! Think of its being called drudgery to take care of a clean, light, airy nursery, to wash and dress and care for two or three children, to mend their clothes, tell them stories, make them playthings, take them out walking or driving; and rather than this, to wear out the whole livelong day, extending often deep into the night, in endless sewing, in a close room of a dressmaking establishment! Is it any less drudgery to stand all day behind a counter, serving customers, than to tend a doorbell and wait on a table? For my part," said my wife, "I have often thought the matter over, and concluded, that, if I were left in straitened circumstances, as many are in a great city, I would seek a position as a servant in one of our good families."

"I envy the family that you even think of in that connection," said I. "I fancy the amazement which would take possession of them as you began to develop among them."

"I have always held," said my wife, "that family work, in many of its branches, can be better performed by an educated woman than an uneducated one. Just as an army where even the bayonets think is superior to one of mere brute force and mechanical training, so, I have heard it said, some of our distinguished modern female reformers show an equal superiority in the domestic sphere, —and I do not doubt it. Family work was never meant to be the special province of untaught brains. I have sometimes thought I should like to show what I could do as a servant."

"Well," said Bob, "to return from all this to the question, What's to be done with her? Are you going to *my* distressed woman? If you are, suppose you take *your* distressed woman along, and ask her to try it. I can promise her a pleasant house, a quiet room by herself, healthful and not too hard work, a kind friend, and some leisure for reading, writing, or whatever other pursuit of her own she may choose for her recreation. We are always quite willing to lend books to any who appreciate them. Our house is surrounded by pleasant grounds, which are open to our servants as to ourselves. So let her come and try us. I am quite sure that country air, quiet security, and moderate exercise in a good home, will bring up her health; and if she is willing to take the one or two disagreeables which may come with all this, let her try us."

"Well," said I, "so be it; and would that all the women seeking homes and employment could thus fall in with women who have homes and are perishing in them for want of educated helpers!"

On this question of woman's work I have yet more to say, but must defer it till another time.

II

WOMAN'S SPHERE

"What do you think of this Woman's Rights question?" said Bob Stephens. "From some of your remarks, I apprehend that you think there is something in it. I may be wrong, but I must confess that I have looked with disgust on the whole movement. No man reverences women as I do; but I reverence them *as* women. I reverence them for those very things in which their sex differs from ours; but when they come upon our ground, and begin to work and fight after our manner and with our weapons, I regard them as fearful anomalies, neither men nor women. These Woman's Rights Conventions appear to me to have ventilated crudities, absurdities, and blasphemies. To hear them talk about men, one would suppose that the two sexes were natural-born enemies, and wonder whether they ever had fathers and brothers. One would think, upon their showing, that all men were a set of ruffians, in league against women,—they seeming, at the same time, to forget how on their very platforms the most constant and gallant defenders of their rights are men. Wendell Phillips and Wentworth Higginson have put at the service of the cause masculine training and manly vehemence, and complacently accepted the wholesale abuse of their own sex at the hands of their warrior sisters. One would think, were all they say of female powers true, that our Joan-of-Arcs ought to have disdained to fight under male captains."

"I think," said my wife, "that, in all this talk about the rights of men, and the rights of women, and the rights of children, the world seems to be forgetting what is quite as important, the *duties* of men and women and children. We all hear of our *rights* till we forget our *duties*; and even theology is beginning to concern itself more with what man has a right to expect of his Creator than what the Creator has a right to expect of man."

"You say the truth," said I; "there is danger of just this overaction; and yet rights must be discussed; because, in order to understand the duties we owe to any class, we must understand their rights. To know our duties to men, women, and children, we must know what the rights of men, women, and children justly are. As to the 'Woman's Rights movement,' it is not peculiar to America, it is part of a great wave in the incoming tide of modern civilization; the swell is felt no less in Europe, but it combs over and breaks on our American shore, because our great wide beach affords the best play for its waters; and as the ocean waves bring with them kelp, seaweed, mud, sand, gravel, and even putrefying débris, which lie unsightly on the shore, and yet, on the whole, are healthful and refreshing, — so the Woman's Rights movement, with its conventions, its speech-makings, its crudities, and eccentricities, is nevertheless a part of a healthful and necessary movement of the human race towards progress. This question of Woman and her Sphere is now, perhaps, the greatest of the age. We have put Slavery under foot, and with the downfall of Slavery the only obstacle to the success of our great democratic experiment is overthrown, and there seems no limit to the splendid possibilities which it may open before the human race.

"In the reconstruction that is now coming there lies more than the reconstruction of States and the arrangement of the machinery of government. We need to know and feel, all of us, that, from the moment of the death of Slavery, we parted finally from the régime and control of all the old ideas formed under old oppressive systems of society, and came upon a new plane of life.

"In this new life we must never forget that we are a peculiar people, that we have to walk in paths unknown to the Old World, — paths where its wisdom cannot guide us, where its precedents can be of little use to us, and its criticisms, in most cases, must be wholly irrelevant. The history of our war has shown us of how little service to us in any important crisis the opinions and advice of the Old World can be. We have been hurt at what seemed to us the want of sympathy, the direct antagonism, of England. We might have been less hurt if we had properly understood that Providence had placed us in a position so far ahead of her ideas or power of comprehension that just judgment or sympathy was not to be expected from her.

"As we went through our great war with no help but that of God, obliged to disregard the misconceptions and impertinences which the foreign press rained down upon us, so, if we are wise, we shall continue to do. Our object must now be to make the principles on which our government is founded permeate consistently the mass of society, and to purge out the leaven of aristocratic and Old World ideas. So long as there is an illogical working in our actual life, so long as there is any class denied equal rights with other classes, so long will there be agitation and trouble."

"Then," said my wife, "you believe that women ought to vote?"

"If the principle on which we founded our government is true, that taxation must not exist without representation, and if women hold property and are taxed, it follows that women should be represented in the State by their votes, or there is an illogical working of our government."

"But, my dear, don't you think that this will have a bad effect on the female character?"

"Yes," said Bob, "it will make women caucus holders, political candidates."

"It may make this of some women, just as of some men," said I. "But all men do not take any great interest in politics; it is very difficult to get some of the best of them to do their duty in voting, and the same will be found true among women."

"But, after all," said Bob, "what do you gain? What will a woman's vote be but a duplicate of that of her husband or father, or whatever man happens to be her adviser?"

"That may be true on a variety of questions; but there are subjects on which the vote of women would, I think, be essentially different from that of men. On the subjects of temperance, public morals, and education, I have no doubt that the introduction of the female vote into legislation, in States, counties, and cities, would produce results very different from that of men alone. There are thousands of women who would close grog-shops, and stop the traffic in spirits, if they had the legislative power; and it would be well for society if they had. In fact, I think that a State can no more afford to dispense with the vote of women in its affairs than a family. Imagine a family where the female has no voice in the housekeeping! A State is but a larger family, and there are many of its concerns which, equally with those of a private household, would be bettered by female supervision."

"But fancy women going to those horrible voting-places! It is more than I can do myself," said Bob.

"But you forget," said I, "that they are horrible and disgusting principally because women never go to them. All places where women are excluded tend downward to barbarism; but the moment she is introduced, there come in with her courtesy, cleanliness, sobriety, and order. When a man can walk up to the ballot-box with his wife or his sister on his arm, voting-places will be far more agreeable than now, and the polls will not be such bear-gardens that refined men will be constantly tempted to omit their political duties there.

"If for nothing else, I would have women vote, that the business of voting may not be so disagreeable and intolerable to men of refinement as it now is; and I sincerely believe that the cause of good morals, good order, cleanliness, and public health would be a gainer not merely by the added feminine vote, but by the added vote of a great many excellent but too fastidious men, who are now kept from the polls by the disagreeables they meet there.

"Do you suppose that, if women had equal representation with men in the municipal laws of New York, its reputation for filth during the last year would have gone so far beyond that of Cologne, or any other city renowned for bad smells? I trow not. I believe a lady mayoress would have brought in a dispensation of brooms and whitewash, and made a terrible searching into dark holes and vile corners, before now. Female New York, I have faith to believe, has yet left in her enough of the primary instincts of womanhood to give us a clean, healthy city, if female votes had any power to do it."

"But," said Bob, "you forget that voting would bring together all the women of the lower classes."

"Yes; but, thanks to the instincts of their sex, they would come in their Sunday clothes; for where is the woman that hasn't her finery, and will not embrace every chance to show it? Biddy's parasol, and hat with pink ribbons, would necessitate a clean shirt in Pat as much as on Sunday. Voting would become a fête, and we should have a population at the polls as well-dressed as at church. Such is my belief."

"I do not see," said Bob, "but you go to the full extent with our modern female reformers."

"There are certain neglected truths, which have been held up by these reformers, that are gradually being accepted and infused into the life of modern society; and their recognition will help to solidify and purify democratic institutions. They are: —

"1. The right of every woman to hold independent property.

"2. The right of every woman to receive equal pay with man for work which she does equally well.

"3. The right of any woman to do any work for which, by her natural organization and talent, she is peculiarly adapted.

"Under the first head, our energetic sisters have already, by the help of their gallant male adjutants, reformed the laws of several of our States, so that a married woman is no longer left the unprotected legal slave of any unprincipled, drunken spendthrift who may be her husband,—but, in case of the imbecility or improvidence of the natural head of the family, the wife, if she have the ability, can conduct business, make contracts, earn and retain money for the good of the household; and I am sure no one can say that immense injustice and cruelty are not thereby prevented.

"It is quite easy for women who have the good fortune to have just and magnanimous husbands to say that they feel no interest in such reforms, and that they would willingly trust their property to the man to whom they give themselves; but they should remember that laws are not made for the restraint of the generous and just, but of the dishonest and base. The law which enables a married woman to hold her own property does not forbid her to give it to the man of her heart, if she so pleases; and it does protect many women who otherwise would be reduced to the extremest misery. I once knew an energetic milliner who had her shop attached four times, and a flourishing business broken up in four different cities, because she was tracked from city to city by a worthless spendthrift, who only waited till she had amassed a little property in a new place to swoop down upon and carry it off. It is to be hoped that the time is not distant when every State will give to woman a fair chance to the ownership and use of her own earnings and her own property.

"Under the head of the right of every woman to do any work for which by natural organization and talent she is especially adapted, there is a word or two to be said.

"The talents and tastes of the majority of women are naturally domestic. The family is evidently their sphere, because in all ways their organization fits them for that more than for anything else.

"But there are occasionally women who are exceptions to the common law, gifted with peculiar genius and adaptations. With regard to such women, there has never seemed to be any doubt in the verdict of mankind that they ought to follow their nature, and that their particular sphere was the one to which they are called. Did anybody ever think that Mrs. Siddons and Mrs. Kemble and Ristori had better have applied themselves sedulously to keeping house, because they were women, and 'woman's noblest station is retreat'?

"The world has always shown a fair average of good sense in this matter, from the days of the fair Hypatia in Alexandria, who, we are told, gave lectures on philosophy behind a curtain, lest her charms should distract the attention of too impressible young men, down to those of Anna Dickinson. Mankind are not, after all, quite fools, and seem in these cases to have a reasonable idea that exceptional talents have exceptional laws, and make their own code of proprieties.

"Now there is no doubt that Miss Dickinson, though as relating to her femininity she is quite as pretty and modest a young woman as any to be found in the most sheltered circle, has yet a most exceptional talent for public speaking, which draws crowds to hear her, and makes lecturing for her a lucrative profession, as well as a means of advocating just and generous sentiments, and of stimulating her own sex to nobler purposes; and the same law which relates to Siddons and Kemble and Ristori relates also to her.

"The doctrine of *vocations* is a good one and a safe one. If a woman mistakes her vocation, so much the worse for her; the world does not suffer, but she does, and the suffering speedily puts her where she belongs. There is not near so much danger from attempts to imitate Anna Dickinson as there is from the more common feminine attempts to rival the *demi-monde* of Paris in fantastic extravagance and luxury.

"As to how a woman may determine whether she has any such vocation, there is a story quite in point. A good Methodist elder was listening to an ardent young mechanic who thought he had a call to throw up his shop and go to preaching.

"'I feel,' said the young ardent, 'that I have a call to preach.'

"'Hast thou noticed whether people seem to have a call to hear thee?' said the shrewd old man. 'I have always noticed that a true call of the Lord may be known by this, that people have a *call* to hear.'"

"Well," said Bob, "the most interesting question still remains: What are to be the employments of woman? What ways are there for her to use her talents, to earn her livelihood and support those who are dear to her, when Providence throws that necessity upon her? This is becoming more than ever one of the pressing questions of our age. The war has deprived so many thousands of women of their natural protectors, that everything must be thought of that may possibly open a way for their self-support."

"Well, let us look over the field," said my wife. "What is there for woman?"

"In the first place," said I, "come the professions requiring natural genius,—authorship, painting, sculpture, with the subordinate arts of photographing, coloring, and finishing; but when all is told, these furnish employment to a very limited number,—almost as nothing to the whole. Then there is teaching, which is profitable in its higher branches, and perhaps the very pleasantest of all the callings open to woman; but teaching is at present an overcrowded profession, the applicants everywhere outnumbering the places. Architecture and landscape gardening are arts every way suited to the genius of woman, and there are enough who have the requisite mechanical skill and mathematical education; and, though never yet thought of for the sex, that I know of, I do not despair of seeing those who shall find in this field a profession at once useful and elegant. When women plan dwelling-houses, the vast body of tenements to be let in our cities will wear a more domestic and comfortable air, and will be built more with reference to the real wants of their inmates."

"I have thought," said Bob, "that agencies of various sorts, as canvassing the country for the sale of books, maps, and engravings, might properly employ a great many women. There is a large class whose health suffers from confinement and sedentary occupations, who might, I think, be both usefully and agreeably employed in business of this sort, and be recruiting their health at the same time."

"Then," said my wife, "there is the medical profession."

"Yes," said I. "The world is greatly obliged to Miss Blackwell and other noble pioneers who faced and overcame the obstacles to the attainment of a thorough medical education by females. Thanks to them, a new and lucrative profession is now open to educated women in relieving the distresses of their own sex; and we may hope that in time, through their intervention, the care of the sick may also become the vocation of cultivated, refined, intelligent women, instead of being left, as heretofore, to the ignorant and vulgar. The experience of our late war has shown us what women of a high class morally and intellectually can do in this capacity. Why should not this experience inaugurate a new and sacred calling for refined and educated women? Why should not NURSING become a vocation equal in dignity and in general esteem to the medical profession, of which it is the right hand? Why should our dearest hopes, in the hour of their greatest peril, be committed into the hands of Sairey Gamps, when the world has seen Florence Nightingales?"

"Yes, indeed," said my wife; "I can testify, from my own experience, that the sufferings and dangers of the sickbed, for the want of intelligent, educated nursing, have been dreadful. A prejudiced, pig-headed, snuff-taking old woman, narrow-minded and vulgar, and more confident in her own way than seven men that can render a reason, enters your house at just the hour and moment when all your dearest earthly hopes are brought to a crisis. She becomes absolute dictator over your delicate, helpless wife and your frail babe, — the absolute dictator of all in the house. If it be her sovereign will and pleasure to enact all sorts of physiological absurdities in the premises, who shall say her nay? 'She knows her business, she hopes!' And if it be her edict, as it was of one of her class whom I knew, that each of her babies shall eat four baked beans the day it is four days old, eat them it must; and if the baby die in convulsions four days after, it is set down as the mysterious will of an overruling Providence.

"I know and have seen women lying upon laced pillows, under silken curtains, who have been bullied and dominated over in the hour of their greatest helplessness by ignorant and vulgar tyrants, in a way that would scarce be thought possible in civilized society, and children that have been injured or done to death by the same means. A celebrated physician told me of a babe whose eyesight was nearly ruined by its nurse taking a fancy to wash its eyes with camphor, — 'to keep it from catching cold,' she said. I knew another infant that was poisoned by the nurse giving it laudanum in some of those patent nostrums which these ignorant creatures carry secretly in their pockets, to secure quiet in their little charges. I knew one delicate woman who never recovered from the effects of being left at her first confinement in the hands of an ill-tempered, drinking nurse, and whose feeble infant was neglected and abused by this woman in a way to cause lasting injury. In the first four weeks of infancy the constitution is peculiarly impressible; and infants of a delicate organization may, if frightened and ill-treated, be the subjects of just such a shock to the nervous system as in mature age comes from the sudden stroke of a great affliction or terror. A bad nurse may affect nerves predisposed to weakness in a manner they never will recover from. I solemnly believe that the constitutions of more women are broken up by bad nursing in their first confinement than by any other cause whatever. And yet there are at the same time hundreds and thousands of women, wanting the means of support, whose presence in a sick-room would be a benediction. I do trust that Miss Blackwell's band of educated nurses will not be long in coming, and that the number of such may increase till they effect a complete revolution in this vocation. A class of cultivated, well-trained, intelligent nurses would soon elevate the employment of attending on the sick into the noble calling it ought to be, and secure for it its appropriate rewards."

"There is another opening for woman," said I,—"in the world of business. The system of commercial colleges now spreading over our land is a new and most important development of our times. There that large class of young men who have either no time or no inclination for an extended classical education can learn what will fit them for that active material life which in our broad country needs so many workers. But the most pleasing feature of these institutions is, that the complete course is open to women no less than to men, and women there may acquire that knowledge of bookkeeping and accounts, and of the forms and principles of business transactions, which will qualify them for some of the lucrative situations hitherto monopolized by the other sex. And the expenses of the course of instruction are so arranged as to come within the scope of very moderate means. A fee of fifty dollars entitles a woman to the benefit of the whole course, and she has the privilege of attending at any hours that may suit her own engagements and convenience."

"Then, again," said my wife, "there are the departments of millinery and dressmaking, and the various branches of needlework, which afford employment to thousands of women; there is typesetting, by which many are beginning to get a living; there are the manufactures of cotton, woolen, silk, and the numberless useful articles which employ female hands in their fabrication,—all of them opening avenues by which, with more or less success, a subsistence can be gained."

"Well, really," said Bob, "it would appear, after all, that there are abundance of openings for women. What is the cause of the outcry and distress? How is it that we hear of women starving, driven to vice and crime by want, when so many doors of useful and profitable employment stand open to them?"

"The question would easily be solved," said my wife, "if you could once see the kind and class of women who thus suffer and starve. There may be exceptions, but too large a portion of them are girls and women who can or will do no earthly thing well,—and, what is worse, are not willing to take the pains to be taught to do anything well. I will describe to you one girl, and you will find in every intelligence-office a hundred of her kind to five thoroughly trained ones.

"Imprimis: she is rather delicate and genteel-looking, and you may know from the arrangement of her hair just what the last mode is of disposing of rats or waterfalls. She has a lace bonnet with roses, a silk mantilla, a silk dress trimmed with velvet, a white skirt with

202

sixteen tucks and an embroidered edge, a pair of cloth gaiters, underneath which are a pair of stockings without feet, the only pair in her possession. She has no under-linen, and sleeps at night in the working-clothes she wears in the day. She never seems to have in her outfit either comb, brush, or tooth-brush of her own,—neither needles, thread, scissors, nor pins; her money, when she has any, being spent on more important articles, such as the lace bonnet or silk mantilla, or the rats and waterfalls that glorify her head. When she wishes to sew, she borrows what is needful of a convenient next neighbor; and if she gets a place in a family as second girl, she expects to subsist in these respects by borrowing of the better-appointed servants, or helping herself from the family stores.

"She expects, of course, the very highest wages, if she condescends to live out; and by help of a trim outside appearance, and the many vacancies that are continually occurring in households, she gets places, where her object is to do just as little of any duty assigned to her as possible, to hurry through her performances, put on her fine clothes, and go a-gadding. She is on free-and-easy terms with all the men she meets, and ready at jests and repartee, sometimes far from seemly. Her time of service in any one place lasts indifferently from a fortnight to two or three months, when she takes her wages, buys her a new parasol in the latest style, and goes back to the intelligence-office. In the different families where she has lived she has been told a hundred times the proprieties of household life, how to make beds, arrange rooms, wash china, glass, and silver, and set tables; but her habitual rule is to try in each place how small and how poor services will be accepted. When she finds less will not do, she gives more. When the mistress follows her constantly, and shows an energetic determination to be well served, she shows that she can serve well; but the moment such attention relaxes, she slides back again. She is as destructive to a house as a fire; the very spirit of wastefulness is in her; she cracks the china, dents the silver, stops the water-pipes with rubbish, and, after she is gone, there is generally a sum equal to half her wages to be expended in repairing the effects of her carelessness. And yet there is one thing to be said for her: she is quite as careful of her employer's things as of her own. The full amount of her mischiefs often does not appear at once, as she is glib of tongue, adroit in apologies, and lies with as much alertness and as little thought of conscience as a blackbird chatters. It is difficult for people who have been trained from childhood in the school of verities,—who have been lectured for even the shadow of a prevarication, and shut up in disgrace for a lie, till truth becomes a habit of their souls,—it is very difficult for people so educated to understand how to get on with those who never speak the truth except by mere accident, who assert any and every thing that comes into their heads with all the assurance and all the energy of perfect verity.

"What becomes of this girl? She finds means, by begging, borrowing, living out, to keep herself extremely trim and airy for a certain length of time, till the rats and waterfalls, the lace hat and parasol, and the glib tongue, have done their work in making a fool of some honest young mechanic who earns three dollars a day. She marries him with no higher object than to have somebody to earn money for her to spend. And what comes of such marriages?

"That is one ending of her career; the other is on the street, in haunts of vice, in prison, in drunkenness, and death.

"Whence come these girls? They are as numerous as yellow butterflies in autumn; they flutter up to cities from the country; they grow up from mothers who ran the same sort of career before them; and the reason why in the end they fall out of all reputable employment and starve on poor wages is, that they become physically, mentally, and morally incapable of rendering any service which society will think worth paying for."

"I remember," said I, "that the head of the most celebrated dressmaking establishment in New York, in reply to the appeals of the needlewomen of the city for sympathy and wages, came out with published statements to this effect: that the difficulty lay, not in unwillingness of employers to pay what work was worth, but in finding any work worth paying for; that she had many applicants, but among them few who could be of real use to her; that she, in common with everybody in this country who has any kind of serious responsibilities to carry, was continually embarrassed for want of skilled work-people who could take and go on with the labor of her various departments without her constant supervision; that, out of a hundred girls, there would not be more than five to whom she could give a dress to be made and dismiss it from her mind as something certain to be properly done.

"Let people individually look around their own little sphere, and ask themselves if they know any woman really excelling in any valuable calling or accomplishment who is suffering for want of work. All of us know seamstresses, dressmakers, nurses, and laundresses who have made themselves such a reputation, and are so beset and overcrowded with work, that the whole neighborhood is constantly on its knees to them with uplifted hands. The fine seamstress, who can cut and make trousseaus and layettes in elegant perfection, is always engaged six months in advance; the pet dressmaker of a neighborhood must be engaged in May for September, and in September for May; a laundress who sends your clothes home in nice order always has all the work that she can do. Good work in any department is the rarest possible thing in our American life; and it is a fact that the great majority of workers, both in the family and out, do only tolerably well,—not so badly that it actually cannot be borne, yet not so well as to be a source of real, thorough satisfaction. The exceptional worker in every neighborhood, who does things really *well*, can always set her own price, and is always having more offering than she can possibly do.

"The trouble, then, in finding employment for women lies deeper than the purses or consciences of the employers: it lies in the want of education in women; the want of *education*, I say,—meaning by education that which fits a woman for practical and profitable employment in life, and not mere common-school learning."

"Yes," said my wife; "for it is a fact that the most troublesome and helpless persons to provide for are often those who have a good medium education, but no feminine habits, no industry, no practical calculation, no muscular strength, and no knowledge of any one of woman's peculiar duties. In the earlier days of New England, women, as a class, had far fewer opportunities for acquiring learning, yet were far better educated, physically and morally, than now. The high school did not exist; at the common school they learned reading, writing, and arithmetic, and practiced spelling; while at home they did the work of the household. They were cheerful, bright, and active, ever on the alert, able to do anything, from the harnessing and driving of a horse to the finest embroidery. The daughters of New England in those days looked the world in the face without a fear. They shunned no labor; they were afraid of none; and they could always find their way to a living."

"But although less instructed in school learning," said I, "they showed no deficiency in intellectual acumen. I see no such women, nowadays, as some I remember of that olden time,—women whose strong minds and ever-active industry carried on reading and study side by side with household toils.

"I remember a young lady friend of mine, attending a celebrated boarding-school, boarded in the family of a woman who had never been to school longer than was necessary to learn to read and write, yet who was a perfect cyclopedia of general information. The young scholar used to take her Chemistry and Natural Philosophy into the kitchen, where her friend was busy with her household work, and read her lessons to her, that she might have the benefit of her explanations; and so, while the good lady scoured her andirons or kneaded her bread, she lectured to her protégée on mysteries of science far beyond the limits of the textbook. Many of the graduates of our modern high schools would find it hard to shine in conversation on the subjects they had studied, in the searching presence of some of these vigorous matrons of the olden time, whose only school had been the leisure hours gained by energy and method from their family cares."

"And in those days," said my wife, "there lived in our families a class of American domestics, women of good sense and good powers of reflection, who applied this sense and power of reflection to household matters. In the early part of my married life, I myself had American 'help'; and they were not only excellent servants, but trusty and invaluable friends. But now, all this class of applicants for domestic service have disappeared, I scarce know why or how. All I know is, there is no more a Betsey or a Lois, such as used to take domestic cares off my shoulders so completely."

"Good heavens! where are they?" cried Bob. "Where do they hide? I would search through the world after such a prodigy!"

"The fact is," said I, "there has been a slow and gradual reaction against household labor in America. Mothers began to feel that it was a sort of *curse*, to be spared, if possible, to their daughters; women began to feel that they were fortunate in proportion as they were able to be entirely clear of family responsibilities. Then Irish labor began to come in, simultaneously with a great advance in female education.

"For a long while nothing was talked of, written of, thought of, in teachers' meetings, conventions, and assemblies, but the neglected state of female education; and the whole circle of the arts and sciences was suddenly introduced into our free-school system, from which needlework as gradually and quietly was suffered to drop out. The girl who attended the primary and high school had so much study imposed on her that she had no time for sewing or housework; and the delighted mother was only too happy to darn her stockings and do the housework alone, that her daughter might rise to a higher plane than she herself had attained to. The daughter, thus educated, had, on coming to womanhood, no solidity of muscle, no manual dexterity, no practice or experience in domestic life; and if she were to seek a livelihood, there remained only teaching, or some feminine trade, or the factory."

"These factories," said my wife, "have been the ruin of hundreds and hundreds of our once healthy farmers' daughters and others from the country. They go there young and unprotected; they live there in great boarding-houses, and associate with a promiscuous crowd, without even such restraints of maternal supervision as they would have in great boarding-schools; their bodies are enfeebled by labor often necessarily carried on in a foul and heated atmosphere; and at the hours when off duty, they are exposed to all the dangers of unwatched intimacy with the other sex.

"Moreover, the factory girl learns and practices but one thing, — some one mechanical movement, which gives no scope for invention, ingenuity, or any other of the powers called into play by domestic labor; so that she is in reality unfitted in every way for family duties.

"Many times it has been my lot to try, in my family service, girls who have left factories; and I have found them wholly useless for any of the things which a woman ought to be good for. They knew nothing of a house, or what ought to be done in it; they had imbibed a thorough contempt of household labor, and looked upon it but as a *dernier ressort*; and it was only the very lightest of its tasks that they could even begin to think of. I remember I tried to persuade one of these girls, the pretty daughter of a fisherman, to take some lessons in washing and ironing. She was at that time engaged to be married to a young mechanic, who earned something like two or three dollars a day.

"'My child,' said I, 'you will need to understand all kinds of housework if you are going to be married.'

"She tossed her little head, —

"'Indeed, she wasn't going to trouble herself about that.'

"'But who will get up your husband's shirts?'

"'Oh, he must put them out. I'm not going to be married to make a slave of myself!'

"Another young factory girl, who came for table and parlor work, was so full of airs and fine notions that it seemed as difficult to treat with her as with a princess. She could not sweep, because it blistered her hands, which, in fact, were long and delicate; she could not think of putting them into hot dish-water, and for that reason preferred washing the dishes in cold water; she required a full hour in the morning to make her toilet; she was laced so tightly that she could not stoop without vertigo; and her hoops were of dimensions which seemed to render it impossible for her to wait upon table; she was quite exhausted with the effort of ironing the table-napkins and chamber-towels: yet she could not think of 'living out' under two dollars a week.

"Both these girls had had a good free-school education, and could read any amount of novels, write a tolerable letter, but had not learned anything with sufficient accuracy to fit them for teachers. They were pretty, and their destiny was to marry and lie a deadweight on the hands of some honest man, and to increase, in their children, the number of incapables."

"Well," said Bob, "what would you have? What is to be done?"

"In the first place," said I, "I would have it felt, by those who are seeking to elevate woman, that the work is to be done, not so much by creating for her new spheres of action as by elevating her conceptions of that domestic vocation to which God and Nature have assigned her. It is all very well to open to her avenues of profit and advancement in the great outer world; but, after all, *to make and keep a home* is, and ever must be, a woman's first glory, her highest aim. No work of art can compare with a perfect home; the training and guiding of a family must be recognized as the highest work a woman can perform; and female education ought to be conducted with special reference to this.

"Men are trained to be lawyers, to be physicians, to be mechanics, by long and self-denying study and practice. A man cannot even make shoes merely by going to the high school and learning reading, writing, and mathematics; he cannot be a bookkeeper or a printer simply from general education.

"Now women have a sphere and profession of their own, — a profession for which they are fitted by physical organization, by their own instincts, and to which they are directed by the pointing and manifest finger of God, — and that sphere is *family life*. Duties to the state and to public life they may have; but the public duties of women must bear to their family ones the same relation that the family duties of men bear to their public ones. The defect in the late efforts to push on female education is, that it has been for her merely general, and that it has left out and excluded all that is professional; and she undertakes the essential duties of womanhood, when they do devolve on her, without any adequate preparation."

"But is it possible for a girl to learn at school the things which fit for her family life?" said Bob.

"Why not?" I replied. "Once it was thought impossible in school to teach girls geometry or algebra, or the higher mathematics; it was thought impossible to put them through collegiate courses; but it has been done, and we see it. Women study treatises on political economy in schools, and why should not the study of domestic economy form a part of every school course? A young girl will stand up at the blackboard, and draw and explain the compound blowpipe, and describe all the processes of making oxygen and hydrogen. Why should she not draw and explain a refrigerator as well as an air-pump? Both are to be explained on philosophical principles. When a schoolgirl, in her chemistry, studies the reciprocal action of acids and alkalies, what is there to hinder the teaching her its application to the various processes of cooking where acids and alkalies are employed? Why should she not be led to see how effervescence and fermentation can be made to perform their office in the preparation of light and digestible bread? Why should she not be taught the chemical substances by which food is often adulterated, and the test by which such adulterations are detected? Why should she not understand the processes of confectionery, and know how to guard against the deleterious or poisonous elements that are introduced into children's sugar-plums and candies? Why, when she learns the doctrine of mordants, the substances by which different colors are set, should she not learn it with some practical view to future life, so that she may know how to set the color of a fading calico or restore the color of a spotted one? Why, in short, when a girl has labored through a profound chemical work, and listened to courses of chemical lectures, should she come to domestic life, which presents a constant series of chemical experiments and changes, and go blindly along as without chart or compass, unable to tell what will take out a stain, or what will brighten a metal, what are common poisons and what their antidotes, and not knowing enough of the laws of caloric to understand how to warm a house, or of the laws of atmosphere to know how to ventilate one? Why should the preparation of food, that subtile art on which life, health, cheerfulness, good temper, and good looks so largely depend, forever be left in the hands of the illiterate and vulgar?

"A benevolent gentleman has lately left a large fortune for the founding of a university for women; and the object is stated to be to give to women who have already acquired a general education the means of acquiring a professional one, to fit themselves for some employment by which they may gain a livelihood.

"In this institution the women are to be instructed in bookkeeping, stenography, telegraphing, photographing, drawing, modeling, and various other arts; but, so far as I remember, there is no proposal to teach domestic economy as at least *one* of woman's professions.

"Why should there not be a professor of domestic economy in every large female school? Why should not this professor give lectures, first on house planning and building, illustrated by appropriate apparatus? Why should not the pupils have presented to their inspection models of houses planned with reference to economy, to ease of domestic service, to warmth, to ventilation, and to architectural appearance? Why should not the professor go on to lecture further on house-fixtures, with models of the best mangles, washing-machines, clothes-wringers, ranges, furnaces, and cooking-stoves, together with drawings and apparatus illustrative of domestic hydraulics, showing the best contrivances for bathing-rooms and the obvious principles of plumbing, so that the pupils may have some idea how to work the machinery of a convenient house when they have it, and to have such conveniences introduced when wanting? If it is thought worth while to provide at great expense apparatus for teaching the revolutions of Saturn's moons and the precession of the equinoxes, why should there not be some also to teach what it may greatly concern a woman's earthly happiness to know?

"Why should not the professor lecture on home chemistry, devoting his first lecture to bread-making? and why might not a batch of bread be made and baked and exhibited to the class, together with specimens of morbid anatomy in the bread line, — the sour cotton bread of the baker; the rough, big-holed bread; the heavy, fossil bread; the bitter bread of too much yeast, — and the causes of their defects pointed out? And so with regard to the various articles of food, — why might not chemical lectures be given on all of them, one after another? In short, it would be easy to trace out a course of lectures on common things to occupy a whole year, and for which the pupils, whenever they come to have homes of their own, will thank the lecturer to the last day of their life.

"Then there is no impossibility in teaching needlework, the cutting and fitting of dresses, in female schools. The thing is done very perfectly in English schools for the working classes. A girl trained at one of these schools came into a family I once knew. She brought with her a sewing-book, in which the process of making various articles was exhibited in miniature. The several parts of a shirt were first shown, each perfectly made, and fastened to a leaf of the book by itself, and then the successive steps of uniting the parts, till finally appeared a miniature model of the whole. The sewing was done with red thread, so that every stitch might show, and any imperfections be at once remedied. The same process was pursued with regard to other garments, and a good general idea of cutting and fitting them was thus given to an entire class of girls.

"In the same manner the care and nursing of young children and the tending of the sick might be made the subject of lectures. Every woman ought to have some general principles to guide her with regard to what is to be done in case of the various accidents that may befall either children or grown people, and of their lesser illnesses, and ought to know how to prepare comforts and nourishment for the sick. Hawthorne's satirical remarks upon the contrast between the elegant Zenobia's conversation, and the smoky porridge she made for him when he was an invalid, might apply to the volunteer cookery of many charming women."

"I think," said Bob, "that your Professor of Domestic Economy would find enough to occupy his pupils."

"In fact," said I, "were domestic economy properly honored and properly taught, in the manner described, it would open a sphere of employment to so many women in the home life, that we should not be obliged to send our women out to California or the Pacific to put an end to an anxious and aimless life.

"When domestic work is sufficiently honored to be taught as an art and science in our boarding-schools and high-schools, then possibly it may acquire also dignity in the eyes of our working classes, and young girls who have to earn their own living may no longer feel degraded in engaging in domestic service. The place of a domestic in a family may become as respectable in their eyes as a place in a factory, in a printing-office, in a dressmaking or millinery establishment, or behind the counter of a shop.

"In America there is no class which will confess itself the lower class, and a thing recommended solely for the benefit of any such class finds no one to receive it.

"If the intelligent and cultivated look down on household work with disdain; if they consider it as degrading, a thing to be shunned by every possible device,—they may depend upon it that the influence

211

of such contempt of woman's noble duties will flow downward, producing a like contempt in every class in life.

"Our sovereign princesses learn the doctrine of equality very quickly, and are not going to sacrifice themselves to what is not considered *de bon ton* by the upper classes; and the girl with the laced hat and parasol, without underclothes, who does her best to 'shirk' her duties as housemaid, and is looking for marriage as an escape from work, is a fair copy of her mistress, who married for much the same reason, who hates housekeeping, and would rather board or do anything else than have the care of a family. The one is about as respectable as the other.

"When housekeeping becomes an enthusiasm, and its study and practice a fashion, then we shall have in America that class of persons to rely on for help in household labors who are now going to factories, to printing-offices, to every kind of toil, forgetful of the best life and sphere of woman."

III

A FAMILY TALK ON RECONSTRUCTION

Our Chimney-Corner, of which we have spoken somewhat, has, besides the wonted domestic circle, its habitués who have a frequent seat there. Among these, none is more welcome than Theophilus Thoro.

Friend Theophilus was born on the shady side of Nature, and endowed by his patron saint with every grace and gift which can make a human creature worthy and available, except the gift of seeing the bright side of things. His bead-roll of Christian virtues includes all the graces of the spirit except hope; and so, if one wants to know exactly the flaw, the defect, the doubtful side, and to take into account all the untoward possibilities of any person, place, or thing, he had best apply to friend Theophilus. He can tell you just where and how the best-laid scheme is likely to fail, just the screw that will fall loose in the smoothest-working machinery, just the flaw in the most perfect character, just the defect in the best-written book, just the variety of thorn that must accompany each particular species of rose.

Yet Theophilus is without guile or malice. His want of faith in human nature is not bitter and censorious, but melting and pitiful. "We are all poor trash, miserable dogs together," he seems to say, as he looks out on the world and its ways. There is not much to be expected of or for any of us; but let us love one another and be patient.

Accordingly, Theophilus is one of the most incessant workers for human good, and perseveringly busy in every scheme of benevolent enterprise, in all which he labors with melancholy steadiness without hope. In religion he has the soul of a martyr,—nothing would suit him better than to be burned alive for his faith; but his belief in the success of Christianity is about on a par with that of the melancholy disciple of old, who, when Christ would go to Judæa, could only say, "Let us also go, that we may die with him." Theophilus is always ready to die for the truth and the right, for which he never sees anything but defeat and destruction ahead.

During the late war, Theophilus has been a despairing patriot, dying daily, and giving all up for lost in every reverse from Bull Run to Fredericksburg. The surrender of Richmond and the capitulation of Lee shortened his visage somewhat; but the murder of the President soon brought it back to its old length. It is true that, while Lincoln lived, he was in a perpetual state of dissent from all his measures. He had broken his heart for years over the miseries of the slaves, but he shuddered at the Emancipation Proclamation; a whirlwind of anarchy was about to sweep over the country, in which the black and the white would dash against each other, and be shivered like potters' vessels. He was in despair at the accession of Johnson, believing the worst of the unfavorable reports that clouded his reputation. Nevertheless he was among the first of loyal citizens to rally to the support of the new administration, because, though he had no hope in that, he could see nothing better.

You must not infer from all this that friend Theophilus is a social wet blanket, a goblin shadow at the domestic hearth. By no means. Nature has gifted him with that vein of humor and that impulse to friendly joviality which are frequent developments in sad-natured men, and often deceive superficial observers as to their real character. He who laughs well and makes you laugh is often called a man of cheerful disposition, yet in many cases nothing can be further from it than precisely this kind of person.

Theophilus frequents our chimney-corner, perhaps because Mrs. Crowfield and myself are, so to speak, children of the light and the day. My wife has precisely the opposite talent to that of our friend. She can discover the good point, the sound spot, where others see only defect and corruption. I myself am somewhat sanguine, and prone rather to expect good than evil, and with a vast stock of faith in the excellent things that may turn up in the future. The millennium is one of the prime articles of my creed; and all the ups and downs of society I regard only as so many jolts on a very rough road that is taking the world on, through many upsets and disasters, to that final consummation.

Theophilus holds the same belief theoretically; but it is apt to sink so far out of sight in the mire of present disaster as to be of very little comfort to him.

"Yes," he said, "we are going to ruin, in my view, about as fast as we can go. Miss Jenny, I will trouble you for another small lump of sugar in my tea."

"You have been saying that, about our going to ruin, every time you have taken tea here for four years past," said Jenny; "but I always noticed that your fears never spoiled your relish either for tea or muffins. People talk about being on the brink of a volcano, and the country going to destruction, and all that, just as they put pepper on

214

their potatoes; it is an agreeable stimulant in conversation,—that's all."

"For my part," said my wife, "I can speak in another vein. When had we ever in all our history so bright prospects, so much to be thankful for? Slavery is abolished; the last stain of disgrace is wiped from our national honor. We stand now before the world self-consistent with our principles. We have come out of one of the severest struggles that ever tried a nation, purer and stronger in morals and religion, as well as more prosperous in material things."

"My dear madam, excuse me," said Theophilus; "but I cannot help being reminded of what an English reviewer once said,—that a lady's facts have as much poetry in them as Tom Moore's lyrics. Of course poetry is always agreeable, even though of no statistical value."

"I see no poetry in my facts," said Mrs. Crowfield. "Is not slavery forever abolished, by the confession of its best friends,—even of those who declare its abolition a misfortune, and themselves ruined in consequence?"

"I confess, my dear madam, that we have succeeded, as we human creatures commonly do, in supposing that we have destroyed an evil, when we have only changed its name. We have contrived to withdraw from the slave just that fiction of property relation which made it for the interest of some one to care for him a little, however imperfectly; and, having destroyed that, we turn him out defenseless to shift for himself in a community every member of which is embittered against him. The whole South resounds with the outcries of slaves suffering the vindictive wrath of former masters; laws are being passed hunting them out of this State and out of that; the animosity of race—at all times the most bitter and unreasonable of animosities—is being aroused all over the land. And the free States take the lead in injustice to them. Witness a late vote of Connecticut on the suffrage question. The efforts of government to protect the rights of these poor defenseless creatures are about as energetic as such efforts always have been and always will be while human nature remains what it is. For a while the obvious rights of the weaker party will be confessed, with some show of consideration, in public speeches; they will be paraded by philanthropic sentimentalists, to give point to their eloquence; they will be here and there sustained in governmental measures, when there is no strong temptation to the contrary, and nothing better to be done; but the moment that political combinations begin to be formed, all the rights and interests of this helpless people will be bandied about as so many make-weights in the political scale. Any troublesome lion will have a negro thrown to him to keep him quiet. All their hopes will be dashed to the ground by the imperious Southern white, no longer feeling for them even the interest of a master, and regarding them with a mixture of hatred and loathing as the cause of all his reverses. Then if, driven to despair, they seek to defend themselves by force, they will be crushed by the power of the government and ground to powder, as the weak have always been under the heel of the strong.

"So much for our abolition of slavery. As to our material prosperity, it consists of an inflated paper currency, an immense debt, a giddy, foolhardy spirit of speculation and stock-gambling, and a perfect furor of extravagance, which is driving everybody to live beyond his means, and casting contempt on the republican virtues of simplicity and economy.

"As to advancement in morals, there never was so much intemperance in our people before, and the papers are full of accounts of frauds, defalcations, forgeries, robberies, assassinations, and arsons. Against this tide of corruption the various organized denominations of religion do nothing effectual. They are an army shut up within their own intrenchments, holding their own with difficulty, and in no situation to turn back the furious assaults of the enemy."

"In short," said Jenny, "according to your showing, the whole country is going to destruction. Now, if things really are so bad, if you really believe all you have been saying, you ought not to be sitting drinking your tea as you are now, or to have spent the afternoon playing croquet with us girls; you ought to gird yourself with sackcloth, and go up and down the land, raising the alarm, and saying, 'Yet forty days and Nineveh shall be overthrown.'"

"Well," said Theophilus, while a covert smile played about his lips, "you know the saying, 'Let us eat and drink, for to-morrow,' etc. Things are not yet gone to destruction, only going, — and why not have a good time on deck before the ship goes to pieces? Your chimney-corner is a tranquil island in the ocean of trouble, and your muffins are absolutely perfect. I'll take another, if you'll please to pass them."

"I've a great mind not to pass them," said Jenny. "Are you in earnest in what you are saying, or are you only saying it for sensation? How can people believe such things and be comfortable? I could not. If I believed all you have been saying I could not sleep nights,—I should be perfectly miserable; and *you* cannot really believe all this, or you would be."

"My dear child," said Mrs. Crowfield, "our friend's picture is the truth painted with all its shadows and none of its lights. All the dangers he speaks of are real and great, but he omits the counterbalancing good. Let *me* speak now. There never has been a time in our history when so many honest and just men held power in our land as now,—never a government before in which the public councils recognized with more respect the just and the right. There never was an instance of a powerful government showing more tenderness in the protection of a weak and defenseless race than ours has shown in the care of the freedmen hitherto. There never was a case in which the people of a country were more willing to give money and time and disinterested labor to raise and educate those who have thus been thrown on their care. Considering that we have had a great, harassing, and expensive war on our hands, I think the amount done by government and individuals for the freedmen unequaled in the history of nations; and I do not know why it should be predicted from this past fact that, in the future, both government and people are about to throw them to the lions, as Mr. Theophilus supposes. Let us wait, at least, and see. So long as government maintains a freedmen's bureau, administered by men of such high moral character, we must think, at all events, that there are strong indications in the right direction. Just think of the immense advance of public opinion within four years, and of the grand successive steps of this advance,—Emancipation in the District of Columbia, the Repeal of the Fugitive Slave Law, the General Emancipation Act, the Amendment of the Constitution. All these do not look as if the black were about to be ground to powder beneath the heel of the white. If the negroes are oppressed in the South, they can emigrate; no laws hold them; active, industrious laborers will soon find openings in any part of the Union."

"No," said Theophilus, "there will be black laws like those of Illinois and Tennessee; there will be turbulent uprisings of the Irish, excited by political demagogues, that will bar them out of Northern States. Besides, as a class, they *will* be idle and worthless. It will not be their fault, but it will be the result of their slave education. All their past observation of their masters has taught them that liberty means licensed laziness, that work means degradation; and therefore they will loathe work, and cherish laziness as the sign of liberty. 'Am not I free? Have I not as good a right to do nothing as you?' will be the cry.

"Already the lazy whites, who never lifted a hand in any useful employment, begin to raise the cry that 'niggers won't work;' and I suspect the cry may not be without reason. Industrious citizens can never be made in a community where the higher class think useful labor a disgrace. The whites will oppose the negro in every effort to rise; they will debar him of every civil and social right; they will set him the worst possible example, as they have been doing for hundreds of years; and then they will hound and hiss at him for being what they made him. This is the old track of the world,—the good, broad, reputable road on which all aristocracies and privileged classes have been always traveling; and it's not likely that we shall have much of a secession from it. The millennium isn't so near us as that, by a great deal."

"It's all very well arguing from human selfishness and human sin in that way," said I; "but you can't take up a newspaper that doesn't contain abundant facts to the contrary. Here, now,"—and I turned to the "Tribune,"—"is one item that fell under my eye accidentally, as you were speaking:—

"'The Superintendent of Freedmen's Affairs in Louisiana, in making up his last Annual Report, says he has 1,952 blacks settled temporarily on 9,650 acres of land, who last year raised crops to the value of $175,000, and that he had but few worthless blacks under his care; and that, as a class, the blacks have fewer vagrants than can be found among any other class of persons.'

"Such testimonies gem the newspapers like stars."

"Newspapers of your way of thinking, very likely," said Theophilus; "but if it comes to statistics, I can bring counter-statements, numerous and dire, from scores of Southern papers, of vagrancy, laziness, improvidence, and wretchedness."

"Probably both are true," said I, "according to the greater or less care which has been taken of the blacks in different regions. Left to themselves, they tend downward, pressed down by the whole weight of semi-barbarous white society; but when the free North protects and guides, the results are as you see."

"And do you think the free North has salt enough in it to save this whole Southern mass from corruption? I wish I could think so; but all I can see in the free North at present is a raging, tearing, headlong chase after *money*. Now money is of significance only as it gives people the power of expressing their ideal of life. And what does this ideal prove to be among us? Is it not to ape all the splendors and vices of old aristocratic society? Is it not to be able to live in idleness, without useful employment, a life of glitter and flutter and show? What do our New York dames of fashion seek after? To avoid family care, to find servants at any price who will relieve them of home responsibilities, and take charge of their houses and children while they shine at ball and opera, and drive in the park. And the servants who learn of these mistresses,—what do they seek after? *They* seek also to get rid of care, to live as nearly as possible without work, to dress and shine in their secondary sphere, as the mistresses do in the primary one. High wages with little work and plenty of company express Biddy's ideal of life, which is a little more respectable than that of her mistress, who wants high wages with no work. The house and the children are not Biddy's; and why should she care more for their well-being than the mistress and the mother?

"Hence come wranglings and moanings. Biddy uses a chest of tea in three months, and the amount of the butcher's bill is fabulous; Jane gives the baby laudanum to quiet it, while she slips out to *her* parties; and the upper classes are shocked at the demoralized state of the Irish, their utter want of faithfulness and moral principle! How dreadful that there are no people who enjoy the self-denials and the cares which they dislike, that there are no people who rejoice in carrying that burden of duties which they do not wish to touch with one of their fingers! The outcry about the badness of servants means just this: that everybody is tired of self-helpfulness,—the servants as thoroughly as the masters and mistresses. All want the cream of life, without even the trouble of skimming; and the great fight now is, who shall drink the skim-milk, which nobody wants. *Work*,—honorable toil,—manly, womanly endeavor,—is just what nobody likes; and this is as much a fact in the free North as in the slave South.

"What are all the young girls looking for in marriage? Some man with money enough to save them from taking any care or having any trouble in domestic life, enabling them, like the lilies of the field, to rival Solomon in all his glory, while they toil not, neither do they spin; and when they find that even money cannot purchase freedom from care in family life, because their servants are exactly of the same mind with themselves, and hate to do their duties as cordially as they themselves do, then are they in anguish of spirit, and wish for slavery, or aristocracy, or anything that would give them power over the lower classes."

"But surely, Mr. Theophilus," said Jenny, "there is no sin in disliking trouble, and wanting to live easily and have a good time in one's life,—it's so very natural."

"No sin, my dear, I admit; but there is a certain amount of work and trouble that somebody must take to carry on the family and the world; and the mischief is, that all are agreed in wanting to get rid of it. Human nature is above all things lazy. I am lazy myself. Everybody is. The whole struggle of society is as to who shall eat the hard bread-and-cheese of labor, which must be eaten by somebody. Nobody wants it,—neither you in the parlor, nor Biddy in the kitchen.

"'The mass ought to labor, and we lie on sofas,' is a sentence that would unite more subscribers than any confession of faith that ever was presented, whether religious or political; and its subscribers would be as numerous and sincere in the free States as in the slave States, or I am much mistaken in my judgment. The negroes are men and women, like any of the rest of us, and particularly apt in the imitation of the ways and ideas current in good society; and consequently to learn to play on the piano and to have nothing in particular to do will be the goal of aspiration among colored girls and woman, and to do housework will seem to them intolerable drudgery, simply because it is so among the fair models to whom they look up in humble admiration. You see, my dear, what it is to live in a democracy. It deprives us of the vantage-ground on which we cultivated people can stand and say to our neighbor,—'The cream is for me, and the skim-milk for you; the white bread for me, and the brown for you. I am born to amuse myself and have a good time, and you are born to do everything that is tiresome and disagreeable to me.' The 'My Lady Ludlows' of the Old World can stand on their platform and lecture the lower classes from the Church Catechism, to 'order themselves lowly and reverently to all their betters;' and they can base their exhortations on the old established law of society by which some are born to inherit the earth, and live a life of ease and pleasure, and others to toil without pleasure or amusement, for their support and aggrandizement. An aristocracy, as I take it, is a combination of human beings to divide life into two parts, one of which shall comprise all social and moral advantages, refinement, elegance, leisure, ease, pleasure, and amusement,—and the other, incessant toil, with the absence of every privilege and blessing of human existence. Life thus divided, we aristocrats keep the good for ourselves and our children, and distribute the evil as the lot of the general mass of mankind. The desire to monopolize and to dominate is the most rooted form of human selfishness; it is the hydra with many heads, and, cut off in one place, it puts out in another.

"Nominally, the great aristocratic arrangement of American society has just been destroyed; but really, I take it, the essential *animus* of the slave system still exists, and pervades the community, North as well as South. Everybody is wanting to get the work done by somebody else, and to take the money himself; the grinding between employers and employed is going on all the time, and the field of controversy has only been made wider by bringing in a whole new class of laborers. The Irish have now the opportunity to sustain their aristocracy over the negro. Shall they not have somebody to look down upon?

"All through free society, employers and employed are at incessant feud; and the more free and enlightened the society, the more bitter the feud. The standing complaint of life in America is the badness of servants; and England, which always follows at a certain rate behind us in our social movements, is beginning to raise very loudly the same complaint. The condition of service has been thought worthy of public attention in some of the leading British prints; and Ruskin, in a summing-up article, speaks of it as a deep ulcer in society, —a thing hopeless of remedy."

"My dear Mr. Theophilus," said my wife, "I cannot imagine whither you are rambling, or to what purpose you are getting up these horrible shadows. You talk of the world as if there were no God in it, overruling the selfishness of men, and educating it up to order and justice. I do not deny that there is a vast deal of truth in what you say. Nobody doubts that, in general, human nature *is* selfish, callous, unfeeling, willing to engross all good to itself, and to trample on the rights of others. Nevertheless, thanks to God's teaching and fatherly care, the world has worked along to the point of a great nation founded on the principles of strict equality, forbidding all monopolies, aristocracies, privileged classes, by its very constitution; and now, by God's wonderful providence, this nation has been brought, and forced, as it were, to overturn and abolish the only aristocratic institution that interfered with its free development. Does not this look as if a Mightier Power than ours were working in and for us, supplementing our weakness and infirmity? and if we believe that man is always ready to drop everything and let it run back to evil, shall we not have faith that God will *not* drop the noble work he has so evidently taken in hand in this nation?"

"And I want to know," said Jenny, "why your illustrations of selfishness are all drawn from the female sex. Why do you speak of girls that marry for money, any more than men? of mistresses of families that want to be free from household duties and responsibilities, rather than of masters?"

"My charming young lady," said Theophilus, "it is a fact that in America, except the slaveholders, women have hitherto been the only aristocracy. Women have been the privileged class,—the only one to which our rough democracy has always and everywhere given the precedence,—and consequently the vices of aristocrats are more developed in them as a class than among men. The leading principle of aristocracy, which is to take pay without work, to live on the toils and earnings of others, is one which obtains more generally among women than among men in this country. The men of our country, as a general thing, even in our uppermost classes, always propose to themselves some work or business by which they may acquire a fortune, or enlarge that already made for them by their fathers. The women of the same class propose to themselves nothing but to live at their ease on the money made for them by the labors of fathers and husbands. As a consequence, they become enervated and indolent,—averse to any bracing, wholesome effort, either mental or physical. The unavoidable responsibilities and cares of a family, instead of being viewed by them in the light of a noble life work, in which they do their part in the general labors of the world, seem to them so many injuries and wrongs; they seek to turn them upon servants, and find servants unwilling to take them; and so selfish are they, that I have heard more than one lady declare that she didn't care if it was unjust, she should like to have slaves, rather than be plagued with servants who had so much liberty. All the novels, poetry, and light literature of the world, which form the general staple of female reading, are based upon aristocratic institutions, and impregnated with aristocratic ideas; and women among us are constantly aspiring to foreign and aristocratic modes of life rather than to those of native republican simplicity. How many women are there, think you, that would not go in for aristocracy and aristocratic prerogatives, if they were only sure that they themselves should be of the privileged class? To be 'My Lady Duchess,' and to have a right by that simple title to the prostrate deference of all the lower orders! How many would have firmness to vote against such an establishment merely because it was bad for society? Tell the fair Mrs. Feathercap, 'In order that you may be a duchess, and have everything a paradise of elegance and luxury around you and your children, a hundred poor families must have no chance for anything better than black bread and muddy water all their lives, a hundred poor men must work all their lives on such wages that a fortnight's sickness will send their families to the almshouse, and that no amount of honesty and forethought can lay up any provision for old age.'"

"Come now, sir," said Jenny, "don't tell me that there are any girls or women so mean and selfish as to want aristocracy or rank so purchased! You are too bad, Mr. Theophilus!"

"Perhaps they might not, were it stated in just these terms; yet I think, if the question of the establishment of an order of aristocracy among us were put to vote, we should find more women than men who would go for it; and they would flout at the consequences to society with the lively wit and the musical laugh which make feminine selfishness so genteel and agreeable.

"No! It is a fact that in America, the women, in the wealthy classes, are like the noblemen of aristocracies, and the men are the workers. And in all this outcry that has been raised about women's wages being inferior to those of men there is one thing overlooked,—and that is, that women's work is generally inferior to that of men, because in every rank they are the pets of society and are excused from the laborious drill and training by which men are fitted for their callings. Our fair friends come in generally by some royal road to knowledge, which saves them the dire necessity of real work,—a sort of feminine hop-skip-and-jump into science or mechanical skill,—nothing like the uncompromising hard labor to which the boy is put who would be a mechanic or farmer, a lawyer or physician.

"I admit freely that we men are to blame for most of the faults of our fair nobility. There is plenty of heroism, abundance of energy, and love of noble endeavor lying dormant in these sheltered and petted daughters of the better classes; but we keep it down and smother it. Fathers and brothers think it discreditable to themselves not to give their daughters and sisters the means of living in idleness; and any adventurous fair one, who seeks to end the ennui of utter aimlessness by applying herself to some occupation whereby she may earn her own living, infallibly draws down on her the comments of her whole circle: 'Keeping school, is she? Isn't her father rich enough to support her? What could possess her?'"

"I am glad, my dear Sir Oracle, that you are beginning to recollect yourself and temper your severities on our sex," said my wife. "As usual, there is much truth lying about loosely in the vicinity of your assertions; but they are as far from being in themselves the truth as would be their exact opposites.

"The class of American women who travel, live abroad, and represent our country to the foreign eye, have acquired the reputation of being Sybarites in luxury and extravagance, and there is much in the modes of life that are creeping into our richer circles to justify this.

"Miss Murray, ex-maid-of-honor to the Queen of England, among other impressions which she received from an extended tour through our country, states it as her conviction that young American girls of the better classes are less helpful in nursing the sick and in the general duties of family life than the daughters of the aristocracy of England; and I am inclined to believe it, because even the Queen has taken special pains to cultivate habits of energy and self-helpfulness in her children. One of the toys of the Princess Royal was said to be a cottage of her own, furnished with every accommodation for cooking and housekeeping, where she from time to time enacted the part of housekeeper, making bread and biscuit, boiling potatoes which she herself had gathered from her own garden-patch, and inviting her royal parents to meals of her own preparing; and report says, that the dignitaries of the German court have been horrified at the energetic determination of the young royal housekeeper to overlook her own linen closets and attend to her own affairs. But as an offset to what I have been saying, it must be admitted that America is a country where a young woman can be self-supporting without forfeiting her place in society. All our New England and Western towns show us female teachers who are as well received and as much caressed in society, and as often contract advantageous marriages, as any women whatever; and the productive labor of American women, in various arts, trades, and callings, would be found, I think, not inferior to that of any women in the world.

"Furthermore, the history of the late war has shown them capable of every form of heroic endeavor. We have had hundreds of Florence Nightingales, and an amount of real hard work has been done by female hands not inferior to that performed by men in the camp and field, and enough to make sure that American womanhood is not yet so enervated as seriously to interfere with the prospects of free republican society."

"I wonder," said Jenny, "what it is in our country that spoils the working classes that come into it. They say that the emigrants, as they land here, are often simple-hearted people, willing to work, accustomed to early hours and plain living, decorous and respectful in their manners. It would seem as if aristocratic drilling had done them good. In a few months they become brawling, impertinent, grasping, want high wages, and are very unwilling to work. I went to several intelligence-offices the other day to look for a girl for Marianne, and I thought, by the way the candidates catechized the ladies, and the airs they took upon them, that they considered themselves the future mistresses interrogating their subordinates.

"'Does ye expect me to do the washin' with the cookin'?'

"'Yes.'

"'Thin I'll niver go to that place!'

"'And does ye expect me to get the early breakfast for yer husband to be off in the train every mornin'?'

"'Yes.'

"'I niver does that,—that ought to be a second girl's work.'

"'How many servants does ye keep, ma'am?'

"'Two.'

"'I niver lives with people that keeps but two servants.'

"'How many has ye in yer family?'

"'Seven.'

"'That's too large a family. Has ye much company?'

"'Yes, we have company occasionally.'

"'Thin I can't come to ye; it'll be too harrd a place.'

"In fact, the thing they were all in quest of seemed to be a very small family, with very high wages, and many perquisites and privileges.

"This is the kind of work-people our manners and institutions make of people that come over here. I remember one day seeing a coachman touch his cap to his mistress when she spoke to him, as is the way in Europe, and hearing one or two others saying among themselves,—

"'That chap's a greenie; he'll get over that soon.'"

"All these things show," said I, "that the staff of power has passed from the hands of gentility into those of labor. We may think the working classes somewhat unseemly in their assertion of self-importance; but, after all, are they, considering their inferior advantages of breeding, any more overbearing and impertinent than the upper classes have always been to them in all ages and countries?

"When Biddy looks long, hedges in her work with many conditions, and is careful to get the most she can for the least labor, is she, after all, doing any more than you or I or all the rest of the world? I myself will not write articles for five dollars a page, when there are those who will give me fifteen. I would not do double duty as an editor on a salary of seven thousand, when I could get ten thousand for less work.

"Biddy and her mistress are two human beings, with the same human wants. Both want to escape trouble, to make their life comfortable and easy, with the least outlay of expense. Biddy's capital is her muscles and sinews; and she wants to get as many greenbacks in exchange for them as her wit and shrewdness will enable her to do. You feel, when you bargain with her, that she is nothing to you, except so far as her strength and knowledge may save you care and trouble; and she feels that you are nothing to her, except so far as she can get your money for her work. The free-and-easy airs of those seeking employment show one thing,—that the country in general is prosperous, and that openings for profitable employment are so numerous that it is not thought necessary to try to conciliate favor. If the community were at starvation-point, and the loss of a situation brought fear of the almshouse, the laboring-class would be more subservient. As it is, there is a little spice of the bitterness of a past age of servitude in their present attitude,—a bristling, self-defensive impertinence, which will gradually smooth away as society learns to accommodate itself to the new order of things."

"Well, but, papa," said Jenny, "don't you think all this a very severe test, if applied to us women particularly, more than to the men? Mr. Theophilus seems to think women are aristocrats, and go for enslaving the lower classes out of mere selfishness; but I say that we are a great deal more strongly tempted than men, because all these annoyances and trials of domestic life come upon us. It is very insidious, the aristocratic argument, as it appeals to us; there seems much to be said in its favor. It does appear to me that it is better to have servants and work-people tidy, industrious, respectful, and decorous, as they are in Europe, than domineering, impertinent, and negligent, as they are here,—and it seems that there is something in our institutions that produces these disagreeable traits; and I presume that the negroes will eventually be traveling the same road as the Irish, and from the same influences.

"When people see all these things, and feel all the inconveniences of them, I don't wonder that they are tempted not to like democracy, and to feel as if aristocratic institutions made a more agreeable state of society. It is not such a blank, bald, downright piece of brutal selfishness as Mr. Theophilus there seems to suppose, for us to wish there were some quiet, submissive, laborious lower class, who would be content to work for kind treatment and moderate wages."

"But, my little dear," said I, "the matter is not left to our choice. Wish it or not wish it, it's what we evidently can't have. The day for that thing is past. The power is passing out of the hands of the cultivated few into those of the strong, laborious many. *Numbers* is the king of our era; and he will reign over us, whether we will hear or whether we will forbear. The sighers for an obedient lower class and the mourners for slavery may get ready their crape and have their pocket-handkerchiefs bordered with black; for they have much weeping to do, and for many years to come. The good old feudal times, when two thirds of the population thought themselves born only for the honor, glory, and profit of the other third, are gone, with all their beautiful devotions, all their trappings of song and story. In the land where such institutions were most deeply rooted and most firmly established, they are assailed every day by hard hands and stout hearts; and their position resembles that of some of the picturesque ruins of Italy, which are constantly being torn away to build prosaic modern shops and houses.

"This great democratic movement is coming down into modern society with a march as irresistible as the glacier moves down from the mountains. Its front is in America,—and behind are England, France, Italy, Prussia, and the Mohammedan countries. In all, the rights of the laboring masses are a living force, bearing slowly and inevitably all before it. Our war has been a marshaling of its armies, commanded by a hard-handed, inspired man of the working-class. An intelligent American, recently resident in Egypt, says it was affecting to notice the interest with which the working classes there were looking upon our late struggle in America, and the earnestness of their wishes for the triumph of the Union. 'It is our cause, it is for us,' they said, as said the cotton spinners of England and the silk weavers of Lyons. The forces of this mighty movement are still directed by a man from the lower orders, the sworn foe of exclusive privileges and landed aristocracies. If Andy Johnson is consistent with himself, with the principles which raised him from a tailor's bench to the head of a mighty nation, he will see to it that the work that Lincoln began is so thoroughly done, that every man and every woman in America, of whatever race or complexion, shall have exactly equal rights before the law, and be free to rise or fall according to their individual intelligence, industry, and moral worth. So long as everything is not strictly in accordance with our principles of democracy, so long as there is in any part of the country an aristocratic upper class who despise labor, and a laboring lower class that is denied equal political rights, so long this grinding and discord between the two will never cease in America. It will make trouble not only in the South, but in the North,—trouble between all employers and employed,—trouble in every branch and department of labor,—trouble in every parlor and every kitchen.

"What is it that has driven every American woman out of domestic service, when domestic service is full as well paid, is easier, healthier, and in many cases far more agreeable, than shop and factory work? It is, more than anything else, the influence of slavery in the South,—its insensible influence on the minds of mistresses, giving them false ideas of what ought to be the position and treatment of a female citizen in domestic service, and its very marked influence on the minds of freedom-loving Americans, causing them to choose *any* position rather than one which is regarded as assimilating them to slaves. It is difficult to say what are the very worst results of a system so altogether bad as that of slavery; but one of the worst is certainly the utter contempt it brings on useful labor, and the consequent utter physical and moral degradation of a large body of the whites; and this contempt of useful labor has been constantly spreading like an infection from the Southern to the Northern States, particularly among women, who, as our friend here has truly said, are by our worship and exaltation of them made peculiarly liable to take the malaria of aristocratic society. Let anybody observe the conversation in good society for an hour or two, and hear the tone in which servant-girls, seamstresses, mechanics, and all who work for their living, are sometimes mentioned, and he will see that, while every one of the speakers professes to regard useful labor as respectable, she is yet deeply imbued with the leaven of aristocratic ideas.

"In the South the contempt for labor bred of slavery has so permeated society, that we see great, coarse, vulgar *lazzaroni* lying about in rags and vermin, and dependent on government rations, maintaining, as their only source of self-respect, that they never have done and never will do a stroke of useful work in all their lives. In the North there are, I believe, no *men* who would make such a boast; but I think there are many women—beautiful, fascinating *lazzaroni* of the parlor and boudoir—who make their boast of elegant helplessness and utter incompetence for any of woman's duties with equal naïveté. The Spartans made their slaves drunk, to teach their children the evils of intoxication; and it seems to be the policy of a large class in the South now to keep down and degrade the only working class they have, for the sake of teaching their children to despise work.

"We of the North, who know the dignity of labor, who know the value of free and equal institutions, who have enjoyed advantages for seeing their operation, ought, in true brotherliness, to exercise the power given us by the present position of the people of the Southern States, and put things thoroughly right for them, well knowing, that, though they may not like it at the moment, they will like it in the end, and that it will bring them peace, plenty, and settled prosperity, such as they have long envied here in the North. It is no kindness to an invalid brother, half recovered from delirium, to leave him a knife to cut his throat with, should he be so disposed. We should rather appeal from Philip drunk to Philip sober, and do real kindness, trusting to the future for our meed of gratitude.

"Giving equal political rights to all the inhabitants of the Southern States will be their shortest way to quiet and to wealth. It will avert what is else almost certain,—a war of races; since all experience shows that the ballot introduces the very politest relations between the higher and lower classes. If the right be restricted, let it be by requirements of property and education, applying to all the population equally.

"Meanwhile, we citizens and citizenesses of the North should remember that Reconstruction means something more than setting things right in the Southern States. We have saved our government and institutions, but we have paid a fearful price for their salvation; and we ought to prove now that they are worth the price.

"The empty chair, never to be filled; the light gone out on its candlestick, never on earth to be rekindled; gallant souls that have exhaled to heaven in slow torture and starvation; the precious blood that has drenched a hundred battlefields,—all call to us with warning voices, and tell us not to let such sacrifices be in vain. They call on us by our clear understanding of the great principles of democratic equality, for which our martyred brethren suffered and died, to show to all the world that their death was no mean and useless waste, but a glorious investment for the future of mankind.

"This war, these sufferings, these sacrifices, ought to make every American man and woman look on himself and herself as belonging to a royal priesthood, a peculiar people. The blood of our slain ought to be a gulf, wide and deep as the Atlantic, dividing us from the opinions and the practices of countries whose government and society are founded on other and antagonistic ideas. Democratic republicanism has never yet been perfectly worked out either in this or any other country. It is a splendid edifice, half built, deformed by rude scaffolding, noisy with the clink of trowels, blinding the eyes with the dust of lime, and endangering our heads with falling brick. We make our way over heaps of shavings and lumber to view the stately apartments,—we endanger our necks in climbing ladders standing in the place of future staircases; but let us not for all this cry out that the old rat-holed mansions of former ages, with their mould, and moss, and cockroaches, are better than this new palace. There is no lime-dust, no clink of trowels, no rough scaffolding there, to be sure, and life goes on very quietly; but there is the foul air of slow and sure decay.

"Republican institutions in America are in a transition state; they have not yet separated themselves from foreign and antagonistic ideas and traditions, derived from old countries; and the labors necessary for the upbuilding of society are not yet so adjusted that there is mutual pleasure and comfort in the relations of employer and employed. We still incline to class distinctions and aristocracies. We incline to the scheme of dividing the world's work into two orders: first, physical labor, which is held to be rude and vulgar, and the province of a lower class; and second, brain labor, held to be refined and aristocratic, and the province of a higher class. Meanwhile, the Creator, who is the greatest of levelers, has given to every human being both a physical system, needing to be kept in order by physical labor, and an intellectual or brain power, needing to be kept in order by brain labor. Work, use, employment, is the condition of health in both; and he who works either to the neglect of the other lives but a half-life, and is an imperfect human being.

"The aristocracies of the Old World claim that their only labor should be that of the brain; and they keep their physical system in order by violent exercise, which is made genteel from the fact only that it is not useful or productive. It would be losing caste to refresh the muscles by handling the plough or the axe; and so foxes and hares must be kept to be hunted, and whole counties turned into preserves, in order that the nobility and gentry may have physical exercise in a way befitting their station,—that is to say, in a way that produces nothing, and does good only to themselves.

"The model republican uses his brain for the highest purposes of brain work, and his muscles in productive physical labor; and useful labor he respects above that which is merely agreeable. When this equal respect for physical and mental labor shall have taken possession of every American citizen, there will be no so-called laboring class; there will no more be a class all muscle without brain power to guide it, and a class all brain without muscular power to execute. The labors of society will be lighter, because each individual will take his part in them; they will be performed better, because no one will be overburdened. In those days, Miss Jenny, it will be an easier matter to keep house, because, housework being no longer regarded as degrading drudgery, you will find a superior class of women ready to engage in it.

"Every young girl and woman, who in her sphere and by her example shows that she is not ashamed of domestic labor, and that she considers the necessary work and duties of family life as dignified and important, is helping to bring on this good day. Louis Philippe once jestingly remarked, 'I have this qualification for being a king in these days, that I have blacked my own boots, and could black them again.'

"Every American ought to cultivate, as his pride and birthright, the habit of self-helpfulness. Our command of the labors of good employees in any department is liable to such interruptions, that he who has blacked his own boots, and can do it again, is, on the whole, likely to secure the most comfort in life.

"As to that which Mr. Ruskin pronounces to be a deep, irremediable ulcer in society, namely, domestic service, we hold that the last workings of pure democracy will cleanse and heal it. When right ideas are sufficiently spread; when everybody is self-helpful and capable of being self-supporting; when there is a fair start for every human being in the race of life, and all its prizes are, without respect of persons, to be obtained by the best runner; when every kind of useful labor is thoroughly respected,—then there will be a clear, just, wholesome basis of intercourse on which employers and employed can move without wrangling or discord.

"Renouncing all claims to superiority on the one hand, and all thought of servility on the other, service can be rendered by fair contracts and agreements, with that mutual respect and benevolence which every human being owes to every other. But for this transition period, which is wearing out the life of so many women, and making so many households uncomfortable, I have some alleviating suggestions, which I shall give in my next chapter."

IV

IS WOMAN A WORKER

"Papa, do you see what the 'Evening Post' says of your New Year's article on Reconstruction?" said Jenny, as we were all sitting in the library after tea.

"I have not seen it."

"Well, then, the charming writer, whoever he is, takes up for us girls and women, and maintains that no work of any sort ought to be expected of us; that our only mission in life is to be beautiful, and to refresh and elevate the spirits of men by being so. If I get a husband, my mission is to be always becomingly dressed, to display most captivating toilettes, and to be always in good spirits, — as, under the circumstances, I always should be, — and thus 'renew his spirits' when he comes in weary with the toils of life. Household cares are to be far from me: they destroy my cheerfulness and injure my beauty.

"He says that the New England standard of excellence as applied to woman has been a mistaken one; and, in consequence, though the girls are beautiful, the matrons are faded, overworked, and uninteresting; and that such a state of society tends to immorality, because, when wives are no longer charming, men are open to the temptation to desert their firesides, and get into mischief generally. He seems particularly to complain of your calling ladies who do nothing the 'fascinating *lazzaroni* of the parlor and boudoir.'"

"There was too much truth back of that arrow not to wound," said Theophilus Thoro, who was ensconced, as usual, in his dark corner, whence he supervises our discussions.

"Come, Mr. Thoro, we won't have any of your bitter moralities," said Jenny; "they are only to be taken as the invariable bay-leaf which Professor Blot introduces into all his recipes for soups and stews, — a little elegant bitterness, to be kept tastefully in the background. You see now, papa, I should like the vocation of being beautiful. It would just suit me to wear point-lace and jewelry, and to have life revolve round me, as some beautiful star, and feel that I had nothing to do but shine and refresh the spirits of all gazers, and that in this way I was truly useful, and fulfilling the great end of my being; but alas for this doctrine! all women have not beauty. The most of us can only hope not to be called ill-looking, and, when we get ourselves up with care, to look fresh and trim and agreeable; which fact interferes with the theory."

"Well, for my part," said young Rudolph, "I go for the theory of the beautiful. If ever I marry, it is to find an asylum for ideality. I don't want to make a culinary marriage or a business partnership. I want a being whom I can keep in a sphere of poetry and beauty, out of the dust and grime of every-lay life."

"Then," said Mr. Theophilus, "you must either be a rich man in your own right, or your fair ideal must have a handsome fortune of her own."

"I never will marry a rich wife," quoth Rudolph. "My wife must be supported by me, not I by her."

Rudolph is another of the habitués of our chimney-corner, representing the order of young knighthood in America, and his dreams and fancies, if impracticable, are always of a kind to make every one think him a good fellow. He who has no romantic dreams at twenty-one will be a horribly dry peascod at fifty; therefore it is that I gaze reverently at all Rudolph's chateaus in Spain, which want nothing to complete them except solid earth to stand on.

"And pray," said Theophilus, "how long will it take a young lawyer or physician, starting with no heritage but his own brain, to create a sphere of poetry and beauty in which to keep his goddess? How much a year will be necessary, as the English say, to *do* this garden of Eden, whereinto shall enter only the poetry of life?"

"I don't know. I haven't seen it near enough to consider. It is because I know the difficulty of its attainment that I have no present thoughts of marriage. Marriage is to me in the bluest of all blue distances, — far off, mysterious, and dreamy as the Mountains of the Moon or sources of the Nile. It shall come only when I have secured a fortune that shall place my wife above all necessity of work or care."

"I desire to hear from you," said Theophilus, "when you have found the sum that will keep a woman from care. I know of women now inhabiting palaces, waited on at every turn by servants, with carriages, horses, jewels, laces, Cashmeres, enough for princesses, who are eaten up by care. One lies awake all night on account of a wrinkle in the waist of her dress; another is dying because no silk of a certain inexpressible shade is to be found in New York; a third has had a dress sent home, which has proved such a failure that life seems no longer worth having. If it were not for the consolations of religion, one doesn't know what would become of her. The fact is, that care and labor are as much correlated to human existence as shadow is to light; there is no such thing as excluding them from any mortal lot. You may make a canary-bird or a gold-fish live in absolute contentment without a care or labor, but a human being you cannot. Human beings are restless and active in their very nature, and will do something, and that something will prove a care, a labor, and a fatigue, arrange it how you will. As long as there is anything to be desired and not yet attained, so long its attainment will be attempted; so long as that attainment is doubtful or difficult, so long will there be care and anxiety. When boundless wealth releases woman from every family care, she immediately makes herself a new set of cares in another direction, and has just as many anxieties as the most toilful housekeeper, only they are of a different kind. Talk of labor, and look at the upper classes in London or in New York in the fashionable season. Do any women work harder? To rush from crowd to crowd all night, night after night, seeing what they are tired of, making the agreeable over an abyss of inward yawning, crowded, jostled, breathing hot air, and crushed in halls and stairways, without a moment of leisure for months and months, till brain and nerve and sense reel, and the country is longed for as a period of resuscitation and relief! Such is the release from labor and fatigue brought by wealth. The only thing that makes all this labor at all endurable is, that it is utterly and entirely useless, and does no good to any one in creation; this alone makes it genteel, and distinguishes it from the vulgar toils of a housekeeper. These delicate creatures, who can go to three or four parties a night for three months, would be utterly desolate if they had to watch one night in a sick-room; and though they can exhibit any amount of physical endurance and vigor in crowding into assembly rooms, and breathe tainted air in an opera-house with the most martyr-like constancy, they could not sit one half-hour in the close room where the sister of charity spends hours in consoling the sick or aged poor."

"Mr. Theophilus is quite at home now," said Jenny; "only start him on the track of fashionable life, and he takes the course like a hound. But hear, now, our champion of the 'Evening Post':—

"'The instinct of women to seek a life of repose, their eagerness to attain the life of elegance, does not mean contempt for labor, but it is a confession of unfitness for labor. Women were not intended to work,—not because work is ignoble, but because it is as disastrous to the beauty of a woman as is friction to the bloom and softness of a flower. Woman is to be kept in the garden of life; she is to rest, to receive, to praise; she is to be kept from the workshop world, where innocence is snatched with rude hands, and softness is blistered into unsightliness or hardened into adamant. No social truth is more in need of exposition and illustration than this one; and, above all, the people of New England need to know it, and, better, they need to believe it.

"'It is therefore with regret that we discover Christopher Crowfield applying so harshly, and, as we think so indiscriminatingly, the theory of work to women, and teaching a society made up of women sacrificed in the workshops of the State, or to the dustpans and kitchens of the house, that women must work, ought to work, and are dishonored if they do not work; and that a woman committed to the drudgery of a household is more creditably employed than when she is charming, fascinating, irresistible, in the parlor or boudoir. The consequence of this fatal mistake is manifest throughout New England, — in New England where the girls are all beautiful and the wives and mothers faded, disfigured, and without charm or attractiveness. The moment a girl marries, in New England, she is apt to become a drudge or a lay figure on which to exhibit the latest fashions. She never has beautiful hands, and she would not have a beautiful face if a utilitarian society could "apply" her face to anything but the pleasure of the eye. Her hands lose their shape and softness after childhood, and domestic drudgery destroys her beauty of form and softness and bloom of complexion after marriage. To correct, or rather to break up, this despotism of household cares, or of work, over woman, American society must be taught that women will inevitably fade and deteriorate, unless it insures repose and comfort to them. It must be taught that reverence for beauty is the normal condition, while the theory of work, applied to women, is disastrous alike to beauty and morals. Work, when it is destructive to men or women, is forced and unjust.

"'All the great masculine or creative epochs have been distinguished by spontaneous work on the part of men, and universal reverence and care for beauty. The praise of work, and sacrifice of women to this great heartless devil of work, belong only to, and are the social doctrine of, a mechanical age and a utilitarian epoch. And if the New England idea of social life continues to bear so cruelly on woman, we shall have a reaction somewhat unexpected and shocking.'"

"Well now, say what you will," said Rudolph, "you have expressed my idea of the conditions of the sex. Woman was not made to work; she was made to be taken care of by man. All that is severe and trying, whether in study or in practical life, is and ought to be in its very nature essentially the work of the male sex. The value of woman is precisely the value of those priceless works of art for which we build museums,—which we shelter and guard as the world's choicest heritage; and a lovely, cultivated, refined woman, thus sheltered, and guarded, and developed, has a worth that cannot be estimated by any gross, material standard. So I subscribe to the sentiments of Miss Jenny's friend without scruple."

"The great trouble in settling all these society questions," said I, "lies in the gold-washing—the cradling I think the miners call it. If all the quartz were in one stratum and all the gold in another, it would save us a vast deal of trouble. In the ideas of Jenny's friend of the 'Evening Post' there is a line of truth and a line of falsehood so interwoven and threaded together that it is impossible wholly to assent or dissent. So with your ideas, Rudolph, there is a degree of truth in them, but there is also a fallacy.

"It is a truth, that woman as a sex ought not to do the hard work of the world, either social, intellectual, or moral. These are evidences in her physiology that this was not intended for her, and our friend of the 'Evening Post' is right in saying that any country will advance more rapidly in civilization and refinement where woman is thus sheltered and protected. And I think, furthermore, that there is no country in the world where women *are* so much considered and cared for and sheltered, in every walk of life, as in America. In England and France,—all over the continent of Europe, in fact,—the other sex are deferential to women only from some presumption of their social standing, or from the fact of acquaintanceship; but among strangers, and under circumstances where no particular rank or position can be inferred, a woman traveling in England or France is jostled and pushed to the wall, and left to take her own chance, precisely as if she were not a woman. Deference to delicacy and weakness, the instinct of protection, does not appear to characterize the masculine population of any other quarter of the world so much as that of America. In France, *les Messieurs* will form a circle round the fire in the receiving-room of a railroad station, and sit, tranquilly smoking their cigars, while ladies who do not happen to be of their acquaintance are standing shivering at the other side of the room. In England, if a lady is incautiously booked for an outside place on a coach, in hope of seeing the scenery, and the day turns out hopelessly rainy, no gentleman in the coach below ever thinks of offering to change seats with her, though it pour torrents. In America, the roughest backwoods steamboat or canal-boat captain always, as a matter of course, considers himself charged with the protection of the ladies. '*Place aux dames*' is written in the heart of many a shaggy fellow who could not utter a French word any more than could a buffalo. It is just as I have before said,—women are the recognized aristocracy, the only aristocracy, of America; and, so far from regarding this fact as objectionable, it is an unceasing source of pride in my country.

"That kind of knightly feeling towards woman which reverences her delicacy, her frailty, which protects and cares for her, is, I think, the crown of manhood; and without it a man is only a rough animal. But our fair aristocrats and their knightly defenders need to be cautioned lest they lose their position, as many privileged orders have before done, by an arrogant and selfish use of power.

"I have said that the vices of aristocracy are more developed among women in America than among men, and that, while there are no men in the Northern States who are not ashamed of living a merely idle life of pleasure, there are many women who make a boast of helplessness and ignorance in woman's family duties which any man would be ashamed to make with regard to man's duties, as if such helplessness and ignorance were a grace and a charm.

"There are women who contentedly live on, year after year, a life of idleness, while the husband and father is straining every nerve, growing prematurely old and gray, abridged of almost every form of recreation or pleasure,—all that he may keep them in a state of careless ease and festivity. It may be very fine, very generous, very knightly, in the man who thus toils at the oar that his princesses may enjoy their painted voyages; but what is it for the women?

"A woman is a moral being—an immortal soul—before she is a woman; and as such she is charged by her Maker with some share of the great burden of work which lies on the world.

"Self-denial, the bearing of the cross, are stated by Christ as indispensable conditions to the entrance into his kingdom, and no exception is made for man or woman. Some task, some burden, some cross, each one must carry; and there must be something done in every true and worthy life, not as amusement, but as duty,—not as play, but as earnest work,—and no human being can attain to the Christian standard without this.

"When Jesus Christ took a towel and girded himself, poured water into a basin, and washed his disciples' feet, he performed a significant and sacramental act, which no man or woman should ever forget. If wealth and rank and power absolve from the services of life, then certainly were Jesus Christ absolved, as he says: 'Ye call me Master, and Lord. If I then, your Lord and Master, have washed your feet, ye also ought to wash one another's feet. For I have given you an example, that ye should do as I have done to you.'

"Let a man who seeks to make a terrestrial paradise for the woman of his heart,—to absolve her from all care, from all labor, to teach her to accept and to receive the labor of others without any attempt to offer labor in return,—consider whether he is not thus going directly against the fundamental idea of Christianity; taking the direct way to make his idol selfish and exacting, to rob her of the highest and noblest beauty of womanhood.

"In that chapter of the Bible where the relation between man and woman is stated, it is thus said, with quaint simplicity: 'It is not good that the man should be alone; I will make him an *help meet* for him.' Woman the *helper* of man, not his toy,—not a picture, not a statue, not a work of art, but a HELPER, a doer,—such is the view of the Bible and the Christian religion.

"It is not necessary that women should work physically or morally to an extent which impairs beauty. In France, where woman is harnessed with an ass to the plough which her husband drives,—where she digs, and wields the pick-axe,—she becomes prematurely hideous; but in America, where woman reigns as queen in every household, she may surely be a good and thoughtful housekeeper, she may have physical strength exercised in lighter domestic toils, not only without injuring her beauty, but with manifest advantage to it. Almost every growing young girl would be the better in health, and therefore handsomer, for two hours of active housework daily; and the habit of usefulness thereby gained would be an equal advantage to her moral development. The labors of modern, well-arranged houses are not in any sense severe; they are as gentle as any kind of exercise that can be devised, and they bring into play muscles that ought to be exercised to be healthily developed.

"The great danger to the beauty of American women does not lie, as the writer of the 'Post' contends, in an overworking of the physical system which shall stunt and deform; on the contrary, American women of the comfortable classes are in danger of a loss of physical beauty from the entire deterioration of the muscular system for want of exercise. Take the life of any American girl in one of our large towns, and see what it is. We have an educational system of public schools which for intellectual culture is a just matter of pride to any country. From the time that the girl is seven years old, her first thought, when she rises in the morning, is to eat her breakfast and be off to her school. There really is no more time than enough to allow her to make that complete toilet which every well-bred female ought to make, and to take her morning meal before her school begins. She returns at noon with just time to eat her dinner, and the afternoon session begins. She comes home at night with books, slate, and lessons enough to occupy her evening. What time is there for teaching her any household work, for teaching her to cut or fit or sew, or to inspire her with any taste for domestic duties? Her arms have no exercise; her chest and lungs, and all the complex system of muscles which are to be perfected by quick and active movement, are compressed while she bends over book and slate and drawing-board; while the ever active brain is kept all the while going at the top of its speed. She grows up spare, thin, and delicate; and while the Irish girl, who sweeps the parlors, rubs the silver, and irons the muslins, is developing a finely rounded arm and bust, the American girl has a pair of bones at her sides, and a bust composed of cotton padding, the work of a skillful dressmaker. Nature, who is no respecter of persons, gives to Colleen Bawn, who uses her arms and chest, a beauty which perishes in the gentle, languid Edith, who does nothing but study and read."

"But is it not a fact," said Rudolph, "as stated by our friend of the 'Post,' that American matrons are perishing, and their beauty and grace all withered, from overwork?"

"It is," said my wife; "but why? It is because they are brought up without vigor or muscular strength, without the least practical experience of household labor, or those means of saving it which come by daily practice; and then, after marriage, when physically weakened by maternity, embarrassed by the care of young children, they are often suddenly deserted by every efficient servant, and the whole machinery of a complicated household left in their weak, inexperienced hands. In the country, you see a household perhaps made void some fine morning by Biddy's sudden departure, and nobody to make the bread, or cook the steak, or sweep the parlors, or do one of the complicated offices of a family, and no bakery, cook-shop, or laundry to turn to for alleviation. A lovely, refined home becomes in a few hours a howling desolation; and then ensues a long season of breakage, waste, distraction, as one wild Irish immigrant after another introduces the style of Irish cottage life into an elegant dwelling.

"Now suppose I grant to the 'Evening Post' that woman ought to rest, to be kept in the garden of life, and all that, how is this to be done in a country where a state of things like this is the commonest of occurrences? And is it any kindness or reverence to woman, to educate her for such an inevitable destiny by a life of complete physical delicacy and incapacity? Many a woman who has been brought into these cruel circumstances would willingly exchange all her knowledge of German and Italian, and all her graceful accomplishments, for a good physical development, and some respectable *savoir faire* in ordinary life.

"Moreover, American matrons are overworked because some unaccountable glamour leads them to continue to bring up their girls in the same inefficient physical habits which resulted in so much misery to themselves. Housework as they are obliged to do it, untrained, untaught, exhausted, and in company with rude, dirty, unkempt foreigners, seems to them a degradation which they will spare to their daughters. The daughter goes on with her schools and accomplishments, and leads in the family the life of an elegant little visitor during all those years when a young girl might be gradually developing and strengthening her muscles in healthy household work. It never occurs to her that she can or ought to fill any of the domestic gaps into which her mother always steps; and she comforts herself with the thought, 'I don't know how; I can't; I haven't the strength. I can't sweep; it blisters my hands. If I should stand at the ironing-table an hour, I should be ill for a week. As to cooking, I don't know anything about it.' And so, when the cook, or the chambermaid, or nurse, or all together, vacate the premises, it is the mamma who is successively cook, and chambermaid, and nurse; and this is the reason why matrons fade and are overworked.

"Now, Mr. Rudolph, do you think a woman any less beautiful or interesting because she is a fully developed physical being, — because her muscles have been rounded and matured into strength, so that she can meet the inevitable emergencies of life without feeling them to be distressing hardships? If there be a competent, well-trained servant to sweep and dust the parlor, and keep all the machinery of the house in motion, she may very properly select her work out of the family, in some form of benevolent helpfulness; but when the inevitable evil hour comes, which is likely to come first or last in every American household, is a woman any less an elegant woman because her love of neatness, order, and beauty leads her to make vigorous personal exertions to keep her own home undefiled? For my part, I think a disorderly, ill-kept home, a sordid, uninviting table, has driven more husbands from domestic life than the unattractiveness of any overworked woman. So long as a woman makes her home harmonious and orderly, so long as the hour of assembling around the family table is something to be looked forward to as a comfort and a refreshment, a man cannot see that the good house fairy, who by some magic keeps everything so delightfully, has either a wrinkle or a gray hair."

"Besides," said I, "I must tell you, Rudolph, what you fellows of twenty-one are slow to believe; and that is, that the kind of ideal paradise you propose in marriage is, in the very nature of things, an impossibility,—that the familiarities of every-day life between two people who keep house together must and will destroy it. Suppose you are married to Cytherea herself, and the next week attacked with a rheumatic fever. If the tie between you is that of true and honest love, Cytherea will put on a gingham wrapper, and with her own sculptured hands wring out the flannels which shall relieve your pains; and she will be no true woman if she do not prefer to do this to employing any nurse that could be hired. True love ennobles and dignifies the material labors of life; and homely services rendered for love's sake have in them a poetry that is immortal.

"No true-hearted woman can find herself, in real, actual life, unskilled and unfit to minister to the wants and sorrows of those dearest to her, without a secret sense of degradation. The feeling of uselessness is an extremely unpleasant one. Tom Hood, in a very humorous paper, describes a most accomplished schoolmistress, a teacher of all the arts and crafts which are supposed to make up fine gentlewomen, who is stranded in a rude German inn, with her father writhing in the anguish of a severe attack of gastric inflammation. The helpless lady gazes on her suffering parent, longing to help him, and thinking over all her various little store of accomplishments, not one of which bears the remotest relation to the case. She could knit him a bead purse, or make him a guard-chain, or work him a footstool, or festoon him with cut tissue-paper, or sketch his likeness, or crust him over with alum crystals, or stick him over with little rosettes of red and white wafers; but none of these being applicable to his present case, she sits gazing in resigned imbecility, till finally she desperately resolves to improvise him some gruel, and, after a laborious turn in the kitchen,—after burning her dress and blacking her fingers,—succeeds only in bringing him a bowl of paste!

"Not unlike this might be the feeling of many an elegant and accomplished woman, whose education has taught and practiced her in everything that woman ought to know, except those identical ones which fit her for the care of a home, for the comfort of a sick-room; and so I say again that, whatever a woman may be in the way of beauty and elegance, she must have the strength and skill of a practical worker, or she is nothing. She is not simply to be the beautiful,—she is to make the beautiful, and preserve it; and she who makes and she who keeps the beautiful must be able to work, and know how to work. Whatever offices of life are performed by women of culture and refinement are thenceforth elevated; they cease to be mere servile toils, and become expressions of the ideas of superior beings. If a true lady makes even a plate of toast, in arranging a *petit souper* for her invalid friend, she does it as a lady should. She does not cut blundering and uneven slices; she does not burn the edges; she does not deluge it with bad butter, and serve it cold; but she arranges and serves all with an artistic care, with a nicety and delicacy, which make it worth one's while to have a lady friend in sickness.

"And I am glad to hear that Monsieur Blot is teaching classes of New York ladies that cooking is not a vulgar kitchen toil, to be left to blundering servants, but an elegant feminine accomplishment, better worth a woman's learning than crochet or embroidery; and that a well-kept culinary apartment may be so inviting and orderly that no lady need feel her ladyhood compromised by participating in its pleasant toils. I am glad to know that his cooking-academy is thronged with more scholars than he can accommodate, and from ladies in the best classes of society.

"Moreover, I am glad to see that in New Bedford, recently, a public course of instruction in the art of bread-making has been commenced by a lady, and that classes of the most respectable young and married ladies in the place are attending them. These are steps in the right direction, and show that our fair countrywomen, with the grand good sense which is their leading characteristic, are resolved to supply whatever in our national life is wanting.

"I do not fear that women of such sense and energy will listen to the sophistries which would persuade them that elegant imbecility and inefficiency are charms of cultivated womanhood or ingredients in the poetry of life. She alone can keep the poetry and beauty of married life who has this poetry in her soul; who with energy and discretion can throw back and out of sight the sordid and disagreeable details which beset all human living, and can keep in the foreground that which is agreeable; who has enough knowledge of practical household matters to make unskilled and rude hands minister to her cultivated and refined tastes, and constitute her skilled brain the guide of unskilled hands. From such a home, with such a mistress, no sirens will seduce a man, even though the hair grow gray, and the merely physical charms of early days gradually pass away. The enchantment that was about her person alone in the days of courtship seems in the course of years to have interfused and penetrated the home which she has created, and which in every detail is only an expression of her personality. Her thoughts, her plans, her provident care, are everywhere; and the home attracts and holds by a thousand ties the heart which before marriage was held by the woman alone."

V

THE TRANSITION

"The fact is, my dear," said my wife, "that you have thrown a stone into a congregation of blackbirds, in writing as you have of our family wars and wants. The response comes from all parts of the country, and the task of looking over and answering your letters becomes increasingly formidable. Everybody has something to say,—something to propose."

"Give me a résumé," said I.

"Well," said my wife, "here are three pages from an elderly gentleman, to the effect that women are not what they used to be,—that daughters are a great care and no help, that girls have no health and no energy in practical life, that the expense of maintaining a household is so great that young men are afraid to marry, and that it costs more now per annum to dress one young woman than it used to cost to carry a whole family of sons through college. In short, the poor old gentleman is in a desperate state of mind, and is firmly of opinion that society is going to ruin by an express train."

"Poor old fellow!" said I, "the only comfort I can offer him is what I take myself,—that this sad world will last out our time at least. Now for the next."

"The next is more concise and spicy," said my wife. "I will read it."

"Christopher Crowfield, Esq.:

"*Sir*,—If you want to know how American women are to be brought back to family work, I can tell you a short method. Pay them as good wages for it as they can make in any other way. I get from seven to nine dollars a week in a shop where I work; if I could make the same in any good family, I should have no objection to doing it.

"Your obedient servant,

"Letitia."

"My correspondent Letitia does not tell me," said I, "how much of this seven or nine dollars she pays out for board and washing, fire and lights. If she worked in a good family at two or three dollars a week, it is easily demonstrable that, at the present cost of these items, she would make as much clear profit as she now does at nine dollars for her shop-work.

"And there are two other things, moreover, which she does not consider: First, that, besides board, washing, fuel, and lights, which she would have in a family, she would have also less unintermitted toil. Shop-work exacts its ten hours per diem; and it makes no allowance for sickness or accident.

"A good domestic in a good family finds many hours when she can feel free to attend to her own affairs. Her work consists of certain definite matters, which being done her time is her own; and if she have skill and address in the management of her duties, she may secure many leisure hours. As houses are now built, and with the many labor-saving conveniences that are being introduced, the physical labor of housework is no more than a healthy woman really needs to keep her in health. In case, however, of those slight illnesses to which all are more or less liable, and which, if neglected, often lead to graver ones, the advantage is still on the side of domestic service. In the shop and factory, every hour of unemployed time is deducted; an illness of a day or two is an appreciable loss of just so much money, while the expense of board is still going on. But in the family a good servant is always considered. When ill, she is carefully nursed as one of the family, has the family physician, and is subject to no deduction from her wages for loss of time. I have known more than one instance in which a valued domestic has been sent, at her employer's expense, to the seaside or some other pleasant locality, for change of air, when her health has been run down.

"In the second place, family work is more remunerative, even at a lower rate of wages, than shop or factory work, because it is better for the health. All sorts of sedentary employment, pursued by numbers of persons together in one apartment, are more or less debilitating and unhealthy, through foul air and confinement.

"A woman's health is her capital. In certain ways of work she obtains more income, but she spends on her capital to do it. In another way she may get less income, and yet increase her capital. A woman cannot work at dressmaking, tailoring, or any other sedentary employment, ten hours a day, year in and out, without enfeebling her constitution, impairing her eyesight, and bringing on a complication of complaints, but she can sweep, wash, cook, and do the varied duties of a well-ordered house with modern arrangements, and grow healthier every year. The times, in New England, when all women did housework a part of every day, were the times when all women were healthy. At present, the heritage of vigorous muscles, firm nerves, strong backs, and cheerful physical life has gone from American women, and is taken up by Irish women. A thrifty young man I have lately heard of married a rosy young Irish girl, quite to the horror of his mother and sisters, but defended himself by the following very conclusive logic: 'If I marry an American girl, I must have an Irish girl to take care of her; and I cannot afford to support both.'

"Besides all this, there is a third consideration, which I humbly commend to my friend Letitia. The turn of her note speaks her a girl of good common sense, with a faculty of hitting the nail square on the head; and such a girl must see that nothing is more likely to fall out than that she will some day be married. Evidently, our fair friend is born to rule; and at this hour, doubtless, her foreordained throne and humble servant are somewhere awaiting her.

"Now domestic service is all the while fitting a girl physically, mentally, and morally for her ultimate vocation and sphere, —to be a happy wife and to make a happy home. But factory work, shop work, and all employments of that sort, are in their nature essentially undomestic, —entailing the constant necessity of a boarding-house life, and of habits as different as possible from the quiet routine of home. The girl who is ten hours on the strain of continued, unintermitted toil feels no inclination, when evening comes, to sit down and darn her stockings, or make over her dresses, or study any of those multifarious economies which turn a wardrobe to the best account. Her nervous system is flagging; she craves company and excitement; and her dull, narrow room is deserted for some place of amusement or gay street promenade. And who can blame her? Let any sensible woman, who has had experience of shop and factory life, recall to her mind the ways and manners in which young girls grow up who leave a father's roof for a crowded boarding-house, without any supervision of matron or mother, and ask whether this is the best school for training young American wives and mothers.

"Doubtless there are discreet and thoughtful women who, amid all these difficulties, do keep up thrifty, womanly habits, but they do it by an effort greater than the majority of girls are willing to make, and greater than they ought to make. To sew or read or study after ten hours of factory or shop work is a further drain on the nervous powers which no woman can long endure without exhaustion.

"When the time arrives that such a girl comes to a house of her own, she comes to it as unskilled in all household lore, with muscles as incapable of domestic labor and nerves as sensitive, as if she had been leading the most luxurious, do-nothing, fashionable life. How different would be her preparation, had the forming years of her life been spent in the labors of a family! I know at this moment a lady at the head of a rich country establishment, filling her station in society with dignity and honor, who gained her domestic education in a kitchen in our vicinity. She was the daughter of a small farmer, and when the time came for her to be earning her living, her parents wisely thought it far better that she should gain it in a way which would at the same time establish her health and fit her for her own future home. In a cheerful, light, airy kitchen, which was kept so tidy always as to be an attractive sitting-room, she and another young country girl were trained up in the best of domestic economies by a mistress who looked well to the ways of her household, till at length they married from the house with honor, and went to practice in homes of their own the lessons they had learned in the home of another. Formerly, in New England, such instances were not uncommon; would that they might become so again!"

"The fact is," said my wife, "the places which the daughters of American farmers used to occupy in our families are now taken by young girls from the families of small farmers in Ireland. They are respectable, tidy, healthy, and capable of being taught. A good mistress, who is reasonable and liberal in her treatment, is able to make them fixtures. They get good wages, and have few expenses. They dress handsomely, have abundant leisure to take care of their clothes and turn their wardrobes to the best account, and they very soon acquire skill in doing it equal to that displayed by any women of any country. They remit money continually to relatives in Ireland, and from time to time pay the passage of one and another to this country,—and whole families have thus been established in American life by the efforts of one young girl. Now, for my part, I do not grudge my Irish fellow citizens these advantages obtained by honest labor and good conduct; they deserve all the good fortune thus accruing to them. But when I see sickly, nervous American women jostling and struggling in the few crowded avenues which are open to mere brain, I cannot help thinking how much better their lot would have been, with good strong bodies, steady nerves, healthy digestion, and the habit of looking any kind of work in the face, which used to be characteristic of American women generally, and of Yankee women in particular."

"The matter becomes still graver," said I, "by the laws of descent. The woman who enfeebles her muscular system by sedentary occupation, and over-stimulates her brain and nervous system, when she becomes a mother perpetuates these evils to her offspring. Her children will be born feeble and delicate, incapable of sustaining any severe strain of body or mind. The universal cry now about the ill health of young American girls is the fruit of some three generations of neglect of physical exercise and undue stimulus of brain and nerves. Young girls now are universally *born* delicate. The most careful hygienic treatment during childhood, the strictest attention to diet, dress, and exercise, succeeds merely so far as to produce a girl who is healthy so long only as she does nothing. With the least strain, her delicate organism gives out, now here, now there. She cannot study without her eyes fail or she has headache, — she cannot get up her own muslins, or sweep a room, or pack a trunk, without bringing on a backache, — she goes to a concert or a lecture, and must lie by all the next day from the exertion. If she skates, she is sure to strain some muscle; or if she falls and strikes her knee or hits her ankle, a blow that a healthy girl would forget in five minutes terminates in some mysterious lameness which confines our poor sibyl for months.

"The young American girl of our times is a creature who has not a particle of vitality to spare, — no reserved stock of force to draw upon in cases of family exigency. She is exquisitely strung, she is cultivated, she is refined; but she is too nervous, too wiry, too sensitive, — she burns away too fast; only the easiest of circumstances, the most watchful of care and nursing, can keep her within the limits of comfortable health; and yet this is the creature who must undertake family life in a country where it is next to an absolute impossibility to have permanent domestics. Frequent change, occasional entire breakdowns, must be the lot of the majority of housekeepers, — particularly those who do not live in cities."

"In fact," said my wife, "we in America have so far got out of the way of a womanhood that has any vigor of outline or opulence of physical proportions that, when we see a woman made as a woman ought to be, she strikes us as a monster. Our willowy girls are afraid of nothing so much as growing stout; and if a young lady begins to round into proportions like the women in Titian's and Giorgione's pictures, she is distressed above measure, and begins to make secret inquiries into reducing diet, and to cling desperately to the strongest corset-lacing as her only hope. It would require one to be better educated than most of our girls are, to be willing to look like the Sistine Madonna or the Venus of Milo.

"Once in a while our Italian opera-singers bring to our shores those glorious physiques which formed the inspiration of Italian painters; and then American editors make coarse jokes about Barnum's fat woman, and avalanches, and pretend to be struck with terror at such dimensions.

"We should be better instructed, and consider that Italy does us a favor, in sending us specimens, not only of higher styles of musical art, but of a warmer, richer, and more abundant womanly life. The magnificent voice is only in keeping with the magnificent proportions of the singer. A voice which has no grate, no strain, which flows without effort,—which does not labor eagerly up to a high note, but alights on it like a bird from above, there carelessly warbling and trilling,—a voice which then without effort sinks into broad, rich, sombre depths of soft, heavy chest-tone,—can come only with a physical nature at once strong, wide, and fine,—from a nature such as the sun of Italy ripens, as he does her golden grapes, filling it with the new wine of song."

"Well," said I, "so much for our strictures on Miss Letitia's letter. What comes next?"

"Here is a correspondent who answers the question, 'What shall we do with her?'—apropos of the case of the distressed young woman which we considered in our first chapter."

"And what does he recommend?"

"He tells us that he should advise us to make our distressed woman Marianne's housekeeper, and to send South for three or four contrabands for her to train, and, with great apparent complacency, seems to think that course will solve all similar cases of difficulty."

"That's quite a man's view of the subject," said Jenny. "They think any woman who isn't particularly fitted to do anything else can keep house."

"As if housekeeping were not the very highest craft and mystery of social life," said I. "I admit that our sex speak too unadvisedly on such topics, and, being well instructed by my household priestesses, will humbly suggest the following ideas to my correspondent.

"1st. A woman is not of course fit to be a housekeeper because she is a woman of good education and refinement.

"2d. If she were, a family with young children in it is not the proper place to establish a school for untaught contrabands, however desirable their training may be.

"A woman of good education and good common sense may learn to be a good housekeeper, as she learns any trade, by going into a good

250

family and practicing first one and then another branch of the business, till finally she shall acquire the comprehensive knowledge to direct all.

"The next letter I will read:—

"DEAR MR. CROWFIELD,—Your papers relating to the domestic problem have touched upon a difficulty which threatens to become a matter of life and death with me.

"I am a young man, with good health, good courage, and good prospects. I have, for a young man, a fair income, and a prospect of its increase. But my business requires me to reside in a country town, near a great manufacturing city. The demand for labor there has made such a drain on the female population of the vicinity, that it seems, for a great part of the time, impossible to keep any servants at all; and what we can hire are of the poorest quality, and want exorbitant wages. My wife was a well-trained housekeeper, and knows perfectly all that pertains to the care of a family; but she has three little children, and a delicate babe only a few weeks old; and can any one woman do all that is needed for such a household? Something must be trusted to servants; and what is thus trusted brings such confusion and waste and dirt into our house, that the poor woman is constantly distraught between the disgust of having them and the utter impossibility of doing without them.

"Now, it has been suggested that we remedy the trouble by paying higher wages; but I find that for the very highest wages I secure only the most miserable service; and yet, poor as it is, we are obliged to put up with it, because there is an amount of work to be done in our family that is absolutely beyond my wife's strength.

"I see her health wearing away under these trials, her life made a burden; I feel no power to help her, and I ask you, Mr. Crowfield, What are we to do? What is to become of family life in this country?

"Yours truly,

"A YOUNG FAMILY MAN."

"My friend's letter," said I, "touches upon the very hinge of the difficulty of domestic life with the present generation.

"The real, vital difficulty, after all, in our American life is, that our country is so wide, so various, so abounding in the richest fields of enterprise, that in every direction the cry is of the plenteousness of the harvest and the fewness of the laborers. In short, there really are not laborers enough to do the work of the country.

"Since the war has thrown the whole South open to the competition of free labor, the demand for workers is doubled and trebled. Manufactories of all sorts are enlarging their borders, increasing their machinery, and calling for more hands. Every article of living is demanded with an imperativeness and over an extent of territory which set at once additional thousands to the task of production. Instead of being easier to find hands to execute in all branches of useful labor, it is likely to grow every year more difficult, as new departments of manufacture and trade divide the workers. The price of labor, even now higher in this country than in any other, will rise still higher, and thus complicate still more the problem of domestic life. Even if a reasonable quota of intelligent women choose domestic service, the demand will be increasingly beyond the supply."

"And what have you to say to this," said my wife, "seeing you cannot stop the prosperity of the country?"

"Simply this,—that communities will be driven to organize, as they now do in Europe, to lessen the labors of individual families by having some of the present domestic tasks done out of the house.

"In France, for example, no housekeeper counts either washing, ironing, or bread-making as part of her domestic cares. All the family washing goes out to a laundry, and being attended to by those who make that department of labor a specialty, it comes home in refreshingly beautiful order.

"We in America, though we pride ourselves on our Yankee thrift, are far behind the French in domestic economy. If all the families of a neighborhood should put together the sums they separately spend in buying or fitting up and keeping in repair tubs, boilers, and other accommodations for washing, all that is consumed or wasted in soap, starch, bluing, fuel, together with the wages and board of an extra servant, the aggregate would suffice to fit up a neighborhood laundry, where one or two capable women could do easily and well what ten or fifteen women now do painfully and ill, and to the confusion and derangement of all other family processes.

"The model laundries for the poor in London had facilities which would enable a woman to do both the washing and ironing of a small family in from two to three hours, and were so arranged that a very few women could, with ease, do the work of a neighborhood.

"But in the absence of an establishment of this sort, the housekeepers of a country village might help themselves very much by owning a mangle in common, to which all the heavier parts of the ironing could be sent. American ingenuity has greatly improved the machinery of the mangle. It is no longer the heavy, cumbersome, structure that it used to be in the Old World, but a compact, neat piece of apparatus, made in three or four different sizes to suit different-sized apartments.

"Mr. H. F. Bond, of Waltham, Massachusetts, now manufactures these articles, and sends them to all parts of the country. The smallest of them does not take up much more room than a sewing-machine, can be turned by a boy of ten or twelve, and thus in the course of an hour or two the heaviest and most fatiguing part of a family ironing may be accomplished.

"I should certainly advise the 'Young Family Man' with a delicate wife and uncertain domestic help to fortify his kitchen with one of these fixtures.

"But after all, I still say that the quarter to which I look for the solution of the American problem of domestic life is a wise use of the principle of association.

"The future model village of New England, as I see it, shall have for the use of its inhabitants not merely a town lyceum hall and a town library, but a town laundry, fitted up with conveniences such as no private house can afford, and paying a price to the operators which will enable them to command an excellence of work such as private families seldom realize. It will also have a town bakery, where the best of family bread, white, brown, and of all grains, shall be compounded; and lastly a town cook-shop, where soup and meats may be bought, ready for the table. Those of us who have kept house abroad remember the ease with which our foreign establishments were carried on. A suite of elegant apartments, a courier, and one female servant were the foundation of domestic life. Our courier boarded us at a moderate expense, and the servant took care of our rooms. Punctually at the dinner hour every day, our dinner came in on the head of a porter from a neighboring cook-shop. A large chest lined with tin, and kept warm by a tiny charcoal stove in the centre, being deposited in an anteroom, from it came forth first soup, then fish, then roasts of various names, and lastly pastry and confections,—far more courses than any reasonable Christian needs to keep him in healthy condition; and dinner being over, our box with its débris went out of the house, leaving a clear field.

"Now I put it to the distressed 'Young Family Man' whether these three institutions of a bakery, a cook-shop, and a laundry, in the village where he lives, would not virtually annihilate his household cares, and restore peace and comfort to his now distracted family.

"There really is no more reason why every family should make its own bread than its own butter,—why every family should do its own washing and ironing than its own tailoring or mantua-making. In France, where certainly the arts of economy are well studied, there is some specialty for many domestic needs for which we keep servants. The beautiful inlaid floors are kept waxed and glossy by a professional gentleman who wears a brush on his foot-sole, skates gracefully over the surface, and, leaving all right, departeth. Many families, each paying a small sum, keep this servant in common.

"Now, if ever there was a community which needed to study the art of living, it is our American one; for, at present, domestic life is so wearing and so oppressive as seriously to affect health and happiness. Whatever has been done abroad in the way of comfort and convenience can be done here; and the first neighborhood that shall set the example of dividing the tasks and burdens of life by the judicious use of the principle of association will initiate a most important step in the way of national happiness and prosperity.

"My solution, then, of the domestic problem may be formulized as follows:—

"1st. That women make self helpfulness and family helpfulness fashionable, and every woman use her muscles daily in enough household work to give her a good digestion.

"2d. That the situation of a domestic be made so respectable and respected that well-educated American women shall be induced to take it as a training-school for their future family life.

"3d. That families by association lighten the multifarious labors of the domestic sphere.

"All of which I humbly submit to the good sense and enterprise of American readers and workers."

VI

BODILY RELIGION: A SERMON ON GOOD HEALTH

One of our recent writers has said, that "good health is physical religion;" and it is a saying worthy to be printed in golden letters. But good health being physical religion, it fully shares that indifference with which the human race regards things confessedly the most important. The neglect of the soul is the trite theme of all religious teachers; and, next to their souls, there is nothing that people neglect so much as their bodies. Every person ought to be perfectly healthy, just as everybody ought to be perfectly religious; but, in point of fact, the greater part of mankind are so far from perfect moral or physical religion that they cannot even form a conception of the blessing beyond them.

The mass of good, well-meaning Christians are not yet advanced enough to guess at the change which a perfect fidelity to Christ's spirit and precepts would produce in them. And the majority of people who call themselves well, because they are not, at present, upon any particular doctor's list, are not within sight of what perfect health would be. That fullness of life, that vigorous tone, and that elastic cheerfulness, which make the mere fact of existence a luxury, that suppleness which carries one like a well-built boat over every wave of unfavorable chance,—these are attributes of the perfect health seldom enjoyed. We see them in young children, in animals, and now and then, but rarely, in some adult human being, who has preserved intact the religion of the body through all opposing influences. Perfect health supposes not a state of mere quiescence, but of positive enjoyment in living. See that little fellow, as his nurse turns him out in the morning, fresh from his bath, his hair newly curled, and his cheeks polished like apples. Every step is a spring or a dance; he runs, he laughs, he shouts, his face breaks into a thousand dimpling smiles at a word. His breakfast of plain bread and milk is swallowed with an eager and incredible delight,—it is so good that he stops to laugh or thump the table now and then in expression of his ecstasy. All day long he runs and frisks and plays; and when at night the little head seeks the pillow, down go the eye-curtains, and sleep comes without a dream. In the morning his first note is a laugh and a crow, as he sits up in his crib and tries to pull papa's eyes open with his fat fingers. He is an embodied joy,—he is sunshine and music and laughter for all the house. With what a magnificent generosity does the Author of life endow a little mortal pilgrim in giving him at the outset of his career such a body as this! How miserable it is to look forward twenty years, when the same child, now grown a man, wakes in the morning with a dull, heavy head, the consequence of smoking and studying till twelve or one the night before; when he rises languidly to a late breakfast, and turns from this and tries that,—wants a deviled bone, or a cutlet with Worcestershire sauce, to make eating possible; and then, with slow and plodding step, finds his way to his office and his books. Verily the shades of the prison-house gather round the growing boy; for, surely, no one will deny that life often begins with health little less perfect than that of the angels.

But the man who habitually wakes sodden, headachy, and a little stupid, and who needs a cup of strong coffee and various stimulating condiments to coax his bodily system into something like fair working order, does not suppose he is out of health. He says, "Very well, I thank you," to your inquiries,—merely because he has entirely forgotten what good health is. He is well, not because of any particular pleasure in physical existence, but well simply because he is not a subject for prescriptions. Yet there is no store of vitality, no buoyancy, no superabundant vigor, to resist the strain and pressure to which life puts him. A checked perspiration, a draught of air ill-timed, a crisis of perplexing business or care, and he is down with a bilious attack or an influenza, and subject to doctors' orders for an indefinite period. And if the case be so with men, how is it with women? How many women have at maturity the keen appetite, the joyous love of life and motion, the elasticity and sense of physical delight in existence, that little children have? How many have any superabundance of vitality with which to meet the wear and strain of life? And yet they call themselves well.

But is it possible, in maturity, to have the joyful fullness of the life of childhood? Experience has shown that the delicious freshness of this dawning hour may be preserved even to midday, and may be brought back and restored after it has been for years a stranger. Nature, though a severe disciplinarian, is still, in many respects, most patient and easy to be entreated, and meets any repentant movement of her prodigal children with wonderful condescension. Take Bulwer's account of the first few weeks of his sojourn at Malvern, and you will read, in very elegant English, the story of an experience of pleasure which has surprised and delighted many a patient at a water-cure. The return to the great primitive elements of health—water, air, and simple food, with a regular system of exercise—has brought to many a jaded, weary, worn-down human being the elastic spirits, the simple, eager appetite, the sound sleep, of a little child. Hence the rude huts and châlets of the peasant Priessnitz were crowded with battered dukes and princesses and notables of every degree, who came from the hot, enervating luxury which had drained them of existence, to find a keener pleasure in peasants' bread under peasants' roofs than in soft raiment and palaces. No arts of French cookery can possibly make anything taste so well to a feeble and palled appetite as plain brown bread and milk taste to a hungry water-cure patient, fresh from bath and exercise.

If the water-cure had done nothing more than establish the fact that the glow and joyousness of early life are things which may be restored after having been once wasted, it would have done a good work. For if Nature is so forgiving to those who have once lost or have squandered her treasures, what may not be hoped for us if we can learn the art of never losing the first health of childhood? And though with us, who have passed to maturity, it may be too late for the blessing, cannot something be done for the children who are yet to come after us?

Why is the first health of childhood lost? Is it not the answer, that childhood is the only period of life in which bodily health is made a prominent object? Take our pretty boy, with cheeks like apples, who started in life with a hop, skip, and dance,—to whom laughter was like breathing, and who was enraptured with plain bread and milk,—how did he grow into the man who wakes so languid and dull, who wants strong coffee and Worcestershire sauce to make his breakfast go down? When and where did he drop the invaluable talisman that once made everything look brighter and taste better to him, however rude and simple, than now do the most elaborate combinations? What is the boy's history? Why, for the first seven years of his life his body is made of some account. It is watched, cared for, dieted, disciplined, fed with fresh air, and left to grow and develop like a thrifty plant. But from the time school education begins, the body is steadily ignored, and left to take care of itself.

The boy is made to sit six hours a day in a close, hot room, breathing impure air, putting the brain and the nervous system upon a constant strain, while the muscular system is repressed to an unnatural quiet. During the six hours, perhaps twenty minutes are allowed for all that play of the muscles which, up to this time, has been the constant habit of his life. After this he is sent home with books, slate, and lessons to occupy an hour or two more in preparing for the next day. In the whole of this time there is no kind of effort to train the physical system by appropriate exercise. Something of the sort was attempted years ago in the infant schools, but soon given up; and now, from the time study first begins, the muscles are ignored in all primary schools. One of the first results is the loss of that animal vigor which formerly made the boy love motion for its own sake. Even in his leisure hours he no longer leaps and runs as he used to; he learns to sit still, and by and by sitting and lounging come to be the habit, and vigorous motion the exception, for most of the hours of the day. The education thus begun goes on from primary to high school, from high school to college, from college through professional studies of law, medicine, or theology, with this steady contempt for the body, with no provision for its culture, training, or development, but rather a direct and evident provision for its deterioration and decay.

The want of suitable ventilation in school-rooms, recitation-rooms, lecture-rooms, offices, court-rooms, conference-rooms, and vestries, where young students of law, medicine, and theology acquire their earlier practice, is something simply appalling. Of itself it would answer for men the question, why so many thousand glad, active children come to a middle life without joy,—a life whose best estate is a sort of slow, plodding endurance. The despite and hatred which most men seem to feel for God's gift of fresh air, and their resolution to breathe as little of it as possible, could only come from a long course of education, in which they have been accustomed to live without it. Let any one notice the conduct of our American people traveling in railroad cars. We will suppose that about half of them are what might be called well-educated people, who have learned in books, or otherwise, that the air breathed from the lungs is laden with impurities,—that it is noxious and poisonous; and yet, travel with these people half a day, and you would suppose from their actions that they considered the external air as a poison created expressly to injure them, and that the only course of safety lay in keeping the cars hermetically sealed, and breathing over and over the vapor from each others' lungs. If a person in despair at the intolerable foulness raises a window, what frowns from all the neighboring seats, especially from great rough-coated men, who always seem the first to be apprehensive! The request to "put down that window" is almost sure to follow a moment or two of fresh air. In vain have rows of ventilators been put in the tops of some of the cars, for conductors and passengers are both of one mind, that these ventilators are inlets of danger, and must be kept carefully closed.

Railroad traveling in America is systematically, and one would think carefully, arranged so as to violate every possible law of health. The old rule to keep the head cool and the feet warm is precisely reversed. A red-hot stove heats the upper stratum of air to oppression, while a stream of cold air is constantly circulating about the lower extremities. The most indigestible and unhealthy substances conceivable are generally sold in the cars or at way-stations for the confusion and distress of the stomach. Rarely can a traveler obtain so innocent a thing as a plain good sandwich of bread and meat, while pie, cake, doughnuts, and all other culinary atrocities are almost forced upon him at every stopping-place. In France, England, and Germany, the railroad cars are perfectly ventilated; the feet are kept warm by flat cases filled with hot water and covered with carpet, and answering the double purpose of warming the feet and diffusing an agreeable temperature through the car, without burning away the vitality of the air; while the arrangements at the refreshment-rooms provide for the passenger as wholesome and well-served a meal of healthy, nutritious food as could be obtained in any home circle.

What are we to infer concerning the home habits of a nation of men who so resignedly allow their bodies to be poisoned and maltreated in traveling over such an extent of territory as is covered by our railroad lines? Does it not show that foul air and improper food are too much matters of course to excite attention? As a writer in "The Nation" has lately remarked, it is simply and only because the American nation like to have unventilated cars, and to be fed on pie and coffee at stopping-places, that nothing better is known to our travelers; if there were any marked dislike of such a state of things on the part of the people, it would not exist. We have wealth enough, and enterprise enough, and ingenuity enough, in our American nation, to compass with wonderful rapidity any end that really seems to us desirable. An army was improvised when an army was wanted,—and an army more perfectly equipped, more bountifully fed, than so great a body of men ever was before. Hospitals, Sanitary Commissions, and Christian Commissions all arose out of the simple conviction of the American people that they must arise. If the American people were equally convinced that foul air was a poison,—that to have cold feet and hot heads was to invite an attack of illness,—that maple-sugar, popcorn, peppermint candy, pie, doughnuts, and peanuts are not diet for reasonable beings,—they would have railroad accommodations very different from those now in existence.

We have spoken of the foul air of court-rooms. What better illustration could be given of the utter contempt with which the laws of bodily health are treated, than the condition of these places? Our lawyers are our highly educated men. They have been through high-school and college training, they have learned the properties of oxygen, nitrogen, and carbonic-acid gas, and have seen a mouse die under an exhausted receiver, and of course they know that foul, unventilated rooms are bad for the health; and yet generation after generation of men so taught and trained will spend the greater part of their lives in rooms notorious for their close and impure air, without so much as an attempt to remedy the evil. A well-ventilated court-room is a four-leaved clover among court-rooms. Young men are constantly losing their health at the bar; lung diseases, dyspepsia, follow them up, gradually sapping their vitality. Some of the brightest ornaments of the profession have actually fallen dead as they stood pleading,—victims of the fearful pressure of poisonous and heated air upon the excited brain. The deaths of Salmon P. Chase of Portland, uncle of our present Chief Justice, and of Ezekiel Webster, the brother of our great statesman, are memorable examples of the calamitous effects of the errors dwelt upon; and yet, strange to say, nothing efficient is done to mend these errors, and give the body an equal chance with the mind in the pressure of the world's affairs.

But churches, lecture-rooms, and vestries, and all buildings devoted especially to the good of the soul, are equally witness of the mind's disdain of the body's needs, and the body's consequent revenge upon the soul. In how many of these places has the question of a thorough provision of fresh air been even considered? People would never think of bringing a thousand persons into a desert place and keeping them there without making preparations to feed them. Bread and butter, potatoes and meat, must plainly be found for them; but a thousand human beings are put into a building to remain a given number of hours, and no one asks the question whether means exist for giving each one the quantum of fresh air needed for his circulation, and these thousand victims will consent to be slowly poisoned, gasping, sweating, getting red in the face, with confused and sleepy brains, while a minister with a yet redder face and a more oppressed brain struggles and wrestles, through the hot, seething vapors, to make clear to them the mysteries of faith. How many churches are there that for six or eight months in the year are never ventilated at all, except by the accidental opening of doors? The foul air generated by one congregation is locked up by the sexton for the use of the next assembly; and so gathers and gathers from week to week, and month to month, while devout persons upbraid themselves, and are ready to tear their hair, because they always feel stupid and sleepy in church. The proper ventilation of their churches and vestries would remove that spiritual deadness of which their prayers and hymns complain. A man hoeing his corn out on a breezy hillside is bright and alert, his mind works clearly, and he feels interested in religion, and thinks of many a thing that might be said at the prayer-meeting at night. But at night, when he sits down in a little room where the air reeks with the vapor of his neighbor's breath and the smoke of kerosene lamps, he finds himself suddenly dull and drowsy,—without emotion, without thought, without feeling,—and he rises and reproaches himself for this state of things. He calls upon his soul and all that is within him to bless the Lord; but the indignant body, abused, insulted, ignored, takes the soul by the throat, and says, "If you won't let *me* have a good time, neither shall you." Revivals of religion, with ministers and with those people whose moral organization leads them to take most interest in them, often end in periods of bodily ill health and depression. But is there any need of this? Suppose that a revival of religion required, as a formula, that all the members of a given congregation should daily take a minute dose of arsenic in concert,— we should not be surprised after a while to hear of various ill effects therefrom; and, as vestries and lecture-rooms are now arranged, a daily prayer-meeting is often nothing more nor less than a number of persons spending half an hour a day breathing poison from each other's lungs. There is not only no need of this, but, on the contrary, a good supply of pure air would make the daily prayer-meeting far more enjoyable. The body, if allowed the slightest degree of fair play, so far from being a contumacious infidel and opposer, becomes a very fair Christian helper, and, instead of throttling the soul, gives it wings to rise to celestial regions.

This branch of our subject we will quit with one significant anecdote. A certain rural church was somewhat famous for its picturesque Gothic architecture, and equally famous for its sleepy atmosphere, the rules of Gothic symmetry requiring very small windows, which could be only partially opened. Everybody was affected alike in this church; minister and people complained that it was like the enchanted ground in the Pilgrim's Progress. Do what they would, sleep was ever at their elbows; the blue, red, and green of the painted windows melted into a rainbow dimness of hazy confusion; and ere they were aware, they were off on a cloud to the land of dreams.

An energetic sister in the church suggested the inquiry, whether it was ever ventilated, and discovered that it was regularly locked up at the close of service, and remained so till opened for the next week.

She suggested the inquiry, whether giving the church a thorough airing on Saturday would not improve the Sunday services; but nobody acted on her suggestion. Finally, she borrowed the sexton's key one Saturday night, and went into the church and opened all the windows herself, and let them remain so for the night. The next day everybody remarked the improved comfort of the church, and wondered what had produced the change. Nevertheless, when it was discovered, it was not deemed a matter of enough importance to call for an order on the sexton to perpetuate the improvement.

The ventilation of private dwellings in this country is such as might be expected from that entire indifference to the laws of health manifested in public establishments. Let a person travel in private conveyance up through the valley of the Connecticut, and stop for a night at the taverns which he will usually find at the end of each day's stage. The bedchamber into which he will be ushered will be the concentration of all forms of bad air. The house is redolent of the vegetables in the cellar,—cabbages, turnips, and potatoes; and this fragrance is confined and retained by the custom of closing the window blinds and dropping the inside curtains, so that neither air nor sunshine enters in to purify. Add to this the strong odor of a new feather bed and pillows, and you have a combination of perfumes most appalling to a delicate sense. Yet travelers take possession of these rooms, sleep in them all night without raising the window or opening the blinds, and leave them to be shut up for other travelers.

The spare chamber of many dwellings seems to be an hermetically closed box, opened only twice a year, for spring and fall cleaning; but for the rest of the time closed to the sun and the air of heaven. Thrifty country housekeepers often adopt the custom of making their beds on the instant after they are left, without airing the sheets and mattresses; and a bed so made gradually becomes permeated with the insensible emanations of the human body, so as to be a steady corrupter of the atmosphere.

In the winter, the windows are calked and listed, the throat of the chimney built up with a tight brick wall, and a close stove is introduced to help burn out the vitality of the air. In a sitting-room like this, from five to ten persons will spend about eight months of the year, with no other ventilation than that gained by the casual opening and shutting of doors. Is it any wonder that consumption every year sweeps away its thousands?—that people are suffering constant chronic ailments,—neuralgia, nervous dyspepsia, and all the host of indefinite bad feelings that rob life of sweetness and flower and bloom?

A recent writer raises the inquiry, whether the community would not gain in health by the demolition of all dwelling-houses. That is, he suggests the question, whether the evils from foul air are not so great and so constant that they countervail the advantages of shelter. Consumptive patients far gone have been known to be cured by long journeys, which have required them to be day and night in the open air. Sleep under the open heaven, even though the person be exposed to the various accidents of weather, has often proved a miraculous restorer after everything else had failed. But surely, if simple fresh air is so healing and preserving a thing, some means might be found to keep the air in a house just as pure and vigorous as it is outside.

An article in the May number of "Harpers' Magazine" presents drawings of a very simple arrangement by which any house can be made thoroughly self-ventilating. Ventilation, as this article shows, consists in two things,—a perfect and certain expulsion from the dwelling of all foul air breathed from the lungs or arising from any other cause, and the constant supply of pure air.

One source of foul air cannot be too much guarded against,—we mean imperfect gas-pipes. A want of thoroughness in execution is the sin of our American artisans, and very few gas-fixtures are so thoroughly made that more or less gas does not escape and mingle with the air of the dwelling. There are parlors where plants cannot be made to live, because the gas kills them; and yet their occupants do not seem to reflect that an air in which a plant cannot live must be dangerous for a human being. The very clemency and long-suffering of Nature to those who persistently violate her laws is one great cause why men are, physically speaking, such sinners as they are. If foul air poisoned at once and completely, we should have well-ventilated houses, whatever else we failed to have. But because people can go on for weeks, months, and years breathing poisons, and slowly and imperceptibly lowering the tone of their vital powers, and yet be what they call "pretty well, I thank you," sermons on ventilation and fresh air go by them as an idle song. "I don't see but we are well enough, and we never took much pains about these things. There's air enough gets into houses, of course. What with doors opening and windows occasionally lifted, the air of houses is generally good enough;"—and so the matter is dismissed.

One of Heaven's great hygienic teachers is now abroad in the world, giving lessons on health to the children of men. The cholera is like the angel whom God threatened to send as leader to the rebellious Israelites. "Beware of him, obey his voice, and provoke him not; for he will not pardon your transgressions." The advent of this fearful messenger seems really to be made necessary by the contempt with which men treat the physical laws of their being. What else could have purified the dark places of New York? What a wiping-up and reforming and cleansing is going before him through the country! At last we find that Nature is in earnest, and that her laws cannot be always ignored with impunity. Poisoned air is recognized at last as an evil,—even although the poison cannot be weighed, measured, or tasted; and if all the precautions that men are now willing to take could be made perpetual, the alarm would be a blessing to the world.

Like the principles of spiritual religion, the principles of physical religion are few and easy to be understood. An old medical apothegm personifies the hygienic forces as the Doctors Air, Diet, Exercise, and Quiet: and these four will be found, on reflection, to cover the whole ground of what is required to preserve human health. A human being whose lungs have always been nourished by pure air, whose stomach has been fed only by appropriate food, whose muscles have been systematically trained by appropriate exercises, and whose mind is kept tranquil by faith in God and a good conscience, has perfect physical religion. There is a line where physical religion must necessarily overlap spiritual religion and rest upon it. No human being can be assured of perfect health, through all the strain and wear and tear of such cares and such perplexities as life brings, without the rest of faith in God. An unsubmissive, unconfiding, unresigned soul will make vain the best hygienic treatment; and, on the contrary, the most saintly religious resolution and purpose may be defeated and vitiated by an habitual ignorance and disregard of the laws of the physical system.

Perfect spiritual religion cannot exist without perfect physical religion. Every flaw and defect in the bodily system is just so much taken from the spiritual vitality: we are commanded to glorify God, not simply in our spirits, but in our bodies and spirits. The only example of perfect manhood the world ever saw impresses us more than anything else by an atmosphere of perfect healthiness. There is a calmness, a steadiness, in the character of Jesus, a naturalness in his evolution of the sublimest truths under the strain of the most absorbing and intense excitement, that could come only from the one perfectly trained and developed body, bearing as a pure and sacred shrine the One Perfect Spirit. Jesus of Nazareth, journeying on foot from city to city, always calm yet always fervent, always steady yet glowing with a white heat of sacred enthusiasm, able to walk and teach all day and afterwards to continue in prayer all night, with unshaken nerves, sedately patient, serenely reticent, perfectly self-controlled, walked the earth, the only man that perfectly glorified God in His body no less than in His spirit. It is worthy of remark, that in choosing His disciples He chose plain men from the laboring classes, who had lived the most obediently to the simple, unperverted laws of nature. He chose men of good and pure bodies, — simple, natural, childlike, healthy men, — and baptized their souls with the inspiration of the Holy Spirit.

The hygienic bearings of the New Testament have never been sufficiently understood. The basis of them lies in the solemn declaration, that our bodies are to be temples of the Holy Spirit, and that all abuse of them is of the nature of sacrilege. Reverence for the physical system, as the outward shrine and temple of the spiritual, is the peculiarity of the Christian religion. The doctrine of the resurrection of the body, and its physical immortality, sets the last crown of honor upon it. That bodily system which God declared worthy to be gathered back from the dust of the grave, and re-created, as the soul's immortal companion, must necessarily be dear and precious in the eyes of its Creator. The one passage in the New Testament in which it is spoken of disparagingly is where Paul contrasts it with the brighter glory of what is to come: "He shall change our vile bodies, that they may be fashioned like his glorious body." From this passage has come abundance of reviling of the physical system. Memoirs of good men are full of abuse of it, as the clog, the load, the burden, the chain. It is spoken of as pollution, as corruption, — in short, one would think that the Creator had imitated the cruelty of some Oriental despots who have been known to chain a festering corpse to a living body. Accordingly, the memoirs of these pious men are also mournful records of slow suicide, wrought by the persistent neglect of the most necessary and important laws of the bodily system; and the body, outraged and downtrodden, has turned traitor to the soul, and played the adversary with fearful power. Who can tell the countless temptations to evil which flow in from a neglected, disordered, deranged nervous system, — temptations to anger, to irritability, to selfishness, to every kind of sin of appetite and passion? No wonder that the poor soul longs for the hour of release from such a companion.

But that human body which God declares expressly was made to be the temple of the Holy Spirit, which he considers worthy to be perpetuated by a resurrection and an immortal existence, cannot be intended to be a clog and a hindrance to spiritual advancement. A perfect body, working in perfect tune and time, would open glimpses of happiness to the soul approaching the joys we hope for in heaven. It is only through the images of things which our bodily senses have taught us, that we can form any conception of that future bliss; and the more perfect these senses, the more perfect our conceptions must be.

The conclusion of the whole matter, and the practical application of this sermon, is, — First, that all men set themselves to form the idea of what perfect health is, and resolve to realize it for themselves and their children. Second, that with a view to this they study the religion of the body, in such simple and popular treatises as those of George Combe, Dr. Dio Lewis, and others, and with simple and honest hearts practice what they there learn. Third, that the training of the bodily system should form a regular part of our common-school education, — every common school being provided with a well-instructed teacher of gymnastics; and the growth and development of each pupil's body being as much noticed and marked as is now the growth of his mind. The same course should be continued and enlarged in colleges and female seminaries, which should have professors of hygiene appointed to give thorough instruction concerning the laws of health.

And when this is all done, we may hope that crooked spines, pimpled faces, sallow complexions, stooping shoulders, and all other signs indicating an undeveloped physical vitality, will, in the course of a few generations, disappear from the earth, and men will have bodies which will glorify God, their great Architect.

The soul of man has got as far as it can without the body. Religion herself stops and looks back, waiting for the body to overtake her. The soul's great enemy and hindrance can be made her best friend and most powerful help; and it is high time that this era were begun. We old sinners, who have lived carelessly, and almost spent our day of grace, may not gain much of its good; but the children, — shall there not be a more perfect day for them? Shall there not come a day when the little child, whom Christ set forth to his disciples as the type of the greatest in the kingdom of heaven, shall be the type no less of our physical than our spiritual advancement, — when men and women shall arise, keeping through long and happy lives the simple, unperverted appetites, the joyous freshness of spirit, the keen delight in mere existence, the dreamless sleep and happy waking of early childhood?

VII

HOW SHALL WE ENTERTAIN OUR COMPANY

"The fact is," said Marianne, "we must have a party. Bob don't like to hear of it, but it must come. We are in debt to everybody: we have been invited everywhere, and never had anything like a party since we were married, and it won't do."

"For my part, I hate parties," said Bob. "They put your house all out of order, give all the women a sick-headache, and all the men an indigestion; you never see anybody to any purpose; the girls look bewitched, and the women answer you at cross-purposes, and call you by the name of your next-door neighbor, in their agitation of mind. We stay out beyond our usual bedtime, come home and find some baby crying, or child who has been sitting up till nobody knows when; and the next morning, when I must be at my office by eight, and wife must attend to her children, we are sleepy and headachy. I protest against making overtures to entrap some hundred of my respectable married friends into this snare which has so often entangled me. If I had my way, I would never go to another party; and as to giving one—I suppose, since my empress has declared her intentions, that I shall be brought into doing it; but it shall be under protest."

"But, you see, we must keep up society," said Marianne.

"But I insist on it," said Bob, "it isn't keeping up society. What earthly thing do you learn about people by meeting them in a general crush, where all are coming, going, laughing, talking, and looking at each other? No person of common sense ever puts forth any idea he cares twopence about, under such circumstances; all that is exchanged is a certain set of commonplaces and platitudes which people keep for parties, just as they do their kid gloves and finery. Now there are our neighbors, the Browns. When they drop in of an evening, she knitting, and he with the last article in the paper, she really comes out with a great deal of fresh, lively, earnest, original talk. We have a good time, and I like her so much that it quite verges on loving; but see her in a party, when she manifests herself over five or six flounces of pink silk and a perfect egg-froth of tulle, her head adorned with a thicket of crêped hair and roses, and it is plain at first view that talking with her is quite out of the question. What has been done to her head on the outside has evidently had some effect within, for she is no longer the Mrs. Brown you knew in her every-day dress, but Mrs. Brown in a party state of mind, and too distracted to think of anything in particular. She has a few words that she answers to everything you say, as for example, 'Oh, very!' 'Certainly!' 'How extraordinary!' 'So happy to,' etc. The fact is, that she has come into a state in which any real communication with her mind and character must be suspended till the party is over and she is rested. Now I like society, which is the reason why I hate parties."

"But you see," said Marianne, "what are we to do? Everybody can't drop in to spend an evening with you. If it were not for these parties, there are quantities of your acquaintances whom you would never meet."

"And of what use is it to meet them? Do you really know them any better for meeting them got up in unusual dresses, and sitting down together when the only thing exchanged is the remark that it is hot or cold, or it rains, or it is dry, or any other patent surface-fact that answers the purpose of making believe you are talking when neither of you is saying a word?"

"Well, now, for my part," said Marianne, "I confess I like parties: they amuse me. I come home feeling kinder and better to people, just for the little I see of them when they are all dressed up and in good humor with themselves. To be sure we don't say anything very profound,—I don't think the most of us have anything profound to say; but I ask Mrs. Brown where she buys her lace, and she tells me how she washes it, and somebody else tells me about her baby, and promises me a new sack-pattern. Then I like to see the pretty, nice young girls flirting with the nice young men; and I like to be dressed up a little myself, even if my finery is all old and many times made over. It does me good to be rubbed up and brightened."

"Like old silver," said Bob.

"Yes, like old silver, precisely; and even if I do come home tired, it does my mind good to have that change of scene and faces. You men do not know what it is to be tied to house and nursery all day, and what a perfect weariness and lassitude it often brings on us women. For my part I think parties are a beneficial institution of society, and that it is worth a good deal of fatigue and trouble to get one up."

"Then there's the expense," said Bob. "What earthly need is there of a grand regale of oysters, chicken salad, ice-creams, coffee, and champagne, between eleven and twelve o'clock at night, when no one of us would ever think of wanting or taking any such articles upon our stomachs in our own homes? If we were all of us in the habit of having a regular repast at that hour, it might be well enough to enjoy one with our neighbor; but the party fare is generally just so much in addition to the honest three meals which we have eaten during the day. Now, to spend from fifty to one, two, or three hundred dollars in giving all our friends an indigestion from a midnight meal seems to me a very poor investment. Yet if we once begin to give the party, we must have everything that is given at the other parties, or wherefore do we live? And caterers and waiters rack their brains to devise new forms of expense and extravagance; and when the bill comes in, one is sure to feel that one is paying a great deal of money for a great deal of nonsense. It is in fact worse than nonsense, because our dear friends are, in half the cases, not only no better, but a great deal worse, for what they have eaten."

"But there is this advantage to society," said Rudolph, —"it helps us young physicians. What would the physicians do if parties were abolished? Take all the colds that are caught by our fair friends with low necks and short sleeves, all the troubles from dancing in tight dresses and inhaling bad air, and all the headaches and indigestion from the *mélange* of lobster salad, two or three kinds of ice-cream, cake, and coffee on delicate stomachs, and our profession gets a degree of encouragement that is worthy to be thought of."

"But the question arises," said my wife, "whether there are not ways of promoting social feeling less expensive, more simple and natural and rational. I am inclined to think that there are."

"Yes," said Theophilus Thoro; "for large parties are not, as a general thing, given with any wish or intention of really improving our acquaintance with our neighbors. In many cases they are openly and avowedly a general tribute paid at intervals to society, for and in consideration of which you are to sit with closed blinds and doors and be let alone for the rest of the year. Mrs. Bogus, for instance, lives to keep her house in order, her closets locked, her silver counted and in the safe, and her china-closet in undisturbed order. Her 'best things' are put away with such admirable precision, in so many wrappings and foldings, and secured with so many a twist and twine, that to get them out is one of the seven labors of Hercules, not to be lightly or unadvisedly taken in hand, but reverently, discreetly, and once for all, in an annual or biennial party. Then says Mrs. Bogus, 'For Heaven's sake, let's have every creature we can think of, and have 'em all over with at once. For pity's sake, let's have no driblets left that we shall have to be inviting to dinner or to tea. No matter whether they can come or not, —only send them the invitation, and our part is done; and, thank Heaven! we shall be free for a year.'"

"Yes," said my wife; "a great stand-up party bears just the same relation towards the offer of real hospitality and good will as Miss Sally Brass's offer of meat to the little hungry Marchioness, when, with a bit uplifted on the end of a fork, she addressed her, 'Will you have this piece of meat? No? Well, then, remember and don't say you haven't had meat *offered* to you!' You are invited to a general jam, at the risk of your life and health; and if you refuse, don't say you haven't had hospitality offered to you. All our debts are wiped out and our slate clean; now we will have our own closed doors, no company and no trouble, and our best china shall repose undisturbed on its shelves. Mrs. Bogus says she never could exist in the way that Mrs. Easygo does, with a constant drip of company,— two or three to breakfast one day, half a dozen to dinner the next, and little evening gatherings once or twice a week. It must keep her house in confusion all the time; yet, for real social feeling, real exchange of thought and opinion, there is more of it in one half-hour at Mrs. Easygo's than in a dozen of Mrs. Bogus's great parties.

"The fact is, that Mrs. Easygo really does like the society of human beings. She is genuinely and heartily social; and, in consequence, though she has very limited means, and no money to spend in giving great entertainments, her domestic establishment is a sort of social exchange, where more friendships are formed, more real acquaintance made, and more agreeable hours spent, than in any other place that can be named. She never has large parties,—great general pay-days of social debts,—but small, well-chosen circles of people, selected so thoughtfully, with a view to the pleasure which congenial persons give each other, as to make the invitation an act of real personal kindness. She always manages to have something for the entertainment of her friends, so that they are not reduced to the simple alternative of gaping at each other's dresses and eating lobster salad and ice-cream. There is either some choice music, or a reading of fine poetry, or a well-acted charade, or a portfolio of photographs and pictures, to enliven the hour and start conversation; and as the people are skillfully chosen with reference to each other, as there is no hurry or heat or confusion, conversation, in its best sense, can bubble up, fresh, genuine, clear, and sparkling as a woodland spring, and one goes away really rested and refreshed. The slight entertainment provided is just enough to enable you to eat salt together in Arab fashion,—not enough to form the leading feature of the evening. A cup of tea and a basket of cake, or a salver of ices, silently passed at quiet intervals, do not interrupt conversation or overload the stomach."

"The fact is," said I, "that the art of society among us Anglo-Saxons is yet in its rudest stages. We are not, as a race, social and confiding, like the French and Italians and Germans. We have a word for home, and our home is often a moated grange, an island, a castle with its drawbridge up, cutting us off from all but our own home-circle. In France and Germany and Italy there are the boulevards and public gardens, where people do their family living in common. Mr. A. is breakfasting under one tree, with wife and children around, and Mr. B. is breakfasting under another tree, hard by; and messages, nods, and smiles pass backward and forward. Families see each other daily in these public resorts, and exchange mutual offices of good will. Perhaps from these customs of society come that naïve simplicity and abandon which one remarks in the Continental, in opposition to the Anglo-Saxon, habits of conversation. A Frenchman or an Italian will talk to you of his feeling and plans and prospects with an unreserve that is perfectly unaccountable to you, who have always felt that such things must be kept for the very innermost circle of home privacy. But the Frenchman or Italian has from a child been brought up to pass his family life in places of public resort, in constant contact and intercommunion with other families; and the social and conversational instinct has thus been daily strengthened. Hence the reunions of these people have been characterized by a sprightliness and vigor and spirit that the Anglo-Saxon has in vain attempted to seize and reproduce. English and American *conversazioni* have very generally proved a failure, from the rooted, frozen habit of reticence and reserve which grows with our growth and strengthens with our strength. The fact is, that the Anglo-Saxon race as a race does not enjoy talking, and, except in rare instances, does not talk well. A daily convocation of people, without refreshments or any extraneous object but the simple pleasure of seeing and talking with each other, is a thing that can scarcely be understood in English or American society. Social entertainment presupposes in the Anglo-Saxon mind something to eat, and not only something, but a great deal. Enormous dinners or great suppers constitute the entertainment. Nobody seems to have formed the idea that the talking—the simple exchange of social feelings—is, of itself, the entertainment, and that being together is the pleasure.

"Madame Rocamier for years had a circle of friends who met every afternoon in her salon from four to six o'clock, for the simple and sole pleasure of talking with each other. The very first wits and men of letters and statesmen and savans were enrolled in it, and each brought to the entertainment some choice morceau which he had laid aside from his own particular field to add to the feast. The daily intimacy gave each one such perfect insight into all the others' habits of thought, tastes, and preferences, that the conversation was like the celebrated music of the Conservatoire in Paris, a concert of perfectly chorded instruments taught by long habit of harmonious intercourse to keep exact time and tune together.

"Real conversation presupposes intimate acquaintance. People must see each other often enough to wear off the rough bark and outside rind of commonplaces and conventionalities in which their real ideas are enwrapped, and give forth without reserve their innermost and best feelings. Now what is called a large party is the first and rudest form of social intercourse. The most we can say of it is, that it is better than nothing. Men and women are crowded together like cattle in a pen. They look at each other, they jostle each other, exchange a few common bleatings, and eat together; and so the performance terminates. One may be crushed evening after evening against men or women, and learn very little about them. You may decide that a lady is good-tempered, when any amount of trampling on the skirt of her new silk dress brings no cloud to her brow. But *is* it good temper, or only wanton carelessness, which cares nothing for waste? You can see that a man is not a gentleman who squares his back to ladies at the supper-table, and devours boned turkey and *paté de foie gras*, while they vainly reach over and around him for something, and that another is a gentleman so far as to prefer the care of his weaker neighbors to the immediate indulgence of his own appetites; but further than this you learn little. Sometimes, it is true, in some secluded corner, two people of fine nervous system, undisturbed by the general confusion, may have a sociable half-hour, and really part feeling that they like each other better, and know more of each other than before. Yet these general gatherings have, after all, their value. They are not so good as something better would be, but they cannot be wholly dispensed with. It is far better that Mrs. Bogus should give an annual party, when she takes down all her bedsteads and throws open her whole house, than that she should never see her friends and neighbors inside her doors at all. She may feel that she has neither the taste nor the talent for constant small reunions. Such things, she may feel, require a social tact which she has not. She would be utterly at a loss how to conduct them. Each one would cost her as much anxiety and thought as her annual gathering, and prove a failure after all; whereas the annual demonstration can be put wholly into the hands of the caterer, who comes in force, with flowers, silver, china, servants, and, taking the house into his own hands, gives her entertainment for her, leaving to her no responsibility but the payment of the bills; and if Mr. Bogus does not quarrel with them, we know no reason why any one else should; and I think Mrs. Bogus merits well of the republic, for doing what she can do towards the hospitalities of the season. I'm sure I never cursed her in my heart, even when her strong coffee has held mine eyes open till morning, and her superlative lobster salads have given me the very darkest views of human life that ever dyspepsia and east wind could engender. Mrs. Bogus is the Eve who offers the apple; but after all, I am the foolish Adam who take and eat what I know is going to hurt me, and I am too gallant to visit my sins on the head of my too obliging tempter. In country places in particular, where little is going on and life is apt to stagnate, a good, large, generous party, which brings the whole neighborhood into one house to have a jolly time, to eat, drink, and be merry, is really quite a work of love and mercy. People see one another in their best clothes, and that is something; the elders exchange all manner of simple pleasantries and civilities, and talk over their domestic affairs, while the young people flirt, in that wholesome manner which is one of the safest of youthful follies. A country party, in fact, may be set down as a work of benevolence, and the money expended thereon fairly charged to the account of the great cause of peace and good will on earth."

"But don't you think," said my wife, "that, if the charge of providing the entertainment were less laborious, these gatherings could be more frequent? You see, if a woman feels that she must have five kinds of cake, and six kinds of preserves, and even ice-cream and jellies in a region where no confectioner comes in to abbreviate her labors, she will sit with closed doors, and do nothing towards the general exchange of life, because she cannot do as much as Mrs. Smith or Mrs. Parsons. If the idea of meeting together had some other focal point than eating, I think there would be more social feeling. It might be a musical reunion, where the various young people of a circle agreed to furnish each a song or an instrumental performance. It might be an impromptu charade party, bringing out something of that taste in arrangement of costume, and capacity for dramatic effect, of which there is more latent in society than we think. It might be the reading of articles in prose and poetry furnished to a common paper or portfolio, which would awaken an abundance of interest and speculation on the authorship, or it might be dramatic readings and recitations. Any or all of these pastimes might make an evening so entertaining that a simple cup of tea and a plate of cake or biscuit would be all the refreshment needed."

"We may with advantage steal a leaf now and then from some foreign book," said I. "In France and Italy, families have their peculiar days set apart for the reception of friends at their own houses. The whole house is put upon a footing of hospitality and invitation, and the whole mind is given to receiving the various friends. In the evening the salon is filled. The guests, coming from week to week, for years, become in time friends; the resort has the charm of a home circle; there are certain faces that you are always sure to meet there. A lady once said to me of a certain gentleman and lady whom she missed from her circle, 'They have been at our house every Wednesday evening for twenty years.' It seems to me that this frequency of meeting is the great secret of agreeable society. One sees, in our American life, abundance of people who are everything that is charming and cultivated, but one never sees enough of them. One meets them at some quiet reunion, passes a delightful hour, thinks how charming they are, and wishes one could see more of them. But the pleasant meeting is like the encounter of two ships in mid-ocean: away we sail, each on his respective course, to see each other no more till the pleasant remembrance has died away. Yet were there some quiet, home-like resort where we might turn in to renew from time to time the pleasant intercourse, to continue the last conversation, and to compare anew our readings and our experiences, the pleasant hour of liking would ripen into a warm friendship.

"But in order that this may be made possible and practicable, the utmost simplicity of entertainment must prevail. In a French salon all is to the last degree informal. The *bouilloire*, the French tea-kettle, is often tended by one of the gentlemen, who aids his fair neighbors in the mysteries of tea-making. One nymph is always to be found at the table dispensing tea and talk; and a basket of simple biscuit and cakes, offered by another, is all the further repast. The teacups and cake-basket are a real addition to the scene, because they cause a little lively social bustle, a little chatter and motion,—always of advantage in breaking up stiffness, and giving occasion for those graceful, airy nothings that answer so good a purpose in facilitating acquaintance.

"Nothing can be more charming than the description which Edmond About gives, in his novel of 'Tolla,' of the reception evenings of an old noble Roman family,—the spirit of repose and quietude through all the apartments; the ease of coming and going; the perfect home-like spirit in which the guests settle themselves to any employment of the hour that best suits them: some to lively chat, some to dreamy, silent lounging, some to a game, others in a distant apartment to music, and others still to a promenade along the terraces.

"One is often in a state of mind and nerves which indisposes for the effort of active conversation; one wishes to rest, to observe, to be amused without an effort; and a mansion which opens wide its hospitable arms, and offers itself to you as a sort of home, where you may rest, and do just as the humor suits you, is a perfect godsend at such times. You are at home there, your ways are understood, you can do as you please,—come early or late, be brilliant or dull,—you are always welcome. If you can do nothing for the social whole to-night, it matters not. There are many more nights to come in the future, and you are entertained on trust, without a challenge.

"I have one friend,—a man of genius, subject to the ebbs and flows of animal spirits which attend that organization. Of general society he has a nervous horror. A regular dinner or evening party is to him a terror, an impossibility; but there is a quiet parlor where stands a much-worn old sofa, and it is his delight to enter without knocking, and be found lying with half-shut eyes on this friendly couch, while the family life goes on around him without a question. Nobody is to mind him, to tease him with inquiries or salutations. If he will, he breaks into the stream of conversation, and sometimes, rousing up from one of these dreamy trances, finds himself, ere he or they know how, in the mood for free and friendly talk. People often wonder, 'How do you catch So-and-so? He is so shy! I have invited and invited, and he never comes.' We never invite, and he comes. We take no note of his coming or his going; we do not startle his entrance with acclamation, nor clog his departure with expostulation; it is fully understood that with us he shall do just as he chooses; and so he chooses to do much that we like.

"The sum of this whole doctrine of society is, that we are to try the value of all modes and forms of social entertainment by their effect in producing real acquaintance and real friendship and good will. The first and rudest form of seeking this is by a great promiscuous party, which simply effects this,—that people at least see each other on the outside, and eat together. Next come all those various forms of reunion in which the entertainment consists of something higher than staring and eating,—some exercise of the faculties of the guests in music, acting, recitation, reading, etc.; and these are a great advance, because they show people what is in them, and thus lay a foundation for a more intelligent appreciation and acquaintance.

These are the best substitute for the expense, show, and trouble of large parties. They are in their nature more refining and intellectual. It is astonishing, when people really put together, in some one club or association, all the different talents for pleasing possessed by different persons, how clever a circle may be gathered, — in the least promising neighborhood. A club of ladies in one of our cities has had quite a brilliant success. It is held every fortnight at the houses of the members, according to alphabetical sequence. The lady who receives has charge of arranging what the entertainment shall be, — whether charade, tableau, reading, recitation, or music; and the interest is much increased by the individual taste shown in the choice of the diversion and the variety which thence follows.

"In the summertime, in the country, open-air reunions are charming forms of social entertainment. Croquet parties, which bring young people together by daylight for a healthy exercise, and end with a moderate share of the evening, are a very desirable amusement. What are called 'lawn teas' are finding great favor in England and some parts of our country. They are simply an early tea enjoyed in a sort of picnic style in the grounds about the house. Such an entertainment enables one to receive a great many at a time, without crowding, and, being in its very idea rustic and informal, can be arranged with very little expense or trouble. With the addition of lanterns in the trees and a little music, this entertainment may be carried on far into the evening with a very pretty effect.

"As to dancing, I have this much to say of it. Either our houses must be all built over and made larger, or female crinolines must be made smaller, or dancing must continue as it now is, the most absurd and ungraceful of all attempts at amusement. The effort to execute round dances in the limits of modern houses, in the prevailing style of dress, can only lead to developments more startling than agreeable. Dancing in the open air, on the shaven green of lawns, is a pretty and graceful exercise, and there only can full sweep be allowed for the present feminine toilet.

"The English breakfast is an institution growing in favor here, and rightfully, too; for a party of fresh, good-natured, well-dressed people, assembled at breakfast on a summer morning, is as nearly perfect a form of reunion as can be devised. All are in full strength from their night's rest; the hour is fresh and lovely, and they are in condition to give each other the very cream of their thoughts, the first keen sparkle of the uncorked nervous system. The only drawback is that, in our busy American life, the most desirable gentlemen often cannot spare their morning hours. Breakfast parties presuppose a condition of leisure; but when they can be compassed, they are perhaps the most perfectly enjoyable of entertainments."

"Well," said Marianne, "I begin to waver about my party. I don't know, after all, but the desire of paying off social debts prompted the idea; perhaps we might try some of the agreeable things suggested. But, dear me! there's the baby. We'll finish the talk some other time."

VIII

HOW SHALL WE BE AMUSED

"One, two, three, four,—this makes the fifth accident on the Fourth of July, in the two papers I have just read," said Jenny.

"A very moderate allowance," said Theophilus Thoro, "if you consider the Fourth as a great national saturnalia, in which every boy in the land has the privilege of doing whatever is right in his own eyes."

"The poor boys!" said Mrs. Crowfield. "All the troubles of the world are laid at their door."

"Well," said Jenny, "they did burn the city of Portland, it appears. The fire arose from firecrackers, thrown by boys among the shavings of a carpenter's shop,—so says the paper."

"And," said Rudolph, "we surgeons expect a harvest of business from the Fourth, as surely as from a battle. Certain to be woundings, fractures, possibly amputations, following the proceedings of our glorious festival."

"Why cannot we Americans learn to amuse ourselves peaceably like other nations?" said Bob Stephens. "In France and Italy, the greatest national festivals pass off without fatal accident, or danger to any one. The fact is, in our country we have not learned *how to be amused*. Amusement has been made of so small account in our philosophy of life, that we are raw and unpracticed in being amused. Our diversions, compared with those of the politer nations of Europe, are coarse and savage,—and consist mainly in making disagreeable noises and disturbing the peace of the community by rude uproar. The only idea an American boy associates with the Fourth of July is that of gunpowder in some form, and a wild liberty to fire off pistols in all miscellaneous directions, and to throw firecrackers under the heels of horses, and into crowds of women and children, for the fun of seeing the stir and commotion thus produced. Now take a young Parisian boy and give him a fête, and he conducts himself with greater gentleness and good breeding, because he is part of a community in which the art of amusement has been refined and perfected, so that he has a thousand resources beyond the very obvious one of making a great banging and disturbance.

"Yes," continued Bob Stephens, "the fact is, that our grim old Puritan fathers set their feet down resolutely on all forms of amusement;

they would have stopped the lambs from wagging their tails, and shot the birds for singing, if they could have had their way; and in consequence of it, what a barren, cold, flowerless life is our New England existence! Life is all, as Mantalini said, one 'demd horrid grind.' 'Nothing here but working and going to church,' said the German emigrants,—and they were about right. A French traveler, in the year 1837, says that attending the Thursday-evening lectures and church prayer-meetings was the only recreation of the young people of Boston; and we can remember the time when this really was no exaggeration. Think of that, with all the seriousness of our Boston east winds to give it force, and fancy the provision for amusement in our society! The consequence is, that boys who have the longing for amusement strongest within them, and plenty of combativeness to back it, are the standing terror of good society, and our Fourth of July is a day of fear to all invalids and persons of delicate nervous organization, and of real, appreciable danger of life and limb to every one."

"Well, Robert," said my wife, "though I agree with you as to the actual state of society in this respect, I must enter my protest against your slur on the memory of our Pilgrim fathers."

"Yes," said Theophilus Thoro, "the New Englanders are the only people, I believe, who take delight in vilifying their ancestry. Every young hopeful in our day makes a target of his grandfather's gravestone, and fires away, with great self-applause. People in general seem to like to show that they are well-born, and come of good stock; but the young New Englanders, many of them, appear to take pleasure in insisting that they came of a race of narrow-minded, persecuting bigots.

"It is true, that our Puritan fathers saw not everything. They made a state where there were no amusements, but where people could go to bed and leave their house doors wide open all night, without a shadow of fear or danger, as was for years the custom in all our country villages. The fact is, that the simple early New England life, before we began to import foreigners, realized a state of society in whose possibility Europe would scarcely believe. If our fathers had few amusements, they needed few. Life was too really and solidly comfortable and happy to need much amusement.

"Look over the countries where people are most sedulously amused by their rulers and governors. Are they not the countries where the people are most oppressed, most unhappy in their circumstances, and therefore in greatest need of amusement? It is the slave who dances and sings, and why? Because he owns nothing, and can own nothing, and may as well dance and forget the fact. But give the slave a farm of his own, a wife of his own, and children of his own, with a schoolhouse and a vote, and ten to one he dances no more. He needs no amusement, because he is happy.

"The legislators of Europe wished nothing more than to bring up a people who would be content with amusements, and not ask after their rights or think too closely how they were governed. 'Gild the dome of the Invalides,' was Napoleon's scornful prescription, when he heard the Parisian population were discontented. They gilded it, and the people forgot to talk about anything else. They were a childish race, educated from the cradle on spectacle and show, and by the sight of their eyes could they be governed. The people of Boston, in 1776, could not have been managed in this way, chiefly because they were brought up in the strict schools of the fathers."

"But don't you think," said Jenny, "that something might be added and amended in the state of society our fathers established here in New England? Without becoming frivolous, there might be more attention paid to rational amusement."

"Certainly," said my wife, "the State and the Church both might take a lesson from the providence of foreign governments, and make liberty, to say the least, as attractive as despotism. It is a very unwise mother that does not provide her children with playthings."

"And yet," said Bob, "the only thing that the Church has yet done is to forbid and to frown. We have abundance of tracts against dancing, whist-playing, ninepins, billiards, operas, theatres,—in short, anything that young people would be apt to like. The General Assembly of the Presbyterian Church refused to testify against slavery, because of political diffidence, but made up for it by ordering a more stringent crusade against dancing. The theatre and opera grow up and exist among us like plants on the windy side of a hill, blown all awry by a constant blast of conscientious rebuke. There is really no amusement young people are fond of, which they do not pursue, in a sort of defiance of the frown of the peculiarly religious world. With all the telling of what the young shall *not* do, there has been very little telling what they shall do.

"The whole department of amusements—certainly one of the most important in education—has been by the Church made a sort of outlaws' ground, to be taken possession of and held by all sorts of spiritual ragamuffins; and then the faults and shortcomings resulting from this arrangement have been held up and insisted on as reasons why no Christian should ever venture into it.

"If the Church would set herself to amuse her young folks, instead of discussing doctrines and metaphysical hair-splitting, she would prove herself a true mother, and not a hard-visaged stepdame. Let her keep this department, so powerful and so difficult to manage, in what are morally the strongest hands, instead of giving it up to the weakest.

"I think, if the different churches of a city, for example, would rent a building where there should be a billiard-table, one or two ninepin-alleys, a reading-room, a garden and grounds for ball playing or innocent lounging, that they would do more to keep their young people from the ways of sin than a Sunday-school could. Nay, more: I would go further. I would have a portion of the building fitted up with scenery and a stage, for the getting up of tableaux or dramatic performances, and thus give scope for the exercise of that histrionic talent of which there is so much lying unemployed in society.

"Young people do not like amusements any better for the wickedness connected with them. The spectacle of a sweet little child singing hymns, and repeating prayers, of a pious old Uncle Tom dying for his religion, has filled theatres night after night, and proved that there really is no need of indecent or improper plays to draw full houses.

"The things that draw young people to places of amusement are not at first gross things. Take the most notorious public place in Paris, — the Jardin Mabille, for instance, — and the things which give it its first charm are all innocent and artistic. Exquisite beds of lilies, roses, gillyflowers, lighted with jets of gas so artfully as to make every flower translucent as a gem; fountains where the gaslight streams out from behind misty wreaths of falling water and calla-blossoms; sofas of velvet turf, canopied with fragrant honeysuckle; dim bowers overarched with lilacs and roses; a dancing-ground under trees whose branches bend with a fruitage of many-colored lamps; enchanting music and graceful motion; in all these there is not only no sin, but they are really beautiful and desirable; and if they were only used on the side and in the service of virtue and religion, if they were contrived and kept up by the guardians and instructors of youth, instead of by those whose interest it is to demoralize and destroy, young people would have no temptation to stray into the haunts of vice.

"In Prussia, under the reign of Frederick William II., when one good, hard-handed man governed the whole country like a strict schoolmaster, the public amusements for the people were made such as to present a model for all states. The theatres were strictly supervised, and actors obliged to conform to the rules of decorum and morality. The plays and performances were under the immediate supervision of men of grave morals, who allowed nothing corrupting to appear; and the effect of this administration and restraint is to be seen in Berlin even to this day. The public gardens are full of charming little resorts, where, every afternoon, for a very moderate sum, one can have either a concert of good music, or a very fair dramatic or operatic performance. Here whole families may be seen enjoying together a wholesome and refreshing entertainment,—the mother and aunts with their knitting, the baby, the children of all ages, and the father,—their faces radiant with that mild German light of contentment and good will which one feels to be characteristic of the nation. When I saw these things, and thought of our own outcast, unprovided boys and young men, haunting the streets and alleys of cities, in places far from the companionship of mothers and sisters, I felt as if it would be better for a nation to be brought up by a good strict schoolmaster king than to try to be a republic."

"Yes," said I, "but the difficulty is to get the good schoolmaster king. For one good shepherd, there are twenty who use the sheep only for their flesh and their wool. Republics can do all that kings can,— witness our late army and sanitary commission. Once fix the idea thoroughly in the public mind that there ought to be as regular and careful provision for public amusement as there is for going to church and Sunday-school, and it will be done. Central Park in New York is a beginning in the right direction, and Brooklyn is following the example of her sister city. There is, moreover, an indication of the proper spirit in the increased efforts that are made to beautify Sunday-school rooms, and make them interesting, and to have Sunday-school fêtes and picnics,—the most harmless and commendable way of celebrating the Fourth of July. Why should saloons and bar-rooms be made attractive by fine paintings, choice music, flowers, and fountains, and Sunday-school rooms be four bare walls? There are churches whose broad aisles represent ten and twenty millions of dollars, and whose sons and daughters are daily drawn to circuses, operas, theatres, because they have tastes and feelings, in themselves perfectly laudable and innocent, for the gratification of which no provision is made in any other place."

"I know one church," said Rudolph, "whose Sunday-school room is as beautifully adorned as any haunt of sin. There is a fountain in the centre, which plays into a basin surrounded with shells and flowers; it has a small organ to lead the children's voices, and the walls are hung with oil paintings and engravings from the best masters. The festivals of the Sabbath school, which are from time to time held in this place, educate the taste of the children, as well as amuse them; and, above all, they have through life the advantage of associating with their early religious education all those ideas of taste, elegance, and artistic culture which too often come through polluted channels.

"When the amusement of the young shall become the care of the experienced and the wise, and the floods of wealth that are now rolling over and over, in silent investments, shall be put into the form of innocent and refined pleasures for the children and youth of the state, our national festivals may become days to be desired, and not dreaded.

"On the Fourth of July, our city fathers do in a certain dim wise perceive that the public owes some attempt at amusement to its children, and they vote large sums, principally expended in bell-ringing, cannon, and fireworks. The sidewalks are witness to the number who fall victims to the temptations held out by grog-shops and saloons; and the papers, for weeks after, are crowded with accounts of accidents. Now, a yearly sum expended to keep up, and keep pure, places of amusement which hold out no temptation to vice, but which excel all vicious places in real beauty and attractiveness, would greatly lessen the sum needed to be expended on any one particular day, and would refine and prepare our people to keep holidays and festivals appropriately."

"For my part," said Mrs. Crowfield, "I am grieved at the opprobrium which falls on the race of *boys*. Why should the most critical era in the life of those who are to be men, and to govern society, be passed in a sort of outlawry,—a rude warfare with all existing institutions? The years between ten and twenty are full of the nervous excitability which marks the growth and maturing of the manly nature. The boy feels wild impulses, which ought to be vented in legitimate and healthful exercise. He wants to run, shout, wrestle, ride, row, skate; and all these together are often not sufficient to relieve the need he feels of throwing off the excitability that burns within.

"For the wants of this period what safe provision is made by the church, or by the state, or any of the boy's lawful educators? In all the Prussian schools amusements are as much a part of the regular school system as grammar or geography. The teacher is with the boys on the playground, and plays as heartily as any of them. The boy has his physical wants anticipated. He is not left to fight his way, blindly stumbling against society, but goes forward in a safe path, which his elders and betters have marked out for him.

"In our country, the boy's career is often a series of skirmishes with society. He wants to skate, and contrives ingeniously to dam the course of a brook and flood a meadow which makes a splendid skating-ground. Great is the joy for a season, and great the skating. But the water floods the neighboring cellars. The boys are cursed through all the moods and tenses,—boys are such a plague! The dam is torn down with emphasis and execration. The boys, however, lie in wait some cold night, between twelve and one, and build it up again; and thus goes on the battle. The boys care not whose cellar they flood, because nobody cares for their amusement. They understand themselves to be outlaws, and take an outlaw's advantage.

"Again, the boys have their sleds; and sliding down hill is splendid fun. But they trip up some grave citizen, who sprains his shoulder. What is the result? Not the provision of a safe, good place, where boys *may* slide down hill without danger to any one, but an edict forbidding all sliding, under penalty of fine.

"Boys want to swim: it is best they should swim; and if city fathers, foreseeing and caring for this want, should think it worth while to mark off some good place, and have it under such police surveillance as to enforce decency of language and demeanor, they would prevent a great deal that now is disagreeable in the unguided efforts of boys to enjoy this luxury.

"It would be cheaper in the end, even if one had to build sliding-piles, as they do in Russia, or to build skating-rinks, as they do in Montreal,—it would be cheaper for every city, town, and village to provide legitimate amusement for boys, under proper superintendence, than to leave them, as they are now left, to fight their way against society.

"In the boys' academies of our country, what provision is made for amusement? There are stringent rules, and any number of them, to prevent boys making any noise that may disturb the neighbors; and generally the teacher thinks that, if he keeps the boys *still*, and sees that they get their lessons, his duty is done. But a hundred boys ought not to be kept still. There ought to be noise and motion among them, in order that they may healthily survive the great changes which nature is working within them. If they become silent, averse to movement, fond of indoor lounging and warm rooms, they are going in far worse ways than any amount of outward lawlessness could bring them to.

"Smoking and yellow-covered novels are worse than any amount of hullabaloo; and the quietest boy is often a poor, ignorant victim, whose life is being drained out of him before it is well begun. If mothers could only see the series of books that are sold behind counters to boarding-school boys, whom nobody warns and nobody cares for,—if they could see the poison, going from pillow to pillow, in books pretending to make clear the great, sacred mysteries of our nature, but trailing them over with the filth of utter corruption! These horrible works are the inward and secret channel of hell, into which a boy is thrust by the pressure of strict outward rules, forbidding that physical and out-of-door exercise and motion to which he ought rather to be encouraged, and even driven.

"It is melancholy to see that, while parents, teachers, and churches make no provision for boys in the way of amusement, the world, the flesh, and the devil are incessantly busy and active in giving it to them. There are ninepin-alleys, with cigars and a bar. There are billiard-saloons, with a bar, and, alas! with the occasional company of girls who are still beautiful, but who have lost the innocence of womanhood, while yet retaining many of its charms. There are theatres, with a bar, and with the society of lost women. The boy comes to one and all of these places, seeking only what is natural and proper he should have,—what should be given him under the eye and by the care of the Church, the school. He comes for exercise and amusement,—he gets these, and a ticket to destruction besides,—and whose fault is it?"

"These are the aspects of public life," said I, "which make me feel that we never shall have a perfect state till women vote and bear rule equally with men. State housekeeping has been, hitherto, like what any housekeeping would be, conducted by the voice and knowledge of man alone.

"If women had an equal voice in the management of our public money, I have faith to believe that thousands which are now wasted in mere political charlatanism would go to provide for the rearing of the children of the state, male and female. My wife has spoken for the boys; I speak for the girls also. What is provided for their physical development and amusement? Hot, gas-lighted theatric and operatic performances, beginning at eight, and ending at midnight;

hot, crowded parties and balls; dancing with dresses tightly laced over the laboring lungs,—these are almost the whole story. I bless the advent of croquet and skating. And yet the latter exercise, pursued as it generally is, is a most terrible exposure. There is no kindly parental provision for the poor, thoughtless, delicate young creature,—not even the shelter of a dressing-room with a fire, at which she may warm her numb fingers and put on her skates when she arrives on the ground, and to which she may retreat in intervals of fatigue; so she catches cold, and perhaps sows the seed which with air-tight stoves and other appliances of hot-house culture may ripen into consumption.

"What provision is there for the amusement of all the shop girls, seamstresses, factory girls, that crowd our cities? What for the thousands of young clerks and operatives? Not long since, in a respectable old town in New England, the body of a beautiful girl was drawn from the river in which she had drowned herself,—a young girl only fifteen, who came to the city, far from home and parents, and fell a victim to the temptation which brought her to shame and desperation. Many thus fall every year who are never counted. They fall into the ranks of those whom the world abandons as irreclaimable.

"Let those who have homes and every appliance to make life pass agreeably, and who yet yawn over an unoccupied evening, fancy a lively young girl all day cooped up at sewing in a close, ill-ventilated room. Evening comes, and she has three times the desire for amusement and three times the need of it that her fashionable sister has. And where can she go? To the theatre, perhaps, with some young man as thoughtless as herself, and more depraved; then to the bar for a glass of wine, and another; and then, with a head swimming and turning, who shall say where else she may be led? Past midnight and no one to look after her,—and one night ruins her utterly and for life, and she as yet only a child!

"John Newton had a very wise saying: 'Here is a man trying to fill a bushel with chaff. Now if I fill it with wheat first, it is better than to fight him.' This apothegm contains in it the whole of what I would say on the subject of amusements."

IX

DRESS, OR WHO MAKES THE FASHIONS

The door of my study being open, I heard in the distant parlor a sort of flutter of silken wings, and chatter of bird-like voices, which told me that a covey of Jenny's pretty young street birds had just alighted there. I could not forbear a peep at the rosy faces that glanced out under pheasants' tails, doves' wings, and nodding humming-birds, and made one or two errands in that direction only that I might gratify my eyes with a look at them.

Your nice young girl, of good family and good breeding, is always a pretty object, and, for my part, I regularly lose my heart (in a sort of figurative way) to every fresh, charming creature that trips across my path. All their mysterious rattletraps and whirligigs,—their curls and networks and crimples and rimples and crisping-pins,—their little absurdities, if you will,—have to me a sort of charm, like the tricks and stammerings of a curly-headed child. I should have made a very poor censor if I had been put in Cato's place: the witches would have thrown all my wisdom into some private chip-basket of their own, and walked off with it in triumph. Never a girl bows to me that I do not see in her eye a twinkle of confidence that she could, if she chose, make an old fool of me. I surrender at discretion on first sight.

Jenny's friends are nice girls,—the flowers of good, staid, sensible families,—not heathen blossoms nursed in the hot-bed heat of wild, high-flying, fashionable society. They have been duly and truly taught and brought up, by good mothers and painstaking aunties, to understand in their infancy that handsome is that handsome does; that little girls must not be vain of their pretty red shoes and nice curls, and must remember that it is better to be good than to be handsome; with all other wholesome truisms of the kind. They have been to school, and had their minds improved in all modern ways,—have calculated eclipses, and read Virgil, Schiller, and La Fontaine, and understand all about the geological strata, and the different systems of metaphysics,—so that a person reading the list of their acquirements might be a little appalled at the prospect of entering into conversation with them. For all these reasons I listened quite indulgently to the animated conversation that was going on about— Well!

What *do* girls generally talk about, when a knot of them get together? Not, I believe, about the sources of the Nile, or the precession of the equinoxes, or the nature of the human understanding, or Dante, or Shakespeare, or Milton, although they have learned all about them in school; but upon a theme much nearer and dearer,—the one all-pervading feminine topic ever since Eve started the first toilet of fig-leaves; and as I caught now and then a phrase of their chatter, I jotted it down in pure amusement, giving to each charming speaker the name of the bird under whose colors she was sailing.

"For my part," said little Humming-Bird, "I'm quite worn out with sewing; the fashions are all *so* different from what they were last year, that everything has to be made over."

"Isn't it dreadful!" said Pheasant. "There's my new mauve silk dress! it was a very expensive silk, and I haven't worn it more than three or four times, and it really looks quite dowdy; and I can't get Patterson to do it over for me for this party. Well, really, I shall have to give up company because I have nothing to wear."

"Who *does* set the fashions, I wonder," said Humming-Bird; "they seem nowadays to whirl faster and faster, till really they don't leave one time for anything."

"Yes," said Dove, "I haven't a moment for reading, or drawing, or keeping up my music. The fact is, nowadays, to keep one's self properly dressed is all one can do. If I were *grande dame* now, and had only to send an order to my milliner and dressmaker, I might be beautifully dressed all the time without giving much thought to it myself; and that is what I should like. But this constant planning about one's toilet, changing your buttons and your fringes and your bonnet-trimmings and your hats every other day, and then being behindhand! It is really too fatiguing."

"Well," said Jenny, "I never pretend to keep up. I never expect to be in the front rank of fashion, but no girl wants to be behind every one; nobody wants to have people say, 'Do see what an old-times, rubbishy looking creature *that* is.' And now, with my small means and my conscience (for I have a conscience in this matter, and don't wish to spend any more time and money than is needed to keep one's self fresh and tasteful), I find my dress quite a fatiguing care."

"Well, now, girls," said Humming-Bird, "do you really know, I have sometimes thought I should like to be a nun, just to get rid of all this labor. If I once gave up dress altogether, and knew I was to have nothing but one plain robe tied round my waist with a cord, it does seem to me as if it would be a perfect repose,—only one is a Protestant, you know."

Now, as Humming-Bird was the most notoriously dressy individual in the little circle, this suggestion was received with quite a laugh. But Dove took it up.

"Well, really," she said, "when dear Mr. S— — preaches those saintly sermons to us about our baptismal vows, and the nobleness of an unworldly life, and calls on us to live for something purer and higher than we are living for, I confess that sometimes all my life seems to me a mere sham,—that I am going to church, and saying solemn words, and being wrought up by solemn music, and uttering most solemn vows and prayers, all to no purpose; and then I come away and look at my life, all resolving itself into a fritter about dress, and sewing-silk, cord, braid, and buttons,—the next fashion of bonnets,—how to make my old dresses answer instead of new,— how to keep the air of the world, while in my heart I am cherishing something higher and better. If there's anything I detest it is hypocrisy; and sometimes the life I lead looks like it. But how to get out of it?—what to do?—"

"I'm sure," said Humming-Bird, "that taking care of my clothes and going into company is, frankly, all I do. If I go to parties, as other girls do, and make calls, and keep dressed,—you know papa is not rich, and one must do these things economically,—it really does take all the time I have. When I was confirmed the Bishop talked to us so sweetly, and I really meant sincerely to be a good girl,—to be as good as I knew how; but now, when they talk about fighting the good fight and running the Christian race, I feel very mean and little, for I am quite sure this isn't doing it. But what is,—and who is?"

"Aunt Betsey Titcomb is doing it, I suppose," said Pheasant.

"Aunt Betsey!" said Humming-Bird, "well, she is. She spends all her money in doing good. She goes round visiting the poor all the time. She is a perfect saint;—but oh girls, how she looks! Well, now, I confess, when I think I must look like Aunt Betsey, my courage gives out. Is it necessary to go without hoops, and look like a dipped candle, in order to be unworldly? Must one wear such a fright of a bonnet?"

"No," said Jenny, "I think not. I think Miss Betsey Titcomb, good as she is, injures the cause of goodness by making it outwardly repulsive. I really think, if she would take some pains with her dress, and spend upon her own wardrobe a little of the money she gives away, that she might have influence in leading others to higher aims; now all her influence is against it. Her *outré* and repulsive exterior arrays our natural and innocent feelings against goodness; for surely it is natural and innocent to wish to look well, and I am really afraid a great many of us are more afraid of being thought ridiculous than of being wicked."

"And after all," said Pheasant, "you know Mr. St. Clair says, 'Dress is one of the fine arts,' and if it is, why of course we ought to cultivate it. Certainly, well-dressed men and women are more agreeable objects than rude and unkempt ones. There must be somebody whose mission it is to preside over the agreeable arts of life; and I suppose it falls to 'us girls.' That's the way I comfort myself, at all events. Then I must confess that I do like dress; I'm not cultivated enough to be a painter or a poet, and I have all my artistic nature, such as it is, in dress. I love harmonies of color, exact shades and matches; I love to see a uniform idea carried all through a woman's toilet,—her dress, her bonnet, her gloves, her shoes, her pocket-handkerchief and cuffs, her very parasol, all in correspondence."

"But, my dear," said Jenny, "anything of this kind must take a fortune!"

"And if I had a fortune, I'm pretty sure I should spend a good deal of it in this way," said Pheasant. "I can imagine such completeness of toilet as I have never seen. How I would like the means to show what I could do! My life, now, is perpetual disquiet. I always feel shabby. My things must all be bought at haphazard, as they can be got out of my poor little allowance,—and things are getting so horridly dear! Only think of it, girls! gloves at two and a quarter! and boots at seven, eight, and ten dollars! and then, as you say, the fashions changing so! Why, I bought a sack last fall and gave forty dollars for it, and this winter I'm wearing it, to be sure, but it has no style at all,—looks quite antiquated!"

"Now I say," said Jenny, "that you are really morbid on the subject of dress; you are fastidious and particular and exacting in your ideas in a way that really ought to be put down. There is not a girl of our set that dresses as nicely as you do, except Emma Seyton, and her father, you know, has no end of income."

"Nonsense, Jenny," said Pheasant. "I think I really look like a beggar; but then, I bear it as well as I can, because, you see, I know papa does all for us he can, and I won't be extravagant. But I do think, as Humming-Bird says, that it would be a great relief to give it up altogether and retire from the world; or, as Cousin John says, climb a tree and pull it up after you, and so be in peace."

"Well," said Jenny, "all this seems to have come on since the war. It seems to me that not only has everything doubled in price, but all the habits of the world seem to require that you shall have double the quantity of everything. Two or three years ago a good balmoral skirt was a fixed fact; it was a convenient thing for sloppy, unpleasant weather. But now, dear me! there is no end to them. They cost fifteen and twenty dollars; and girls that I know have one or two every season, besides all sorts of quilled and embroidered and ruffled and tucked and flounced ones. Then, in dressing one's hair, what a perfect overflow there is of all manner of waterfalls, and braids, and rats, and mice, and curls, and combs; when three or four years ago we combed our own hair innocently behind our ears, and put flowers in it, and thought we looked nicely at our evening parties! I don't believe we look any better now, when we are dressed, than we did then,—so what's the use?"

"Well, did you ever see such a tyranny as this of fashion?" said Humming-Bird. "We know it's silly, but we all bow down before it; we are afraid of our lives before it; and who makes all this and sets it going? The Paris milliners, the Empress, or who?"

"The question where fashions come from is like the question where pins go to," said Pheasant. "Think of the thousands and millions of pins that are being used every year, and not one of them worn out. Where do they all go to? One would expect to find a pin mine somewhere."

"Victor Hugo says they go into the sewers in Paris," said Jenny.

"And the fashions come from a source about as pure," said I, from the next room.

"Bless me, Jenny, do tell us if your father has been listening to us all this time!" was the next exclamation; and forthwith there was a whir and rustle of the silken wings, as the whole troop fluttered into my study.

"Now, Mr. Crowfield, you are too bad!" said Humming-Bird, as she perched upon a corner of my study-table, and put her little feet upon an old "Froissart" which filled the armchair.

"To be listening to our nonsense!" said Pheasant.

"Lying in wait for us!" said Dove.

"Well, now, you have brought us all down on you," said Humming-Bird, "and you won't find it so easy to be rid of us. You will have to answer all our questions."

"My dears, I am at your service, as far as mortal man may be," said I.

"Well, then," said Humming-Bird, "tell us all about everything,— how things come to be as they are. Who makes the fashions?"

"I believe it is universally admitted that, in the matter of feminine toilet, France rules the world," said I.

"But who rules France?" said Pheasant. "Who decides what the fashions shall be there?"

"It is the great misfortune of the civilized world, at the present hour," said I, "that the state of morals in France is apparently at the very lowest ebb, and consequently the leadership of fashion is entirely in the hands of a class of women who could not be admitted into good society, in any country. Women who can never have the name of wife,—who know none of the ties of family,—these are the dictators whose dress and equipage and appointments give the law, first to France, and through France to the civilized world. Such was the confession of Monsieur Dupin, made in a late speech before the French Senate, and acknowledged, with murmurs of assent on all sides, to be the truth. This is the reason why the fashions have such an utter disregard of all those laws of prudence and economy which regulate the expenditures of families. They are made by women whose sole and only hold on life is personal attractiveness, and with whom to keep this up, at any cost, is a desperate necessity. No moral quality, no association of purity, truth, modesty, self-denial, or family love, comes in to hallow the atmosphere about them, and create a sphere of loveliness which brightens as mere physical beauty fades. The ravages of time and dissipation must be made up by an unceasing study of the arts of the toilet. Artists of all sorts, moving in their train, rack all the stores of ancient and modern art for the picturesque, the dazzling, the grotesque; and so, lest these Circes of society should carry all before them, and enchant every husband, brother, and lover, the staid and lawful Penelopes leave the hearth and home to follow in their triumphal march and imitate their arts. Thus it goes in France; and in England, virtuous and domestic princesses and peeresses must take obediently what has been decreed by their rulers in the *demi-monde* of France; and we in America have leaders of fashion, who make it their pride and glory to turn New York into Paris, and to keep even step with everything that is going on there. So the whole world of womankind is marching under the command of those leaders. The love of dress and glitter and fashion is getting to be a morbid, unhealthy epidemic, which really eats away the nobleness and purity of women.

"In France, as Monsieur Dupin, Edmond About, and Michelet tell us, the extravagant demands of love for dress lead women to contract debts unknown to their husbands, and sign obligations which are paid by the sacrifice of honor, and thus the purity of the family is continually undermined. In England there is a voice of complaint, sounding from the leading periodicals, that the extravagant demands of female fashion are bringing distress into families, and making marriages impossible; and something of the same sort seems to have begun here. We are across the Atlantic, to be sure; but we feel the swirl and drift of the great whirlpool; only, fortunately, we are far enough off to be able to see whither things are tending, and to stop ourselves if we will.

"We have just come through a great struggle, in which our women have borne an heroic part,—have shown themselves capable of any kind of endurance and self-sacrifice; and now we are in that reconstructive state which makes it of the greatest consequence to ourselves and the world that we understand our own institutions and position, and learn that, instead of following the corrupt and worn-out ways of the Old World, we are called on to set the example of a new state of society,—noble, simple, pure, and religious; and women can do more towards this even than men, for women are the real architects of society.

"Viewed in this light, even the small, frittering cares of women's life—the attention to buttons, trimmings, thread, and sewing-silk— may be an expression of their patriotism and their religion. A noble-hearted woman puts a noble meaning into even the commonplace details of life. The women of America can, if they choose, hold back their country from following in the wake of old, corrupt, worn-out, effeminate European society, and make America the leader of the world in all that is good."

"I'm sure," said Humming-Bird, "we all would like to be noble and heroic. During the war, I did so long to be a man! I felt so poor and insignificant because I was nothing but a girl!"

"Ah, well," said Pheasant, "but then one wants to do something worth doing, if one is going to do anything. One would like to be grand and heroic, if one could; but if not, why try at all? One wants to be *very* something, *very* great, *very* heroic; or if not that, then at least very stylish and very fashionable. It is this everlasting mediocrity that bores me."

"Then, I suppose, you agree with the man we read of, who buried his one talent in the earth, as hardly worth caring for."

"To say the truth, I always had something of a sympathy for that man," said Pheasant. "I can't enjoy goodness and heroism in homœopathic doses. I want something appreciable. What I can do, being a woman, is a very different thing from what I should try to do if I were a man, and had a man's chances: it is so much less—so poor—that it is scarcely worth trying for."

"You remember," said I, "the apothegm of one of the old divines, that if two angels were sent down from heaven, the one to govern a kingdom, and the other to sweep a street, they would not feel any disposition to change works."

"Well, that just shows that they are angels, and not mortals," said Pheasant; "but we poor human beings see things differently."

"Yet, my child, what could Grant or Sherman have done, if it had not been for the thousands of brave privates who were content to do each their imperceptible little,—if it had not been for the poor, unnoticed, faithful, never-failing common soldiers, who did the work and bore the suffering? No *one* man saved our country, or could save it; nor could the men have saved it without the women. Every mother that said to her son, Go; every wife that strengthened the hands of her husband; every girl who sent courageous letters to her betrothed; every woman who worked for a fair; every grandam whose trembling hands knit stockings and scraped lint; every little maiden who hemmed shirts and made comfort-bags for soldiers,— each and all have been the joint doers of a great heroic work, the doing of which has been the regeneration of our era. A whole generation has learned the luxury of thinking heroic thoughts and being conversant with heroic deeds, and I have faith to believe that all this is not to go out in a mere crush of fashionable luxury and folly and frivolous emptiness,—but that our girls are going to merit the high praise given us by De Tocqueville, when he placed first among the causes of our prosperity the *noble character of American women*. Because foolish female persons in New York are striving to outdo the *demi-monde* of Paris in extravagance, it must not follow that every sensible and patriotic matron, and every nice, modest young girl, must forthwith and without inquiry rush as far after them as they possibly can. Because Mrs. Shoddy opens a ball in a two-thousand-dollar lace dress, every girl in the land need not look with shame on her modest white muslin. Somewhere between the fast women of Paris and the daughters of Christian American families there should be established a *cordon sanitaire*, to keep out the contagion of manners, customs, and habits with which a noble-minded, religious democratic people ought to have nothing to do."

"Well now, Mr. Crowfield," said the Dove, "since you speak us so fair, and expect so much of us, we must of course try not to fall below your compliments; but, after all, tell us what is the right standard about dress. Now we have daily lectures about this at home. Aunt Maria says that she never saw such times as these, when mothers and daughters, church-members and worldly people, all seem to be going one way, and sit down together and talk, as they will, on dress and fashion, — how to have this made and that altered. We used to be taught, she said, that church-members had higher things to think of, — that their thoughts ought to be fixed on something better, and that they ought to restrain the vanity and worldliness of children and young people; but now, she says, even before a girl is born, dress is the one thing needful, — the great thing to be thought of; and so, in every step of the way upward, her little shoes, and her little bonnets, and her little dresses, and her corals and her ribbons, are constantly being discussed in her presence, as the one all-important object of life. Aunt Maria thinks mamma is dreadful, because she has maternal yearnings over our toilet successes and fortunes; and we secretly think Aunt Maria is rather soured by old age, and has forgotten how a girl feels."

"The fact is," said I, "that the love of dress and outside show has been always such an exacting and absorbing tendency, that it seems to have furnished work for religionists and economists, in all ages, to keep it within bounds. Various religious bodies, at the outset, adopted severe rules in protest against it. The Quakers and the Methodists prescribed certain fixed modes of costume as a barrier against its frivolities and follies. In the Romish Church an entrance on any religious order prescribed entire and total renunciation of all thought and care for the beautiful in person or apparel, as the first step towards saintship. The costume of the *religieuse* seemed to be purposely intended to imitate the shroudings and swathings of a corpse and the lugubrious color of a pall, so as forever to remind the wearer that she was dead to the world of ornament and physical beauty. All great Christian preachers and reformers have leveled their artillery against the toilet, from the time of St. Jerome downward; and Tom Moore has put into beautiful and graceful verse St. Jerome's admonitions to the fair churchgoers of his time.

WHO IS THE MAID?

ST. JEROME'S LOVE.

Who is the maid my spirit seeks,
　　Through cold reproof and slander's blight?
Has *she* Love's roses on her cheeks?
　　Is *hers* an eye of this world's light?
No: wan and sunk with midnight prayer
　　Are the pale looks of her I love;
Or if, at times, a light be there,
　　Its beam is kindled from above.

I chose not her, my heart's elect,
　　From those who seek their Maker's shrine
In gems and garlands proudly decked,
　　As if themselves were things divine.
No: Heaven but faintly warms the breast
　　That beats beneath a broidered veil;
And she who comes in glittering vest
　　To mourn her frailty, still is frail.

Not so the faded form I prize
　　And love, because its bloom is gone;
The glory in those sainted eyes
　　Is all the grace *her* brow puts on.
And ne'er was Beauty's dawn so bright,
　　So touching, as that form's decay,
Which, like the altar's trembling light,
　　In holy lustre wastes away.

"But the defect of all these modes of warfare on the elegances and refinements of the toilet was that they were too indiscriminate. They were in reality founded on a false principle. They took for granted that there was something radically corrupt and wicked in the body and in the physical system. According to this mode of viewing things, the body was a loathsome and pestilent prison, in which the soul was locked up and enslaved, and the eyes, the ears, the taste, the smell, were all so many corrupt traitors in conspiracy to poison her. Physical beauty of every sort was a snare, a Circean enchantment, to be valiantly contended with and straitly eschewed. Hence they preached, not moderation, but total abstinence from all pursuit of physical grace and beauty.

"Now, a resistance founded on an over-statement is constantly tending to reaction. People always have a tendency to begin thinking for themselves; and when they so think, they perceive that a good and wise God would not have framed our bodies with such exquisite care only to corrupt our souls,—that physical beauty, being created in such profuse abundance around us, and we being possessed with such a longing for it, must have its uses, its legitimate sphere of exercise. Even the poor, shrouded nun, as she walks the convent garden, cannot help asking herself why, if the crimson velvet of the rose was made by God, all colors except black and white are sinful for her; and the modest Quaker, after hanging all her house and dressing all her children in drab, cannot but marvel at the sudden outstreaking of blue and yellow and crimson in the tulip-beds under her window, and reflect how very differently the great All-Father arrays the world's housekeeping. The consequence of all this has been, that the reforms based upon these severe and exclusive views have gradually gone backward. The Quaker dress is imperceptibly and gracefully melting away into a refined simplicity of modern costume, which in many cases seems to be the perfection of taste. The obvious reflection, that one color of the rainbow is quite as much of God as another, has led the children of gentle dove-colored mothers to appear in shades of rose-color, blue, and lilac; and wise elders have said, it is not so much the color or the shape that we object to, as giving too much time and too much money,—if the heart be right with God and man, the bonnet ribbon may be of any shade you please."

"But don't you think," said Pheasant, "that a certain fixed dress, marking the unworldly character of a religious order, is desirable? Now, I have said before that I am very fond of dress. I have a passion for beauty and completeness in it; and as long as I am in the world and obliged to dress as the world does, it constantly haunts me, and tempts me to give more time, more thought, more money, to these things than I really think they are worth. But I can conceive of giving up this thing altogether as being much easier than regulating it to the precise point. I never read of a nun's taking the veil without a certain thrill of sympathy. To cut off one's hair, to take off and cast from her, one by one, all one's trinkets and jewels, to lie down and have the pall thrown over one, and feel one's self once for all dead to the world,—I cannot help feeling as if this were real, thorough, noble renunciation, and as if one might rise up from it with a grand, calm consciousness of having risen to a higher and purer atmosphere, and got above all the littlenesses and distractions that beset us here. So I have heard charming young Quaker girls, who in more thoughtless days indulged in what for them was a slight shading of worldly conformity, say that it was to them a blessed rest when they put on the strict, plain dress, and felt that they really had taken up the cross and turned their backs on the world. I can conceive of doing this, much more easily than I can of striking the exact line between worldly conformity and noble aspiration, in the life I live now."

"My dear child," said I, "we all overlook one great leading principle of our nature, and that is, that we are made to find a higher pleasure in self-sacrifice than in any form of self-indulgence. There is something grand and pathetic in the idea of an entire self-surrender, to which every human soul leaps up, as we do to the sound of martial music.

"How many boys of Boston and New York, who had lived effeminate and idle lives, felt this new power uprising in them in our war! How they embraced the dirt and discomfort and fatigue and watchings and toils of camp-life with an eagerness of zest which they had never felt in the pursuit of mere pleasure, and wrote home burning letters that they never were so happy in their lives! It was not that dirt and fatigue and discomfort and watchings and weariness were in themselves agreeable, but it was a joy to feel themselves able to bear all and surrender all for something higher than self. Many a poor Battery bully of New York, many a street rowdy, felt uplifted by the discovery that he too had hid away under the dirt and dust of his former life this divine and precious jewel. He leaped for joy to find that he too could be a hero. Think of the hundreds of thousands of plain ordinary workingmen, and of seemingly ordinary boys, who, but for such a crisis, might have passed through life never knowing this to be in them, and who courageously endured hunger and thirst and cold, and separation from dearest friends, for days and weeks and months, when they might, at any day, have bought a respite by deserting their country's flag! Starving boys, sick at heart, dizzy in head, pining for home and mother, still found warmth and comfort in the one thought that they could suffer, die, for their country; and the graves at Salisbury and Andersonville show in how many souls this noble power of self-sacrifice to the higher good was lodged,—how many there were, even in the humblest walks of life, who preferred death by torture to life in dishonor.

"It is this heroic element in man and woman that makes self-sacrifice an ennobling and purifying ordeal in any religious profession. The man really is taken into a higher region of his own nature, and finds a pleasure in the exercise of higher faculties which he did not suppose himself to possess. Whatever sacrifice is supposed to be duty, whether the supposition be really correct or not, has in it an ennobling and purifying power; and thus the eras of conversion from one form of the Christian religion to another are often marked with a real and permanent exaltation of the whole character. But it does not follow that certain religious beliefs and ordinances are in themselves just, because they thus touch the great heroic master-chord of the human soul. To wear sackcloth and sleep on a plank may have been of use to many souls, as symbolizing the awakening of this higher nature; but, still, the religion of the New Testament is plainly one which calls to no such outward and evident sacrifices.

"It was John the Baptist, and not the Messiah, who dwelt in the wilderness and wore garments of camel's hair; and Jesus was commented on, not for his asceticism, but for his cheerful, social acceptance of the average innocent wants and enjoyments of humanity. 'The Son of man came eating and drinking.' The great, and never ceasing, and utter self-sacrifice of his life was not signified by any peculiarity of costume, or language, or manner; it showed itself only as it unconsciously welled up in all his words and actions, in his estimates of life, in all that marked him out as a being of a higher and holier sphere."

"Then you do not believe in influencing this subject of dress by religious persons' adopting any particular laws of costume?" said Pheasant.

"I do not see it to be possible," said I, "considering how society is made up. There are such differences of taste and character,—people move in such different spheres, are influenced by such different circumstances,—that all we can do is to lay down certain great principles, and leave it to every one to apply them according to individual needs."

"But what are these principles? There is the grand inquiry."

"Well," said I, "let us feel our way. In the first place, then, we are all agreed in one starting-point,—that beauty is not to be considered as a bad thing,—that the love of ornament in our outward and physical life is not a sinful or a dangerous feeling, and only leads to evil, as all other innocent things do, by being used in wrong ways. So far we are all agreed, are we not?"

"Certainly," said all the voices.

"It is, therefore, neither wicked nor silly nor weak-minded to like beautiful dress, and all that goes to make it up. Jewelry, diamonds, pearls, emeralds, rubies, and all sorts of pretty things that are made of them, are as lawful and innocent objects of admiration and desire, as flowers or birds or butterflies, or the tints of evening skies. Gems, in fact, are a species of mineral flower; they are the blossoms of the dark, hard mine; and what they want in perfume they make up in durability. The best Christian in the world may, without the least inconsistency, admire them, and say, as a charming, benevolent old Quaker lady once said to me, 'I do so love to look at beautiful jewelry!' The love of beautiful dress, in itself, therefore, so far from being in a bad sense worldly, may be the same indication of a refined and poetical nature that is given by the love of flowers and of natural objects.

"In the third place, there is nothing in itself wrong, or unworthy a rational being, in a certain degree of attention to the fashion of society in our costume. It is not wrong to be annoyed at unnecessary departures from the commonly received practices of good society in the matter of the arrangement of our toilet; and it would indicate rather an unamiable want of sympathy with our fellow beings, if we were not willing, for the most part, to follow what they indicate to be agreeable in the disposition of our outward affairs."

"Well, I must say, Mr. Crowfield, you are allowing us all a very generous margin," said Humming-Bird.

"But now," said I, "I am coming to the restrictions. When is love of dress excessive and wrong? To this I answer by stating my faith in one of old Plato's ideas, in which he speaks of beauty and its uses. He says there were two impersonations of beauty worshiped under the name of Venus in the ancient times,—the one celestial, born of the highest gods, the other earthly. To the earthly Venus the sacrifices were such as were more trivial; to the celestial, such as were more holy. 'The worship of the earthly Venus,' he says, 'sends us oftentimes on unworthy and trivial errands, but the worship of the celestial to high and honorable friendships, to noble aspirations and heroic actions.'

"Now it seems to me that, if we bear in mind this truth in regard to beauty, we shall have a test with which to try ourselves in the matter of physical adornment. We are always excessive when we sacrifice the higher beauty to attain the lower one. A woman who will sacrifice domestic affection, conscience, self-respect, honor, to love of dress, we all agree, loves dress too much. She loses the true and higher beauty of womanhood for the lower beauty of gems and flowers and colors. A girl who sacrifices to dress all her time, all her strength, all her money, to the neglect of the cultivation of her mind and heart, and to the neglect of the claims of others on her helpfulness, is sacrificing the higher to the lower beauty; her fault is not the love of beauty, but loving the wrong and inferior kind.

"It is remarkable that the directions of Holy Writ, in regard to the female dress, should distinctly take note of this difference between the higher and the lower beauty which we find in the works of Plato. The Apostle gives no rule, no specific costume, which should mark the Christian woman from the Pagan; but says, 'whose adorning, let it not be that outward adorning of plaiting the hair, and of wearing of gold, or of putting on of apparel; but let it be the hidden man of the heart, in that which is not corruptible, even the ornament of a meek and quiet spirit, which is in the sight of God of great price.' The gold and gems and apparel are not forbidden; but we are told not to depend on them for beauty, to the neglect of those imperishable, immortal graces that belong to the soul. The makers of fashion among whom Christian women lived when the Apostle wrote were the same class of brilliant and worthless Aspasias who make the fashions of modern Paris; and all womankind was sunk into slavish adoration of more physical adornment when the gospel sent forth among them this call to the culture of a higher and immortal beauty.

"In fine, girls," said I, "you may try yourselves by this standard. You love dress too much when you care more for your outward adornings than for your inward dispositions, when it afflicts you more to have torn your dress than to have lost your temper, when you are more troubled by an ill-fitting gown than by a neglected duty,—when you are less concerned at having made an unjust comment, or spread a scandalous report, than at having worn a passé bonnet, when you are less troubled at the thought of being found at the last great feast without the wedding garment, than at being found at the party to-night in the fashion of last year. No Christian woman, as I view it, ought to give such attention to her dress as to allow it to take up *all* of three very important things, viz:—

All her time.
All her strength.
All her money.

Whoever does this lives not the Christian, but the Pagan life,— worships not at the Christian's altar of our Lord Jesus, but at the shrine of the lower Venus of Corinth and Rome."

"Oh now, Mr. Crowfield, you frighten me," said Humming-Bird. "I'm so afraid, do you know, that I am doing exactly that."

"And so am I," said Pheasant; "and yet, certainly, it is not what I mean or intend to do."

"But how to help it," said Dove.

"My dears," said I, "where there is a will there is a way. Only resolve that you will put the true beauty first,—that, even if you do have to seem unfashionable, you will follow the highest beauty of womanhood,—and the battle is half gained. Only resolve that your time, your strength, your money, such as you have, shall not all—nor more than half—be given to mere outward adornment, and you will go right. It requires only an army of girls animated with this noble purpose to declare independence in America, and emancipate us from the decrees and tyrannies of French actresses and ballet-dancers. *En avant*, girls! You yet can, if you will, save the republic."

X

WHAT ARE THE SOURCES OF BEAUTY IN DRESS

The conversation on dress which I had held with Jenny and her little covey of Birds of Paradise appeared to have worked in the minds of the fair council, for it was not long before they invaded my study again in a body. They were going out to a party, but called for Jenny, and of course gave me and Mrs. Crowfield the privilege of seeing them equipped for conquest.

Latterly, I must confess, the mysteries of the toilet rites have impressed me with a kind of superstitious awe. Only a year ago my daughter Jenny had smooth dark hair, which she wreathed in various soft, flowing lines about her face, and confined in a classical knot on the back of her head. Jenny had rather a talent for coiffure, and the arrangement of her hair was one of my little artistic delights. She always had something there, — a leaf, a spray, a bud or blossom, that looked fresh, and had a sort of poetical grace of its own.

But in a gradual way all this has been changing. Jenny's hair first became slightly wavy, then curly, finally frizzly, presenting a tumbled and twisted appearance, which gave me great inward concern; but when I spoke upon the subject I was always laughingly silenced with the definitive settling remark: "Oh, it's the fashion, papa! Everybody wears it so."

I particularly objected to the change on my own small account, because the smooth, breakfast-table coiffure, which I had always so much enjoyed, was now often exchanged for a peculiarly bristling appearance; the hair being variously twisted, tortured, woven, and wound, without the least view to immediate beauty or grace. But all this, I was informed, was the necessary means towards crimping for some evening display of a more elaborate nature than usual.

Mrs. Crowfield and myself are not party-goers by profession, but Jenny insists on our going out at least once or twice in a season, just, as she says, to keep up with the progress of society; and at these times I have been struck with frequent surprise by the general untidiness which appeared to have come over the heads of all my female friends. I know, of course, that I am only a poor, ignorant, bewildered man creature; but to my uninitiated eyes they looked as if they had all, after a very restless and perturbed sleep, come out of bed without smoothing their tumbled and disordered locks. Then, every young lady, without exception, seemed to have one kind of hair, and that the kind which was rather suggestive of the term "woolly." Every sort of wild abandon of frowzy locks seemed to be in vogue; in some cases the hair appearing to my vision nothing but a confused snarl, in which glittered tinklers, spangles, and bits of tinsel, and from which waved long pennants and streamers of different colored ribbons.

I was in fact very greatly embarrassed by my first meeting with some very charming girls, whom I thought I knew as familiarly as my own daughter Jenny, and whose soft, pretty hair had often formed the object of my admiration. Now, however, they revealed themselves to me in coiffures which forcibly reminded me of the electrical experiments which used to entertain us in college, when the subject stood on the insulated stool, and each particular hair of his head bristled and rose, and set up, as it were, on its own account. This high-flying condition of the tresses, and the singularity of the ornaments which appeared to be thrown at haphazard into them, suggested so oddly the idea of a bewitched person, that I could scarcely converse with any presence of mind, or realize that these really were the nice, well-informed, sensible little girls of my own neighborhood,—the good daughters, good sisters, Sunday-school teachers, and other familiar members of our best educated circles; and I came away from the party in a sort of blue maze, and hardly in a state to conduct myself with credit in the examination through which I knew Jenny would put me as to the appearance of her different friends.

I know not how it is, but the glamour of fashion in the eyes of girlhood is so complete that the oddest, wildest, most uncouth devices find grace and favor in the eyes of even well-bred girls, when once that invisible, ineffable aura has breathed over them which declares them to be fashionable. They may defy them for a time,—they may pronounce them horrid; but it is with a secretly melting heart, and with a mental reservation to look as nearly like the abhorred spectacle as they possibly can on the first favorable opportunity.

On the occasion of the visit referred to, Jenny ushered her three friends in triumph into my study; and, in truth, the little room seemed to be perfectly transformed by their brightness. My honest, nice, lovable little Yankee fireside girls were, to be sure, got up in a style that would have done credit to Madame Pompadour, or any of the most questionable characters of the time of Louis XIV. or XV. They were frizzled and powdered, and built up in elaborate devices; they wore on their hair flowers, gems, streamers, tinklers, humming-birds, butterflies, South American beetles, beads, bugles, and all imaginable rattletraps, which jingled and clinked with every motion; and yet, as they were three or four fresh, handsome, intelligent, bright-eyed girls, there was no denying the fact that they did look extremely pretty; and as they sailed hither and thither before me, and gazed down upon me in the saucy might of their rosy girlhood, there was a gay defiance in Jenny's demand, "Now, papa, how do you like us?"

"Very charming," answered I, surrendering at discretion.

"I told you, girls, that you could convert him to the fashions, if he should once see you in party trim."

"I beg pardon, my dear; I am not converted to the fashion, but to you, and that is a point on which I didn't need conversion; but the present fashions, even so fairly represented as I see them, I humbly confess I dislike."

"Oh, Mr. Crowfield!"

"Yes, my dears, I do. But then, I protest, I'm not fairly treated. I think, for a young American girl, who looks as most of my fair friends do look, to come down with her bright eyes and all her little panoply of graces upon an old fellow like me, and expect him to like a fashion merely because *she* looks well in it, is all sheer nonsense. Why, girls, if you wore rings in your noses, and bangles on your arms up to your elbows, if you tied your hair in a war-knot on the top of your heads like the Sioux Indians, you would still look pretty. The question isn't, as I view it, whether you look pretty, — for that you do, and that you will, do what you please and dress how you will. The question is whether you might not look prettier, whether another style of dress, and another mode of getting up, would not be far more becoming. I am one who thinks that it would."

"Now, Mr. Crowfield, you positively are too bad," said Humming-Bird, whose delicate head was encircled by a sort of crêpy cloud of bright hair, sparkling with gold-dust and spangles, in the midst of which, just over her forehead, a gorgeous blue butterfly was perched, while a confused mixture of hairs, gold-powder, spangles, stars, and tinkling ornaments fell in a sort of cataract down her pretty neck. "You see, we girls think everything of you; and now we don't like it that you don't like our fashions."

"Why, my little princess, so long as I like *you* better than your fashions, and merely think they are not worthy of you, what's the harm?"

"Oh yes, to be sure. You sweeten the dose to us babies with that sugarplum. But really, Mr. Crowfield, why don't you like the fashions?"

"Because, to my view, they are in great part in false taste, and injure the beauty of the girls," said I. "They are inappropriate to their characters, and make them look like a kind and class of women whom they do not, and I trust never will, resemble internally, and whose mark therefore they ought not to bear externally. But there you are, beguiling me into a sermon which you will only hate me in your hearts for preaching. Go along, children! You certainly look as well as anybody can in that style of getting up; so go to your party, and to-morrow night, when you are tired and sleepy, if you'll come with your crochet, and sit in my study, I will read you Christopher Crowfield's dissertation on dress."

"That will be amusing, to say the least," said Humming-Bird; "and, be sure, we will all be here. And mind, you have to show good reasons for disliking the present fashion."

So the next evening there was a worsted party in my study, sitting in the midst of which I read as follows: —

WHAT ARE THE SOURCES OF BEAUTY IN DRESS

"The first one is *appropriateness*. Colors and forms and modes, in themselves graceful or beautiful, can become ungraceful and ridiculous simply through inappropriateness. The most lovely bonnet that the most approved modiste can invent, if worn on the head of a coarse-faced Irishwoman bearing a market-basket on her arm, excites no emotion but that of the ludicrous. The most elegant and brilliant evening dress, if worn in the daytime in a railroad car, strikes every one with a sense of absurdity; whereas both these objects in appropriate associations would excite only the idea of beauty. So a mode of dress obviously intended for driving strikes us as *outré* in a parlor; and a parlor dress would no less shock our eyes on horseback. In short, the course of this principle through all varieties of form can easily be perceived. Besides appropriateness to time, place, and circumstances, there is appropriateness to age, position, and character. This is the foundation of all our ideas of professional propriety in costume. One would not like to see a clergyman in his external air and appointments resembling a gentleman of the turf; one would not wish a refined and modest scholar to wear the outward air of a fast fellow, or an aged and venerable statesman to appear with all the peculiarities of a young dandy. The flowers, feathers, and furbelows which a light-hearted young girl of seventeen embellishes by the airy grace with which she wears them, are simply ridiculous when transferred to the toilet of her serious, well-meaning mamma, who bears them about with an anxious face, merely because a loquacious milliner has assured her, with many protestations, that it is the fashion, and the only thing remaining for her to do.

"There are, again, modes of dress in themselves very beautiful and very striking, which are peculiarly adapted to theatrical representation and to pictures, but the adoption of which as a part of unprofessional toilet produces a sense of incongruity. A mode of dress maybe in perfect taste on the stage, that would be absurd in an evening party, absurd in the street, absurd, in short, everywhere else.

"Now you come to my first objection to our present American toilet,—its being to a very great extent *inappropriate* to our climate, to our habits of life and thought, and to the whole structure of ideas on which our life is built. What we want, apparently, is some court of inquiry and adaptation that shall pass judgment on the fashions of other countries, and modify them to make them a graceful expression of our own national character, and modes of thinking and living. A certain class of women in Paris at this present hour makes the fashions that rule the feminine world. They are women who live only for the senses, with as utter and obvious disregard of any moral or intellectual purpose to be answered in living as a paroquet or a macaw. They have no family ties; love, in its pure domestic sense, is an impossibility in their lot; religion in any sense is another impossibility; and their whole intensity of existence, therefore, is concentrated on the question of sensuous enjoyment, and that personal adornment which is necessary to secure it. When the great ruling country in the world of taste and fashion has fallen into such a state that the virtual leaders of fashion are women of this character, it is not to be supposed that the fashions emanating from them will be of a kind well adapted to express the ideas, the thoughts, the state of society, of a great Christian democracy such as ours ought to be.

"What is called, for example, the Pompadour style of dress, so much in vogue of late, we can see to be perfectly adapted to the kind of existence led by dissipated women whose life is one revel of excitement; and who, never proposing to themselves any intellectual employment or any domestic duty, can afford to spend three or four hours every day under the hands of a waiting-maid, in alternately tangling and untangling their hair. Powder, paint, gold-dust and silver-dust, pomatums, cosmetics, are all perfectly appropriate where the ideal of life is to keep up a false show of beauty after the true bloom is wasted by dissipation. The woman who never goes to bed till morning, who never even dresses herself, who never takes a needle in her hand, who never goes to church, and never entertains one serious idea of duty of any kind, when got up in Pompadour style, has, to say the truth, the good taste and merit of appropriateness. Her dress expresses just what she is,—all false, all artificial, all meretricious and unnatural; no part or portion of her from which it might be inferred what her Creator originally designed her to be.

"But when a nice little American girl, who has been brought up to cultivate her mind, to refine her taste, to care for her health, to be a helpful daughter and a good sister, to visit the poor and teach in Sunday schools; when a good, sweet, modest little puss of this kind combs all her pretty hair backward till it is one mass of frowsy confusion; when she powders, and paints under her eyes; when she adopts, with eager enthusiasm, every *outré*, unnatural fashion that comes from the most dissipated foreign circles,—she is in bad taste, because she does not represent either her character, her education, or her good points. She looks like a second-rate actress, when she is, in fact, a most thoroughly respectable, estimable, lovable little girl, and on the way, as we poor fellows fondly hope, to bless some one of us with her tenderness and care in some nice home in the future.

"It is not the fashion in America for young girls to have waiting-maids,—in foreign countries it is the fashion. All this meretricious toilet—so elaborate, so complicated, and so contrary to nature—must be accomplished, and it is accomplished, by the busy little fingers of each girl for herself; and so it seems to be very evident that a style of hair-dressing which it will require hours to disentangle, which must injure and in time ruin the natural beauty of the hair, ought to be one thing which a well-regulated court of inquiry would reject in our American fashions.

"Again, the genius of American life is for simplicity and absence of ostentation. We have no parade of office: our public men wear no robes, no stars, garters, collars, etc.; and it would, therefore, be in good taste in our women to cultivate simple styles of dress. Now I object to the present fashions, as adopted from France, that they are flashy and theatrical. Having their origin with a community whose senses are blunted, drugged, and deadened with dissipation and ostentation, they reject the simpler forms of beauty, and seek for startling effects, for odd and unexpected results. The contemplation of one of our fashionable churches, at the hour when its fair occupants pour forth, gives one a great deal of surprise. The toilets there displayed might have been in good keeping among showy Parisian women in an opera house, but even their original inventors would have been shocked at the idea of carrying them into a church. The rawness of our American mind as to the subject of propriety in dress is nowhere more shown than in the fact that no apparent distinction is made between church and opera house in the adaptation of attire. Very estimable and we trust very religious young women sometimes enter the house of God in a costume which makes their utterance of the words of the litany and the acts of prostrate devotion in the service seem almost burlesque. When a brisk little creature comes into a pew with hair frizzed till it stands on end in a most startling manner, rattling strings of beads and bits of tinsel, mounting over all some pert little hat with a red or green feather standing saucily upright in front, she may look exceedingly pretty and piquant; and, if she came there for a game of croquet or a tableau party, would be all in very good taste; but as she comes to confess that she is a miserable sinner, that she has done the things she ought not to have done, and left undone the things she ought to have done, — as she takes upon her lips most solemn and tremendous words, whose meaning runs far beyond life into a sublime eternity, — there is a discrepancy which would be ludicrous if it were not melancholy.

"One is apt to think, at first view, that St. Jerome was right in saying,

"'She who comes in glittering vest
To mourn her frailty, still is frail.'

But St. Jerome was in the wrong, after all; for a flashy, unsuitable attire in church is not always a mark of an undevout or entirely worldly mind; it is simply a mark of a raw, uncultivated taste. In Italy, the ecclesiastical law prescribing a uniform black dress for the churches gives a sort of education to European ideas of propriety in toilet, which prevents churches from being made theatres for the same kind of display which is held to be in good taste at places of public amusement. It is but justice to the inventors of Parisian fashions to say that, had they ever had the smallest idea of going to church and Sunday school, as our good girls do, they would immediately have devised toilets appropriate to such exigencies. If it were any part of their plan of life to appear statedly in public to confess themselves 'miserable sinners,' we should doubtless have sent over here the design of some graceful penitential habit, which would give our places of worship a much more appropriate air than they now have. As it is, it would form a subject for such a court of inquiry and adaptation as we have supposed, to draw a line between the costume of the theatre and the church.

"In the same manner, there is a want of appropriateness in the costume of our American women, who display in the street promenade a style of dress and adornment originally intended for showy carriage drives in such great exhibition grounds as the Bois de Boulogne. The makers of Parisian fashions are not generally walkers. They do not, with all their extravagance, have the bad taste to trail yards of silk and velvet over the mud and dirt of a pavement, or promenade the street in a costume so pronounced and striking as to draw the involuntary glance of every eye; and the showy toilets displayed on the *pavé* by American young women have more than once exposed them to misconstruction in the eyes of foreign observers.

"Next to appropriateness, the second requisite to beauty in dress I take to be unity of effect. In speaking of the arrangement of rooms in the 'House and Home Papers,' I criticised some apartments wherein were many showy articles of furniture, and much expense had been incurred, because, with all this, there was no *unity of result*. The carpet was costly, and in itself handsome; the paper was also in itself handsome and costly; the tables and chairs also in themselves very elegant; and yet, owing to a want of any unity of idea, any grand harmonizing tint of color, or method of arrangement, the rooms had a jumbled, confused air, and nothing about them seemed particularly pretty or effective. I instanced rooms where thousands of dollars had been spent, which, because of this defect, never excited admiration; and others in which the furniture was of the cheapest description, but which always gave immediate and universal pleasure. The same rule holds good in dress. As in every apartment, so in every toilet, there should be one ground-tone or dominant color, which should rule all the others, and there should be a general style of idea to which everything should be subjected.

"We may illustrate the effect of this principle in a very familiar case. It is generally conceded that the majority of women look better in mourning than they do in their ordinary apparel; a comparatively plain person looks almost handsome in simple black. Now why is this? Simply because mourning requires a severe uniformity of color and idea, and forbids the display of that variety of colors and objects which go to make up the ordinary female costume, and which very few women have such skill in using as to produce really beautiful effects.

"Very similar results have been attained by the Quaker costume, which, in spite of the quaint severity of the forms to which it adhered, has always had a remarkable degree of becomingness, because of its restriction to a few simple colors and to the absence of distracting ornament.

"But the same effect which is produced in mourning or the Quaker costume may be preserved in a style of dress admitting color and ornamentation. A dress may have the richest fullness of color, and still the tints may be so chastened and subdued as to produce the impression of a severe simplicity. Suppose, for example, a golden-haired blonde chooses for the ground-tone of her toilet a deep shade of purple, such as affords a good background for the hair and complexion. The larger draperies of the costume being of this color, the bonnet may be of a lighter shade of the same, ornamented with lilac hyacinths, shading insensibly towards rose-color. The effect of such a costume is simple, even though there be much ornament, because it is ornament artistically disposed towards a general result.

"A dark shade of green being chosen as the ground-tone of a dress, the whole costume may, in like manner, be worked up through lighter and brighter shades of green, in which rose-colored flowers may appear with the same impression of simple appropriateness that is made by the pink blossom over the green leaves of a rose. There have been times in France when the study of color produced artistic effects in costume worthy of attention, and resulted in styles of dress of real beauty. But the present corrupted state of morals there has introduced a corrupt taste in dress; and it is worthy of thought that the decline of moral purity in society is often marked by the deterioration of the sense of artistic beauty. Corrupt and dissipated social epochs produce corrupt styles of architecture and corrupt styles of drawing and painting, as might easily be illustrated by the history of art. When the leaders of society have blunted their finer perceptions by dissipation and immorality, they are incapable of feeling the beauties which come from delicate concords and truly artistic combinations. They verge towards barbarism, and require things that are strange, odd, dazzling, and peculiar to captivate their jaded senses. Such we take to be the condition of Parisian society now. The tone of it is given by women who are essentially impudent and vulgar, who override and overrule, by the mere brute force of opulence and luxury, women of finer natures and moral tone. The court of France is a court of adventurers, of parvenus; and the palaces, the toilets, the equipage, the entertainments, of the mistresses outshine those of the lawful wives. Hence comes a style of dress which is in itself vulgar, ostentatious, pretentious, without simplicity, without unity, seeking to dazzle by strange combinations and daring contrasts.

"Now, when the fashions emanating from such a state of society come to our country, where it has been too much the habit to put on and wear, without dispute and without inquiry, any or every thing that France sends, the results produced are often things to make one wonder. A respectable man, sitting quietly in church or other public assembly, may be pardoned sometimes for indulging a silent sense of the ridiculous in the contemplation of the forest of bonnets which surround him, as he humbly asks himself the question, Were these meant to cover the head, to defend it, or to ornament it? and, if they are intended for any of these purposes, how?

"I confess, to me nothing is so surprising as the sort of things which well-bred women serenely wear on their heads with the idea that they are ornaments. On my right hand sits a good-looking girl with a thing on her head which seems to consist mostly of bunches of grass, straws, with a confusion of lace, in which sits a draggled bird, looking as if the cat had had him before the lady. In front of her sits another, who has a glittering confusion of beads swinging hither and thither from a jaunty little structure of black and red velvet. An anxious-looking matron appears under the high eaves of a bonnet with a gigantic crimson rose crushed down into a mass of tangled hair. She is *ornamented*! she has no doubt about it.

"The fact is, that a style of dress which allows the use of everything in heaven above or earth beneath requires more taste and skill in disposition than falls to the lot of most of the female sex to make it even tolerable. In consequence, the flowers, fruits, grass, hay, straw, oats, butterflies, beads, birds, tinsel, streamers, jinglers, lace, bugles, crape, which seem to be appointed to form a covering for the female head, very often appear in combinations so singular, and the results, taken in connection with all the rest of the costume, are such, that we really think the people who usually assemble in a Quaker meeting-house are, with their entire absence of ornament, more becomingly attired than the majority of our public audiences. For if one considers his own impression after having seen an assemblage of women dressed in Quaker costume, he will find it to be, not of a confusion of twinkling finery, but of many fair, sweet faces, of charming, nice-looking women, and not of articles of dress. Now this shows that the severe dress, after all, has better answered the true purpose of dress, in setting forth the *woman*, than our modern costume, where the woman is but one item in a flying mass of colors and forms, all of which distract attention from the faces they are supposed to adorn. The dress of the Philadelphian ladies has always been celebrated for its elegance of effect, from the fact, probably, that the early Quaker parentage of the city formed the eye and the taste of its women for uniform and simple styles of color, and for purity and chastity of lines. The most perfect toilets that have ever been achieved in America have probably been those of the class familiarly called the gay Quakers,—children of Quaker families, who, while abandoning the strict rules of the sect, yet retain their modest and severe reticence, relying on richness of material, and soft, harmonious coloring, rather than striking and dazzling ornament.

"The next source of beauty in dress is the impression of truthfulness and reality. It is a well-known principle of the fine arts, in all their branches, that all shams and mere pretenses are to be rejected,—a truth which Ruskin has shown with the full lustre of his many-colored prose-poetry. As stucco pretending to be marble, and graining pretending to be wood, are in false taste in building, so false jewelry and cheap fineries of every kind are in bad taste; so also is powder instead of natural complexion, false hair instead of real, and flesh-painting of every description. I have even the hardihood to think and assert, in the presence of a generation whereof not one woman in twenty wears her own hair, that the simple, short-cropped locks of Rosa Bonheur are in a more beautiful style of hair-dressing than the most elaborate edifice of curls, rats, and waterfalls that is erected on any fair head nowadays."

"Oh, Mr. Crowfield! you hit us all now," cried several voices.

"I know it, girls,—I know it. I admit that you are all looking very pretty; but I do maintain that you are none of you doing yourselves justice, and that Nature, if you would only follow her, would do better for you than all these elaborations. A short crop of your own hair, that you could brush out in ten minutes every morning, would have a more real, healthy beauty than the elaborate structures which cost you hours of time, and give you the headache besides. I speak of the short crop,—to put the case at the very lowest figure,—for many of you have lovely hair of different lengths, and susceptible of a variety of arrangements, if you did not suppose yourself obliged to build after a foreign pattern, instead of following out the intentions of the great Artist who made you.

"Is it necessary absolutely that every woman and girl should look exactly like every other one? There are women whom Nature makes with wavy or curly hair: let them follow her. There are those whom she makes with soft and smooth locks, and with whom crinkling and crêping is only a sham. They look very pretty with it, to be sure; but, after all, is there but one style of beauty? and might they not look prettier in cultivating the style which Nature seemed to have intended for them?

"As to the floods of false jewelry, glass beads, and tinsel finery which seem to be sweeping over the toilet of our women, I must protest that they are vulgarizing the taste, and having a seriously bad effect on the delicacy of artistic perception. It is almost impossible to manage such material and give any kind of idea of neatness or purity; for the least wear takes away their newness. And, of all disreputable things, tumbled, rumpled, and tousled finery is the most disreputable. A simple white muslin, that can come fresh from the laundry every week, is, in point of real taste, worth any amount of spangled tissues. A plain straw bonnet, with only a ribbon across it, is in reality in better taste than rubbishy birds or butterflies, or tinsel ornaments.

"Finally, girls, don't dress at haphazard; for dress, so far from being a matter of small consequence, is in reality one of the fine arts, — so far from trivial, that each country ought to have a style of its own, and each individual such a liberty of modification of the general fashion as suits and befits her person, her age, her position in life, and the kind of character she wishes to maintain.

"The only motive in toilet which seems to have obtained much as yet among young girls is the very vague impulse to look 'stylish,'—a desire which must answer for more vulgar dressing than one would wish to see. If girls would rise above this, and desire to express by their dress the attributes of true ladyhood, nicety of eye, fastidious neatness, purity of taste, truthfulness, and sincerity of nature, they might form, each one for herself, a style having its own individual beauty, incapable of ever becoming common and vulgar.

"A truly trained taste and eye would enable a lady to select from the permitted forms of fashion such as might be modified to her purposes, always remembering that simplicity is safe, that to attempt little and succeed is better than to attempt a great deal and fail.

"And now, girls, I will finish by reciting to you the lines old Ben Jonson addressed to the pretty girls of his time, which form an appropriate ending to my remarks: —

"'Still to be dressed
As you were going to a feast;
Still to be powdered, still perfumed;
Lady, it is to be presumed,
Though art's hid causes are not found,
All is not sweet, all is not sound.

"'Give me a look, give me a face,
That makes simplicity a grace, —
Robes loosely flowing, hair as free:
Such sweet neglect more taketh me
Than all the adulteries of art,
That strike my eyes, but not my heart.'"

XI

THE CATHEDRAL

"I am going to build a cathedral one of these days," said I to my wife, as I sat looking at the slant line of light made by the afternoon sun on our picture of the Cathedral of Milan.

"That picture is one of the most poetic things you have among your house ornaments," said Rudolph. "Its original is the world's chief beauty,—a tribute to religion such as Art never gave before and never can again,—as much before the Pantheon as the Alps, with their virgin snows and glittering pinnacles, are above all temples made with hands. Say what you will, those Middle Ages that you call Dark had a glory of faith that never will be seen in our days of cotton-mills and Manchester prints. Where will you marshal such an army of saints as stands in yonder white-marble forest, visibly transfigured and glorified in that celestial Italian air? Saintship belonged to the medieval Church; the heroism of religion has died with it."

"That's just like one of your assertions, Rudolph," said I. "You might as well say that Nature has never made any flowers since Linnæus shut up his herbarium. We have no statues and pictures of modern saints; but saints themselves, thank God, have never been wanting. 'As it was in the beginning, is now, and ever shall be'"—

"But what about your cathedral?" said my wife.

"Oh yes!—my cathedral,—yes. When my stocks in cloud-land rise, I'll build a cathedral larger than Milan's; and the men, but more particularly the women, thereon, shall be those who have done even more than Saint Paul tells of in the saints of old, who 'subdued kingdoms, wrought righteousness, quenched the violence of fire, escaped the edge of the sword, out of weakness were made strong, waxed valiant in fight, turned to flight the armies of the aliens.' I am not now thinking of Florence Nightingale, nor of the host of women who have been walking worthily in her footsteps, but of nameless saints of more retired and private state,—domestic saints, who have tended children not their own through whooping-cough and measles, and borne the unruly whims of fretful invalids,—stocking-darning, shirt-making saints,—saints who wore no visible garment of haircloth, bound themselves with no belts of spikes and nails, yet in their inmost souls were marked and seared with the red cross of a lifelong self-sacrifice,—saints for whom the mystical terms self-annihilation and self-crucifixion had a real and tangible meaning, all the stronger because their daily death was marked by no outward sign. No mystical rites consecrated them; no organ-music burst forth in solemn rapture to welcome them; no habit of their order proclaimed to themselves and the world that they were the elect of Christ, the brides of another life: but small, eating cares, daily prosaic duties, the petty friction of all the littleness and all the inglorious annoyances of every day, were as dust that hid the beauty and grandeur of their calling even from themselves; they walked unknown even to their households, unknown even to their own souls; but when the Lord comes to build his New Jerusalem, we shall find many a white stone with a new name thereon, and the record of deeds and words which only He that seeth in secret knows. Many a humble soul will be amazed to find that the seed it sowed in such weakness, in the dust of daily life, has blossomed into immortal flowers under the eye of the Lord.

"When I build my cathedral, that woman," I said, pointing o a small painting by the fire, "shall be among the first of my saints. You see her there, in an every-day dress-cap with a mortal thread-lace border, and with a very ordinary worked collar, fastened by a visible and terrestrial breastpin. There is no nimbus around her head, no sign of the cross upon her breast; her hands are clasped on no crucifix or rosary. Her clear, keen, hazel eye looks as if it could sparkle with mirthfulness, as in fact it could; there are in it both the subtile flash of wit and the subdued light of humor; and though the whole face smiles, it has yet a certain decisive firmness that speaks the soul immutable in good. That woman shall be the first saint in my cathedral, and her name shall be recorded as Saint Esther. What makes saintliness in my view, as distinguished from ordinary goodness, is a certain quality of magnanimity and greatness of soul that brings life within the circle of the heroic. To be really great in little things, to be truly noble and heroic in the insipid details of every-day life, is a virtue so rare as to be worthy of canonization, — and this virtue was hers. New England Puritanism must be credited with the making of many such women. Severe as was her discipline, and harsh as seems now her rule, we have yet to see whether women will be born of modern systems of tolerance and indulgence equal to those grand ones of the olden times whose places now know them no more. The inconceivable austerity and solemnity with which Puritanism invested this mortal life, the awful grandeur of the themes which it made household words, the sublimity of the issues which it hung upon the commonest acts of our earthly existence, created characters of more than Roman strength and greatness; and the good men and women of Puritan training excelled the saints of the Middle Ages, as a soul fully developed intellectually, educated to closest thought, and exercised in reasoning, is superior to a soul great merely through impulse and sentiment.

"My earliest recollections of Aunt Esther, for so our saint was known, were of a bright-faced, cheerful, witty, quick-moving little middle-aged person, who came into our house like a good fairy whenever there was a call of sickness or trouble. If an accident happened in the great roystering family of eight or ten children (and when was not something happening to some of us?), and we were shut up in a sick-room, then duly as daylight came the quick step and cheerful face of Aunt Esther,—not solemn and lugubrious like so many sick-room nurses, but with a never failing flow of wit and story that could beguile even the most doleful into laughing at their own afflictions. I remember how a fit of the quinsy—most tedious of all sicknesses to an active child—was gilded and glorified into quite a fête by my having Aunt Esther all to myself for two whole days, with nothing to do but amuse me. She charmed me into smiling at the very pangs which had made me weep before, and of which she described her own experiences in a manner to make me think that, after all, the quinsy was something with an amusing side to it. Her knowledge of all sorts of medicines, gargles, and alleviatives, her perfect familiarity with every canon and law of good nursing and tending, was something that could only have come from long experience in those good old New England days when there were no nurses recognized as a class in the land, but when watching and the care of the sick were among those offices of Christian life which the families of a neighborhood reciprocally rendered each other. Even from early youth she had obeyed a special vocation as sister of charity in many a sick-room, and, with the usual keen intelligence of New England, had widened her powers of doing good by the reading of medical and physiological works. Her legends of nursing in those days of long typhus fever and other formidable and protracted forms of disease were to our ears quite wonderful, and we regarded her as a sort of patron saint of the sick-room. She seemed always so cheerful, so bright, and so devoted, that it never occurred to us youngsters to doubt that she enjoyed, above all things, being with us, waiting on us all day, watching over us by night, telling us stories, and answering, in her lively and always amusing and instructive way, that incessant fire of questions with which a child persecutes a grown person.

"Sometimes, as a reward of goodness, we were allowed to visit her in her own room, a neat little parlor in the neighborhood, whose windows looked down a hillside on one hand, under the boughs of an apple-orchard, where daisies and clover and bobolinks always abounded in summer time; and on the other faced the street, with a green yard flanked by one or two shady elms between them and the street. No nun's cell was ever neater, no bee's cell ever more compactly and carefully arranged; and to us, familiar with the confusion of a great family of little ones, there was always something inviting about its stillness, its perfect order, and the air of thoughtful repose that breathed over it. She lived there in perfect independence, doing, as it was her delight to do, every office of life for herself. She was her own cook, her own parlor and chamber maid, her own laundress; and very faultless the cooking, washing, ironing, and care of her premises were. A slice of Aunt Esther's gingerbread, one of Aunt Esther's cookies, had, we all believed, certain magical properties such as belonged to no other mortal mixture. Even a handful of walnuts that were brought from the depths of her mysterious closet had virtues in our eyes such as no other walnuts could approach. The little shelf of books that hung suspended by cords against her wall was sacred in our regard; the volumes were like no other books; and we supposed that she derived from them those stores of knowledge on all subjects which she unconsciously dispensed among us,—for she was always telling us something of metals, or minerals, or gems, or plants, or animals, which awakened our curiosity, stimulated our inquiries, and, above all, led us to wonder where she had learned it all. Even the slight restrictions which her neat habits imposed on our breezy and turbulent natures seemed all quite graceful and becoming. It was right, in our eyes, to cleanse our shoes on scraper and mat with extra diligence, and then to place a couple of chips under the heels of our boots when we essayed to dry our feet at her spotless hearth. We marveled to see our own faces reflected in a thousand smiles and winks from her bright brass andirons,—such andirons we thought were seen on earth in no other place,—and a pair of radiant brass candlesticks, that illustrated the mantelpiece, were viewed with no less respect.

"Aunt Esther's cat was a model for all cats,—so sleek, so intelligent, so decorous and well-trained, always occupying exactly her own cushion by the fire, and never transgressing in one iota the proprieties belonging to a cat of good breeding. She shared our affections with her mistress, and we were allowed as a great favor and privilege, now and then, to hold the favorite on our knees, and stroke her satin coat to a smoother gloss.

"But it was not for cats alone that she had attractions. She was in sympathy and fellowship with everything that moved and lived; knew every bird and beast with a friendly acquaintanceship. The squirrels that inhabited the trees in the front yard were won in time by her blandishments to come and perch on her window-sills, and thence, by trains of nuts adroitly laid, to disport themselves on the shining cherry tea-table that stood between the windows; and we youngsters used to sit entranced with delight as they gamboled and waved their feathery tails in frolicsome security, eating rations of gingerbread and bits of seedcake with as good a relish as any child among us.

"The habits, the rights, the wrongs, the wants, and the sufferings of the animal creation formed the subject of many an interesting conversation with her; and we boys, with the natural male instinct of hunting, trapping, and pursuing, were often made to pause in our career, remembering her pleas for the dumb things which could not speak for themselves.

"Her little hermitage was the favorite resort of numerous friends. Many of the young girls who attended the village academy made her acquaintance, and nothing delighted her more than that they should come there and read to her the books they were studying, when her superior and wide information enabled her to light up and explain much that was not clear to the immature students.

"In her shady retirement, too, she was a sort of Egeria to certain men of genius, who came to read to her their writings, to consult her in their arguments, and to discuss with her the literature and politics of the day,—through all which her mind moved with an equal step, yet with a sprightliness and vivacity peculiarly feminine.

"Her memory was remarkably retentive, not only of the contents of books, but of all that great outlying fund of anecdote and story which the quaint and earnest New England life always supplied. There were pictures of peculiar characters, legends of true events stranger than romance, all stored in the cabinets of her mind; and these came from her lips with the greater force because the precision of her memory enabled her to authenticate them with name, date, and circumstances of vivid reality. From that shadowy line of incidents which marks the twilight boundary between the spiritual world and the present life she drew legends of peculiar clearness, but invested with the mysterious charm which always dwells in that uncertain region; and the shrewd flash of her eye, and the keen, bright smile with which she answered the wondering question,

'What *do* you suppose it was?' or, 'What could it have been?' showed how evenly rationalism in her mind kept pace with romance.

"The retired room in which she thus read, studied, thought, and surveyed from afar the whole world of science and literature, and in which she received friends and entertained children, was perhaps the dearest and freshest spot to her in the world. There came a time, however, when the neat little independent establishment was given up, and she went to associate herself with two of her nieces in keeping house for a boarding-school of young girls. Here her lively manners and her gracious interest in the young made her a universal favorite, though the cares she assumed broke in upon those habits of solitude and study which formed her delight. From the day that she surrendered this independency of hers, she had never, for more than a score of years, a home of her own, but filled the trying position of an accessory in the home of others. Leaving the boarding-school, she became the helper of an invalid wife and mother in the early nursing and rearing of a family of young children,—an office which leaves no privacy and no leisure. Her bed was always shared with some little one; her territories were exposed to the constant inroads of little pattering feet; and all the various sicknesses and ailments of delicate childhood made absorbing drafts upon her time.

"After a while she left New England with the brother to whose family she devoted herself. The failing health of the wife and mother left more and more the charge of all things in her hands; servants were poor, and all the appliances of living had the rawness and inconvenience which in those days attended Western life. It became her fate to supply all other people's defects and deficiencies. Wherever a hand failed, there must her hand be. Whenever a foot faltered, she must step into the ranks. She was the one who thought for and cared for and toiled for all, yet made never a claim that any one should care for her.

"It was not till late in my life that I became acquainted with the deep interior sacrifice, the constant self-abnegation, which all her life involved. She was born with a strong, vehement, impulsive nature,—a nature both proud and sensitive,—a nature whose tastes were passions, whose likings and whose aversions were of the most intense and positive character. Devoted as she always seemed to the mere practical and material, she had naturally a deep romance and enthusiasm of temperament which exceeded all that can be written in novels. It was chiefly owing to this that a home and a central affection of her own were never hers. In her early days of attractiveness, none who would have sought her could meet the high requirements of her ideality; she never saw her hero, and so never married. Family cares, the tending of young children, she often confessed, were peculiarly irksome to her. She had the head of a student, a passionate love for the world of books. A Protestant convent, where she might devote herself without interruption to study, was her ideal of happiness. She had, too, the keenest appreciation of poetry, of music, of painting, and of natural scenery. Her enjoyment in any of these things was intensely vivid whenever, by chance, a stray sunbeam of the kind darted across the dusty path of her life; yet in all these her life was a constant repression. The eagerness with which she would listen to any account from those more fortunate ones who had known these things, showed how ardent a passion was constantly held in check. A short time before her death, talking with a friend who had visited Switzerland, she said, with great feeling: 'All my life my desire to visit the beautiful places of this earth has been so intense, that I cannot but hope that after my death I shall be permitted to go and look at them.'

"The completeness of her self-discipline may be gathered from the fact that no child could ever be brought to believe she had not a natural fondness for children, or that she found the care of them burdensome. It was easy to see that she had naturally all those particular habits, those minute pertinacities in respect to her daily movements and the arrangement of all her belongings, which would make the meddling, intrusive demands of infancy and childhood peculiarly hard for her to meet. Yet never was there a pair of toddling feet that did not make free with Aunt Esther's room, never a curly head that did not look up, in confiding assurance of a welcome smile, to her bright eyes. The inconsiderate and never ceasing requirements of children and invalids never drew from her other than a cheerful response; and to my mind there is more saintship in this than in the private wearing of any number of haircloth shirts or belts lined with spikes.

"In a large family of careless, noisy children there will be constant losing of thimbles and needles and scissors; but Aunt Esther was always ready, without reproach, to help the careless and the luckless. Her things, so well kept and so treasured, she was willing to lend, with many a caution and injunction, it is true, but also with a relish of right good will. And, to do us justice, we generally felt the sacredness of the trust, and were more careful of her things than of our own. If a shade of sewing-silk were wanting, or a choice button, or a bit of braid or tape, Aunt Esther cheerfully volunteered something from her well-kept stores, not regarding the trouble she made herself in seeking the key, unlocking the drawer, and searching out in bag or parcel just the treasure demanded. Never was more perfect precision, or more perfect readiness to accommodate others.

"Her little income, scarcely reaching a hundred dollars yearly, was disposed of with a generosity worthy a fortune. One tenth was sacredly devoted to charity, and a still further sum laid by every year for presents to friends. No Christmas or New Year ever came round that Aunt Esther, out of this very tiny fund, did not find something for children and servants. Her gifts were trifling in value, but well timed,—a ball of thread-wax, a paper of pins, a pin-cushion,—something generally so well chosen as to show that she had been running over our needs, and noting what to give. She was no less gracious as receiver than as giver. The little articles that we made for her, or the small presents that we could buy out of our childish resources, she always declared were exactly what she needed; and she delighted us by the care she took of them and the value she set upon them.

"Her income was a source of the greatest pleasure to her, as maintaining an independence without which she could not have been happy. Though she constantly gave to every family in which she lived services which no money could repay, it would have been the greatest trial to her not to be able to provide for herself. Her dress, always that of a true gentlewoman,—refined, quiet, and neat,—was bought from this restricted sum, and her small traveling expenses were paid out of it. She abhorred anything false or flashy: her caps were trimmed with real thread lace, and her silk dresses were of the best quality, perfectly well made and kept; and, after all, a little sum always remained over in her hands for unforeseen exigencies.

"This love of independence was one of the strongest features of her life, and we often playfully told her that her only form of selfishness was the monopoly of saintship,—that she who gave so much was not willing to allow others to give to her; that she who made herself servant of all was not willing to allow others to serve her.

"Among the trials of her life must be reckoned much ill health, borne, however, with such heroic patience that it was not easy to say when the hand of pain was laid upon her. She inherited, too, a tendency to depression of spirits, which at times increased to a morbid and distressing gloom. Few knew or suspected these sufferings, so completely had she learned to suppress every outward manifestation that might interfere with the happiness of others. In her hours of depression she resolutely forbore to sadden the lives of those around her with her own melancholy, and often her darkest moods were so lighted up and adorned with an outside show of wit and humor, that those who had known her intimately were astonished to hear that she had ever been subject to depression.

"Her truthfulness of nature amounted almost to superstition. From her promise once given she felt no change of purpose could absolve her; and therefore rarely would she give it absolutely, for she *could not* alter the thing that had gone forth from her lips. Our belief in the certainty of her fulfilling her word was like our belief in the immutability of the laws of nature. Whoever asked her got of her the absolute truth on every subject, and, when she had no good thing to say, her silence was often truly awful. When anything mean or ungenerous was brought to her knowledge, she would close her lips resolutely; but the flash in her eyes showed what she would speak were speech permitted. In her last days she spoke to a friend of what she had suffered from the strength of her personal antipathies. 'I thank God,' she said, 'that I believe at last I have overcome all that too, and that there has not been, for some years, any human being toward whom I have felt a movement of dislike.'

"The last year of her life was a constant discipline of unceasing pain, borne with that fortitude which could make her an entertaining and interesting companion even while the sweat of mortal agony was starting from her brow. Her own room she kept as a last asylum, to which she would silently retreat when the torture became too intense for the repression of society, and there alone, with closed doors, she wrestled with her agony. The stubborn independence of her nature took refuge in this final fastness, and she prayed only that she might go down to death with the full ability to steady herself all the way, needing the help of no other hand.

"The ultimate struggle of earthly feeling came when this proud self-reliance was forced to give way, and she was obliged to leave herself helpless in the hands of others. 'God requires that I should give up my last form of self-will,' she said; 'now I have resigned this, perhaps He will let me go home.'

"In a good old age, Death, the friend, came and opened the door of this mortal state, and a great soul, that had served a long appenticeship to little things, went forth into the joy of its Lord; a life of self-sacrifice and self-abnegation passed into a life of endless rest."

"But," said Rudolph, "I rebel at this life of self-abnegation and self-sacrifice. I do not think it the duty of noble women, who have beautiful natures and enlarged and cultivated tastes, to make themselves the slaves of the sick-room and nursery."

"Such was not the teaching of our New England faith," said I. "Absolute unselfishness,—the death of self,—such were its teachings, and such as Esther's the characters it made. 'Do the duty nearest thee' was the only message it gave to 'women with a mission;' and from duty to duty, from one self-denial to another, they rose to a majesty of moral strength impossible to any form of mere self-indulgence. It is of souls thus sculptured and chiseled by self-denial and self-discipline that the living temple of the perfect hereafter is to be built. The pain of the discipline is short, but the glory of the fruition is eternal."

XII

THE NEW YEAR

[1865.]

Here comes the First of January, Eighteen Hundred and Sixty-Five, and we are all settled comfortably into our winter places, with our winter surroundings and belongings; all cracks and openings are calked and listed, the double windows are in, the furnace dragon in the cellar is ruddy and in good liking, sending up his warming respirations through every pipe and register in the house; and yet, though an artificial summer reigns everywhere, like bees we have our swarming place, — in my library. There is my chimney-corner, and my table permanently established on one side of the hearth; and each of the female genus has, so to speak, pitched her own winter tent within sight of the blaze of my camp-fire. I discerned to-day that Jenny had surreptitiously appropriated one of the drawers of my study-table to knitting-needles and worsted; and wicker work-baskets and stands of various heights and sizes seem to be planted here and there for permanence among the bookcases. The canary-bird has a sunny window, and the plants spread out their leaves and unfold their blossoms as if there were no ice and snow in the street, and Rover makes a hearth-rug of himself in winking satisfaction in front of my fire, except when Jenny is taken with a fit of discipline, when he beats a retreat, and secretes himself under my table.

Peaceable, ah, how peaceable, home and quiet and warmth in winter! And how, when we hear the wind whistle, we think of you, O our brave brothers, our saviors and defenders, who for our sake have no home but the muddy camp, the hard pillow of the barrack, the weary march, the uncertain fare, — you, the rank and file, the thousand unnoticed ones, who have left warm fires, dear wives, loving little children, without even the hope of glory or fame, — without even the hope of doing anything remarkable or perceptible for the cause you love, — resigned only to fill the ditch or bridge the chasm over which your country shall walk to peace and joy! Good men and true, brave unknown hearts, we salute you, and feel that we, in our soft peace and security, are not worthy of you! When we think of you, our simple comforts seem luxuries all too good for us, who give so little when you give all!

But there are others to whom from our bright homes, our cheerful firesides, we would fain say a word, if we dared.

Think of a mother receiving a letter with such a passage as this in it! It is extracted from one we have just seen, written by a private in the army of Sheridan, describing the death of a private. "He fell instantly, gave a peculiar smile and look, and then closed his eyes. We laid him down gently at the foot of a large tree. I crossed his hands over his breast, closed his eyelids down, but the smile was still on his face. I wrapt him in his tent, spread my pocket-handkerchief over his face, wrote his name on a piece of paper, and pinned it on his breast, and there we left him: we could not find pick or shovel to dig a grave." There it is!—a history that is multiplying itself by hundreds daily, the substance of what has come to so many homes, and must come to so many more before the great price of our ransom is paid!

What can we say to you, in those many, many homes where the light has gone out forever?—you, O fathers, mothers, wives, sisters, haunted by a name that has ceased to be spoken on earth,—you, for whom there is no more news from the camp, no more reading of lists, no more tracing of maps, no more letters, but only a blank, dead silence! The battlecry goes on, but for you it is passed by! the victory comes, but, oh, never more to bring him back to you! your offering to this great cause has been made, and been taken; you have thrown into it *all* your living, even all that you had, and from henceforth your house is left unto you desolate! O ye watchers of the cross, ye waiters by the sepulchre, what can be said to you? We could almost extinguish our own home-fires, that seem too bright when we think of your darkness; the laugh dies on our lip, the lamp burns dim through our tears, and we seem scarcely worthy to speak words of comfort, lest we seem as those who mock a grief they cannot know.

But is there no consolation? Is it nothing to have had such a treasure to give, and to have given it freely for the noblest cause for which ever battle was set,—for the salvation of your country, for the freedom of all mankind? Had he died a fruitless death, in the track of common life, blasted by fever, smitten or rent by crushing accident, then might his most precious life seem to be as water spilled upon the ground; but now it has been given for a cause and a purpose worthy even the anguish of your loss and sacrifice. He has been counted worthy to be numbered with those who stood with precious incense between the living and the dead, that the plague which was consuming us might be stayed. The blood of these young martyrs shall be the seed of the future church of liberty, and from every drop shall spring up flowers of healing. O widow! O mother! blessed among bereaved women! there remains to you a treasure that

327

belongs not to those who have lost in any other wise,—the power to say, "He died for his country." In all the good that comes of this anguish you shall have a right and share by virtue of this sacrifice. The joy of freedmen bursting from chains, the glory of a nation new-born, the assurance of a triumphant future for your country and the world,—all these become yours by the purchase-money of that precious blood.

Besides this, there are other treasures that come through sorrow, and sorrow alone. There are celestial plants of root so long and so deep that the land must be torn and furrowed, ploughed up from the very foundation, before they can strike and nourish; and when we see how God's plough is driving backward and forward and across this nation, rending, tearing up tender shoots, and burying soft wild-flowers, we ask ourselves, What is He going to plant?

Not the first year, nor the second, after the ground has been broken up, does the purpose of the husbandman appear. At first we see only what is uprooted and ploughed in,—the daisy drabbled, and the violet crushed,—and the first trees planted amid the unsightly furrows stand dumb and disconsolate, irresolute in leaf, and without flower or fruit. Their work is under the ground. In darkness and silence they are putting forth long fibres, searching hither and thither under the black soil for the strength that years hence shall burst into bloom and bearing.

What is true of nations is true of individuals. It may seem now winter and desolation with you. Your hearts have been ploughed and harrowed and are now frozen up. There is not a flower left, not a blade of grass, not a bird to sing,—and it is hard to believe that any brighter flowers, any greener herbage, shall spring up than those which have been torn away; and yet there will. Nature herself teaches you to-day. Outdoors nothing but bare branches and shrouding snow; and yet you know that there is not a tree that is not patiently holding out at the end of its boughs next year's buds, frozen indeed, but unkilled. The rhododendron and the lilac have their blossoms all ready, wrapped in cere-cloth, waiting in patient faith. Under the frozen ground the crocus and the hyacinth and the tulip hide in their hearts the perfect forms of future flowers. And it is even so with you: your leaf buds of the future are frozen, but not killed; the soil of your heart has many flowers under it cold and still now, but they will yet come up and bloom.

The dear old book of comfort tells of no present healing for sorrow. No chastening for the present seemeth joyous, but grievous, but afterwards it yieldeth peaceable fruits of righteousness. We, as individuals, as a nation, need to have faith in that AFTERWARDS. It is sure to come, — sure as spring and summer to follow winter.

There is a certain amount of suffering which must follow the rending of the great cords of life, suffering which is natural and inevitable; it cannot be argued down; it cannot be stilled; it can no more be soothed by any effort of faith and reason than the pain of a fractured limb, or the agony of fire on the living flesh. All that we can do is to brace ourselves to bear it, calling on God, as the martyrs did in the fire, and resigning ourselves to let it burn on. We must be willing to suffer, since God so wills. There are just so many waves to go over us, just so many arrows of stinging thought to be shot into our soul, just so many faintings and sinkings and revivings only to suffer again, belonging to and inherent in our portion of sorrow; and there is a work of healing that God has placed in the hands of Time alone.

Time heals all things at last; yet it depends much on us in our suffering, whether time shall send us forth healed, indeed, but maimed and crippled and callous, or whether, looking to the great Physician of sorrows, and co-working with him, we come forth stronger and fairer even for our wounds.

We call ourselves a Christian people, and the peculiarity of Christianity is that it is a worship and doctrine of sorrow. The five wounds of Jesus, the instruments of the passion, the cross, the sepulchre, — these are its emblems and watchwords. In thousands of churches, amid gold and gems and altars fragrant with perfume, are seen the crown of thorns, the nails, the spear, the cup of vinegar mingled with gall, the sponge that could not slake that burning death-thirst; and in a voice choked with anguish the Church in many lands and divers tongues prays from age to age, "By thine agony and bloody sweat, by thy cross and passion, by thy precious death and burial!" —mighty words of comfort, whose meaning reveals itself only to souls fainting in the cold death-sweat of mortal anguish! They tell all Christians that by uttermost distress alone was the Captain of their salvation made perfect as a Saviour.

Sorrow brings us into the true unity of the Church, —that unity which underlies all external creeds, and unites all hearts that have suffered deeply enough to know that when sorrow is at its utmost there is but one kind of sorrow, and but one remedy. What matter, *in extremis*, whether we be called Romanist, or Protestant, or Greek, or Calvinist?

We suffer, and Christ suffered; we die, and Christ died; he conquered suffering and death, he rose and lives and reigns, —and we shall conquer, rise, live, and reign. The hours on the cross were long, the thirst was bitter, the darkness and horror real, —*but they ended*. After the wail, "My God, why hast thou forsaken me?" came the calm, "It is finished;" pledge to us all that our "It is finished" shall come also.

Christ arose, fresh, joyous, no more to die; and it is written that, when the disciples were gathered together in fear and sorrow, he stood in the midst of them, and showed unto them his hands and his side; and then were they glad. Already had the healed wounds of Jesus become pledges of consolation to innumerable thousands; and those who, like Christ, have suffered the weary struggles, the dim horrors of the cross, —who have lain, like him, cold and chilled in the hopeless sepulchre, —if his spirit wakes them to life, shall come forth with healing power for others who have suffered and are suffering.

Count the good and beautiful ministrations that have been wrought in this world of need and labor, and how many of them have been wrought by hands wounded and scarred, by hearts that had scarcely ceased to bleed!

How many priests of consolation is God now ordaining by the fiery imposition of sorrow! how many Sisters of the Bleeding Heart, Daughters of Mercy, Sisters of Charity, are receiving their first vocation in tears and blood!

The report of every battle strikes into some home; and heads fall low, and hearts are shattered, and only God sees the joy that is set before them, and that shall come out of their sorrow. He sees our morning at the same moment that He sees our night, —sees us comforted, healed, risen to a higher life, at the same moment that He sees us crushed and broken in the dust; and so, though tenderer than we, He bears our great sorrows for the joy that is set before us.

After the Napoleonic wars had desolated Europe, the country was, like all countries after war, full of shattered households, of widows and orphans and homeless wanderers. A nobleman of Silesia, the Baron von Kottwitz, who had lost his wife and all his family in the reverses and sorrows of the times, found himself alone in the world, which looked more dreary and miserable through the multiplying lenses of his own tears. But he was one of those whose heart had been quickened in its death anguish by the resurrection voice of Christ; and he came forth to life and comfort. He bravely resolved to do all that one man could to lessen the great sum of misery. He sold his estates in Silesia, bought in Berlin a large building that had been used as barracks for the soldiers, and, fitting it up in plain, commodious apartments, formed there a great family-establishment, into which he received the wrecks and fragments of families that had been broken up by the war,—orphan children, widowed and helpless women, decrepit old people, disabled soldiers. These he made his family, and constituted himself their father and chief. He abode with them, and cared for them as a parent. He had schools for the children; the more advanced he put to trades and employments; he set up a hospital for the sick; and for all he had the priestly ministrations of his own Christ-like heart. The celebrated Professor Tholuck, one of the most learned men of modern Germany, was an early protégé of the old Baron's, who, discerning his talents, put him in the way of a liberal education. In his earlier years, like many others of the young who play with life, ignorant of its needs, Tholuck piqued himself on a lordly skepticism with regard to the commonly received Christianity, and even wrote an essay to prove the superiority of the Mohammedan to the Christian religion. In speaking of his conversion, he says,—"What moved me was no argument, nor any spoken reproof, but simply that divine image of the old Baron walking before my soul. That life was an argument always present to me, and which I never could answer; and so I became a Christian." In the life of this man we see the victory over sorrow. How many with means like his, when desolated by like bereavements, have lain coldly and idly gazing on the miseries of life, and weaving around themselves icy tissues of doubt and despair,—doubting the being of a God, doubting the reality of a Providence, doubting the divine love, embittered and rebellious against the power which they could not resist, yet to which they would not submit! In such a chill heart-freeze lies the danger of sorrow. And it is a mortal danger. It is a torpor that must be resisted, as the man in the whirling snows must bestir himself, or he will perish. The apathy of melancholy must be broken by an effort of religion and duty. The stagnant blood must be made to flow by active work, and the cold hand warmed by clasping the hands outstretched towards it in sympathy or supplication. One orphan child taken in, to be fed, clothed, and nurtured, may save a heart from freezing to death: and God knows this war is making but too many orphans!

It is easy to subscribe to an orphan asylum, and go on in one's despair and loneliness. Such ministries may do good to the children who are thereby saved from the street, but they impart little warmth and comfort to the giver. One destitute child housed, taught, cared for, and tended personally, will bring more solace to a suffering heart than a dozen maintained in an asylum. Not that the child will probably prove an angel, or even an uncommonly interesting mortal. It is a prosaic work, this bringing-up of children, and there can be little rose-water in it. The child may not appreciate what is done for him, may not be particularly grateful, may have disagreeable faults, and continue to have them after much pains on your part to eradicate them,—and yet it is a fact, that to redeem one human being from destitution and ruin, even in some homely every-day course of ministrations, is one of the best possible tonics and alteratives to a sick and wounded spirit.

But this is not the only avenue to beneficence which the war opens. We need but name the service of hospitals, the care and education of the freedmen,—for these are charities that have long been before the eyes of the community, and have employed thousands of busy hands: thousands of sick and dying beds to tend, a race to be educated, civilized, and Christianized, surely were work enough for one age; and yet this is not all. War shatters everything, and it is hard to say what in society will not need rebuilding and binding up and strengthening anew. Not the least of the evils of war are the vices which a great army engenders wherever it moves,—vices peculiar to military life, as others are peculiar to peace. The poor soldier perils for us not merely his body, but his soul. He leads a life of harassing and exhausting toil and privation, of violent strain on the nervous energies, alternating with sudden collapse, creating a craving for stimulants, and endangering the formation of fatal habits. What furies and harpies are those that follow the army, and that seek out the soldier in his tent, far from home, mother, wife and sister, tired, disheartened, and tempt him to forget his troubles in a momentary exhilaration, that burns only to chill and to destroy! Evil angels are always active and indefatigable, and there must be good angels enlisted to face them; and here is employment for the slack hand of grief. Ah, we have known mothers bereft of sons in this war, who have seemed at once to open wide their hearts, and to become mothers to every brave soldier in the field. They have lived only to work,—and in place of one lost, their sons have been counted by thousands.

And not least of all the fields for exertion and Christian charity opened by this war is that presented by womanhood. The war is abstracting from the community its protecting and sheltering elements, and leaving the helpless and dependent in vast disproportion. For years to come, the average of lone women will be largely increased; and the demand, always great, for some means by which they may provide for themselves, in the rude jostle of the world, will become more urgent and imperative.

Will any one sit pining away in inert grief, when two streets off are the midnight dance-houses, where girls of twelve, thirteen, and fourteen are being lured into the way of swift destruction? How many of these are daughters of soldiers who have given their hearts' blood for us and our liberties!

Two noble women of the Society of Friends have lately been taking the gauge of suffering and misery in our land, visiting the hospitals at every accessible point, pausing in our great cities, and going in their purity to those midnight orgies where mere children are being trained for a life of vice and infamy. They have talked with these poor bewildered souls, entangled in toils as terrible and inexorable as those of the slave-market, and many of whom are frightened and distressed at the life they are beginning to lead, and earnestly looking for the means of escape. In the judgment of these holy women, at least one third of those with whom they have talked are children so recently entrapped, and so capable of reformation, that there would be the greatest hope in efforts for their salvation. While such things are to be done in our land, is there any reason why any one should die of grief? One soul redeemed will do more to lift the burden of sorrow than all the blandishments and diversions of art, all the alleviations of luxury, all the sympathy of friends.

In the Roman Catholic Church there is an order of women called the Sisters of the Good Shepherd, who have renounced the world to devote themselves, their talents and property, entirely to the work of seeking out and saving the fallen of their own sex; and the wonders worked by their self-denying love on the hearts and lives of even the most depraved are credible only to those who know that the Good Shepherd himself ever lives and works with such spirits engaged in such a work. A similar order of women exists in New York, under the direction of the Episcopal Church, in connection with St. Luke's Hospital; and another in England, who tend the "House of Mercy" of Clewer.

Such benevolent associations offer objects of interest to that class which most needs something to fill the void made by bereavement. The wounds of grief are less apt to find a cure in that rank of life where the sufferer has wealth and leisure. The *poor* widow, whoso husband was her all, *must* break the paralysis of grief. The hard necessities of life are her physicians; they send her out to unwelcome, yet friendly toil, which, hard as it seems, has yet its healing power. But the sufferer surrounded by the appliances of wealth and luxury may long indulge the baleful apathy, and remain in the damp shadows of the valley of death till strength and health are irrecoverably lost. How Christ-like is the thought of a woman, graceful, elegant, cultivated, refined, whose voice has been trained to melody, whose fingers can make sweet harmony with every touch, whose pencil and whose needle can awake the beautiful creations of art, devoting all these powers to the work of charming back to the sheepfold those wandering and bewildered lambs whom the Good Shepherd still calls his own! Jenny Lind once, when she sang at a concert for destitute children, exclaimed in her enthusiasm, "Is it not beautiful that I can sing so?" And so may not every woman feel, when her graces and accomplishments draw the wanderer, and charm away evil demons, and soothe the sore and sickened spirit, and make the Christian fold more attractive than the dizzy gardens of false pleasure?

In such associations, and others of kindred nature, how many of the stricken and bereaved women of our country might find at once a home and an object in life! Motherless hearts might be made glad in a better and higher motherhood; and the stock of earthly life that seemed cut off at the root, and dead past recovery, may be grafted upon with a shoot from the tree of life which is in the Paradise of God.

So the beginning of this eventful 1865, which finds us still treading the wine-press of our great conflict, should bring with it a serene and solemn hope, a joy such as those had with whom in the midst of the fiery furnace there walked one like unto the Son of God.

The great affliction that has come upon our country is so evidently the purifying chastening of a Father, rather than the avenging anger of a Destroyer, that all hearts may submit themselves in a solemn and holy calm still to bear the burning that shall make us clean from dross and bring us forth to a higher national life. Never, in the whole course of our history, have such teachings of the pure abstract Right been so commended and forced upon us by Providence. Never have public men been so constrained to humble themselves before God, and to acknowledge that there is a Judge that ruleth in the earth. Verily his inquisition for blood has been strict and awful; and for every stricken household of the poor and lowly hundreds of households of the oppressor have been scattered. The land where the family of the slave was first annihilated, and the negro, with all the loves and hopes of a man, was proclaimed to be a beast to be bred and sold in market with the horse and the swine, —that land, with its fair name, Virginia, has been made a desolation so signal, so wonderful, that the blindest passer-by cannot but ask for what sin so awful a doom has been meted out. The prophetic visions of Nat Turner, who saw the leaves drop blood and the land darkened, have been fulfilled. The work of justice which he predicted is being executed to the uttermost.

But when this strange work of judgment and justice is consummated, when our country, through a thousand battles and ten thousands of precious deaths, shall have come forth from this long agony, redeemed and regenerated, then God himself shall return and dwell with us, and the Lord God shall wipe away all tears from all faces, and the rebuke of his people shall he utterly take away.

XIII

THE NOBLE ARMY OF MARTYRS

When the first number of the Chimney-Corner appeared, the snow lay white on the ground, the buds on the trees were closed and frozen, and beneath the hard frost-bound soil lay buried the last year's flower-roots, waiting for a resurrection.

So in our hearts it was winter,—a winter of patient suffering and expectancy,—a winter of suppressed sobs, of inward bleedings,—a cold, choked, compressed anguish of endurance, for how long and how much God only could tell us.

The first paper of the Chimney-Corner, as was most meet and fitting, was given to those homes made sacred and venerable by the cross of martyrdom,—by the chrism of a great sorrow. That Chimney-Corner made bright by home firelight seemed a fitting place for a solemn act of reverent sympathy for the homes by whose darkness our homes had been preserved bright, by whose emptiness our homes had been kept full, by whose losses our homes had been enriched; and so we ventured with trembling to utter these words of sympathy and cheer to those whom God had chosen to this great sacrifice of sorrow.

The winter months passed with silent footsteps, spring returned, and the sun, with ever waxing power, unsealed the snowy sepulchre of buds and leaves,—birds reappeared, brooks were unchained, flowers filled every desolate dell with blossoms and perfume. And with returning spring, in like manner, the chill frost of our fears and of our dangers melted before the breath of the Lord. The great war, which lay like a mountain of ice upon our hearts, suddenly dissolved and was gone. The fears of the past were as a dream when one awaketh, and now we scarce realize our deliverance. A thousand hopes are springing up everywhere, like spring flowers in the forest. All is hopefulness, all is bewildering joy.

But this our joy has been ordained to be changed into a wail of sorrow. The kind hard hand, that held the helm so steadily in the desperate tossings of the storm, has been stricken down just as we entered port,—the fatherly heart that bore all our sorrows can take no earthly part in our joys. His were the cares, the watchings, the toils, the agonies, of a nation in mortal struggle; and God, looking down, was so well pleased with his humble faithfulness, his patient continuance in well-doing, that earthly rewards and honors seemed all too poor for him, so he reached down and took him to immortal glories. "Well done, good and faithful servant, enter thou into the joy of thy Lord!"

Henceforth the place of Abraham Lincoln is first among that noble army of martyrs who have given their blood to the cause of human freedom. The eyes are yet too dim with tears that would seek calmly to trace out his place in history. He has been a marvel and a phenomenon among statesmen, a new kind of ruler in the earth. There has been something even unearthly about his extreme unselfishness, his utter want of personal ambition, personal self-valuation, personal feeling.

The most unsparing criticism, denunciation, and ridicule never moved him to a single bitter expression, never seemed to awaken in him a single bitter thought. The most exultant hour of party victory brought no exultation to him; he accepted power not as an honor, but as a responsibility; and when, after a severe struggle, that power came a second time into his hands, there was something preternatural in the calmness of his acceptance of it. The first impulse seemed to be a disclaimer of all triumph over the party that had strained their utmost to push him from his seat, and then a sober girding up of his loins to go on with the work to which he was appointed. His last inaugural was characterized by a tone so peculiarly solemn and free from earthly passion, that it seems to us now, who look back on it in the light of what has followed, as if his soul had already parted from earthly things, and felt the powers of the world to come. It was not the formal state paper of the chief of a party in an hour of victory, so much as the solemn soliloquy of a great soul reviewing its course under a vast responsibility, and appealing from all earthly judgments to the tribunal of Infinite Justice. It was the solemn clearing of his soul for the great sacrament of Death, and the words that he quoted in it with such thrilling power were those of the adoring spirits that veil their faces before the throne, —"Just and true are thy ways, thou King of saints!"

Among the rich treasures which this bitter struggle has brought to our country, not the least is the moral wealth which has come to us in the memory of our martyrs. Thousands of men, women, and children too, in this great conflict, have "endured tortures, not accepting deliverance," counting not their lives dear unto them in the holy cause; and they have done this as understandingly and thoughtfully as the first Christians who sealed their witness with their blood.

Let us in our hour of deliverance and victory record the solemn vow, that our right hand shall forget her cunning before we forget them and their sufferings,—that our tongue shall cleave to the roof of our mouth if we remember them not above our chief joy.

Least suffering among that noble band were those who laid down their lives on the battlefield, to whom was given a brief and speedy passage to the victor's meed. The mourners who mourn for such as these must give place to another and more august band, who have sounded lower deeps of anguish, and drained bitterer drops out of our great cup of trembling.

The narrative of the lingering tortures, indignities, and sufferings of our soldiers in Rebel prisons has been something so harrowing that we have not dared to dwell upon it. We have been helplessly dumb before it, and have turned away our eyes from what we could not relieve, and therefore could not endure to look upon. But now, when the nation is called to strike the great and solemn balance of justice, and to decide measures of final retribution, it behooves us all that we should at least watch with our brethren for one hour, and take into our account what they have been made to suffer for us.

Sterne said he could realize the miseries of captivity only by setting before him the image of a miserable captive with hollow cheek and wasted eye, notching upon a stick, day after day, the weary record of the flight of time. So we can form a more vivid picture of the sufferings of our martyrs from one simple story than from any general description; and therefore we will speak right on, and tell one story which might stand as a specimen of what has been done and suffered by thousands.

In the town of Andover, Massachusetts, a boy of sixteen, named Walter Raymond, enlisted among our volunteers. He was under the prescribed age, but his eager zeal led him to follow the footsteps of an elder brother who had already enlisted; and the father of the boy, though these two were all the sons he had, instead of availing himself of his legal right to withdraw him, indorsed the act in the following letter addressed to his captain:—

ANDOVER, MASS., *August 15, 1862.*

CAPTAIN HUNT,—My eldest son has enlisted in your company. I send you his younger brother. He is, and always has been, in perfect health, of more than the ordinary power of endurance, honest, truthful, and courageous. I doubt not you will find him on trial all you can ask, except his age, and that I am sorry to say is only sixteen; yet if our country needs his service, take him.

Your obedient servant,

SAMUEL RAYMOND.

The boy went forth to real service, and to successive battles at Kingston, at Whitehall, and at Goldsborough; and in all this did his duty bravely and faithfully. He met the temptations and dangers of a soldier's life with the pure-hearted firmness of a Christian child, neither afraid nor ashamed to remember his baptismal vows, his Sunday-school teachings, and his mother's wishes.

He had passed his promise to his mother against drinking and smoking, and held it with a simple, childlike steadiness. When in the midst of malarious swamps, physicians and officers advised the use of tobacco. The boy writes to his mother: "A great many have begun to smoke, but I shall not do it without your permission, though I think it does a great deal of good."

In his leisure hours, he was found in his tent reading; and before battle he prepared his soul with the beautiful psalms and collects for the day, as appointed by his church, and writes with simplicity to his friends: —

"I prayed God that he would watch over me, and if I fell, receive my soul in heaven; and I also prayed that I might not forget the cause I was fighting for, and turn my back in fear."

After nine months' service, he returned with a soldier's experience, though with a frame weakened by sickness in a malarious region. But no sooner did health and strength return than he again enlisted, in the Massachusetts cavalry service, and passed many months of constant activity and adventure, being in some severe skirmishes and battles with that portion of Sheridan's troops who approached nearest to Richmond, getting within a mile and a half of the city. At the close of this raid, so hard had been the service, that only thirty horses were left out of seventy-four in his company, and Walter and two others were the sole survivors among eight who occupied the same tent.

On the sixteenth of August, Walter was taken prisoner in a skirmish; and from the time that this news reached his parents, until the 18th of the following March, they could ascertain nothing of his fate. A general exchange of prisoners having been then effected, they learned that he had died on Christmas Day in Salisbury Prison, of hardship and privation.

What these hardships were is, alas! easy to be known from those too well-authenticated accounts published by our government of the treatment experienced by our soldiers in the Rebel prisons.

Robbed of clothing, of money, of the soldier's best friend, his sheltering blanket,—herded in shivering nakedness on the bare ground,—deprived of every implement by which men of energy and spirit had soon bettered their lot,—forbidden to cut in adjacent forests branches for shelter, or fuel to cook their coarse food,—fed on a pint of corn-and-cob-meal per day, with some slight addition of molasses or rancid meat,—denied all mental resources, all letters from home, all writing to friends,—these men were cut off from the land of the living while yet they lived,—they were made to dwell in darkness as those that have been long dead.

By such slow, lingering tortures,—such weary, wasting anguish and sickness of body and soul,—it was the infernal policy of the Rebel government either to wring from them an abjuration of their country, or by slow and steady draining away of the vital forces to render them forever unfit to serve in her armies.

Walter's constitution bore four months of this usage, when death came to his release. A fellow sufferer, who was with him in his last hours, brought the account to his parents.

Through all his terrible privations, even the lingering pains of slow starvation, Walter preserved his steady simplicity, his faith in God, and unswerving fidelity to the cause for which he was suffering.

When the Rebels had kept the prisoners fasting for days, and then brought in delicacies to tempt their appetite, hoping thereby to induce them to desert their flag, he only answered, "I would rather be carried out in that dead-cart!"

When told by some that he must steal from his fellow sufferers, as many did, in order to relieve the pangs of hunger, he answered, "No, I was not brought up to that!" And so when his weakened system would no longer receive the cobmeal which was his principal allowance, he set his face calmly towards death. He grew gradually weaker and weaker and fainter and fainter, and at last disease of the lungs set in, and it became apparent that the end was at hand.

On Christmas Day, while thousands among us were bowing in our garlanded churches or surrounding festive tables, this young martyr

340

lay on the cold, damp ground, watched over by his destitute friends, who sought to soothe his last hours with such scanty comforts as their utter poverty afforded,—raising his head on the block of wood which was his only pillow, and moistening his brow and lips with water, while his life ebbed slowly away, until about two o'clock, when he suddenly roused himself, stretched out his hand, and, drawing to him his dearest friend among those around him, said, in a strong, clear voice:—

"I am going to die. Go tell my father I am ready to die, for I die for God and my country,"—and, looking up with a triumphant smile, he passed to the reward of the faithful.

And now, men and brethren, if this story were a single one, it were worthy to be had in remembrance; but Walter Raymond is not the only noble-hearted boy or man that has been slowly tortured and starved and done to death, by the fiendish policy of Jefferson Davis and Robert Edmund Lee. No,—wherever this simple history shall be read, there will arise hundreds of men and women who will testify, "Just so died my son!" "So died my brother!" "So died my husband!" "So died my father!" The numbers who have died in these lingering tortures are to be counted, not by hundreds, or even by thousands, but by tens of thousands.

And is there to be no retribution for a cruelty so vast, so aggravated, so cowardly and base? And if there is retribution, on whose head should it fall? Shall we seize and hang the poor, ignorant, stupid, imbruted semi-barbarians who were set as jailers to keep these hells of torment and inflict these insults and cruelties? or shall we punish the educated, intelligent chiefs who were the head and brain of the iniquity?

If General Lee had been determined not to have prisoners starved or abused, does any one doubt that he could have prevented these things? Nobody doubts it. His raiment is red with the blood of his helpless captives. Does any one doubt that Jefferson Davis, living in ease and luxury in Richmond, knew that men were dying by inches in filth and squalor and privation in the Libby Prison, within bowshot of his own door? Nobody doubts it. It was his will, his deliberate policy, thus to destroy those who fell into his hands. The chief of a so-called Confederacy, who could calmly consider among his official documents incendiary plots for the secret destruction of ships, hotels, and cities full of peaceable people, is a chief well worthy to preside over such cruelties; but his only just title is

President of Assassins, and the whole civilized world should make common cause against such a miscreant.

There has been, on both sides of the water, much weak, ill-advised talk of mercy and magnanimity to be extended to these men, whose crimes have produced a misery so vast and incalculable. The wretches who have tortured the weak and the helpless, who have secretly plotted to supplement, by dastardly schemes of murder and arson, that strength which failed them in fair fight, have been commiserated as brave generals and unfortunate patriots, and efforts are made to place them within the comities of war.

It is no feeling of personal vengeance, but a sense of the eternal fitness of things, that makes us rejoice, when criminals who have so outraged every sentiment of humanity are arrested and arraigned and awarded due retribution at the bar of their country's justice. There are crimes against God and human nature which it is treason alike to God and man not to punish; and such have been the crimes of the traitors who were banded together in Richmond.

If there be those whose hearts lean to pity, we can show them where all the pity of their hearts may be better bestowed than in deploring the woes of assassins. Let them think of the thousands of fathers, mothers, wives, sisters, whose lives will be forever haunted with memories of the slow tortures in which their best and bravest were done to death.

The sufferings of those brave men are ended. Nearly a hundred thousand are sleeping in those sad nameless graves, — and may their rest be sweet! "There the wicked cease from troubling; and there the weary be at rest. There the prisoners rest together; they hear not the voice of the oppressor." But, O ye who have pity to spare, spare it for the broken-hearted friends, who, to life's end, will suffer over and over all that their dear ones endured. Pity the mothers who hear their sons' faint calls in dreams, who in many a weary night-watch see them pining and wasting, and yearn with a lifelong, unappeasable yearning to have been able to soothe those forsaken, lonely death-beds. O man or woman, if you have pity to spare, spend it not on Lee or Davis, — spend it on their victims, on the thousands of living hearts which these men of sin have doomed to an anguish that will end only with life!

Blessed are the mothers whose sons passed in battle, — a quick, a painless, a glorious death! Blessed in comparison, — yet we weep for them. We rise up and give place at sight of their mourning-garments. We reverence the sanctity of their sorrow. But before this other sorrow we are dumb in awful silence. We find no words with which to console such grief. We feel that our peace, our liberties, have been bought at a fearful price, when we think of the sufferings of our martyred soldiers. Let us think of them. It was for *us* they bore hunger and cold and nakedness. They might have had food and raiment and comforts, if they would have deserted our cause,—and they did not. Cut off from all communication with home or friends or brethren, dragging on the weary months, apparently forgotten,— still they would not yield, they would not fight against us; and so for us at last they died.

What return can we make them? Peace has come, and we take up all our blessings restored and brightened; but if we look, we shall see on every blessing a bloody cross.

When three brave men broke through the ranks of the enemy, to bring to King David a draught from the home well, for which he longed, the generous-hearted prince would not drink it, but poured it out as an offering before the Lord; for he said, "Is not this the blood of the men that went in jeopardy of their lives?"

Thousands of noble hearts have been slowly consumed to secure to us the blessings we are rejoicing in. We owe a duty to these our martyrs,—the only one we can pay.

In every place, honored by such a history and example, let a monument be raised at the public expense, on which shall be inscribed the names of those who died for their country, and the manner of their death. Such monuments will educate our young men in heroic virtue, and keep alive to future ages the flame of patriotism. And thus, too, to the aching heart of bereaved love shall be given the only consolation of which its sorrows admit, in the reverence which is paid to its lost loved ones.

OUR SECOND GIRL

Our establishment on Beacon Street had been for some days in a revolutionary state, owing to the fact that our second girl had gone from us into the holy estate of matrimony. Alice was a pretty, tidy, neat-handed creature, and, like many other blessings of life, so good as to be little appreciated while with us. It was not till she had left us that we began to learn that clean glass, bright silver, spotless and untumbled table-linen, and, in short, all the appetizing arrangements and appointments of our daily meals, were not always and in all hands matters of course.

In a day or two, our silver began to have the appearance of old pewter, and our glass looked as if nothing but muddy water could be found. On coming down to our meals, we found the dishes in all sorts of conversational attitudes on the table, —the meat placed diagonally, the potatoes crosswise, and the other vegetables scattered here and there, —while the table itself stood rakishly aslant, and wore the air of a table slightly intoxicated.

Our beautiful china, moreover, began to have little chipped places in the edges, most unusual and distressing to our eyes; the handles vanished from our teacups, and here and there a small mouthful appeared to be bitten out of the nose of some pretty fancy pitchers, which had been the delight of my eyes.

Now, if there is anything which I specially affect, it is a refined and pretty table arrangement, and at our house for years and years such had prevailed. All of us had rather a weakness for china, and the attractions of the fragile world, as presented in the great crockery-stores, had been many times too much for our prudence and purse. Consequently we had all sorts of little domestic idols of the breakfast and dinner table, —Bohemian-glass drinking-mugs of antique shape, lovely bits of biscuit choicely moulded in classic patterns, beauties, oddities, and quaintnesses in the way of especial teacups and saucers, devoted to different members of the family, wherein each took a particular and individual delight. Our especial china or glass pets of the table often started interesting conversations on the state of the plastic arts as applied to every-day life, and the charm of being encircled, even in the material act of feeding our mortal bodies, with a sort of halo of art and beauty.

All this time none of us ever thought in how great degree our feeling for elegance and refinement owed its gratification at the hour of meals to the care, the tidiness, and neat handling of our now lost and wedded Alice.

Nothing presents so forlorn an appearance as battered and neglected finery of any kind; and elegant pitchers with their noses knocked off, cut glass with cracked edges, and fragments of artistic teacups and saucers on a tumbled tablecloth, have a peculiarly dismal appearance. In fact, we had really occasion to wonder at the perfectly weird and bewitched effect which one of our two Hibernian successors to the pretty Alice succeeded in establishing in our table department. Every caprice in the use and employment of dishes, short of serving cream in the gravy-boats and using the sugar-bowl for pickled oysters and the cream-pitcher for vinegar, seemed possible and permissible. My horror was completed one morning on finding a china hen, artistically represented as brooding on a nest, made to cover, not boiled eggs, but a lot of greasy hash, over which she sat so that her head and tail bewilderingly projected beyond the sides of the nest, instead of keeping lengthwise within it, as a respectable hen in her senses might be expected to do. There certainly is a great amount of native vigor shown by these untrained Hibernians in always finding an unexpected wrong way of doing the simplest thing. It quite enlarges one's ideas of human possibilities.

In a paroxysm of vexation, I reviled matrimony and Murphy O'Connor, who had stolen our household treasure, and further expressed my griefs, as elder sons are apt to do, by earnest expostulations with the maternal officer on the discouraging state of things; declaring most earnestly, morning, noon, and night, that all was going to ruin, that everything was being spoiled, that nothing was even decent, and that, if things went on so much longer, I should be obliged to go out and board,—by which style of remark I nearly drove that long-suffering woman frantic.

"Do be reasonable, Tom," said she. "Can I make girls to order? Can I do anything more than try such as apply, when they seem to give promise of success? Delicacy of hand, neatness, nicety of eye, are not things likely to be cultivated in the Irish boarding-houses from which our candidates emerge. What chance have the most of them had to learn anything except the most ordinary rough housework? A trained girl is rare as a nugget of gold amid the sands of the washings; but let us persevere in trying, and one will come at last."

"Well, I hope, at any rate, you have sent off that Bridget," I said, in high disdain. "I verily believe, if that girl stays a week longer, I shall have to leave the house."

"Compose yourself," said my mother; "Bridget's bundle is made up, and she is going. I'm sorry for her too, poor thing; for she seemed anxious to keep the place."

At this moment the doorbell rang. "I presume that's the new girl whom they have sent round for me to see," said my mother.

I opened the door, and there in fact stood a girl dressed in a neat-fitting dark calico, with a straw bonnet, simply tied with some dark ribbon, and a veil which concealed her face.

"Is Mrs. Seymour at home?"

"She is."

"I was told that she wanted a girl."

"She does; will you walk in?"

I pique myself somewhat on the power of judging character, and there was something about this applicant which inspired hope; so that, before I introduced her into the room, I felt it necessary to enlighten my mother with a little of my wisdom. I therefore whispered in her ear, with the decisive tone of an eldest son, "I think, mother, this one will do; you had better engage her at once."

"Have you lived out much?" said my mother, commencing the usual inquiries.

"I have not, ma'am. I am but lately come to the city."

"Are you Irish?"

"No, ma'am; I am American."

"Have you been accustomed to the care of the table, — silver, glass, and china?"

"I think, ma'am, I understand what is necessary for that."

All this while the speaker remained standing with her veil down; her answers seemed to be the briefest possible; and yet, notwithstanding the homely plainness of her dress, there was something about her that impressed both my mother and me with an idea of cultivation and refinement above her apparent station, — there was a composure and quiet decision in her manner of speaking which produced the same impression on us both.

"What wages do you expect?" said my mother.

"Whatever you have been accustomed to give to a girl in that place will satisfy me," she said.

"There is only one thing I would like to ask," she added, with a slight hesitation and embarrassment of manner; "would it be convenient for me to have a room by myself?"

I nodded to my mother to answer in the affirmative.

The three girls who composed our establishment had usually roomed in one large apartment, but there was a small closet of a room which I had taken for books, fishing-rods, guns, and any miscellaneous property of my own. I mentally turned these out, and devoted the room to the newcomer, whose appearance interested me.

And, as my mother hesitated, I remarked, with the assured tone of master of the house, that "certainly she could have a small room to herself."

"It is all I ask," she briefly answered. "In that case, I will come for the same wages you paid the last girl in my situation."

"When will you come?" said my mother.

"I am ready to come immediately. I only want time to go and order my things to be sent here."

She rose and left us, saying that we might expect her that afternoon.

"Well, sir," said my mother, "you seem to have taken it upon you to settle this matter on your own authority."

"My dear little mother," said I, in a patronizing tone, "I have an instinctive certainty that she will do. I wanted to make sure of a prize for you."

"But the single room."

"Never mind; I'll move all my traps out of the little third-story room. It's my belief that this girl or woman has seen better days; and if she has, a room to herself will be a necessity of her case,—poor thing!"

"I don't know," said my mother hesitatingly. "I never wish to employ in my service those above their station,—they always make trouble; and there is something in this woman's air and manner and pronunciation that makes me feel as if she had been born and bred in cultivated society."

"Supposing she has," said I; "it's quite evident that she, for some reason, means to conform to this position. You seldom have a girl apply for work who comes dressed with such severe simplicity; her manner is retiring, and she seemed perfectly willing and desirous to undertake any of the things which you mentioned as among her daily tasks."

On the afternoon of that day our new assistant came, and my mother was delighted with the way she set herself at work. The china-closet, desecrated and disordered in the preceding reigns of terror and confusion, immediately underwent a most quiet but thorough transformation. Everything was cleaned, brightened, and arranged with a system and thoroughness which showed, as my mother remarked, a good head; and all this was done so silently and quietly that it seemed like magic. By the time we came down to breakfast the next morning, we perceived that the reforms of our new prime minister had extended everywhere. The dining-room was clean, cool, thoroughly dusted, and freshly aired; the tablecloth and napkins were smooth and clean; the glass glittered like crystal, and the silver wore a cheerful brightness. Added to this were some extra touches of refinement, which I should call table coquetry. The cold meat was laid out with green fringes of parsley; and a bunch of heliotrope, lemon verbena, and mignonette, with a fresh rosebud, all culled from our little back yard, stood in a wineglass on my mother's waiter.

"Well, Mary, you have done wonders," said my mother, as she took her place; "your arrangements restore appetite to all of us."

Mary received our praises with a gracious smile, yet with a composed gravity which somewhat puzzled me. She seemed perfectly obliging and amiable, yet there was a serious reticence about her that quite piqued my curiosity. I could not help recurring to the idea of a lady in disguise; though I scarcely knew to what circumstance about her I could attach the idea. So far from the least effort to play the lady, her dress was, in homely plainness, a perfect contrast to that of the girls who had preceded her. It consisted of strong dark-blue stuff, made perfectly plain to her figure, with a narrow band of white linen around her throat. Her dark brown hair was brushed smoothly away from her face, and confined simply behind in a net; there was not the slightest pretension to coquetry in its arrangement; in fact, the object seemed to be to get it snugly out of the way, rather than to make it a matter of ornament. Nevertheless, I could not help remarking that there was a good deal of it, and that it waved very prettily, notwithstanding the care that had been taken to brush the curl out of it.

She was apparently about twenty years of age. Her face was not handsome, but it was a refined and intelligent one. The skin had a sallow hue, which told of ill health or of misfortune; there were lines of trouble about the eye; but the mouth and chin had that unmistakable look of firmness which speaks a person able and resolved to do a quiet battle with adverse fate, and to go through to the end with whatever is needed to be done, without fretfulness and without complaint. She had large, cool, gray eyes, attentive and thoughtful, and she met the look of any one who addressed her with an honest firmness; she seemed to be, in fact, simply and only interested to know and to do the work she had undertaken,—but what there might be behind and beyond that I could not conjecture.

One thing about her dress most in contrast with that of the other servants was that she evidently wore no crinoline. The exuberance of this article in the toilet of our domestics had become threatening of late, apparently requiring that the kitchens and pantries should be torn down and rebuilt. As matters were, our three girls never could be in our kitchen at one time without reefings and manœuvrings of their apparel which much impeded any other labor, and caused some loss of temper; and our china-closet was altogether too small for the officials who had to wash the china there, and they were constantly at odds with my mother for her firmness in resisting their tendency to carry our china and silver to the general mêlée of the kitchen sink. Moreover, our dining-room not having been constructed with an eye to modern expansions of the female toilet, it happened that, if our table was to be enlarged for guests, there arose serious questions of the waiter's crinoline to complicate the calculations; and for all these reasons, I was inclined to look with increasing wonder on a being in female form who could so far defy the tyranny of custom as to dress in a convenient and comfortable manner, adapted to the work which she undertook to perform. A good-looking girl without crinoline had a sort of unworldly freshness of air that really constituted a charm. If it had been a piece of refined coquetry,—as certainly it was not,—it could not have been better planned.

Nothing could be more perfectly proper than the demeanor of this girl in relation to all the proprieties of her position. She seemed to give her whole mind to it with an anxious exactness; but she appeared to desire no relations with the family other than those of a mere business character. It was impossible to draw her into conversation. If a good-natured remark was addressed to her on any subject such as in kindly disposed families is often extended as an invitation to a servant to talk a little with an employer, Mary met it with the briefest and gravest response that was compatible with propriety, and with a definite and marked respectfulness of demeanor which had precisely the effect of throwing us all at a distance, like ceremonious politeness in the intercourse of good society.

"I cannot make out our Mary," said I to my mother; "she is a perfect treasure, but who or what do you suppose she is?"

"I cannot tell you," said my mother. "All I know is, she understands her business perfectly, and does it exactly; but she no more belongs to the class of common servants than I do."

"Does she associate with the other girls?"

"Not at all—except at meal-times, and when about her work."

"I should think that would provoke the pride of sweet Erin," said I.

"One would think so," said my mother; "but she certainly has managed her relations with them with a curious kind of tact. She always treats them with perfect consideration and politeness, talks with them during the times that they necessarily are thrown together in the most affable and cheerful manner, and never assumes any airs of supremacy with them. Her wanting a room to herself gave them at first an idea that she would hold herself aloof from them, and in fact, for the first few days, there was a subterranean fire in the kitchen ready to burst forth; but now all that is past, and in some way or other, without being in the least like any of them, she has contrived to make them her fast friends. I found her last night in the kitchen writing a letter for the cook, and the other day she was sitting in her room trimming a bonnet for Katy; and her opinion seems to be law in the kitchen. She seldom sits there, and spends most of her leisure in her own room, which is as tidy as a bee's cell."

"What is she doing there?"

"Reading, sewing, and writing, as far as I can see. There are a few books, and a portfolio, and a small inkstand there,—and a neat little work-basket. She is very nice with her needle, and obliging in putting her talents to the service of the other girls; but towards me she is the most perfectly silent and reserved being that one can conceive. I can't make conversation with her; she keeps me off by a most rigid respectfulness of demeanor which seems to say that she wants nothing from me but my orders. I feel that I could no more ask her a question about her private affairs, than I could ask one of Mrs. McGregor in the next street. But then it is a comfort to have some one so entirely trustworthy as she is in charge of all the nice little articles which require attention and delicate handling. She is the only girl I ever had whom I could trust to arrange a parlor and a table without any looking after. Her eye and hand, and her ideas, are certainly those of a lady, whatever her position may have been."

In time our Mary became quite a family institution for us, seeming to fill a thousand little places in the domestic arrangement where a hand or an eye was needed. She was deft at mending glass and china, and equally so at mending all sorts of household things. She darned the napkins and tablecloths in a way that excited my mother's admiration, and was always so obliging and ready to offer her services that, in time, a resort to Mary's work-basket and ever ready needle became the most natural thing in the world to all of us. She seemed to have no acquaintance in the city, never went out visiting, received no letters, — in short, seemed to live a completely isolated life, and to dwell in her own thoughts in her own solitary little room.

By that talent for systematic arrangement which she possessed, she secured for herself a good many hours to spend there. My mother, seeing her taste for reading, offered her the use of our books; and one volume after another spent its quiet week or fortnight in her room, and returned to our shelves in due time. They were mostly works of solid information, — history, travels, — and a geography and atlas which had formed part of the school outfit of one of the younger children she seemed interested to retain for some time. "It is my opinion," said my mother, "that she is studying, — perhaps with a view to getting some better situation."

"Pray keep her with us," said I, "if you can. Why don't you raise her wages? You know that she does more than any other girl ever did before in her place, and is so trustworthy that she is invaluable to us. Persons of her class are worth higher wages than common uneducated servants."

My mother accordingly did make a handsome addition to Mary's wages, and by the time she had been with us a year the confidence which her quiet manner had inspired was such that, if my mother wished to be gone for a day or two, the house, with all that was in it, was left trustingly in Mary's hands, as with a sort of housekeeper. She was charged with all the last directions, as well as the keys to the jellies, cakes, and preserves, with discretionary power as to their use; and yet, for some reason, such was the ascendency she contrived to keep over her Hibernian friends in the kitchen, all this confidence evidently seemed to them quite as proper as to us.

"She ain't quite like us," said Biddy one day, mysteriously, as she looked after her. "She's seen better days, or I'm mistaken; but she don't take airs on her. She knows how to take the bad luck quiet like, and do the best she can."

"Has she ever told you anything of herself, Biddy?" said my mother.

"Me? No. It's a quiet tongue she keeps in her head. She is ready enough to do good turns for us, and to smooth out our ways, and hear our stories, but it's close in her own affairs she is. Maybe she don't like to be talkin', when talkin' does no good, — poor soul!"

Matters thus went on, and I amused myself now and then with speculating about Mary. I would sometimes go to her to ask some of those little charities of the needle which our sex are always needing from feminine hands; but never, in the course of any of these little transactions, could I establish the slightest degree of confidential communication. If she sewed on a shirt-button, she did it with as abstracted an air as if my arm were a post which she was required to handle, and not the arm of a good-looking youth of twenty-five, — as I fondly hoped I was. And certain remarks which I once addressed to her in regard to her studies and reading in her own apartment were met with that cool, wide-open gaze of her calm gray eyes, that seemed to say, "Pray, what is that to your purpose, sir?" and she merely answered, "Is there anything else that you would like me to do, sir?" with a marked deference that was really defiant.

But one day I fancied I had got hold of a clue. I was standing in our lower front hall, when I saw young McPherson, whom I used to know in New York, coming up the doorsteps.

At the moment that he rung the doorbell, our Mary, who had seen him from the chamber window, suddenly grew pale, and said to my mother, "Please, ma'am, will you be so good as to excuse my going to the door? I feel faint."

My mother spoke over the banisters, and I opened the door, and let in McPherson.

He and I were jolly together, as old classmates are wont to be, and orders were given to lay a plate for him at dinner.

Mary prepared the service with her usual skill and care, but pleaded that her illness increased so that it would be impossible for her to wait on table. Now, nobody in the house thought there was anything peculiar about this but myself. My mother, indeed, had noticed that Mary's faintness had come on very suddenly, as she looked out on the street; but it was I who suggested to her that McPherson might have some connection with it.

"Depend upon it, mother, he is somebody whom she has known in her former life, and doesn't wish to meet," said I.

"Nonsense, Tom; you are always getting up mysteries, and fancying romances."

Nevertheless, I took a vicious pleasure in experimenting on the subject; and therefore, a day or two after, when I had got Mary fairly within eye-range, as she waited on table, I remarked to my mother carelessly, "By the bye, the McPhersons are coming to Boston to live."

There was a momentary jerk of Mary's hand, as she was filling a tumbler, and then I could see the restraint of self-command passing all over her. I had hit something, I knew; so I pursued my game.

"Yes," I continued, "Jim is here to look at houses; he is thinking strongly of one in the next block."

There was a look of repressed fear and distress on Mary's face as she hastily turned away, and made an errand into the china-closet.

"I have found a clue," I said to my mother triumphantly, going to her room after dinner. "Did you notice Mary's agitation when I spoke of the McPhersons coming to Boston? By Jove! but the girl is plucky, though; it was the least little start, and in a minute she had her visor down and her armor buckled. This certainly becomes interesting."

"Tom, I certainly must ask you what business it is of yours," said my mother, settling back into the hortatory attitude familiar to mothers. "Supposing the thing is as you think,—suppose that Mary is a girl of refinement and education, who, from some unfortunate reason, has no resource but her present position,—why should you hunt her out of it? If she is, as you think, a lady, there is the strongest reason why a gentleman should respect her feelings. I fear the result of all this restless prying and intermeddling of yours will be to drive her away; and really, now I have had her, I don't know how I ever could do without her. People talk of female curiosity," said my mother, with a slightly belligerent air; "I never found but men had fully as much curiosity as women. Now, what will become of us all if your restlessness about this should be the means of Mary's leaving us? You know the perfectly dreadful times we had before she came, and I don't know anybody who has less patience to bear such things than you."

In short, my mother was in that positive state of mind which is expressed by the colloquial phrase of being on her high horse. I—as the male part of creation always must in such cases—became very meek and retiring, and promised to close my eyes and ears, and not dream, or think, or want to know, anything which it was not agreeable to Mary and my mother that I should. I would not look towards the doorbell, nor utter a word about the McPhersons, who, by the bye, decided to take the house in our neighborhood.

But though I was as exemplary as one of the saints, it did no good. Mary, for some reasons known to herself, became fidgety, nervous, restless, and had frequent headaches and long crying spells in her own private apartment, after the manner of women when something is the matter with them.

My mother was, as she always is with every creature in her employ, maternal and sympathetic, and tried her very best to get into her confidence.

Mary only confessed to feeling a little unwell, and hinted obscurely that perhaps she should be obliged to leave the place. But it was quite evident that her leaving was connected with the near advent of the McPhersons in the next block; for I observed that she always showed some little irrepressible signs of nervousness whenever that subject was incidentally alluded to. Finally, on the day that their furniture began to arrive, and to provide abundant material for gossip and comment to the other members of the kitchen cabinet, Mary's mind appeared suddenly made up. She came into my mother's room looking as a certain sort of women do when they have made a resolution which they mean to stand by,—very pale, very quiet, and very decided. She asked to see my mother alone, and in that interview she simply expressed gratitude for all her kindness to her, but said that circumstances would oblige her to go to New York.

My mother now tried her best to draw from her her history, whatever that might be. She spoke with tact and tenderness, and with the respect due from one human being to another; for my mother always held that every soul has its own inviolable private door which it has a right to keep closed, and at which even queens and duchesses, if they wish to enter, must knock humbly and reverently.

Mary was almost overcome by her kindness. She thanked her over and over; at times my mother said she looked at her wistfully, as if on the very point of speaking, and then, quietly gathering herself within herself, she remained silent. All that could be got from her was, that it was necessary for her hereafter to live in New York.

The servants in the kitchen, with the warm-heartedness of their race, broke out into a perfect Irish howl of sorrow; and at the last moment, Biddy, our fat cook, fell on her neck and lifted up her voice and wept, almost smothering her with her tumultuous embraces; and the whole party of them would go with her to the New York station, one carrying her shawl, another her hand-bag and parasol, with emulous affection; and so our very pleasant and desirable second girl disappeared, and we saw her no more.

Six months after this, when our Mary had become only a memory of the past, I went to spend a week or two in Newport, and took, among other matters and things, a letter of introduction to Mrs. McIntyre, a Scotch lady, who had just bought a pretty cottage there, and, as my friend who gave it told me, would prove an interesting acquaintance.

"She has a pretty niece," said he, "who I'm told is heiress to her property, and is called a very nice girl."

So, at the proper time, I lounged in one morning, and found a very charming, cosy, home-like parlor, arranged with all those little refined touches and artistic effects by which people of certain tastes and habits at once recognize each other in all parts of the world, as by the tokens of freemasonry. I felt perfectly acquainted with Mrs. McIntyre from the first glance at her parlor, — where the books, the music, the birds, the flowers, and that everlasting variety of female small-work prepared me for a bright, chatty, easy-going, home-loving kind of body, such as I found Mrs. McIntyre to be. She was, as English and Scotch ladies are apt to be, very oddly dressed in very nice and choice articles. It takes the eye of the connoisseur to appreciate these oddly dressed Englishwomen. They are like antique china; but a discriminating eye soon sees the real quality that underlies their quaint adornment. Mrs. McIntyre was scrupulously, exquisitely neat. All her articles of dress were of the choicest quality. The yellow and tumbled lace that was fussed about her neck and wrists might have been the heirloom of a countess; her satin gown, though very short and very scanty, was of a fabulous richness; and the rings that glittered on her withered hands were of the fashion of two centuries ago, but of wonderful brilliancy.

She was very gracious in her reception, as my letter was from an old friend, and said many obliging things of me; so I was taken at once to her friendship, with the frankness characteristic of people of her class when they make up their minds to know you at all.

"I must introduce you to my Mary," she said; "she has just gone into the garden to cut flowers for the vases."

In a moment more "Mary" entered the room, with a little white apron full of flowers, and a fresh bloom on her cheeks; and I was — as the reader has already anticipated — to my undisguised amazement, formally introduced to Miss Mary McIntyre, our second girl.

Of all things for which I consider women admirable, there is no trait which fills me with such positive awe as their social tact and self-command. Evidently this meeting was quite as unexpected to Mary as to me; but except for a sudden flash of amused astonishment in the eyes, and a becoming flush of complexion, she met me as any thoroughbred young lady meets a young man properly presented by her maternal guardian.

For my part, I had one of those dreamy periods of existence in which people doubt whether they are awake or asleep. The world seemed all turning topsy-turvy. I was filled with curiosity, which I could with difficulty keep within the limits of conventional propriety.

"I see, Mr. Seymour, that you are very much astonished," said Mary to me, when Mrs. McIntyre had left the room to give some directions to the servants.

"Upon my word," said I, "I never was more so; I feel as if I were in the midst of a fairy tale."

"Nothing so remarkable as that," she said. "But since I saw you, a happy change, as I need not tell you now, has come over my life through the coming of my mother's sister to America. When my mother died, my aunt was in India. The letters that I addressed to her in Scotland were a long time in reaching her, and then it took a long time for her to wind up her affairs there, and find her way to this country."

"But," said I, "what could" —

"What could induce me to do as I did? Well, I knew your mother's character,—no matter how. I needed a support and protection, and I resolved for a time to put myself under her wing. I knew that in case of any real trouble I should find in her a true friend and a safe adviser, and I hoped to earn her esteem and confidence by steadily doing my duty. Some other time, perhaps, I will tell you more," she added.

The return of Mrs. McIntyre put an end to our private communication, but she insisted, with true old-world hospitality, on my remaining to dinner.

Here I was precipitated into a romance at once. Mary had just enough of that perverse feminine pleasure in teasing to keep my interest alive. The fact was, she saw me becoming entangled from day to day without any more misgivings of conscience than the celebrated spider of the poem felt when she invited the fly to walk into her parlor.

Mrs. McIntyre took me in a very marked way into her good graces, and I had every opportunity to ride, walk, sketch, and otherwise to attend upon Mary; and Mary was gracious also, but so quietly and discreetly mistress of herself that I could not for the life of me tell what to make of her. There were all sorts of wonders and surmises boiling up within me. What was it about McPherson? Was there anything there? Was Mary engaged? Or was there any old affair? etc., etc. Not that it was any business of mine; but then a fellow likes to know his ground before—Before *what*? I thought to myself, and that unknown WHAT every day assumed new importance in my eyes. Mary had many admirers. Her quiet, easy, self-possessed manners, her perfect tact and grace, always made her a favorite; but I could not help hoping that between her and me there was that confidential sense of a mutually kept secret which it is delightful to share with the woman you wish to please.

Why won't women sometimes enlighten a fellow a little in this dark valley that lies between intimate acquaintance and the awful final proposal? To be sure, there are kind souls who will come more than halfway to meet you, but they are always sure to be those you don't want to meet. The woman you want is always as reticent as a nut, and leaves you the whole work of this last dread scene without a bit of help on her part. To be sure, she smiles on you; but what of that? You see she smiles also on Tom, Dick, and Harry.

> "Bright as the sun her eyes the gazers strike;
> And, like the sun, they shine on all alike."

I fought out a battle of two or three weeks with my fair foe, trying to get in advance some hint from her as to what she would do with me if I put myself at her mercy. No use. Our sex may as well give up first as last before one of these quiet, resolved, little pieces of femininity, who are perfect mistresses of all the peculiar weapons, defensive and offensive, of womanhood. There was nothing for it but to surrender at discretion; but when I had done this, I was granted all the honors of war. Mrs. McIntyre received me with an old-fashioned maternal blessing, and all was as happy as possible.

"And now," said Mary, "I suppose, sir, you will claim a right to know all about me."

"Something of the sort," I said complacently.

"I know you have been dying of curiosity ever since I was waiting behind your lordship's chair at your mother's. I knew you suspected something then, — confess now."

"But what could have led you there?"

"Just hear. My mother, who was Mrs. McIntyre's sister, had by a first marriage only myself. Shortly after my father's death, she married a widower with several children. As long as she lived, I never knew what want or care or trouble was; but just as I was entering upon my seventeenth year she died. A year after her death, my stepfather, who was one of those men devoted to matrimony at all hazards, married another woman, by whom he had children.

"In a few years more, he died; and his affairs, on examination, proved to be in a very bad state; there was, in fact, scarcely anything for us to live on. Our stepmother had a settlement from her brother. The two other daughters of my father were married, and went to houses of their own; and I was left, related really to nobody, without property and without home.

"I suppose hundreds of young girls are from one reason or other left just in this way, and have, without any previous preparation in their education and habits, to face the question, How can I get a living?

"I assure you it is a serious question for a young girl who has grown up in the easy manner in which I had. My stepfather had always been a cheery, kindly, generous man, one of those who love to see people enjoy themselves, and to have things done handsomely, and had kept house in a free, abundant, hospitable manner; so that when I came to look myself over in relation to the great uses of life, I could make out very little besides expensive tastes and careless habits.

"I had been to the very best schools, but then I had studied, as most girls in easy circumstances do, without a thought of using my knowledge for any practical purpose. I could speak very fair English; but how I did it, or why, I didn't know,—all the technical rules of grammar had passed from my head like a dream. I could play a little on the piano, and sing a few songs; but I did not know enough of music to venture to propose myself as a teacher; and so with every other study. All the situations of profit in the profession of teaching are now crowded and blocked by girls who have been studying for that express object,—and what could I hope among them?

"My mother-in-law was a smart, enterprising, driving woman of the world, who told all her acquaintance that, of course, she should give me a home, although I was no kind of relation to her, and who gave me to understand that I was under infinite obligations to her on this account, and must pay for the privilege by making myself generally useful. I soon found that this meant doing a servant's work without wages. During six months I filled, I may say, the place of a seamstress and nursery governess to some very ungoverned children, varying with occasional weeks of servant's work, when either the table girl or the cook left a place vacant. For all this I received my board, and some cast-off dresses and underclothes to make over for myself. I was tired of this, and begged my stepmother to find me some place where I could earn my own living. She was astonished and indignant at the demand. When Providence had provided me a good home, under respectable protection, she said, why should I ask to leave it? For her part, she thought the situation of a young lady making herself generally useful in domestic life, in the family of her near connections, was a delightful one. She had no words to say how much more respectable and proper it was thus to live in the circle of family usefulness and protection, than to go out in the world looking for employment.

"I did not suggest to her that the chief difference in the cases would be, that in a hired situation I should have regular wages and regular work; whereas in my present position it was irregular work, and no wages.

"Her views on the subject were perhaps somewhat beclouded by the extreme convenience she found in being able to go into company, and to range about the city at all hours, unembarrassed by those family cares which generally fall to the mistress, but which her views of what constituted general usefulness devolved upon me.

"I had no retirement, no leisure, no fixed place anywhere. My bed was in the nursery, where the children felt always free to come and go; and even this I was occasionally requested to resign, to share the couch of the housemaid, when sickness in the family or a surplus of guests caused us to be crowded for room.

"I grew very unhappy, my health failed, and the demands upon me were entirely beyond my strength, and without any consideration. The doer of all the odds and ends in a family has altogether the most work and least praise of any, as I discovered to my cost. I found one thing after another falling into my long list of appointed duties, by a regular progress. Thus first it would be, 'Mary, won't you see to the dusting of the parlors? for Bridget is'—etc., etc.; this would be the form for a week or two, and then, 'Mary, have you dusted the parlors?' and at last, 'Mary, why have you not dusted the parlors?'

"As I said, I never studied anything to practical advantage; and though I had been through arithmetic and algebra, I had never made any particular use of my knowledge. But now, under the influence of misfortune, my thoughts took an arithmetical turn. By inquiring among the servants, I found that, in different families in the neighborhood, girls were receiving three dollars a week for rendering just such services as mine. Here was a sum of a hundred and fifty-six dollars yearly, in ready money, put into their hands, besides their board, the privilege of knowing their work exactly, and having a control of their own time when certain definite duties were performed. Compared with what I was doing and receiving, this was riches and ease and rest.

"After all, I thought to myself, why should not I find some respectable, superior, motherly woman, and put myself under her as a servant, make her my friend by good conduct, and have some regular hours and some definite income, instead of wearing out my life in service without pay? Nothing stood in my way but the traditionary shadow of gentility, and I resolved it should not stop me.

"Years before, when I was only eight or ten years old, I had met your mother with your family at the seaside, where my mother took me. I had seen a great deal of her, and knew all about her. I remembered well her habitual consideration for the nurses and servants in her employ. I knew her address in Boston, and I resolved to try to find a refuge in her family. And so there is my story. I left a note with my stepmother, saying that I was going to seek independent employment, and then went to Boston to your house. There I hoped to find a quiet asylum,—at least, till I could hear from my aunt in Scotland. The delay of hearing from her during those two years at your house often made me low-spirited."

"But what made you so afraid of McPherson?" said I nervously. "I remember your faintness, and all that, the day he called."

"Oh, that? Why, it was merely this,—they were on intimate visiting terms with my mother-in-law, and I knew that it would be all up with my plans if they were to be often at the house."

"Why didn't you tell my mother?" said I.

"I did think of it, but then"—She gave me a curious glance.

"But what, Mary?"

"Well, I could see plainly enough that there were no secrets between you and her, and I did not wish to take so fine a young gentleman into my confidence," said Mary. "You will observe I was not out seeking flirtations, but an honest independence."

My mother was apprised of our engagement in due form, and came to Newport, all innocence, to call on Miss McIntyre, her intended daughter-in-law. Her astonishment at the moment of introduction was quite satisfactory to me.

For the rest, Mary's talents in making a home agreeable have had since then many years of proof; and where any of the little domestic chasms appear which are formed by the shifting nature of the American working-class, she always slides into the place with a quiet grace, and reminds me, with a humorous twinkle of the eye, that she is used to being second girl.

A SCHOLAR'S ADVENTURES IN THE COUNTRY

"If we could only live in the country," said my wife, "how much easier it would be to live!"

"And how much cheaper!" said I.

"To have a little place of our own, and raise our own things!" said my wife. "Dear me! I am heartsick when I think of the old place at home, and father's great garden. What peaches and melons we used to have! what green peas and corn! Now one has to buy every cent's worth of these things—and how they taste! Such wilted, miserable corn! Such peas! Then, if we lived in the country, we should have our own cow, and milk and cream in abundance; our own hens and chickens. We could have custard and ice-cream every day."

"To say nothing of the trees and flowers, and all that," said I.

The result of this little domestic duet was that my wife and I began to ride about the city of — — to look up some pretty, interesting cottage, where our visions of rural bliss might be realized. Country residences, near the city, we found to bear rather a high price; so that it was no easy matter to find a situation suitable to the length of our purse; till, at last, a judicious friend suggested a happy expedient.

"Borrow a few hundred," he said, "and give your note; you can save enough, very soon, to make the difference. When you raise everything you eat, you know it will make your salary go a wonderful deal further."

"Certainly it will," said I. "And what can be more beautiful than to buy places by the simple process of giving one's note?—'tis so neat, and handy, and convenient!"

"Why," pursued my friend, "there is Mr. B., my next-door neighbor—'tis enough to make one sick of life in the city to spend a week out on his farm. Such princely living as one gets! And he assures me that it costs him very little—scarce anything perceptible, in fact."

"Indeed!" said I; "few people can say that."

"Why," said my friend, "he has a couple of peach-trees for every month, from June till frost, that furnish as many peaches as he, and his wife, and ten children can dispose of. And then he has grapes, apricots, etc.; and last year his wife sold fifty dollars' worth from her strawberry patch, and had an abundance for the table besides. Out of the milk of only one cow they had butter enough to sell three or four pounds a week, besides abundance of milk and cream; and madam has the butter for her pocket money. This is the way country people manage."

"Glorious!" thought I. And my wife and I could scarcely sleep, all night, for the brilliancy of our anticipations!

To be sure our delight was somewhat damped the next day by the coldness with which my good old uncle, Jeremiah Standfast, who happened along at precisely this crisis, listened to our visions.

"You'll find it pleasant, children, in the summer time," said the hard-fisted old man, twirling his blue-checked pocket-handkerchief; "but I'm sorry you've gone in debt for the land."

"Oh, but we shall soon save that—it's so much cheaper living in the country!" said both of us together.

"Well, as to that, I don't think it is, to city-bred folks."

Here I broke in with a flood of accounts of Mr. B.'s peach-trees, and Mrs. B.'s strawberries, butter, apricots, etc., etc.; to which the old gentleman listened with such a long, leathery, unmoved quietude of visage as quite provoked me, and gave me the worst possible opinion of his judgment. I was disappointed, too; for as he was reckoned one of the best practical farmers in the county, I had counted on an enthusiastic sympathy with all my agricultural designs.

"I tell you what, children," he said, "a body can live in the country, as you say, amazin' cheap; but then a body must *know how*,"—and my uncle spread his pocket-handkerchief thoughtfully out upon his knees, and shook his head gravely.

I thought him a terribly slow, stupid old body, and wondered how I had always entertained so high an opinion of his sense.

"He is evidently getting old," said I to my wife; "his judgment is not what it used to be."

At all events, our place was bought, and we moved out, well pleased, the first morning in April, not at all remembering the ill savor of that day for matters of wisdom. Our place was a pretty cottage, about two miles from the city, with grounds that had been tastefully laid out. There was no lack of winding paths, arbors, flower borders, and rosebushes, with which my wife was especially pleased. There was a little green lot, strolling off down to a brook, with a thick grove of trees at the end, where our cow was to be pastured.

The first week or two went on happily enough in getting our little new pet of a house into trimness and good order; for as it had been long for sale, of course there was any amount of little repairs that had been left to amuse the leisure hours of the purchaser. Here a doorstep had given way, and needed replacing; there a shutter hung loose, and wanted a hinge; abundance of glass needed setting; and as to painting and papering, there was no end to that. Then my wife wanted a door cut here, to make our bedroom more convenient, and a china closet knocked up there, where no china closet before had been. We even ventured on throwing out a bay-window from our sitting-room, because we had luckily lighted on a workman who was so cheap that it was an actual saving of money to employ him. And to be sure our darling little cottage did lift up its head wonderfully for all this garnishing and furbishing. I got up early every morning, and nailed up the rosebushes, and my wife got up and watered geraniums, and both flattered ourselves and each other on our early hours and thrifty habits. But soon, like Adam and Eve in Paradise, we found our little domain to ask more hands than ours to get it into shape. So says I to my wife, "I will bring out a gardener when I come next time, and he shall lay the garden out, and get it into order; and after that I can easily keep it by the work of my leisure hours."

Our gardener was a very sublime sort of man,—an Englishman, and of course used to laying out noblemen's places,—and we became as grasshoppers in our own eyes when he talked of Lord This and That's estate, and began to question us about our carriage drive and conservatory; and we could with difficulty bring the gentleman down to any understanding of the humble limits of our expectations; merely to dress out the walks, and lay out a kitchen garden, and plant potatoes, turnips, beets and carrots, was quite a descent for him. In fact, so strong were his æsthetic preferences, that he persuaded my wife to let him dig all the turf off from a green square opposite the bay window, and to lay it out into divers little triangles, resembling small pieces of pie, together with circles, mounds, and various other geometrical ornaments, the planning and planting of which soon engrossed my wife's whole soul. The planting of the potatoes, beets, carrots, etc., was intrusted to a raw Irishman; for as to me, to confess the truth, I began to fear that digging did not agree with me. It is true that I was exceedingly vigorous at first, and actually planted with my own hands two or three long rows of potatoes; after which I got a turn of rheumatism in my shoulder, which lasted me a week. Stooping down to plant beets and radishes gave me a vertigo, so that I was obliged to content myself with a general superintendence of the garden; that is to say, I charged my Englishman to see that my Irishman did his duty properly, and then got on to my horse and rode to the city. But about one part of the matter, I must say, I was not remiss; and that is, in the purchase of seed and garden utensils. Not a day passed that I did not come home with my pockets stuffed with choice seeds, roots, etc.; and the variety of my garden utensils was unequaled. There was not a priming hook of any pattern, not a hoe, rake, or spade great or small, that I did not have specimens of; and flower seeds and bulbs were also forthcoming in liberal proportions. In fact, I had opened an account at a thriving seed store; for when a man is driving business on a large scale, it is not always convenient to hand out the change for every little matter, and buying things on account is as neat and agreeable a mode of acquisition as paying bills with one's notes.

"You know we must have a cow," said my wife, the morning of our second week. Our friend the gardener, who had now worked with us at the rate of two dollars a day for two weeks, was at hand in a moment in our emergency. We wanted to buy a cow, and he had one to sell—a wonderful cow, of a real English breed. He would not sell her for any money, except to oblige particular friends; but as we had patronized him, we should have her for forty dollars. How much we were obliged to him! The forty dollars were speedily forthcoming, and so also was the cow.

"What makes her shake her head in that way?" said my wife, apprehensively, as she observed the interesting beast making sundry demonstrations with her horns. "I hope she's gentle."

The gardener fluently demonstrated that the animal was a pattern of all the softer graces, and that this head-shaking was merely a little nervous affection consequent on the embarrassment of a new position. We had faith to believe almost anything at this time, and therefore came from the barn yard to the house as much satisfied with our purchase as Job with his three thousand camels and five hundred yoke of oxen. Her quondam master milked her for us the first evening, out of a delicate regard to her feelings as a stranger, and we fancied that we discerned forty dollars' worth of excellence in the very quality of the milk.

But alas! the next morning our Irish girl came in with a most rueful face. "And is it milking that baste you'd have me be after?" she said; "sure, and she won't let me come near her."

"Nonsense, Biddy!" said I; "you frightened her, perhaps; the cow is perfectly gentle;" and with the pail on my arm I sallied forth. The moment madam saw me entering the cow yard, she greeted me with a very expressive flourish of her horns.

"This won't do," said I, and I stopped. The lady evidently was serious in her intentions of resisting any personal approaches. I cut a cudgel, and, putting on a bold face, marched towards her, while Biddy followed with her milking stool. Apparently the beast saw the necessity of temporizing, for she assumed a demure expression, and Biddy sat down to milk. I stood sentry, and if the lady shook her head I shook my stick; and thus the milking operation proceeded with tolerable serenity and success.

"There!" said I, with dignity, when the frothing pail was full to the brim. "That will do, Biddy," and I dropped my stick. Dump! came madam's heel on the side of the pail, and it flew like a rocket into the air, while the milky flood showered plentifully over me, and a new broadcloth riding-coat that I had assumed for the first time that morning. "Whew!" said I, as soon as I could get my breath from this extraordinary shower bath; "what's all this?" My wife came running towards the cow yard, as I stood with the milk streaming from my hair, filling my eyes, and dropping from the tip of my nose; and she and Biddy performed a recitative lamentation over me in alternate strophes, like the chorus in a Greek tragedy. Such was our first morning's experience; but as we had announced our bargain with some considerable flourish of trumpets among our neighbors and friends, we concluded to hush the matter up as much as possible.

"These very superior cows are apt to be cross," said I; "we must bear with it as we do with the eccentricities of genius; besides, when she gets accustomed to us, it will be better."

Madam was therefore installed into her pretty pasture lot, and my wife contemplated with pleasure the picturesque effect of her appearance, reclining on the green slope of the pasture lot, or standing ankle deep in the gurgling brook, or reclining under the deep shadows of the trees. She was, in fact, a handsome cow, which may account, in part, for some of her sins; and this consideration inspired me with some degree of indulgence towards her foibles.

But when I found that Biddy could never succeed in getting near her in the pasture, and that any kind of success in the milking operations required my vigorous personal exertions morning and evening, the matter wore a more serious aspect, and I began to feel quite pensive and apprehensive. It is very well to talk of the pleasures of the milkmaid going out in the balmy freshness of the purple dawn; but imagine a poor fellow pulled out of bed on a drizzly, rainy morning, and equipping himself for a scamper through a wet pasture lot, rope in hand, at the heels of such a termagant as mine! In fact, madam established a regular series of exercises, which had all to be gone through before she would suffer herself to be captured; as, first, she would station herself plump in the middle of a marsh, which lay at the lower part of the lot, and look very innocent and absent-minded, as if reflecting on some sentimental subject. "Suke! Suke! Suke!" I ejaculate, cautiously tottering along the edge of the marsh, and holding out an ear of corn. The lady looks gracious, and comes forward, almost within reach of my hand. I make a plunge to throw the rope over her horns, and away she goes, kicking up mud and water into my face in her flight, while I, losing my balance, tumble forward into the marsh. I pick myself up, and, full of wrath, behold her placidly chewing her cud on the other side, with the meekest air imaginable, as who should say, "I hope you are not hurt, sir." I dash through swamp and bog furiously, resolving to carry all by a *coup de main*. Then follows a miscellaneous season of dodging, scampering, and bopeeping, among the trees of the grove, interspersed with sundry occasional races across the bog aforesaid. I always wondered how I caught her every day; and when I had tied her head to one post and her heels to another, I wiped the sweat from my brow, and thought I was paying dear for the eccentricities of genius. A genius she certainly was, for besides her surprising agility, she had other talents equally extraordinary. There was no fence that she could not take down; nowhere that she could not go. She took the pickets off the garden fence at her pleasure, using her horns as handily as I could use a claw hammer. Whatever she had a mind to, whether it were a bite in the cabbage garden, or a run in the corn patch, or a foraging expedition into the flower borders, she made herself equally welcome and at home. Such a scampering and driving, such cries of "Suke here" and "Suke there," as constantly greeted our ears, kept our little establishment in a constant commotion. At last, when she one morning made a plunge at the skirts of my new broadcloth frock coat, and carried off one flap on her horns, my patience gave out, and I determined to sell her.

As, however, I had made a good story of my misfortunes among my friends and neighbors, and amused them with sundry whimsical accounts of my various adventures in the cow-catching line, I found, when I came to speak of selling, that there was a general coolness on the subject, and nobody seemed disposed to be the recipient of my responsibilities. In short, I was glad, at last, to get fifteen dollars for her, and comforted myself with thinking that I had at least gained twenty-five dollars worth of experience in the transaction, to say nothing of the fine exercise.

I comforted my soul, however, the day after, by purchasing and bringing home to my wife a fine swarm of bees.

"Your bee, now," says I, "is a really classical insect, and breathes of Virgil and the Augustan age,—and then she is a domestic, tranquil, placid creature. How beautiful the murmuring of a hive near our honeysuckle of a calm, summer evening! Then they are tranquilly and peacefully amassing for us their stores of sweetness, while they lull us with their murmurs. What a beautiful image of disinterested benevolence!"

My wife declared that I was quite a poet, and the beehive was duly installed near the flower plots, that the delicate creatures might have the full benefit of the honeysuckle and mignonette. My spirits began to rise. I bought three different treatises on the rearing of bees, and also one or two new patterns of hives, and proposed to rear my bees on the most approved model. I charged all the establishment to let me know when there was any indication of an emigrating spirit, that I might be ready to receive the new swarm into my patent mansion.

Accordingly, one afternoon, when I was deep in an article that I was preparing for the "North American Review," intelligence was brought me that a swarm had risen. I was on the alert at once, and discovered, on going out, that the provoking creatures had chosen the top of a tree about thirty feet high to settle on. Now my books had carefully instructed me just how to approach the swarm and cover them with a new hive; but I had never contemplated the possibility of the swarm being, like Haman's gallows, forty cubits high. I looked despairingly upon the smooth-bark tree, which rose, like a column, full twenty feet, without branch or twig. "What is to be done?" said I, appealing to two or three neighbors. At last, at the recommendation of one of them, a ladder was raised against the tree, and, equipped with a shirt outside of my clothes, a green veil over my head, and a pair of leather gloves on my hands, I went up with a saw at my girdle to saw off the branch on which they had settled, and lower it by a rope to a neighbor, similarly equipped, who stood below with the hive.

As a result of this manœuvre the fastidious little insects were at length fairly installed at housekeeping in my new patent hive, and, rejoicing in my success, I again sat down to my article.

That evening my wife and I took tea in our honeysuckle arbor, with our little ones and a friend or two, to whom I showed my treasures, and expatiated at large on the comforts and conveniences of the new patent hive.

But alas for the hopes of man! The little ungrateful wretches—what must they do but take advantage of my oversleeping myself, the next morning, to clear out for new quarters without so much as leaving me a P. P. C.! Such was the fact; at eight o'clock I found the new patent hive as good as ever; but the bees I have never seen from that day to this!

"The rascally little conservatives!" said I; "I believe they have never had a new idea from the days of Virgil down, and are entirely unprepared to appreciate improvements."

Meanwhile the seeds began to germinate in our garden, when we found, to our chagrin, that, between John Bull and Paddy, there had occurred sundry confusions in the several departments. Radishes had been planted broadcast, carrots and beets arranged in hills, and here and there a whole paper of seed appeared to have been planted bodily. My good old uncle, who, somewhat to my confusion, made me a call at this time, was greatly distressed and scandalized by the appearance of our garden. But by a deal of fussing, transplanting, and replanting, it was got into some shape and order. My uncle was rather troublesome, as careful old people are apt to be—annoying us by perpetual inquiries of what we gave for this and that, and running up provoking calculations on the final cost of matters; and we began to wish that his visits might be as short as would be convenient.

But when, on taking leave, he promised to send us a fine young cow of his own raising, our hearts rather smote us for our impatience.

"'Tain't any of your new breeds, nephew," said the old man, "yet I can say that she's a gentle, likely young crittur, and better worth forty dollars than many a one that's cried up for Ayrshire or Durham; and you shall be quite welcome to her."

We thanked him, as in duty bound, and thought that if he was full of old-fashioned notions, he was no less full of kindness and good will.

And now, with a new cow, with our garden beginning to thrive under the gentle showers of May, with our flower borders blooming, my wife and I began to think ourselves in Paradise. But alas! the same sun and rain that warmed our fruit and flowers brought up from the earth, like sulky gnomes, a vast array of purple-leaved weeds, that almost in a night seemed to cover the whole surface of the garden beds. Our gardeners both being gone, the weeding was expected to be done by me—one of the anticipated relaxations of my leisure hours.

"Well," said I, in reply to a gentle intimation from my wife, "when my article is finished, I'll take a day and weed all up clean."

Thus days slipped by, till at length the article was dispatched, and I proceeded to my garden. Amazement! Who could have possibly foreseen that anything earthly could grow so fast in a few days! There were no bounds, no alleys, no beds, no distinction of beet and carrot, nothing but a flourishing congregation of weeds nodding and bobbing in the morning breeze, as if to say, "We hope you are well, sir—we've got the ground, you see!" I began to explore, and to hoe, and to weed. Ah! did anybody ever try to clean a neglected carrot or beet bed, or bend his back in a hot sun over rows of weedy onions! He is the man to feel for my despair! How I weeded, and sweat, and sighed! till, when high noon came on, as the result of all my toils, only three beds were cleaned! And how disconsolate looked the good seed, thus unexpectedly delivered from its sheltering tares, and laid open to a broiling July sun! Every juvenile beet and carrot lay flat down wilted, and drooping, as if, like me, they had been weeding, instead of being weeded.

"This weeding is quite a serious matter," said I to my wife; "the fact is, I must have help about it!"

"Just what I was myself thinking," said my wife. "My flower borders are all in confusion, and my petunia mounds so completely overgrown, that nobody would dream what they were meant for!"

In short, it was agreed between us that we could not afford the expense of a full-grown man to keep our place; yet we must reinforce ourselves by the addition of a boy, and a brisk youngster from the vicinity was pitched upon as the happy addition. This youth was a fellow of decidedly quick parts, and in one forenoon made such a clearing in our garden that I was delighted. Bed after bed appeared to view, all cleared and dressed out with such celerity that I was quite ashamed of my own slowness, until, on examination, I discovered that he had, with great impartiality, pulled up both weeds and vegetables.

This hopeful beginning was followed up by a succession of proceedings which should be recorded for the instruction of all who seek for help from the race of boys. Such a loser of all tools, great and small; such an invariable leaver-open of all gates, and letter-down of bars; such a personification of all manner of anarchy and ill luck, had never before been seen on the estate. His time, while I was gone to the city, was agreeably diversified with roosting on the fence, swinging on the gates, making poplar whistles for the children, hunting eggs, and eating whatever fruit happened to be in season, in which latter accomplishment he was certainly quite distinguished. After about three weeks of this kind of joint gardening, we concluded to dismiss Master Tom from the firm, and employ a man.

"Things must be taken care of," said I, "and I cannot do it. 'Tis out of the question." And so the man was secured.

But I am making a long story, and may chance to outrun the sympathies of my readers. Time would fail me to tell of the distresses manifold that fell upon me—of cows dried up by poor milkers; of hens that wouldn't set at all, and hens that, despite all law and reason, would set on one egg; of hens that, having hatched families, straightway led them into all manner of high grass and weeds, by which means numerous young chicks caught premature colds and perished; and how, when I, with manifold toil, had driven one of these inconsiderate gadders into a coop, to teach her domestic habits, the rats came down upon her and slew every chick in one night; how my pigs were always practicing gymnastic exercises over the fence of the sty, and marauding in the garden. I wonder that Fourier never conceived the idea of having his garden land ploughed by pigs; for certainly they manifest quite a decided elective attraction for turning up the earth.

When autumn came, I went soberly to market, in the neighboring city, and bought my potatoes and turnips like any other man; for, between all the various systems of gardening pursued, I was obliged to confess that my first horticultural effort was a decided failure. But though all my rural visions had proved illusive, there were some very substantial realities. My bill at the seed store, for seeds, roots, and tools, for example, had run up to an amount that was perfectly unaccountable; then there were various smaller items, such as horseshoeing, carriage mending—for he who lives in the country and does business in the city must keep his vehicle and appurtenances. I had always prided myself on being an exact man, and settling every account, great and small, with the going out of the old year; but this season I found myself sorely put to it. In fact, had not I received a timely lift from my good old uncle, I should have made a complete break down. The old gentleman's troublesome habit of ciphering and calculating, it seems, had led him beforehand to foresee that I was not exactly in the money-making line, nor likely to possess much surplus revenue to meet the note which I had given for my place; and, therefore, he quietly paid it himself, as I discovered, when, after much anxiety and some sleepless nights, I went to the holder to ask for an extension of credit.

"He was right, after all," said I to my wife; "'to live cheap in the country, a body must know how.'"

TRIALS OF A HOUSEKEEPER

I have a detail of very homely grievances to present; but such as they are, many a heart will feel them to be heavy—the trials of a housekeeper.

"Poh!" says one of the lords of creation, taking his cigar out of his mouth, and twirling it between his two first fingers, "what a fuss these women do make of this simple matter of managing a family! I can't see for my life as there is anything so extraordinary to be done in this matter of housekeeping: only three meals a day to be got and cleared off—and it really seems to take up the whole of their mind from morning till night. *I* could keep house without so much of a flurry, I know."

Now, prithee, good brother, listen to my story, and see how much you know about it. I came to this enlightened West about a year since, and was duly established in a comfortable country residence within a mile and a half of the city, and there commenced the enjoyment of domestic felicity. I had been married about three months, and had been, previously *in love* in the most approved romantic way, with all the proprieties of moonlight walks, serenades, sentimental billets doux, and everlasting attachment.

After having been allowed, as I said, about three months to get over this sort of thing, and to prepare for realities, I was located for life as aforesaid. My family consisted of myself and husband, a female friend as a visitor, and two brothers of my good man, who were engaged with him in business.

I pass over the first two or three days, spent in that process of hammering boxes, breaking crockery, knocking things down and picking them up again, which is commonly called getting to housekeeping. As usual, carpets were sewed and stretched, laid down, and taken up to be sewed over; things were formed, and *re*formed, *trans*formed, and *con*formed, till at last a settled order began to appear. But now came up the great point of all. During our confusion we had cooked and eaten our meals in a very miscellaneous and pastoral manner, eating now from the top of a barrel, and now from a fireboard laid on two chairs, and drinking, some from teacups, and some from saucers, and some from tumblers, and some from a pitcher big enough to be drowned in, and sleeping, some on sofas, and some on straggling beds and mattresses thrown down here and there wherever there was room. All these pleasant barbarities were now at an end. The house was in order, the dishes put up in their places; three regular meals were to be administered in one day, all in an orderly, civilized form; beds were to be made, rooms swept and dusted, dishes washed, knives scoured, and all the et cetera to be attended to. Now for getting "help," as Mrs. Trollope says; and where and how were we to get it? We knew very few persons in the city; and how were we to accomplish the matter? At length the "house of employment" was mentioned; and my husband was dispatched thither regularly every day for a week, while I, in the mean time, was very nearly *dispatched* by the abundance of work at home. At length, one evening, as I was sitting completely exhausted, thinking of resorting to the last feminine expedient for supporting life, viz., a good fit of crying, my husband made his appearance, with a most triumphant air, at the door. "There, Margaret, I have got you a couple at last—cook and chambermaid." So saying, he flourished open the door, and gave to my view the picture of a little, dry, snuffy-looking old woman, and a great, staring Dutch girl, in a green bonnet with red ribbons, with mouth wide open, and hands and feet that would have made a Greek sculptor open *his* mouth too. I addressed forthwith a few words of encouragement to each of this cultivated-looking couple, and proceeded to ask their names; and forthwith the old woman began to snuffle and to wipe her face with what was left of an old silk pocket-handkerchief preparatory to speaking, while the young lady opened her mouth wider, and looked around with a frightened air, as if meditating an escape. After some preliminaries, however, I found out that my old woman was Mrs. Tibbins, and my Hebe's name was *Kotterin*; also, that she knew much more Dutch than English, and not any too much of either. The old lady was the cook. I ventured a few inquiries. "Had she ever cooked?"

"Yes, ma'am, sartain; she had lived at two or three places in the city."

"I suspect, my dear," said my husband confidently, "that she is an experienced cook, and so your troubles are over;" and he went to reading his newspaper. I said no more, but determined to wait till morning. The breakfast, to be sure, did not do much honor to the talents of my official; but it was the first time, and the place was new to her. After breakfast was cleared away I proceeded to give directions for dinner; it was merely a plain joint of meat, I said, to be roasted in the tin oven. The experienced cook looked at me with a stare of entire vacuity. "The tin oven," I repeated, "stands there," pointing to it.

She walked up to it, and touched it with such an appearance of suspicion as if it had been an electrical battery, and then looked round at me with a look of such helpless ignorance that my soul was moved. "I never see one of them things before," said she.

"Never saw a tin oven!" I exclaimed. "I thought you said you had cooked in two or three families."

"They does not have such things as them, though," rejoined my old lady. Nothing was to be done, of course, but to instruct her into the philosophy of the case; and having spitted the joint, and given numberless directions, I walked off to my room to superintend the operations of Kotterin, to whom I had committed the making of my bed and the sweeping of my room, it never having come into my head that there could be a wrong way of making a bed; and to this day it is a marvel to me how any one could arrange pillows and quilts to make such a nondescript appearance as mine now presented. One glance showed me that Kotterin also was *"just caught,"* and that I had as much to do in her department as in that of my old lady.

Just then the doorbell rang. "Oh, there is the doorbell," I exclaimed. "Run, Kotterin, and show them into the parlor."

Kotterin started to run, as directed, and then stopped, and stood looking round on all the doors and on me with a wofully puzzled air. "The street door," said I, pointing towards the entry. Kotterin blundered into the entry, and stood gazing with a look of stupid wonder at the bell ringing without hands, while I went to the door and let in the company before she could be fairly made to understand the connection between the ringing and the phenomenon of admission.

As dinner time approached, I sent word into my kitchen to have it set on; but recollecting the state of the heads of department there, I soon followed my own orders. I found the tin oven standing out in the middle of the kitchen, and my cook seated *à la Turc* in front of it, contemplating the roast meat with full as puzzled an air as in the morning. I once more explained the mystery of taking it off, and assisted her to get it on to the platter, though somewhat cooled by having been so long set out for inspection. I was standing holding the spit in my hands, when Kotterin, who had heard the doorbell ring, and was determined this time to be in season, ran into the hall, and, soon returning, opened the kitchen door, and politely ushered in three or four fashionable looking ladies, exclaiming, "Here she is." As these were strangers from the city, who had come to make their first call, this introduction was far from proving an eligible one—the look of thunderstruck astonishment with which I greeted their first appearance, as I stood brandishing the spit, and the terrified snuffling and staring of poor Mrs. Tibbins, who again had recourse to her old pocket-handkerchief, almost entirely vanquished their gravity, and it was evident that they were on the point of a broad laugh; so, recovering my self-possession, I apologized, and led the way to the parlor.

Let these few incidents be a specimen of the four mortal weeks that I spent with these "helps," during which time I did almost as much work, with twice as much anxiety, as when there was nobody there; and yet everything went wrong besides. The young gentlemen complained of the patches of starch grimed to their collars, and the streaks of black coal ironed into their dickies, while one week every pocket-handkerchief in the house was starched so stiff that you might as well have carried an earthen plate in your pocket; the tumblers looked muddy; the plates were never washed clean or wiped dry unless I attended to each one; and as to eating and drinking, we experienced a variety that we had not before considered possible.

At length the old woman vanished from the stage, and was succeeded by a knowing, active, capable damsel, with a temper like a steel-trap, who remained with me just one week, and then went off in a fit of spite. To her succeeded a rosy, good-natured, merry lass, who broke the crockery, burned the dinner, tore the clothes in ironing, and knocked down everything that stood in her way about the house, without at all discomposing herself about the matter. One night she took the stopper from a barrel of molasses, and came singing off upstairs, while the molasses ran soberly out into the cellar bottom all night, till by morning it was in a state of universal emancipation. Having done this, and also dispatched an entire set of tea things by letting the waiter fall, she one day made her disappearance.

Then, for a wonder, there fell to my lot a tidy, efficient, trained English girl; pretty, and genteel, and neat, and knowing how to do everything, and with the sweetest temper in the world. "Now," said I to myself, "I shall rest from my labors." Everything about the house began to go right, and looked as clean and genteel as Mary's own pretty self. But, alas! this period of repose was interrupted by the vision of a clever, trim-looking young man, who for some weeks could be heard scraping his boots at the kitchen door every Sunday night; and at last Miss Mary, with some smiling and blushing, gave me to understand that she must leave in two weeks.

"Why, Mary," said I, feeling a little mischievous, "don't you like the place?"

"Oh, yes, ma'am."

"Then why do you look for another?"

"I am not going to another place."

"What, Mary, are you going to learn a trade?"

"No, ma'am."

"Why, then, what do you mean to do?"

"I expect to keep house myself, ma'am," said she, laughing and blushing.

"Oh ho!" said I, "that is it;" and so in two weeks I lost the best little girl in the world: peace to her memory.

After this came an interregnum, which put me in mind of the chapter in Chronicles that I used to read with great delight when a child, where Basha, and Elah, and Tibni, and Zimri, and Omri, one after the other, came on to the throne of Israel, all in the compass of half a dozen verses. We had one old woman, who stayed a week, and went away with the misery in her tooth; one young woman, who ran away and got married; one cook, who came at night and went off before light in the morning; one very clever girl, who stayed a month, and then went away because her mother was sick; another, who stayed six weeks, and was taken with the fever herself; and during all this time, who can speak the damage and destruction wrought in the domestic paraphernalia by passing through these multiplied hands?

What shall we do? Shall we give up houses, have no furniture to take care of, keep merely a bag of meal, a porridge pot, and a pudding stick, and sit in our tent door in real patriarchal independence? What shall we do?

Lightning Source UK Ltd.
Milton Keynes UK
UKHW010630190721
387400UK00001B/7